FLYING TO AMERICA

* * *

Other Books by Donald Barthelme

/

FLYING TO AMERICA

45 More Stories

BY DONALD BARTHELME

★   ★   ★

Edited and with a Preface by Kim Herzinger

Shoemaker Hoard

Library of Congress Cataloging-in-Publication Data
Barthelme, Donald.
Flying to America : 45 more stories / Donald Barthelme ;
edited and with a preface by Kim Herzinger.
p. cm.
Includes bibliographical references.
ISBN-13: 978-1-59376-172-1
ISBN-10: 1-59376-172-4
1. Experimental fiction, American.
I. Herzinger, Kim A., 1946–   II. Title
PS3552.A76F59 2007
813'.54—dc22   2007015211

Jacket design by Gerilyn Attebery
Interior design by David Bullen
Printed in the United States of America

Shoemaker ▓ Hoard
www.shoemakerhoard.com

10 9 8 7 6 5 4 3 2 1

CONTENTS

Preface

In the fifteen years since we began the project of putting together all of Donald Barthelme's unpublished and uncollected work, we've published his satires, parodies, fables, illustrated stories, plays, essays, reviews, occasional pieces, and interviews. But the crown of the project was always understood to be the publication of Barthelme's unpublished and uncollected stories. The stories, after all, established his genius and influence, and radically transformed what twentieth-century American literature could be. Saddening as it is to have to accept that after these there will be no more stories, there is still reason to celebrate. All of Donald Barthelme's work is now available in book form, and the importance of his achievement can now be fully appreciated.

Sixty Stories, it was once said, was Barthelme's attempt to establish his canon. *Forty Stories*, then, might be seen as his attempt to enlarge it. *Flying to America: 45 More Stories*, which contains every story not collected in *Sixty Stories* and *Forty Stories*, twelve stories never collected in any of the individual published volumes, and three previously unpublished stories, is a crucial addition—perhaps *the* crucial addition—to his existing canon.

The forty-five stories in *Flying to America* display the range of Barthelme's talents as well as a rare peek into the working methods of a supreme literary collagist. Some of Barthelme's most dedicatedly experimental stories are available here. "Florence Green Is 81," "The Sea of Hesitation," "The Viennese Opera Ball," "Bone Bubbles," and "Flying to America," for instance, demonstrate that any assumptions a reader might bring to a Barthelme story will be subject to challenge and disruption. "Florence Green Is 81," the first story in Barthelme's very first book, announced immediately and definitively that Barthelme's kind of joking was not going to be joking around. As the title of that first book, *Come Back, Dr. Caligari*, suggests, "Florence Green Is 81" was a statement as well as a plea—Barthelme clearly thought that it was the likes of Caligari, that dislocated and aesthetically challenging figure, that required a comeback. We had had quite enough of that well-worn hero, Shane, and the forms and formulae that had created and sustained him. "Bone Bubbles" is a piece in which Barthelme's experiment in word collision reminds us of such tablet breakers as Joyce, Beckett, Burroughs, or even Mallarmé. The title story, "Flying to America," is a superb example of Barthelme's collage method of construction, a story that itself absorbed bits and pieces of previously published work, and then lent itself—in bits and pieces—to no fewer than three subsequently published stories.

Many of the stories in *Flying to America* were generated by the aesthetic and cultural issues that engaged Barthelme throughout his writing career: the perils of the unfulfilled life; the modern tendency toward conformist nonconformity; the blindness of obsession; the relationship between art and life, politics and life, sex and life; the necessity of continuing to ask questions even as we are aware of the inevitability of not knowing the answers. "Perpetua," to call on one example, features a woman perpetually in search of an authentic, nonconformist individualism, only to demonstrate that the very act of consciously setting out to make herself different can become the worst kind of cliche, leading to a kind of drained theatrical one-upmanship of idiosyncrasy that she is doomed to repeat—perpetually. "To London and Rome" offers a vision of married life mechanistically attached to money and acquisition, where the flatness and terror of the unfulfilled life portrayed in the main text is juxtaposed to a column of statements and "stage directions" that remind us of the joy-stripped world of Harold Pinter's theater of menace. The marvelous "Tickets," the last story Barthelme published in *The New Yorker*, features that numbingly formal, almost-British voice he so often used—a voice we associate with Evelyn Waugh and Anthony Powell, not to speak of that great line of English comic writers from Wodehouse and Sir Henry Howard Bashford to Joe Orton and Tom Stoppard—completely absorbed in its own obsessions, delivered by a character whose unremitting confidence only serves to reveal his incomparable blindness. "The Agreement," to call on one last example, is constructed around one man's series of recurring and increasingly anxious questions, questions that are unanswerable because, to quote Barthelme himself, "the Project Life is in some sense beyond his abilities."

Here are stories in which the attitudes and processes of two seemingly mutually exclusive worlds are wonderfully mixed or transposed and thereby refreshed. In "The Police Band," for instance, a police riot squad trains to perform its job of calming crowds and maintaining order, not with guns and truncheons, but with saxophones and drums and renditions of "Perdido"—a "triumph of art over good sense." Like so many of the best romantic ideas circa *annus terribilus* 1968, when the story appeared in *Unspeakable Practices, Unnatural Acts*, such a band was "an idea of a very Romantic kind," as Barthelme tells us, but it was also "an idea that didn't work."

And here, too, are stories motivated by Barthelme's persistent anger at institutional bureaucracy and, especially, at the dangerous follies of government. "Subpoena," "The Reference," "The New Member," come to mind, as does "The Mothball Fleet," in which an "Admiral" who once believed in the mission of those destroyers and battleships, and the meaning of the flag they flew, now gathers the same ships to attack a government he no longer trusts. "I believed," the Admiral tells us. "Then, over time, I discovered that they were lying. Consistently. With exemplary skill, in a hundred languages. I decided to take the ships." It is the kind of Vietnam-era story we might have expected Barthelme to write, a furious comic parable restrained by its own seriousness, but sustained by an irony which is his last defense against a government which has rendered him helpless, angry, and immensely sad. It is the kind of story we might, perhaps, expect Barthelme to write now, if he had lived to see something of the Vietnam era making its ugly return.

In the papers examined after Barthelme's death, in 1989, there were a number of "fits and starts"—fragments, beginnings, and unfinished pieces. But for a writer who published significantly and continuously for almost thirty years, there just weren't *that* many. Nor were there many unpublished pieces that we could say were complete. Of them, "Among the Beanwoods" and "Heather" both revisit the linguistic torque we find in Barthelme's best work. "Pandemonium," on the other hand, was a piece Barthelme was working on very late in his life, and is very likely an early draft, a sketch of what he intended eventually to do. Unpolished as it may be, "Pandemonium" is still a lively little thing, and serves at the very least to provide us a look at his writing in process.

As was the case with *The Teachings of Don B.* and *Not-Knowing*, the two companion volumes to *Flying to America*, the work that appears in this book falls into four categories: (1) unpublished work; (2) uncollected work; (3) work—other than the novels—that did not appear in his two compendium collections, *Sixty Stories* and *Forty Stories*; and (4) work that, though perhaps later collected, first (or in one case later) appeared in significantly different form. Editorial information has been kept to a minimum, but certain crucial information has been included in the "Notes" at the back of the book.

For those truly dedicated followers of Barthelmismo who already know and love Donald Barthelme's work, *Flying to America* is a rare and wonderful treat—to have in your hands at long last a handsome number of previously uncollected and even a few unseen stories. For those new to Barthelme, here is an opportunity to discover the literary giant whose influence was singular to many of today's most celebrated writers. Picking up where *Sixty Stories* and *Forty Stories* left off, here—sadly but thankfully—are the final forty-five.

Kim Herzinger

FLYING TO AMERICA

Flying to America

18 March

Sing, goddess, the brilliance of Perpetua, who came then to lend her salt-sweet God-gift beauty to the film. Sing the beauty of the breasts of a Perpetua, like unto the cancelment of action at law against you, sing the redness of her hair, like unto the anger of Peleus' son who put pains a thousandfold upon the Achaeans. Sing the hauteur of Perpetua, like unto that of a thief of fine porcelains, sing the movement of her naked leg under the long gray gown, like unto the progress of that sad song, the Borodin Quartet in D Major. Sing the whiteness of her brow, like unto a failed poem pulped into Erasable Bond, sing her sudden smile, like unto the shriek of that swan which hid Zeus the powerful. Sing, goddess, the rancor of Perpetua, which is plain to see, sing her gold-glistering trumpet, with which she promulgates her rancor and earns her daily bread, by the sweat of her lip. Sing, goddess, the mystery of Perpetua, of which I cannot speak, without undue emotion, sing her stern eye, which tells me that, among the sons of men, I am not worthy.

Perpetua showed us her breasts.

"Yes, they're wonderful," I said.

All of the members of the crew were smiling.

She has just left her husband, Harold.

3

"Order is not interesting," Perpetua said. "Disorder is interesting."

"Thank you, Perpetua. Ezra will call you when we're ready for you."

20 March

Two days of inactivity.

The script is terrible.

Ezra said: "This script is no good."

I maintained a grave and thoughtful silence. Then I asked: "Who have you hired?"

"Joan," Ezra said. "Marty. Mitch. Marcello."

"Who are they?"

"Marty," Ezra said, "is a C.O. whose draft board requires him to work for extremely low pay at some hardship in a job with provable social utility."

"Are we that?"

"I presented us as a leprosarium."

This was reasonable.

"Mitch," Ezra said, "has come from the asylum."

"Which?"

"The Maryland Motherhouse of Our Lady of Perpetual Chagrin."

"Is he a nun?"

"He is not."

"In what capacity was he there?"

"In the capacity, borderline case."

"Very good. Go on."

"The podesta's brief against Marcello," Ezra said, and paused, "I have chosen to disbelieve."

"And Joan?"

"Mail fraud."

Mail fraud is not something that bothers me much.

"O.K., Ezra. You have done a good job. Monday we begin."

"How?" Ezra asked. "With this script?"

"Have you never heard of grace?"

4

21 March

I heard a noise outside. I looked out of the window. An old woman was bent over my garbage can, borrowing some of my garbage. They do that all over the city, old men and old women. They borrow your garbage and they never bring it back.

My apartment is nearly empty. I've thrown everything out. Books, pictures, most of the furniture. The parquet needs a waxing, its brown has changed to brown-gray. The plants are withering because I don't water them. My wife and child are gone.

The telephone rang. It was the genius (one of the people we've hired for the film).

"They haf removed the tooth," he told me.

"Fine. Did it hurt?"

"Not so much. But I am worrying."

"What about?"

"I haf the tooth. Which in your opinion museum should I donate it to—the Smithsonian or rather the Metropolitan?"

"The Smithsonian. Absolutely the Smithsonian."

22 March

Thinking about the "Flying to America" sequence. This will be the film's climax. But am I capable of mounting such a spectacle? And will the man from Brewers' Natural (the bank that put up the money for the film) understand?

23 March

The first day of shooting. It took the crew to the desert. Perpetua came along to watch. It was necessary for me not to watch Perpetua watching.

"Tom," Ezra said, "we should have stars."

"No stars," I said.

"Stars have bigger heads than ordinary people," Ezra argued. "Bigger heads photograph better."

"No stars."

Shooting in the desert was a mistake but an instructive mistake. I blew my whistle. The crew gathered around. I explained

5

the sequence. We'd be shooting two parallel blue lines each one a mile long. I could smell resistance. Resistance-pheromones being released all around me.

Ezra took me aside. "What they object to is not the sequence but the whistle. They don't like to be whistled at."

I threw the whistle high in the air.

The whistle stayed up in the air for a long time.

Everyone looked at the whistle.

We shot the two parallel blue lines each a mile long.

Something wrong. The scene has no movement, no impact.

What about printing the words of Christ in red, across the bottom of each frame?

Dismal to want to succeed but I can't help it. I watched the whistle, still in the air.

25 March

I was once a monster of a kind. I was bookish. Half man, half book.

No longer. Now I am worried about making the film.

Even today I am tempted to go to the library and find a book about great trumpet playing and read it so that when the moment comes (Perpetua is a trumpet player, with the New World Symphony Orchestra) I can discourse knowledgeably on the subject. I resist the impulse.

"And is it not the case," said Ezra when we first met, "that I have been associated with the production of nineteen major motion pictures of such savage originality, scalding *vérité*, and honey-warm sexual indecency that the very theaters chained their doors rather than permit exhibition of these major motion pictures on their ammonia-scented gum-daubed premises? And is it not the case," said Ezra, "that I myself with my two sinewy hands and strong-wrought God-gift brain have participated in the changing of seven high-class literary works of the first water and four of the second water and two of the third water into major muscatel? And is it not the living truth," said Ezra, "that I was the very man, I myself and none other without exception, who clung to the underside of the camera of the great Dreyer, clung with my two sinewy hands and noble well-wrought thighs and cunning-muscled knees both dexter and sinister, during the cinematization of the master's 'Gertrud,' clung there to slow the movement of said camera to that exquisite slowness that distinguishes this masterpiece from all other masterpieces of its water? And is it not chapter and verse," said Ezra, "that I was the comrade of all the comrades of the Dziga-Vertov Group who was first in no-saying, firmest in no-saying, most final in no-saying, to all honey-sweet commercial seductions of whatever water and capitalist blandishments of whatever water and ideological incorrectitudes of whatever water whatsoever? And is it not as true as Saul become Paul," Ezra said, "that you require a man, a firm-limbed long-winded good true man, and that *I am the man* standing before you in his very blood and bones?"

"You are hired, Ezra," I said.

27 March

Thinking of sequences for the film.
A frenzy of desire?
Sensible lovers taking precautions?
Swimming with horses?

28 March

Today we filmed the genius. I made no attempt to frame or place him. We simply stood him in front of the camera and let him speak.

"Divorce in Indonesia now costs a penny," the genius began. "Architecture students in China must now build with their own hands whatever they design. The plan . . . the plan offers metabolic support to ninety-nine percent of reality as well as peak load servicing of maximum social stress. Under omni-favorable conditions no one will ask you any questions and you will be able to go your way utilizing our two great options, trial and error.

"There is no limit to what can be accomplished," the genius said. "That is unfortunate, I would prefer a limit. The latest schedules call for a rate of growth in the corruption of public officials of something like twenty-two percent per annum. This 'noise' in the system is a good thing. Successful administration endangers anti-growth positions.

"The sudden world population bulge offers no threat, contrary to certain opinions expressed in the newspaper. Preterminal mummification of the deserving poor has been spoken of but I don't think we'll actually do it—not yet. Managerial capabilities and leadership potential may yet be discovered in you, predicted by your colored felt-pen drawings as a child, but not noticed at that time. These qualities offer possible new solutions that should not be discounted until progressive failure phases have been worked through. 'Pipe' dreams, which allow brine to cool passions and oil to flow under the ice, should be sought after. Better people yet unborn will evolve still other methods, doubtless superior to our own, yet retaining a flavor of improvisation, poking around, smashed thumbs, chemical accidents. It is difficult to do anything right, the first time. As one erects slatted fences in order to control dune formation, so we mix vodka and vermouth in a fully bundled hard- and software operation designed to soothe those of our clients whose jitters incapacitate them for ordinary life. Cyclic event-recurrences distress those who had hoped that rewards and punishments would change places, that painting things with red lead would retard lust, that Breton would not patent the soluble fish, that in the fires along the coasts at midsummer, witches are not being burnt, really. That is all I have to say, at this time."

"You did very well," I said to the genius.

"Yes!" he said. "I think so!"

2 April

Just saw, on the street, a man in yellow shorts, orange shirt, orange straw hat. He was carrying three naked putters and a book, the latter decently dust-jacketed. And he was shouting, shouting at the top of his lungs:

"I am angry!"

"I am very angry!

"I am *extremely* angry!

"Oh, I am so angry!
"I am furious!"
Something for the film?

3 April

Today we shot "country music." These country boys, despised and admired, know what they're about. The way they pull on their strings—the strings of their instruments and the strings of their fates. Bringing up the bass line here, inserting "fills" there, in their expensive forty-dollar Western shirts and plain ordinary eight-dollar jeans. We're filming a big battle dance in Rogers, Tennessee. It's the first time the crew really has had something to chew upon, and everyone is slightly excited. We set up backstage trying not to get in the way. Four bands are competing at the Masonic Temple. The musicians are unscrewing their flasks and tasting the bourbon inside, when they are not lighting their joints and pipes and hookahs. Meanwhile they're looking over the house, a big pile of stone erected in 1928, and wondering whether the wiring will be adequate to the demands of their art. The flasks and joints are being passed around, and everyone is wiping his mouth on his sleeve. And so the ropes holding the equipment to the roofs of the white station wagons are untied, and the equipment is carried onto the stage, with its closed curtain and its few spotty worklights shining. The various groups send out for supper, ordering steak sandwiches on a bun, hold the onions or hold the lettuce, as individual taste dictates. We send out for supper, too. The most junior member of each group or a high-ranking groupie goes over to the café with the list, an envelope on which all the orders have been written, and reads off the orders to the counterman there, and the counterman says, "You with the band?" and the go-for says, "Yup," succinct and not putting too fine a point on it. Meanwhile the ushers have arrived, all high-school girls who are members of the Daughters of the Mystic Shrine Auxiliary, wearing white blouses and blue miniskirts, with a red sash slung across their breasts tied at the hip, a badge of office. These, the flower of Rogers' young girls, all go backstage to look at the musicians, and this is their privilege, because the performance doesn't begin for

9

another hour, and they stand around looking at the musicians, and the musicians look back at them, and certain thoughts push their way into all of the minds gathered there, under the worklights, but then are pushed out again, because there is music to be performed this night! and one of the amplifiers has just blown its slo-blo fuse, and nobody can remember where the spare fuses were packed, and also the microphones provided by the Temple are freaking out, if one can say that about a microphone, and in addition the second band's drummer discovers that his heads are soggy (probably a result of that situation outside Tulsa, where the bridge was out and the station wagon more or less forded the river) but luckily he has brought along a hot plate to deal with this sort of contingency, and he plugs it in and begins toasting his heads, to bring them back to the right degree of brashness for the performance. And now the first people are filling up the seats, out in front of the curtain, some of them sitting in seats that are better, strictly speaking, than those they had paid for, in the hope that the real owners of the seats will not show up, having been detained by a medical emergency. All of the musicians take turns in looking out over the auditorium through a hole in the closed curtain, counting the house and looking for girls who are especially beautiful. And now the m.c. arrives, a very jovial man in a big Western hat, such as the Stetson company has stopped making, and he goes around shaking hands with everybody, cutting up old touches, and the musicians tolerate this, because it is part of their life. And now everybody is tuning up, and you hear parts of lots of different songs, fragments clashing with each other, because each musician has a different favorite bit that he likes to tune up with, although sometimes two musicians will start in on the same piece at the same time, because they are thinking alike, at that moment. And now the hall is filling up with people who are well- or ill-dressed, according to the degree that St. Pecula has smiled upon them, and the Daughters of the Mystic Shrine are outside, with their programs, which contain advertisements from the Bart Lumber Yard, and the Sons and Daughters of I Will Arise, and the House of Blue Lights, and the Sunbeam Vacuum Cleaner Company, and the Okay Funeral Home.

A man comes backstage with a piece of paper on which is written the order in which the various performers will appear. The leaders of the various groups drift over to this man and look at his piece of paper, to see what spot on the bill has been given to each band, while the bandsmen talk to each other, in enthusiastic or desultory fashion, according to their natures. "Where'd you git that shirt?" "Took it off a cop in Texarkana." "How much you give for it?" "Dollar and a half." And now everybody is being careful not to drink too much, because drinking too much slows down your attack, and if there is one thing you don't want in this kind of situation it is having your attack slowed down. Of course some people are into drinking and smoking a lot *more* before they play, but that's another idea, and now the audience on the other side of the closed curtain is a loud presence, and everyone has the feeling of something important about to happen, and the first band to perform gets into position, with the three guitar players in a kind of skirmish line in front, the drummer spread out behind them, and the electric-piano player off to the side somewhat, more or less parallel to the drummer, and the happy m.c. standing in front of the guitar players, with his piece of paper in his hand, and the stage manager looking alternately at his watch and at the people out front. One of the musicians borrows a last cigarette from another musician, and all of the musicians are fiddling with the controls of their instruments, and the drummer is tightening his snares, and the stage manager says "O.K." to the m.c., and the m.c. holds up his piece of paper and prepares to read what is written there into the bunch of microphones before him, and the houselights go down as the stage lights come up, and the m.c. looks at the leader of the first group, who nods complacently, and the m.c. shouts into the microphones (from behind the closed curtain) in a hearty voice, "From Rogers, Tennessee, the Masonic Temple Battle of the Bands, it's Bill Tippey and the Unhappy Valley Boys!" and the band crashes into "When Your Tender Body Touches Mine," and the curtains part, and the crowd roars.

We filmed all this, for the film.

9 April

A brief exchange with Perpetua about revolutionary praxis.

"But I thought," I said, "that there had been a sexual revolution and everybody could sleep with anybody who was a consenting adult."

"In theory," Perpetua said. "In theory. But sleeping with somebody also has a political dimension. One does not, for example go to bed with running dogs of imperialism."

I thought: But who will care for and solace the running dogs of imperialism? Who will bring them their dog food, who will tuck the covers tight as they dream their imperialistic dreams?

"My group says I should not be associated with you or with the film," Perpetua said. "They say you have no more political consciousness than a cat."

"But that's what the priests used to say. They said I had no more religion than a cat!"

"The group says you're a skeptic."

In truth I am a monster or ex-monster. But ex-monstrousness however hard won is not a position entitling one to ride the first elephant in this particular parade.

"I'll work on it, Perpetua."

12 April

Somebody knocked on my door (a rare event). I undid the various locks top to bottom—like unbuttoning a shirt. A man standing there. He handed me a business card.

L. JOHN SILVERMAN
ATTORNEY-AT-LAW

"Did you want to see me?"
"Are you Mr. Rush?"
"Come in."
Mr. Silverman was a large man with a red face who looked a great deal like the late Wallace Beery.
"What can I do for you, Mr. Silverman? Have a seat."

"It's about your picture," Mr. Silverman said. "I represent some folks—a consortium, you might call it—who are very interested. The long and short of it is, we'd like to buy in."

"Why?"

"From what we've heard you're making a very peculiar picture. Idiosyncratic and kinky."

"Oh, I wouldn't say that. Not exactly."

I thought: Isn't consorting a crime?

Mr. Silverman leaned forward earnestly.

"You young filmmakers are the key to the whole situation today. The rest of the industry is arse over teacup."

"Mr. Silverman, I can hardly be called a young filmmaker. I'm thirty-nine."

"Don't matter. Don't matter. I hear your picture is solid gold."

"I'm just shooting a lot of raw material right now."

"The question is, will you let us come aboard?"

"I'd rather not, to be frank. Brewers' Natural is handling the whole deal and our relations with them are a little delicate and I'd hate to rock the boat at this point."

Mr. Silverman became agitated. He reached into his coat pocket and withdrew a plastic vial containing yellow pills and popped one into his mouth without even asking for a glass of water. The pills were not hard to recognize—Valium, a tranquilizer I've often used myself.

"I know, I know," Mr. Silverman said, catching my expression. "It's a crutch." Then, businesslike: "Mr. Rush, I just want to leave you with one thought."

"One thought?"

"There's such a thing as too much individualism."

"There's such a thing as too much individualism?"

"You'll be hearing from us," he said, and stomped from the room.

13 April

Then I Thomas son of Titus took thought with myself about what measures might be taken against the threat. I devised then in my mind many fine punishments of the first water for anyone who might dare trifle with our enterprise in any way great or small. On the first day the trifler will be hung well wrapped with strong cords upside down from a flagpole at a height of twenty stories. On the second day the trifler will be turned right side up and rehung from the same staff, so as to empty the blood from his head and prepare him for the third day. On the third day the trifler will be unwrapped and attended by a licensed D.D.S., who will extract every tooth from the top part of his jaw and every other tooth from the bottom part of his jaw, the extractions to be mismatching according to the blueprint supplied. On the fourth day the trifler will be given hard things to eat. On the fifth day the trifler will be comforted with soft fine garments and flagons and the love of lithesome women' so as to make the shock of the sixth day the more severe. On the sixth day the trifler will be confined alone in a small room with the music of Karlheinz Stockhausen. On the seventh day the trifler will be pricked with nettles. On the eighth day the trifler will be slid naked down a thousand-foot razor blade to the music of Karlheinz Stockhausen. On the ninth day the trifler will be sewn together by children. On the tenth day . . .

14 April

Thinking about my father.

My father was a drinker, favoring vodka. Vodka is for people who wish to conceal their anger. Sometimes my father concealed his anger in the middle of the afternoon, mostly he concealed his anger around dinnertime. Once in a while at breakfast, when he concealed it in Minute Maid orange juice.

A banging on my door. I opened it. A little man was standing there. He handed me a folded piece of paper.

"What the hell is this?"

But the man was already scampering down the stairs.

I unfolded the paper. There was nothing on it except, in the center of the sheet, a black circle.

I had been tipped the black spot.

15 April

Today we photographed fear, a distressing emotion aroused by impending danger, real or imagined.

I'm interested in fear not only for its own sweet sake but because it seems the one emotion among the emotions that presents itself pure, unmediated. One does not so much observe oneself experiencing fear as experience it directly.

Perpetua watching, sitting in a folding chair, hands in her lap. Her breasts hiding beneath the long gray gown. She has red hair!

We filmed the startle pattern—shrinking, blinking, all that. We did the sham-rage reaction and also "panting." Mitch panted. Then we shot some stuff in which a primitive person (my bare arm as stand-in for the primitive person) kills an enemy by pointing a magic bone at him.

"O.K., who's got the magic bone?"

The magic bone was brought. I pointed the magic bone and the actor playing the enemy fell to the ground. I had carefully explained to the actor that the magic bone would not really kill him, probably.

Then, the thrill of fear along the buttocks. We used a girl named Heidi for this sequence because her buttocks are the most beautiful I know. This was a silent bit so that everyone could talk as Heidi's buttocks thrilled.

"Hope is the very sign of lack-of-happiness," Heidi said, stomach down on the couch.

"Fame is a palliative for doubt," I said.

"Wealth-formation is a source of fear for both winners and losers," Ezra said.

"Civilization aims at making all good things available even to cowards," said the actor who had played dead, quoting Nietzsche.

Perpetua said nothing. How can I persuade her to have a drink with me? She does her parts of the film (mostly disquisitions upon revolutionary tactics and the oppression of women) in a stern and serious and workmanlike manner and refuses to have a drink with me afterward.

I took the magic bone home with me. I don't believe in it, exactly, but you never know.

17 April

Thinking about "Flying to America." Will it really say what I want it to say?

A telephone call. The Bill Bones Forwarding Company. Mr. Bones speaking.

"Listen, Rush. You want to finish that picture?"

"Who is this?

"You got our message."

"The black spot?"

"We want two hundred thousand."

"You're out of your mind. We don't have that kind of money."

"Put in to the bank for an overrun."

"If the bank ever saw what I'm doing—"

A pause.

"You mean you're ripping off the bank?"

"Not exactly."

"O.K.," Mr. Bones said patiently. "Put us on the picture as consultants."

"Who is this?"

"L. J. Silverman Incorporated."

"I thought you were Bill Bones Forwarding."

"Bill Bones Forwarding is a subsidiary of Pew Associates, which is part of a conglomerate called L. J. Silverman Incorporated. Make the check out to L. J. Silverman but send it with a letter of transmittal to Bill Bones Forwarding. And a blind copy to Pew Associates. Ha ha."

"Do I have any options?"

We considered this together.

"I don't see any," he said. "Do you? And I want to leave you with one thought."

"I know," I said. "There's such a thing as . . ."

On the tenth day the trifler will be nibbled at by bald eagles. On the eleventh day . . .

Then I had a slosh and then another slosh and then another slosh. Then another slosh and another slosh and another slosh. A total of six, in a quarter of an hour. Then I skittered and skated and bounced and danced, in my mind, and felt myself kin to Zeus the immortal whose breath makes the waves mount even to the height of the mast of a tall ship and whose breath makes the dust of the earth leap up and form into whirlwinds and whose frown makes the high-reaching many-branched trees split asunder showing their marrow and whose frown makes the white-terrible snow rush from the mountaintops in house-destroying rushes and whose smile is never seen, but rather hid behind his hand, because it roasts the eyes. Then the mood changed and I felt not kin to Zeus the well-feared but rather myself, Thomas—Thomas the fuddled, Thomas of the putty spear, Thomas of the fell-short arrow, Thomas the kithless, Thomas of the gnashed teeth, Thomas the ricked wrenched twisted and maimed, Thomas the marrowless, Thomas the reduced, Thomas of the overdraft, Thomas of the last legs. I was, in fine, depressed.

I thought: Perhaps I drink too much?

20 April

Perpetua smiled at me today. Why?

I asked her if she wanted to have a drink after we finished shooting.

"Sure," she said.

In the bar she asked: "Are you going to give them the money?"

"Who told you?"

"Ezra."

"I don't have the money."

She thought about this. Then she said: "I like people who are struggling with dark malefic forces."

25 April

No shooting for three days. It's been raining and I don't have any interiors scheduled. That is to say: No ideas.

I wanted to film everything but there are things we're not getting.

17

The wild ass is in danger in Ethiopia—we've got nothing on that. We've got nothing on intellectual elitism funded out of public money, an important subject. We've got nothing on ball lightning and nothing on the National Grid and not a foot on the core-mantle problem, the problem of a looped economy, or the problem of praxis vs. theory. I wanted to get it all but there's only so much time, so much energy. There's an increasing resistance to antibiotics world-wide and liquid metal fast-breeder reactors are subject to swelling and a large proportion of Quakers are colorblind but our film will have not a shred of material on any of these matters.

Tonight I got rid of my rocking chair. It was a bentwood rocker made by Thonet in 18-something and of all the physical objects I once owned I liked it best. I had it recaned nineteen times. I carried it down the stairs and set it in front of the building and hurried back to the window of the apartment to see who the lucky legatee would be.

It was not two seconds before a young couple paused in front of my rocker. They could not believe their eyes, peered all about like thieves, and then were off down the street with it, the girl in front and the boy in back. Looking for all the world like a Siberian sleigh pursued by wolves.

26 April

A day of crises.

Then did the umbrage of the gods fall upon Thomas son of Titus, Thomas the unbuckled, Thomas the not-together, Thomas the weeper of night-weeps, Thomas the bald-someday. As when sacrifice is made incorrectly not according to custom, as when Father Zeus' fair-wrought altar is affronted by a goat not fresh-killed but killed many days before and sending forth a foul odor, as when guests disposed about a feast board neglect to pour upon the ground the sweet-souled wine in offering to Athene, so calamities arose.

The crew festered and fought. Marty said he'd rather go to jail than work one more day on the film, and Mitch said the same thing vis-à-vis the asylum. Joan began sending things through the mail again—nude photographs of herself together with a spurious Annual

Report suggesting a considerable net worth. Marcello approached Ezra with a garrote in one hand and an oubliette in the other.

And Brewers' Natural slapped a lien on the film.

They sent a lien officer around for the purpose. Ezra gave him a drink, and then another drink, and then many more drinks. But the lien officer had a head as clear as the decimal system, as clear as capitalism.

"How can you tell anything about the film until it's finished and cut?" Ezra asked the lien officer, and the lien officer said, "I can tell." He slapped the lien.

Pew Associates called and said they were no longer interested in coming aboard and would we please send the black spot back.

Perpetua remained warm and beautiful. She sat in the cutting room near the Moviola and looked over my shoulder at the soft, shrunken lengths of film and said, "Probably the music will help it a lot." That is the worst thing you can say in the film business.

She placed a hand on my arm.

"I like that part of the film where the genius says, 'It is difficult to do anything right, the first time,'" she said. "That was really inspiring."

I looked at her.

"And I liked that part where the counterman looks at the groupie and says, 'You with the band?' And I like the part with the magic bone."

I looked at her, amazed. Parts of the film had remained, had stuck, in her memory—not even her own parts. *The film was able to move from the screen into a human mind.*

I thought: But what more do I want?

27 April

Votes of no confidence on every side. The principal American distributor does not wish to distribute the film. Suggests that we have it dubbed into Mandarin and approach again, from the East. Well and good. The lab will not make additional prints without additional money. Can't blame them. The networks are not interested in a film that runs for four hours and cannot be interrupted for commercial announcements. That's sensible. The university and art-house circuits say that the film, what they've of seen it, is not "relevant." That's true. The overseas exhibitors have said "No" in all major languages. Quite properly so. Most of our equipment has been repossessed by Brewers' Natural. As is only natural. The film itself is in a vault with the lien liening against it. I am forbidden by injunction to enter the vault or even the building. Well, yes.

My answering service refuses to speak to me.

30 April

I am being bothered by doves.

Walking down the street, I notice a white dove (out of the corner of my eye) making an approach at three o'clock.

The dove dives, then shears off. He hovers for a bit, then begins to descend, then shears off again. This has happened today, yesterday, and the day before yesterday.

I thought: Doves.

Ezra and Mitch have gotten very tight. Ezra has explained to Mitch his feelings about Dreyer and Mitch has described to Ezra the inner workings of the Maryland Motherhouse of Our Lady of Perpetual Chagrin. The patients there, Mitch said, were tied to trees, in good weather. In bad weather they were allowed to act out historical pageants, such as the winter at Valley Forge.

"Real blood," Mitch said. "Our blood."

"I am better than he is," Perpetua told me.

"Than who?"

"Waverly Branch. Our first-desk man."

"I believe you."

"But he is a man," Perpetua said. "Therefore—"

"I see what you mean," I said.

"There was nothing the matter with Harold that is not also the matter with all of you," she said. "I am thinking of becoming a fanatic."

"Don't," I said. "Give us time."

"Time!" she said. "You've had centuries." And then: "Why is that white dove making passes at your head?"

"It's something that's been happening to me lately."

I thought: It could not be. I am not worthy.

"For food," Mitch said to Ezra, "we had gruel. One oat per bowl."

"I am tempted to bust Waverly in the mouth," Perpetua said, "definitively."

I thought: What are the preconditions for being splashed with grace? I'll have to look it up.

1 May

Now we are shooting "Flying to America."

The one hundred and twelve pilots check their watches.

If they all turn on their machines at once . . .

Flying to America.

(But did I remember to—?)

"Where is the blimp?" Marcello shouts. "I can't find the—"

Ropes dangling from the sky.

I'm using forty-seven cameras, the outermost of which is posted in the Dover marshes.

The Atlantic is calm in some parts, angry in others. This will affect the air.

A blueprint four miles long is the flight plan.

Every detail coordinated with the air-sea rescue services of all nations.

Victory through Air Power! I seem to remember that slogan from somewhere.

Hovercraft flying to America. Flying boats flying to America. F-111s flying to America. The China Clipper!

Seaplanes, bombers, Flying Wings flying to America.

A shot of a pilot named Jellybelly. He opens the cockpit door and speaks to the passengers. "America is only two thousand miles away now," he says. The passengers break out in smiles.

Balloons flying to America (they are painted in red and white stripes). Spads and Fokkers flying to America. Self-improvement is the big theme of flying to America. "Nowhere is self-realization more a possibility than in America," a man says.

Perpetua watching the clouds of craft in the air . . .

Gliders gliding to America. One man has constructed a huge paper airplane, seventy-two feet in length. It is doing better than we had any right to expect. But then great expectations are a part of flying to America.

Rich people are flying to America, and poor people, and people of moderate means. This aircraft is powered by twelve rubber bands, each rubber band thicker than a man's leg—can it possibly survive the turbulence over Greenland?

Is this the end of the film? Or is it rather the beginning? I can't decide.

Long thoughts are extended to enwrap the future American experience of the people who are flying to America . . .

"Sit down," Perpetua says. I look at her. She is holding my rocking chair!

"Where did you get that?"

"Sit down," she says again. "Relax. Watch the sky. Let Ezra do the rest."

I sit down in my rocking chair. I rock and watch the sky. Ezra does the rest. He is waving his hands in the air and shouting into a walkie-talkie.

"Why don't we have a child?" I say to Perpetua. "Or something."

"Good God," she says. "You are optimistic. What's got into you?"

"Once in a while I say something spontaneously. Something ill-considered."

"Flying to America," she says.

"Well, yes."

Perpetua

Now Perpetua was living alone. She had told her husband that she didn't want to live with him any longer.

"Why not?" he had asked.

"For all the reasons you know," she said.

Harold's farewell gift was a Blue Cross Blue Shield insurance policy, paid up for one year. Now Perpetua was putting valve oil on her trumpet. One of the valves was sticking. She was fourth-chair trumpet with the New World Symphony Orchestra.

Perpetua thought: That time he banged the car door on my finger. I am sure it was deliberate. That he locked me out while I was pregnant and I had to walk four miles after midnight to my father's house. One does not forget.

Perpetua smiled at the new life she saw spread out before her like a red velvet map.

Back in the former house, Harold watched television.

Perpetua remembered the year she was five. She had to learn to be nice, all in one year. She only learned part of it. She was not fully nice until she was seven.

Now I must obtain a lover, she thought. Perhaps more than one. One for Monday, one for Tuesday, one for Wednesday . . .

2.

Harold was looking at a picture of the back of a naked girl, in a magazine for men. The girl was pulling a dress over her head, in the picture. This girl has a nice-looking back, Harold thought. I wonder where she lives?

Perpetua sat on the couch in her new apartment smoking dope with a handsome bassoon player. A few cats walked around.

"Our art contributes nothing to the revolution," the bassoon player said. "We cosmeticize reality."

"We are trustees of Form," Perpetua said.

"It is hard to make the revolution with a bassoon," the bassoon player said.

"Sabotage?" Perpetua suggested.

"Sabotage would get me fired," her companion replied. "The sabotage would be confused with ineptness anyway."

I am tired of talking about the revolution, Perpetua thought.

"Go away," she said. The bassoon player put on his black raincoat and left.

It is wonderful to be able to tell them to go away, she reflected. Then she said aloud, "Go away. Go away. Go away."

Harold went to visit his child, Peter. Peter was at school in New England. "How do you like school?" Harold asked Peter.

"It's O.K.," Peter said. "Do you have a light?"

Harold and Peter watched the game together. Peter's school won. After the game, Harold went home.

3.

Perpetua went to her mother's house for Christmas. Her mother was cooking the eighty-seventh turkey of her life. "God damn this turkey!" Perpetua's mother shouted. "If anyone knew how I hate, loathe, and despise turkeys. If I had known that I would cook eighty-seven separate and distinct turkeys in my life, I would have split forty-four years ago. I would have been long gone for the tall timber."

Perpetua's mother showed her a handsome new leather coat.

"Tanned in the bile of matricides," her mother said, with a meaningful look.

Harold wrote to the magazine for men asking for the name and address of the girl whose back had bewitched him. The magazine answered his letter saying that it could not reveal this information. The magazine was not a pimp, it said.

Harold, enraged, wrote to the magazine and said that if the magazine was not a pimp, what was it? The magazine answered that while it could not in all conscience give Harold the girl's address, it would be glad to give him her grid coordinates. Harold, who had had map reading in the Army, was delighted.

4.

Perpetua sat in the trumpet section of the New World Symphony Orchestra. She had a good view of the other players because the sections were on risers and the trumpet section sat on the highest riser of all. They were playing Brahms. A percussionist had just split a head on the bass drum. "I luff Brahms," he explained.

Perpetua thought: I wish this so-called conductor would get his movie together.

After the concert she took off her orchestra uniform and put on her suede jeans, her shirt made of a lot of colored scarves sewn together, her carved-wood neck bracelet, and her D'Artagnan cape with its silver lining.

Perpetua could not remember what was this year and what was last year. Had something just happened, or had it happened a long time ago? She met many new people. "You are different," Perpetua said to Sunny Marge. "Very few of the girls I know wear a tattoo of the head of Marshal Foch on their backs."

"I am different," Sunny Marge agreed. "Since I posed for that picture in that magazine for men, many people have been after my back. My back has become practically an international incident. So I decided to alter it."

"Will it come off? Ever?"

"I hope and pray."

Perpetua slept with Robert in his loft. His children were sleeping on mattresses in the other room. It was cold. Robert said that when he was a child he was accused by his teacher of being "pert."

"Pert?"

Perpetua and Robert whispered to each other, on the mattress.

5.

Perpetua said, "Now, I am alone. I have thrown my husband away. I remember him. Once he seemed necessary to me, or at least important, or at least interesting. Now none of these things is true. Now he is as strange to me as something in the window of a pet shop. I gaze into the pet-shop window, the Irish setters move about, making their charming moves, I see the moves and see that they are charming, yet I am not charmed. An Irish setter is what I do not need. I remember my husband awaking in the morning, inserting his penis in his penis sheath, placing ornaments of bead and feather on his upper arms, smearing his face with ochre and umber—broad lines under the eyes and across the brow. I remember him taking his blowpipe from the umbrella stand and leaving for the office. What he did there I never knew. Slew his enemies, he said. Our dinner table was decorated with the heads of his enemies, whom he had slain. It was hard to believe one man could have so many enemies. Or maybe they were the same enemies, slain over and over and over. He said he saw girls going down the street who broke his heart, in their loveliness. I no longer broke his heart, he said. I had not broken his heart for at least a year, perhaps more than a year, with my loveliness. Well screw that, I said, screw that. My oh my, he said, my oh my, what a mouth. He meant that I was foulmouthed. This, I said, is just the beginning."

In the desert, Harold's Land-Rover had a flat tire. Harold got out of the Land-Rover and looked at his map. Could this be the wrong map?

6.

Perpetua was scrubbing Sunny Marge's back with a typewriter eraser.

"Oh. Ouch. Oh. Ouch."

"I'm not making much progress," Perpetua said.

"Well I suppose it will have to be done by the passage of time," Sunny Marge said, looking at her back in the mirror.

"Years are bearing us to Heaven," Perpetua agreed.

Perpetua and Sunny Marge went cruising, on the boulevard. They saw a man coming toward them.

"He's awfully clean-looking," Perpetua said.

"Probably he's from out of town," Sunny Marge said.

Edmund was a small farmer.

"What is your cash crop?" Sunny Marge asked.

"We have two hundred acres in hops," the farmer replied. "That reminds me, would you ladies like a drink?"

"*I'd* like a drink," Perpetua said.

"I'd like a drink too," Sunny Marge said. "Do you know anywhere he can go, in those clothes?"

"Maybe we'd better go back to my place," Perpetua said.

At Perpetua's apartment Edmund recounted the history of hops.

"Would you like to see something interesting?" Sunny Marge asked Edmund.

"What is it?"

"A portrait of Marshal Foch, a French hero of World War I."

"Sure," Edmund said.

The revolution called and asked Perpetua if she would tape an album of songs of the revolution.

"Sure," Perpetua said.

Harold took ship for home. He shared a cabin with a man whose hobby was building scale models of tank battles.

"This is a *Sturmgeschütz* of the 1945 period," the man said. "Look at the bullet nicks. The bullet nicks are done by applying a small touch of gray paint with a burst effect of flat white. For small holes in the armor, I pierce with a hot nail."

The floor of Harold's cabin was covered with tanks locked in duels to the death.

Harold hurried to the ship's bar. I wonder how Perpetua is doing, he thought. I wonder if she is happier without me. Probably she is. Probably she has found deep contentment by now. But maybe not.

1.

Perpetua met many new people. She met Henry, who was a cathedral builder. He built cathedrals in places where there were no cathedrals—Twayne, Nebraska, for example. Every American city needed a cathedral, Henry said. The role of the cathedral in the building of the national soul was well known. We should punish ourselves in our purses, Henry said, to shape up the national soul. An arch never sleeps, Henry said, pointing to the never-sleeping arches in his plans. Architecture is memory, Henry said, and the nation that had no cathedrals to speak of had no memory to speak of either. He did it all, Henry said, with a 30-man crew composed of 1 superintendent 1 masonry foreman 1 ironworker foreman 1 carpenter foreman 1 pipefitter foreman 1 electrician foreman 2 journeyman masons 2 journeyman pipefitters 2 journeyman electricians 1 mason's helper 1 ironworker's helper 1 carpenter's helper 1 pipefitter's helper 1 electrician's helper 3 gargoyle carvers 1 grimer 1 clerk-of-the-works 1 master fund-raiser 2 journeyman fund-raisers and 1 fund-raiser's helper. Cathedrals are mostly a matter of thrusts, Henry said. You got to balance your thrusts. The ribs of your vaults intersect collecting the vertical and lateral thrusts at fixed points which are then buttressed or grounded although that's not so important anymore when you use a steel skeleton as we do which may be cheating but I always say that cheating in the Lord's name is O.K. as long as He don't catch you at it. Awe and grace, Henry said, awe and grace, that's what we're selling and we offer a Poet's Corner where any folks who were poets or even suspected of being poets can be buried, just like Westminster Abbey. The financing is the problem, Henry said. What we usually do is pick out some old piece of ground that was a cornfield or something like that, and put it in the Soil Bank. We take that piece of ground out of production and promise the government we won't grow no more corn on it no matter how they beg and plead with us. Well the government sends a man around from the Agriculture Department and he agrees with us that there certainly ain't no corn growing there. So we ask him about how much he thinks we can get from the Soil Bank and he says it looks like around a hundred and fifty thousand a year to him but that he will have to check with the home office and we can't expect the money before the middle of next week. We tell him that will be fine and we all go have a drink over to the Holiday Inn. Of course the hundred and fifty thousand is just a spit in the ocean but it pays for the four-color brochures. By this time we got our artist's rendering of the Twayne Undenominational Cathedral sitting right in the lobby of the Valley National Bank on a card table covered with angel hair left over from Christmas, and the money is just pouring in. And I'm worrying about how we're going to *staff* this cathedral. We need a sexton and a bellringer and a beadle and maybe an undenominational archbishop, and that last is hard to come by. Pretty soon the ground is broken and the steel is up, and the Bell Committee is wrangling about whether the carillon is going to be sixteen bells or thirty-two. There is something about cathedral building that men like, Henry said, this has often been noticed. And the first thing you know it's Dedication Day and the whole state is there, it seems like, with long lines of little girls carrying bouquets of mistflowers and the Elks Honor Guard presenting arms with M-16s sent back in pieces from Nam and reassembled for domestic use, and the band is playing the Albinoni Adagio in G Minor which is the saddest piece of music ever written by mortal man and the light is streaming through the guaranteed stained-glass windows and the awe is so thick you could cut it with a knife.

"You are something else, Henry," Perpetua said.

8.

Perpetua and André went over to have dinner with Sunny Marge and Edmund.

"This is André," Perpetua said.

André, a well-dressed graduate of the École du Regard, managed a large industry in Reims.

Americans were very strange, André said. They did not have a stable pattern of family life, as the French did. This was attributable to the greater liberty—perhaps license was not too strong a term—permitted to American women by their husbands and lovers. American women did not know where their own best interests lay, André said. The intoxication of modern life, which was in part a result of the falling away of former standards of conduct . . .

Perpetua picked up a chicken leg and tucked it into the breast pocket of André's coat.

"Goodbye, André."

Peter called Perpetua from his school in New England.

"What's the matter, Peter?"

"I'm lonesome."

"Do you want to come stay with me for a while?"

"No. Can you send me fifty dollars?"

"Yes. What do you want it for?"

"I want to buy some blue racers."

Peter collected snakes. Sometimes Perpetua thought that the snakes were dearer to him than she was.

9.

Harold walked into Perpetua's apartment.

"Harold," Perpetua said.

"I just want to ask you one question," Harold said. "Are you happier now than you were before?"

"Sure," Perpetua said.

Edward and Pia

E dward looked at his red beard in the tableknife. Then Edward and Pia went to Sweden, to the farm. In the mailbox Pia found a check for Willie from the government of Sweden. It was for twenty-three hundred crowns and had a rained-on look. Pia put the check in the pocket of her brown coat. Pia was pregnant. In London she had been sick every day. In London Pia and Edward had seen the Marat/Sade at the Aldwych Theatre. Edward bought a bottle of white stuff for Pia in London. It was supposed to make her stop vomiting. Edward walked out to the wood barn and broke up wood for the fire. Snow in patches lay on the ground still. Pia wrapped cabbage leaves around chopped meat. She was still wearing her brown coat. Willie's check was still in the pocket. It was still Sunday.

"What are you thinking about?" Edward asked Pia and she said she was thinking about Willie's hand. Willie had hurt his hand in a machine in a factory in Markaryd. The check was for compensation.

Edward turned away from the window. Edward received a cable from his wife in Maine. "Many happy birthdays," the cable said. He was thirty-four. His father was in the hospital. His mother was in the hospital. Pia wore white plastic boots with her brown coat. When Edward inhaled sharply—a sharp intake of breath—they could hear a peculiar noise in his chest. Edward inhaled sharply. Pia heard the noise. She looked up. "When will you go to the doctor?" "I have to get something to read," Edward said. "Something in English." They walked to Markaryd. Pia wore a white plastic hat. At the train station they bought a *Life* magazine with a gold-painted girl on the cover. "Shall we eat something?" Edward asked. Pia said no. They bought a crowbar for the farm. Pia was sick on the way back. She vomited into a ditch.

Pia and Edward walked the streets of Amsterdam. They were hungry. Edward wanted to go to bed with Pia but she didn't feel like it. "There's something wrong," he said. "The wood isn't catching." "It's too wet," she said, "perhaps." "I *know* it's too wet," Edward said. He went out to the wood barn and broke up more wood. He wore a leather glove on his right hand. Pia told Edward that she had been raped once, when she was twenty-two, in the Botanical Gardens. "The man that raptured me has a shop by the Round Tower. Still." Edward walked out of the room. Pia looked after him placidly. Edward reentered the room. "How would you like to have some Southern fried chicken?" he asked. "It's the most marvelous-tasting thing in the world. Tomorrow I'll make some. Don't say 'rapture.' In English it's 'rape.' What did you do about it?" "Nothing," Pia said. Pia wore green rings, dresses with green sleeves, a green velvet skirt.

Edward put flour in a paper bag and then the pieces of chicken, which had been dipped in milk. Then he shook the paper bag violently. He stood behind Pia and tickled her. Then he hugged her tightly. But she didn't want to go to bed. Edward decided that he would never go to bed with Pia again. The telephone rang. It was for Fru Schmidt. Edward explained that Fru Schmidt was in Rome, that she would return in three months, that he, Edward, was renting the flat from Fru Schmidt, that he would be happy to make a note of the caller's name, and that he would be delighted to call this note to the attention of Fru Schmidt when she returned, from Rome, in three months. Pia vomited. Pia lay on the bed sleeping. Pia wore a red dress, green rings on her fingers.

Then Edward and Pia went to the cinema to see an Eddie Constantine picture. The film was very funny. Eddie Constantine broke up a great deal of furniture chasing international bad guys. Edward read two books he had already read. He didn't remember that he had read them until he reached the last page of each. Then he read four paperback mysteries by Ross Macdonald. They were excellent. He felt slightly sick. Pia walked about with her hands clasped together in front of her chest, her shoulders bent. "Are you cold?" Edward asked. "What are you thinking about?" he asked her, and she said she was thinking about Amboise, where she had contrived to get locked in a chateau after visiting hours. She was *also* thinking, she said, about the green-and-gold wooden horses they had seen in Amsterdam. "I would like enormously to have one for this flat," she said. "Even though the flat is not ours." Edward asked Pia if she felt like making love now. Pia said no.

It was Sunday. Edward went to the bakery and bought bread. Then he bought milk. Then he bought cheese and the Sunday newspaper, which he couldn't read. Pia was asleep. Edward made coffee for himself and looked at the pictures in the newspaper. Pia woke up and groped her way to the bathroom. She vomited. Edward bought Pia a white dress. Pia made herself a necklace of white glass and red wood beads. Edward worried about his drinking. Would there be enough gin? Enough ice? He went out to the kitchen and looked at the bottle of Gordon's gin. Two inches of gin.

Edward and Pia went to Berlin on the train. Pia's father thrust flowers through the train window. The flowers were wrapped in green paper. Edward and Pia climbed into the Mercedes-Benz taxi. "Take us to the Opera if you will, please," Edward said to the German taxi-driver in English. "*Ich verstehe nicht,*" the driver said. Edward looked at Pia's belly. It was getting larger, all right. Edward paid the driver. Pia wondered if the Germans were as loud in Germany as they were abroad. Edward and Pia listened for loudness.

Edward received a letter from London, from Bedford Square Office Equipment, Ltd. "We have now completed fitting new parts and adjusting the Olivetti portable that was unfortunately dropped by you. The sum total of parts and labour comes to £7.10.0 and I am adding £1.00.0 hire charges, which leaves a balance of £1.10.0 from your initial deposit of £10. Yours." Yours. Yours. Edward received a letter

33

from Rome, from Fru Schmidt, the owner of the flat in Frederiksberg Allé. "Here are many Americans who have more opportunities to wear their mink capes than they like, I guess! I wish I had one, just one of rabbit or cat, it is said to be just as warm! but I left all my mink clothes behind me in Denmark! We spend most of our time in those horrible subways-metros which are like the rear entrance to Hell and what can you see of a city from there? Well you are from New York and so are used to it but I was born as a human being and not as a—" Here there was a sketch of a rat, in plan. Kurt poured a fresh cup of coffee for Edward. There were three people Pia and Edward did not know in the room, two men and a woman. Everyone watched Kurt pouring a cup of coffee for Edward. Edward explained the American position in South Vietnam. The others looked dubious. Edward and Pia discussed leaving each other.

Pia slept on the couch. She had pulled the red-and-brown blanket up over her feet. Edward looked in the window of the used-radio store. It was full of used radios. Edward and Pia drank more sherry. "What are you thinking about?" he asked her and she said she was wondering if they should separate. "You don't seem happy," she said. "You don't seem happy either," he said. Edward tore the cover off a book. The book cover showed a dog's head surrounded by flowers. The dog wore a black domino. Edward went to the well for water. He lifted the heavy wooden well cover. He was wearing a glove on his right hand. He carried two buckets of water to the kitchen. Then he went to the back of the farmhouse and built a large wooden veranda, roofed, thirty metres by nine metres. Fortunately there was a great deal of new lumber stacked in the barn. In the Frederiksberg Allé apartment in Copenhagen he stared at the brass mail slot in the door. Sometimes red-and-blue airmail envelopes came through the slot.

Edward put his hands on Pia's breasts. The nipples were the largest he had ever seen. Then he counted his money. He had two hundred and forty crowns. He would have to get some more money from somewhere. Maurice came in. "My house is three times the size of this one," Maurice said. Maurice was Dutch. Pia and Edward went to Maurice's house with Maurice. Maurice's wife Randy made coffee. Maurice's son Pieter cried in his wooden box. Maurice's cats walked around. There was an open fire in Maurice's kitchen. There were forty empty beer bottles in a corner. Randy said she was a witch. She pulled a long dark hair from her head. Randy said she could tell if the baby was going to be a boy or a girl. She slipped a gold ring from her finger and, suspending the ring on the hair, dangled it over Pia's belly. "It has to be real gold," Randy said, referring to the ring. Randy was rather pretty.

Pia and Edward and Ole and Anita sat on a log in France drinking white Algerian wine. It was barely drinkable. Everyone wiped the mouth of the bottle as it was passed from hand to hand. Edward wanted to sleep with Pia. "Yes," Pia said. They left the others. Edward looked at his red beard in the shiny bottom part of the kerosene lantern. Pia thought about her first trip to the Soviet Union. Edward sat at the bar in Le Ectomorph listening to the music. Pia thought about her first trip to the Soviet Union. There had been a great deal of singing. Edward listened to the music. Don Cherry was playing trumpet. Steve Lacey was playing soprano sax. Kenny Drew was playing piano. The drummer and bassist were Scandinavians. Pia remembered a Russian boy she had known. Edward talked to a Swede. "You want to know who killed Kennedy?" the Swede said. "*You* killed Kennedy." "No," Edward said. "I did not." Edward went back to Frederiksberg Allé. Pia was sleeping. She was naked. Edward lifted the blankets and looked at Pia sleeping. Pia moved in the bed and grabbed at the blankets. Edward went into the other room and tried to find something to read. Edward had peculiar-looking hair. Parts of it were too short and parts of it were too long. Edward and Pia telephoned friends in another city. "Come stay with us," Edward and Pia said. "Please!"

Edward regarded Pia. Pia felt sick: "Why doesn't he leave me alone sometimes?" Edward told Pia about Harry. Once he had gotten Harry out of jail. "Harry was drunk. A cop told him to sit down. Harry stood up. Blam! Five stitches." "What are stitches?" Edward looked it up in the Dansk-Engelsk Ordbog. Edward had several manuscripts that were designed to have an effect on Pia. One of them was washing the dishes. At other times he was sour for several hours. In Leningrad they visited Pia's former lover, Paul. The streets in Leningrad are extremely wide. Paul called his friend Igor, who played the guitar. Paul called Igor on the telephone. Pia and Paul were happy to see each other again. Paul talked to Edward about South Vietnam. There was tea. Edward thought that he, Edward, was probably being foolish. But how could he tell? Edward wanted more dishes. Igor's fingers moved quickly among the frets. Edward had drunk too much tea. Edward had drunk too much brandy. Edward was in bed with Pia. "You look beautiful," Edward said to Pia. Pia thought: I feel sick.

In Copenhagen Edward bought *The Penguin English Dictionary*. Sixteen crowns. Pia told a story about one of the princesses. "She is an archeologist, you know? Her picture comes in the newspaper standing over a great hole with her end sticking up in the air." Pia's little brother wore a black turtleneck sweater and sang "We Shall Overcome." He played the guitar. Kurt played the guitar. Kirsten played the guitar. Anita and Ole played the guitar. Deborah played the flute. Edward read *Time* and *Newsweek*. On Tuesday Edward read *Newsweek*, and on Wednesday, *Time*. Pia bought a book about babies. Then she painted her nails silver. Pia's nails were very long. Organ music played by Finn Viderø was heard on the radio. Edward suggested that Pia go back to the university. He suggested that Pia study French, Russian, English, guitar, flute, and cooking. Pia's cooking was rotten. Suddenly she wished she was with some other man and not with Edward. Edward was listening to the peculiar noise inside his chest. Pia looked at Edward. She looked at his red beard, his immense spectacles. I don't like him, she thought. That red beard, those immense spectacles. Saab jets roared overhead. Edward turned off the radio.

Pia turned on the radio. Edward made himself a dry vermouth on the rocks with two onions. It was a way of not drinking. Edward felt sick. He had been reading *Time* and *Newsweek*. It was Thursday. Pia said to Edward that he was the only person she had ever loved for this long. "How long is it?" Edward asked. It was seven months. Edward cashed a check at American Express. The girl gave him green-and-blue Scandinavian money. Edward was pleased. Little moans of pleasure. He cashed another check at Cook's. More money. Edward sold Pia's farm for eighteen thousand crowns. Much more money. Pia was pleased. Edward sold Pia's piano for three thousand crowns. General rejoicing. Klaus opened the door. Edward showed him the money. Pia made a chocolate cake with little red-and-white flags on the top. Pia lay in bed. She felt sick. They plugged in an electric heater. The lights went out. Herr Kepper knocked on the door. "Is here an electric heater?" Edward showed him the money. Pia hid the electric heater.

Edward watched the brass slot on the door. Pia read to Edward from the newspaper. She read a story about four Swedes sent to prison for rapture. Edward asked Pia if she wanted to make love. "No," she said. Edward said something funny. Pia tried to laugh. She was holding a piece of cake with a red-and-white flag on top. Edward bought a flashlight. Pia laughed. Pia still didn't want to go to bed with Edward. It was becoming annoying. He owed the government back home a thousand dollars. Edward laughed and laughed. "I owe the government a thousand dollars," Edward said to Pia, "did you know that?" Edward laughed. Pia laughed. They had another glass of wine. Pia was pregnant. They laughed and laughed. Edward turned off the radio. "The lights went out," he said in Danish. Pia and Edward laughed. "What are you thinking about?" Edward asked Pia and she said she couldn't tell him just then because she was laughing.

The Piano Player

Outside his window five–year–old Priscilla Hess, square and squat as a mailbox (red sweater, blue lumpy corduroy pants), looked around poignantly for someone to wipe her overflowing nose. There was a butterfly locked inside that mailbox, surely; would it ever escape? Or was the quality of mailboxness stuck to her forever, like her parents, like her name? The sky was sunny and blue. A filet of green Silly Putty disappeared into fat Priscilla Hess and he turned to greet his wife who was crawling through the door on her hands and knees.

"Yes?" he said. "What now?"

"I'm ugly," she said, sitting back on her haunches. "Our children are ugly."

"Nonsense," Brian said sharply. "They're wonderful children. Wonderful and beautiful. Other people's children are ugly, not our children. Now get up and go back to the smokeroom. You're supposed to be curing a ham."

"The ham died," she said. "I couldn't cure it. I tried everything. You don't love me anymore. The penicillin was stale. I'm ugly and so are the children. It said to tell you goodbye."

"It?"

38

"The ham," she said. "Is one of our children named Ambrose? Somebody named Ambrose has been sending us telegrams. How many do we have now? Four? Five? Do you think they're heterosexual?" She made a *moue* and ran a hand through her artichoke hair. "The house is rusting away. Why did you want a steel house? Why did I think I wanted to live in Connecticut? I don't know."

"Get up," he said softly, "get up, dearly beloved. Stand up and sing. Sing *Parsifal*."

"I want a Triumph," she said from the floor. "A TR–4. Everyone in Stamford, every single person, has one but me. If you gave me a TR–4 I'd put our ugly children in it and drive away. To Wellfleet. I'd take all the ugliness out of your life."

"A green one?"

"A *red* one," she said menacingly. "Red with leather seats."

"Aren't you supposed to be chipping paint?" he asked. "I bought us an electronic data processing system. An IBM."

"I want to go to Wellfleet," she said. "I want to talk to Edmund Wilson and take him for a ride in my red TR–4. The children can dig clams. We have a lot to talk about, Bunny and me."

"Why don't you remove those shoulder pads?" Brian said kindly. "It's too bad about the ham."

"*I loved that ham,*" she said viciously. "When you galloped into the University of Texas on your roan Volvo, I thought you were going to *be somebody*. I gave you my hand. You put rings on it. Rings that my mother gave me. I thought you were going to be distinguished, like Bunny."

He showed her his broad-shouldered back. "Everything is in flitters," he said. "Play the piano, won't you?"

"You always were afraid of my piano," she said. "My four or five children are afraid of the piano. *You taught them to be afraid of it.* The giraffe is on fire, but I suppose you don't care."

"What can we eat," he asked, "with the ham gone?"

"There's Silly Putty in the deepfreeze," she said tonelessly.

"Rain is falling," he observed. "Rain or something."

"When you graduated from the Wharton School of Business," she said, "I thought *at last!* I thought *now we can move to Stamford and have interesting neighbors.* But they're not interesting. The giraffe is interesting but he sleeps so much of the time. The mailbox is *rather* interesting. The man didn't open it at 3:31 P.M. today. He was five minutes late. The government lied again."

With a gesture of impatience, Brian turned on the light. The great burst of electricity illuminated her upturned tiny face. Eyes like snow peas, he thought. Tamar dancing. My name is in the dictionary, in the back. The Law of Bilateral Good Fortune. Piano bread perhaps. A nibble of pain running through the Western World. Coriolanus.

"Oh God," she said, from the floor. "Look at my knees."

Brian looked. Her knees were blushing.

"It's senseless, senseless, senseless," she said, "I've been caulking the medicine chest. What for? I don't know. You've got to give me more money. Ben is bleeding. Bessie wants to be an S.S. man. She's reading *The Rise and Fall.* She's identified with Himmler. Is that her name? Bessie?"

"Yes. Bessie."

"What's the other one's name? The blond one?"

"Billy. Named after your father. Your Dad."

"You've got to get me an air hammer. To clean the children's teeth. What's the name of that disease? They'll all have it, every single one, if you don't get me an air hammer."

"And a compressor," Brian said. "And a Pinetop Smith record. I remember."

She lay on her back. The shoulder pads clattered against the terrazzo. Her number, 17, was written large on her chest. Her eyes were screwed tight shut. "Altman's is having a sale," she said. "Maybe I should go in."

"Listen," he said. "Get up. Go into the grape arbor. I'll trundle the piano out there. You've been chipping too much paint."

"You wouldn't touch that piano," she said. "Not in a million years."

"You really think I'm afraid of it?"

40

"Not in a million years," she said, "you phony."

"All right," Brian said quietly. "All *right.*" He strode over to the piano. He took a good grip on its black varnishedness. He began to trundle it across the room, and, after slight hesitation, it struck him dead.

Henrietta and Alexandra

Alexandra was reading Henrietta's manuscript.

"This," she said, pointing with her finger, "is inane."

Henrietta got up and looked over Alexandra's shoulder at the sentence.

"Yes," she said. "I prefer the inane, sometimes. The ane is often inutile to the artist."

There was a moment of contemplation.

"I have been offered a thousand florins for it," Henrietta said. "The Dutch rights."

"How much is that in our money?"

"Two hundred sixty-six dollars."

"Bless Babel," Alexandra said, and took her friend in her arms.

Henrietta said: "Once I was a young girl, very much like any other young girl, interested in the same things, I was exemplary. I was told what I was, that is to say a young girl, and I knew what I was because I had been told and because there were other young girls all around me who had been told the same things and knew the same things, and looking at them and hearing again in my head the things I had been told I knew what a young girl was. We had all been told the same things. I had not been told, for example, that some wine was

42

piss and some not and I had not been told . . . other things. Still I had not been told a great many things all very useful but I had not been told that I was going to die in any way that would allow me to realize that I really was going to die and that it would all be over, then, and that this was all there was and that I had damned well better make the most of it. That I discovered for myself and covered with shame and shit as I was I made the most of it. I had not been told how to make the most of it but I figured it out. Then I moved through a period of depression, the depression engendered by the realization that I had placed myself beyond the pale, there I was, beyond the pale. Then I discovered that there were other people beyond the pale with me, that there were quite as many people on the wrong side of the pale as there were on the right side of the pale and that the people on the wrong side of the pale were as complex as the people on the right side of the pale, as unhappy, as subject to time, as subject to death. So what the fuck? I said to myself in the colorful language I had learned on the wrong side of the pale. By this time I was no longer a young girl. I was mature."

Alexandra had a special devotion to the Sacred Heart.

THEORIES OF THE SACRED HEART

LOSS AND RECOVERY OF THE SACRED HEART

CONFLICTING CLAIMS OF THE GREAT CATHEDRALS

THE SACRED HEART IN CONTEMPORARY ICONOGRAPHY

APPEARANCE OF SPURIOUS SACRED HEARTS AND HOW THEY MAY BE
DISTINGUISHED FROM THE TRUE ONE

LOCATION OF THE TRUE SACRED HEART REVEALED

HOW THE ABBÉ ST. GERMAIN PRESERVED THE TRUE SACRED HEART
FROM THE HANDS OF THE BARBARIANS

WHY THE SACRED HEART IS FREQUENTLY REPRESENTED SURMOUNTED
BY A CROWN OF THORNS

MEANING OF THE TINY TONGUE OF FLAME

ORDERS AND CEREMONIES IN THE VENERATION OF THE SACRED HEART

ROLE OF THE SACRED HEART SOCIETY IN THE VENERATION OF THE
SACRED HEART

Alexandra was also a member of the Knights of St. Dympna, patroness of the insane.

Alexandra and Henrietta were walking down the street in their long gowns. A man looked at them and laughed. Alexandra and Henrietta rushed at him and scratched his eyes out.

As a designer of artificial ruins, Alexandra was well-known. She designed ruins in the manners of Langley, Effner, Robert Adam, and Carlo Marchionni, as well as her own manner. She was working on a ruin for a park in Tempe, Arizona, consisting of a ruined wall nicely disintegrated at the top and one end, two classical columns upright and one fallen, vines, and a number of broken urns. The urns were difficult because it was necessary to produce them from intact urns and the workmen at the site were often reluctant to do violence to the urns. Sometimes she pretended to lose her temper. *"Hurl the bloody urn, Umberto!"*

Alexandra looked at herself in the mirror. She admired her breasts, her belly, and her legs, which were, she felt, her best feature.

"Now I will go into the other room and astonish Henrietta, who is also beautiful."

Henrietta stood up and, with a heaving motion, threw the manuscript of her novel into the fire. The manuscript of the novel she had been working on ceaselessly, night and day, for the last ten years.

"Alexandra! Aren't you going to rush to the fire and pull the manuscript of my novel out of it?"

"No."

Henrietta rushed to the fire and pulled the manuscript out of it. Only the first and last pages were fully burned, and luckily, she remembered what was written there.

Henrietta decided that Alexandra did not love her enough. And how could nuances of despair be expressed if you couldn't throw your novel into the fire safely?

Alexandra was sending a petition to Rome. She wanted her old marriage, a dim marriage ten years old to a man named Black Dog, annulled. Alexandra read the rules about sending petitions to Rome to Henrietta.

"All applications to be sent to Rome should be written on good paper, and a double sheet, 8⅛ inches x 10¾ inches, should be employed. The writing of petitions should be done with ink of a good quality, that will remain legible for a long time. Petitions are generally composed in the Latin language, but the use of the French and Italian languages is also permissible.

"The fundamental rule to be observed is that all petitions must be addressed to the Pope, who, directly or indirectly, grants the requested favors. Hence the regulation form of address in all petitions reads *Beatissime Pater*. Following this the petition opens with the customary deferential phrase *ad pedes Sanctitatis Vestrae humillime provolutus*. The concluding formula is indicated by its opening words: *Et Deus* . . . expressing the prayer of blessing which the grateful petitioner addresses in advance to God for the expected favor.

"After introduction, body, and conclusion of the petition have been duly drawn, the sheet is evenly folded length-wise, and on its back, to the right of the fold line, are indited the date of the presentation and the petitioner's name.

"The presentation of petitions is generally made through an agent, whose name is inscribed in the right-hand corner on the back of the petition. This signature is necessary because the agent will call for the grant, and the Congregations deliver rescripts to no one but the agent whose name is thus recorded. The agents, furthermore, pay the fee and taxes for the requested rescripts of favor, give any necessary explanations and comments that may be required, and are at all times in touch with the authorities in order to correct any mistakes or defects in the petitions. Between the hours of nine and one o'clock the agents gather in the offices of the Curial administration to hand in new petitions and to inquire about the fate of those not yet decided. Many of them also go to the anterooms of secretaries in order to discuss important matters personally with the leading officials.

"For lay persons it is as a rule useless to forward petitions through the mails to the Roman Congregations, because as a matter of principle they will not be considered. Equally useless, of course, would be the enclosing of postage stamps with such petitions. Applications by telegraph are not permitted because of their publicity. Nor are decisions ever given by telegraph."

Alexandra stopped reading.

"Jesus Christ!" Henrietta said.

"This wine is piss," Alexandra said.

"You needn't drink it then."

"I'll have another glass."

"You wanted me to buy California wine," Henrietta said.

"But there's no reason to buy absolute vinegar, is there? I mean couldn't you have asked the man at the store?"

"They don't always tell the truth."

"I remember that time in Chicago," Alexandra said. "That was a good bottle. And afterwards . . ."

"How much did we pay for that bottle?" Henrietta asked, incuriously.

"Twelve dollars. Or ten dollars. Ten or twelve."

"The hotel," Henrietta said. "Snapdragons on the night table."

"You were . . . exquisite."

"I was mature," Henrietta said.

"If you were mature then, what are you now?"

"More mature," Henrietta said. "Maturation is a process that is ongoing."

"When are you old?" Alexandra asked.

"Not while love is here," Henrietta said.

Henrietta said: "Now I am mature. In maturity I found a rich world beyond the pale and found it possible to live in that world with a degree of enthusiasm. My mother says I am deluded but I have stopped talking to my mother. My father is dead and thus has no opinion. Alexandra continues to heap up indulgences by exclaiming 'Jesus, Mary, and Joseph!' which is worth an indulgence of fifty days each time it is exclaimed. Some of the choicer ejaculations are worth seven years and seven quarantines and these she pursues with the innocent cupidity of the small investor. She keeps her totals in a little book. I love her. She has to date worked off eighteen thousand years in the flames of Purgatory. I tell her that the whole thing is a shuck but she refuses to consider my views on this point. Alexandra is immature in that she thinks she will live forever, live after she is dead at the right hand of God in His glory with His power and His angels and His whatnot and I cannot persuade her otherwise. Joseph Conrad will live forever but Alexandra will not. I love her. Now we are going out."

Henrietta and Alexandra went walking. They were holding each other's arms. Alexandra moved a hand sensuously with a circular motion around one of Henrietta's breasts. Henrietta did the same thing to Alexandra. People were looking at them with strange expressions on their faces. They continued walking, under the shaped trees of the boulevard. They were swooning with pleasure, more or less. Someone called the police.

Presents

In the middle of a forest. Parked there is a handsome 1932 Ford, its left rear door open. Two young women are pausing, about to step into the car. Each has one foot on the running board. Both are naked. They have their arms around each other's waist in sisterly embrace. The woman on the left is dark, the one on the right fair. Their white, graceful backs are in sharp contrast to the shiny black of the Ford. The woman on the right has turned her head to hear something her companion is saying.

* * *

At a dinner party. The eight guests are seated, in shining white plastic shells mounted on steel pedestals, in a luxurious kitchen. They sit around a long table of polished rosewood, at one end of which there is a wicker basket filled with fruit, pineapples, bananas, pears, and at the other a wicker basket containing loaves of burnt-orange bread. The kitchen floor is polished black tile; electric ovens with bronze fronts are set into the polished off-white walls. On thick glass shelves above the diners, handsome pots with herbs, jams, jellies, and tall glass jars with half-a-dozen varieties of raw pasta. Six of the guests, men and women, are conventionally clothed. The two young women (one dark, one fair) are naked, smoking cigarillos. One of them unfolds a large white linen napkin and smoothes it over her companion's lap.

* * *

Ten o'clock in the morning. Marble, more marble, together with walnut paneling, a terrazzo floor, on the left a long (sixty feet) black-topped counter behind which the tellers sit, on the right a beige-carpeted area with three rows (three times three) of bank officers, suited and gowned. At the back, the great vault door open, functionary seated at desk reading a Gothic novel. In the center, long lines of depositors channeled to the tellers by a flattened S-curve of blue velvet ropes. Uniformed guards, etc., the American flag drooping on its standard near the vault. Two young women enter. They are naked except for black masks. One is dark, one fair. They place themselves back-to-back in the center of the banking floor. The guards rush toward them, then rush away again.

* * *

A woman seated on a plain wooden chair under a canopy. She is wearing white overalls and has a pleased expression on her face. Watching her, two dogs, German shepherds, at rest. Behind the dogs, with their backs to us, a row of naked women kneeling, sitting on their heels, their buttocks perfect as eggs or O's—OOOOOOOOOOOOO. In profile to the scene, at the far right, Henry James—his calm, accepting gaze.

* * *

Two young women wrapped as gifts. But the gift-wrapping is indistinguishable from ordinary clothing. Or there is a distinction, in that what they are wearing is perhaps a shade newer, brighter, more studied than ordinary clothing, proclaims the specialness of what is wrapped, argues for immediate unwrapping, or if not that, unwrapping at leisure, with wine, cheese, sour cream.

* * *

Two young women, naked, tied together by a long red thread. One is dark, one is fair.

* * *

Large (eight by ten feet) sheets of white paper on the floor, six or eight of them. The total area covered is perhaps 200 feet square; some of the sheets overlap. A string quartet is playing at one edge of this area, and irregular rows of handsomely-dressed spectators border another. A large bucket of blue paint sits on the paper. Two young women, naked. Each has her hair rolled up in a bun; each has been splashed, breasts, belly, and thighs, with blue paint. One, on her belly, is being dragged across the paper by the other, who is standing, gripping the first woman's wrists. Their backs are not painted. Or not painted with. The artist is Yves Klein.

* * *

Two young men, wrapped as gifts. They have wrapped themselves carefully, tight pants, open-throated shirts, shoes with stacked heels, gold jewelry on right and left wrists, codpieces stuffed with credit cards. They stand, under a Christmas tree big as an office building, the women rush toward them. Or they stand, under a Christmas tree big as an office building, and no women rush toward them. A voice singing inappropriate Easter songs, hallelujahs.

* * *

Two young men, artists, naked in a loft on Broome Street, are paint-ing a joint portrait of four young women, fully clothed, who are standing in a row with their backs to the artists, who are sipping coffee from paper cups (the paper cup held in the left hand, the brush or palette knife in the right) and carefully regarding the backs of the women, who from time to time let slip from the sides of their mouths comments (encouraging or disparaging) about the artists, who for their part are not intimidated by these comments which have mostly to do with the weather and future projects but in some cases with the comparative beauty and masculinity (because of course the women have opinions about these matters, expressed in whispers just loud enough to be overheard) of the naked artists, who are mostly worried about the stamina and comfort (four or five hours' work yet ahead) of the women, who are feeling rather hot and peevish in the white-painted, rather stuffy (although the big windows have been opened) loft of the artists, who are perfectly comfortable themselves, being naked, but do recognize the fact that some discomfort may be engendered by the heavy overcoats worn by the women, who are in truth pulling and tugging irritably upon these gross garments, increasing the nervousness of the artists, who are also concerned about the effect the scene might have upon someone who just blundered into it, such as the four lovers of the women, who are thinking now (by coincidence) of those selfsame lovers, Luke, Matt, John, and Mark, and what they might say if, battered by the heat of the hot sun, they staggered into an air-conditioned art gallery and there beheld a sixteen-by-forty foot painting of four backs, backs that they know intimately even through the layers of clothes, and begin to wonder whether the clothes on those backs had just been painted on (but of course they had been painted on, like everything else on the canvas) but had been really there while the women were posing for the naked artists, who are as character types notoriously . . .

* * *

Nowhere—the middle of it, its exact center. Standing there, a telephone booth, green with tarnished aluminum, the word PHONE and the system's symbol (bell in ring) in medium blue. Inside the telephone booth, two young women, one dark, one fair, facing each other. Their breasts and thighs brush lightly (one holding the receiver to the other's ear) as they place phone calls to their mothers in California and Maine. In profile to the scene, at far right, Henry James, wearing white overalls.

* * *

Henry James, wearing white overalls (Iron Boy brand) is attending a film. On the screen two young women, naked, are playing ping-pong. One makes a swipe with her paddle at a ball the other has placed just over the net and misses, bruising her right leg. The other puts down her paddle and walks around the table (gracefully) to examine the bruise; she places her hands on either side of the raw, ugly mark, then bends to kiss it. Henry James picks up his hat and walks thoughtfully from the theatre. Behind the popcorn machine in the lobby stand two young women, naked, one dark and one fair. Henry James approaches the popcorn stand and purchases, for 35¢, a bag of M & Ms. He opens the bag with his teeth. The women smile at each other.

* * *

Two young women wearing web belts to which canteens are attached, nothing more, marching down Broadway again. They are followed by a large crowd, bands, etc.

* * *

A plaza or open space. Two young women on their hands and knees. They are separated by a distance of eight feet, both facing in the same direction. Rough wooden boards (one by tens) have been laid across their backs to form a sort of table. On top of the table are piled bags and bags of M & Ms, hundreds of bags some of which have been opened spilling the chocolate out onto the table. A small army of insects, not ants but other chocolate-loving insects, informed of this prime target by scouts, is advancing across the plaza toward the rear of the table. The vanguard (the insects are a half-inch long and, closely inspected, resemble tiny black toothbrushes) reaches the left leg of the young woman on the left side of the table. The boldest members leap upon the leg, a line of insects runs up the leg toward the cleft of the buttocks. The table shudders and collapses.

* * *

The world of work. Two young women, one dark, one fair, wearing web belts to which canteens are attached, nothing more. They are sitting side-by-side on high stools (OO OO) before a pair of draughting tables, inking-in pencil drawings. Or, in a lumberyard in Southern Illinois, they are unloading a railroad car containing several hundred thousand board feet of Southern yellow pine. Or, in the composing room of a medium-sized Akron daily, they are passing long pieces of paper through a machine which deposits a thin coating of wax on the back side, and then positioning the type on a page. Or, they are driving two Yellow cabs which are racing side-by-side up Park Avenue with frightened passengers, each driver trying to beat the other to a hole in the traffic in front of them. Or, they are seated at adjacent desks in the beige-carpeted area set apart for officers in a bank (possibly the very same bank they had entered, naked, masked, several days ago), refusing loans. Or, they are standing bent over, hands on knees, peering into the site of an archaeological dig in the Cameroons. Or, they are teaching, in adjacent classrooms, Naked Physics—in the classroom on the left, Naked Physics I, and in the classroom on the right, Naked Physics II. These courses are very popular. Or, they are kneeling, sitting on their heels, before a pair of shoeshine stands, polishing the expensive boots, suave loafers, of their admiring customers. OO OO.

*   *   *

Two women, one dark and one fair, wearing parkas, blue wool watch caps on their heads, inspecting a row of naked satyrs, hairy-legged, split-footed, tailed and tufted, who hang on hooks in a meat locker where the temperature is a constant 18 degrees. The women are tickling the satyrs under the tail, where they are most vulnerable, with their long white (nimble) fingers tipped with long curved scarlet nails. The satyrs squirm and dance under this treatment, hanging from hooks, while other women, seated in red plush armchairs, in the meat locker, applaud, or scold, or hug and kiss, in the meat locker.

*   *   *

Two women, one dark and one fair, wearing parkas, blue wool watch caps on their heads, inspecting a row of naked young men, hairy-legged, many-toed, pale and shivering, who hang on hooks in a meat locker where the temperature is a constant 18 degrees. The women are tickling the young men under the tail, where they are most vulnerable, with their long white (nimble) fingers tipped with long curved scarlet nails. The young men squirm and dance under this treatment, hanging from hooks, while giant eggs, seated in red plush chairs, boil.

* * *

Two young women, naked, trundle the giant boiled eggs to market in wheelbarrows. They move through double rows of shouting civilians who applaud the size, whiteness, and exquisite shape of the eggs, and the humor and good cheer of the women. The grandest eggs ever seen in this part of the country, and the most gloriously-powered wheelbarrows! There is no end to the intoxicating noise. The women are sweating, moisture visible on their backs, on their legs and breasts, on their white, beautifully-formed shoulders. Yet they smile, and smile, and smile, their hands on the handles of the wheelbarrows, their sturdy sweating backs bent into the work. Like Henry James writing a novel, they trundle onward, placing one foot in front of the other in sweet, determined, dogged bliss—the achievement of a task.

* * *

Bliss: A condition of extreme happiness, euphoria. The nakedness of young women, especially in pairs (that is to say, a plenitude) often produces bliss in the eye of the beholder, male or female. If you have an elbow in your mouth, then you are occupied, for the moment, but your mind often wanders away, toward more bliss, wondering if you should be doing something else, with your arms and legs, so as to provide more static along the surface of the situation, wherein the two (naked) young women lie unfolded before you, waiting for you to fold them up again in new, interesting ways. Oh they are good kids, no doubt about it, and brave and forthright too, and mind their manners and their eggs, and have hope and ambitions, and are supportive and giving as well as chilly and austere—most of all, naked. That is a delight, let us confess the fact, and that is why we are considering all these different ways in which naked young women may be conceptualized, in the privacy of our studies, dealt out like cards from a deck of thin, flexible, six-foot-tall mirrors. Doubtless women do the same sort of thing in regard to us, in the privacy of their studies, or even better things, things we have not yet been able to imagine, or possibly nothing at all—maybe they just sit there, the beauty of a naked thumb, for example, or a passionate, interestingly-historied wrist. What if they don't care? If this is the case, send them to the elephants, let them sit around all day listening to the elephants cry "Long live King Babar! Long live Queen Celeste!" Few naked young women can take much of this.

*　*　*

Back to business: Two naked young women are walking, with an older man in a white suit, on a plain in British Columbia. The older man has told them that he is Henry James, returned to earth in a special dispensation accorded those whose works, in life, have added to the gaiety of nations. They do not quite believe him, yet he is stately, courteous, beautifully-spoken, full of anecdotes having to do with the upper levels of London society. One of the naked young women reaches across the chest of Henry James to pinch, lightly, the rosy, full breast of the second young woman, who—

Among the Beanwoods

T he already-beautiful do not, as a rule, run.

I am, at the moment, seated.

Ireland and Scotland are remote; Wales fares little better. Here in this forest of tall, white beanwoods, the already-beautiful saunter. Some of them carry plump red hams, already cooked.

I am, at the moment, seated. On a chair in the forest, listening. I will rise, shortly, to hold the ladder for you. Every beanwood will have its chandelier scattering light on my exercise machine, which is made of cane. The beans you have glued together are as nothing to the difficulty of working with cane, at night, in the dark, in the wind, watched by insects. I will not allow my exercise machine to be photographed. It sings, as I exercise, like an unaccompanied cello. I will not allow my exercise machine to be recorded.

Tombs are scattered through the beanwoods, made of perfectly ordinary gray stone. All are empty. The chandeliers, at night, scatter light over the tombs, little houses in which I sleep, from time to time, with the already-beautiful, and they with me. We call to each other, at night, saying "Hello, hello" and "Who, who, who?" That one has her hips exposed, for rubbing.

Holding the ladder, I watch you glue additional chandeliers to appropriate limbs. You are tiring, you have worked very hard. Iced beanwater will refresh you, and these wallets made of ham. *I have been meaning to speak to you.* I have set bronze statues of alert, crouching Indian boys around the periphery of the forest, for ornamentation. Each alert, crouching Indian boy is accompanied by a large, bronze, wolf-like dog, finely polished.

I have been meaning to speak to you. I have many pages of notes. I have a note about cameras, a note about recorders, a note about steel wool, a note about the invitations. On weightier matters I will speak without notes, freely and passionately, as if inspired, at night, in a rage, slapping myself, great tremendous slaps to the brow which will fell me to the earth. The already-beautiful will stand and watch, in a circle, cradling, each, an animal in mothering arms—green monkey, meadow mouse, tucotuco. That one has her hips exposed, for study. I make careful notes. You snatch the notebook from my hands.

The pockets of your smock swinging heavily with the lights of chandeliers. *Your light-by-light, bean-by-bean career.*

I am, at this time, prepared to dance. The already-beautiful have, historically, danced. The music made by my exercise machine is, we agree, danceable. The women partner themselves with large bronze hares, which have been cast in the attitudes of dancers. The beans you have glued together are as nothing to the difficulty of casting hares in the attitudes of dancers, at night, in the foundry, the sweat, the glare. Thieves have been invited to dinner, along with the deans of the great cathedrals. The thieves will rest upon the bosoms of the deans, at dinner, among the beanwoods. Soft benedictions will ensue.

I am privileged, privileged, to be able to hold your ladder.

Pillows are placed in the tombs, together with pot holders and dust cloths. The already-beautiful strut. England is far away, and France is scarcely nearer. I am, for the time being, reclining. In a warm tomb, with Concordia, who is beautiful. Mad with bean wine she has caught me by the belt buckle and demanded that I hear her times tables. Her voice enchants me. Tirelessly you glue. The forest will soon exist on some maps, a tribute to the quickness of the world's cartographers. This life is better than any life I have lived, previously. I order more smoke, which is delivered in heavy glass demi-johns, twelve to a crate. Beautiful hips abound, bloom. Your sudden movement toward red kidney beans has proved, in the event, masterly. Everywhere we see formal gowns of red kidney beans, which have been polished to the fierceness of carnelians. No ham hash does not contain two beans, polished to the fierceness of carnelians.

Spain is distant, Portugal wrapped in an impenetrable haze. These noble beans, glued by you, are mine. Thousand-pound sacks are off-loaded at the quai, against our future needs. The thieves are willing workers, the deans, straw bosses of extraordinary tact. I polish hares, dogs, Indian boys in the chill of early morning. Your weather reports have been splendid. The fall of figs you predicted did in fact occur. There is nothing like ham in fig sauce, or almost nothing. I am, at the moment, feeling very jolly. Hey hey, I say. It is remarkable how well human affairs can be managed, with care.

You Are as Brave as Vincent Van Gogh

You eavesdrop in three languages. Has no one ever told you not to pet a leashed dog? We wash your bloody hand with Scotch from the restaurant.

Children. *I want one,* you say, pointing to a mother pushing a pram. And there's not much time. But the immense road-mending machine (yellow) cannot have children, even though it is a member of a family, it has siblings—the sheep's-foot roller, the air hammer.

You ask: Will there be fireworks?

I would never pour lye in your eyes, you say.

Where do you draw the line? I ask. Top Job?

Shall we take a walk? Is there a trout stream? Can one rent a car? Is there dancing? Sailing? Dope? Do you know Saint-Exupéry? Wind? Sand? Stars? Night flights?

You don't offer to cook dinner for me again today.

The air hammer with the miserable sweating workman hanging on to the handles. I assimilated the sexual significance of the air hammer long ago. It's new to you. You are too young.

You move toward the pool in your black bikini, you will open people's pop-top Pepsis for them, explicate the Torah, lave the brown shoulders of new acquaintances with Bain de Soleil.

You kick me in the backs of the legs while I sleep.

59

You are staring at James. James is staring back. There are six of us sitting on the floor around a low, glass-topped table. I become angry. Is there no end to it?

See, there is a boy opening a fire hydrant, you stand closer, see, he has a large wrench on top of the hydrant and he is turning the wrench, the water rushes from the hydrant, you bend to feel the water on your hand.

You are reading *From Ritual to Romance*, by Jessie L. Weston. But others have read it before you. Practically everyone has read it.

At the pool, you read Saint-Exupéry. But wait, there is a yellow nylon cord crossing the pool, yellow nylon supported by red-and-blue plastic floats, it divides the children's part from the deeper part, you are in the pool investigating, flexing the nylon cord, pulling on it, yes, it is firmly attached to the side of the pool, to both sides of the pool. And in the kitchen you regard the salad chef, a handsome young Frenchman, he stares at you, at your tanned breasts, at your long dark (wet) hair, can one, would it be possible, at this hour, a cup of coffee, or perhaps tea . . .

Soon you will be thirty.

And the giant piece of yellow road-mending equipment enters the pool, silently, you are in the cab, manipulating the gears, levers, shove this one forward and the machine swims. Swims toward the man in the Day-Glo orange vest who is waving his Day-Glo orange flags in the air, this way, this way, here!

He's a saint, you said. Did you ever try to live with a saint?

You telephone to tell me you love me before going out to do something I don't want you to do.

If you are not asking for fireworks you are asking for Miles Davis bound hand and foot, or Iceland. You make no small plans.

See, there is a blue BOAC flight bag, open, on the floor, inside it is a folded newspaper, a towel, and something wrapped in silver foil. You bend over the flight bag (whose is it? you don't know) and begin to unwrap the object wrapped in silver foil. Half a loaf of bread. Satisfied, you wrap it up again.

You return from California too late to vote. One minute too late. I went across the street to the school with you. They had locked the doors. I remember your banging on the doors. No one came to open them. Tears. *What difference does one minute make?* you screamed, in the direction of the doors.

Your husband, you say, is a saint.

And did no one ever tell you that the staircase you climbed in your dream, carrying the long brown velvet skirt, in your dream is a very old staircase?

I remind myself to tell you that you are abnormally intelligent. You kick me in the backs of the legs again, while I sleep.

Parades, balloons, fêtes, horse races.

You feel your time is limited. Tomorrow, you think, there will be three deep creases in your forehead. You offer to quit your job, if that would please me. I say that you cannot quit your job, because you are abnormally intelligent. Your job needs you.

The salad chef moves in your direction, but you are lying on your back on the tennis court, parallel with and under the net, turning your head this way and that, applauding the players, one a tall man with a rump as big as his belly, which is huge, the other a fourteen-year-old girl, intent, lean stringy hair, sorry, good shot, nice one, your sunglasses stuck in your hair. You rush toward the mountain which is furnished with trees, ski lifts, power lines, deck chairs, wedding invitations, you invade the mountain as if it were a book, leaping into the middle, checking the ending, ignoring the beginning. And look there, a locked door! You try the handle, first lightly, then viciously.

You once left your open umbrella outside the A & P, tied to the store with a string. When you came out of the store with your packages, you were surprised to find it gone.

The three buildings across the street from my apartment—one red, one yellow, one brown—are like a Hopper in the slanting late-afternoon light. See? Like a Hopper.

Is that a rash on my chest? Between the breasts? Those little white marks? Look, those people at the next table, all have ordered escargots, seven dozen in garlic butter arriving all at once, eighty-four dead snails on a single surface, in garlic butter. And last night, when it was so hot, I opened the doors to the balcony, I couldn't sleep, I lay awake, I thought I heard something, I imagined someone climbing over the balcony, I got up to see but there was no one.

You are as beautiful as twelve Hoppers.

You are as brave as Vincent Van Gogh.

I make the fireworks for you:

* ! * !] * !! * [! * ! * and * % % * +&+&+ * % % *.

If he is a saint, why did you marry him? It makes no sense. Outside in the street, some men with a cherry picker are placing new high-intensity bulbs in all the street lights, so that our criminals will be scalded, transfigured with light.

Yesterday you asked me for the Princeton University Press.

The Princeton University Press is not a toy, I said.

It's not?

And then: Can we go to a *movie* in which there are fireworks?

But there are fireworks in all movies, that is what movies are for—what they do for us.

You should not have left the baby on the lawn. In a hailstorm. When we brought him inside, he was covered with dime-size blue bruises.

The Agreement

Where is my daughter?

Why is she there? What crucial error did I make? Was there more than one?

Why have I assigned myself a task that is beyond my abilities?

Having assigned myself a task that is beyond my abilities, why do I then pursue it with all of the enthusiasm of one who believes himself capable of completing the task?

Having assigned myself a task that is beyond my abilities, why do I then do that which is most certain to preclude my completing the task? To ensure failure? To excuse failure? Ordinary fear of failure?

When I characterize the task as beyond my abilities, do I secretly believe that it is within my powers?

Was there only one crucial error, or was there a still more serious error earlier, one that I did not recognize as such at the time?

Was there a series of errors?

Are they in any sense forgivable? If so, who is empowered to forgive me?

If I fail in the task that is beyond my abilities, will my lover laugh?

Will the mailman laugh? The butcher?

When will the mailman bring me a letter from my daughter?

Why do I think my daughter might be dead or injured when I know that she is almost certainly well and happy? If I fail in the task that is beyond my abilities, will my daughter's mother laugh?

But what if the bell rings and I go down the stairs and answer the door and find there an old woman with white hair wearing a bright-red dress, and when I open the door she immediately begins spitting blood, a darker red down the front of her bright-red dress?

If I fail in the task that is beyond my abilities, will my doctor laugh?

Why do I conceal from my doctor what it is necessary for him to know?

Is my lover's lover a man or a woman?

Will my father and mother laugh? Are they already laughing, secretly, behind their hands?

If I succeeded in the task that is beyond my abilities, will I win the approval of society? If I win the approval of society, does this mean that the (probable) series of errors already mentioned will be forgiven, or, if not forgiven, viewed in a more sympathetic light? Will my daughter then be returned to me?

Will I deceive myself about the task that is beyond my abilities, telling myself that I have successfully completed it when I have not?

Will others aid in the deception?

Will others unveil the deception?

But what if the bell rings and I go down the stairs and answer the door and find there an old man with white hair wearing a bright-red dress, and when I open the door he immediately begins spitting blood, a darker red down the front of his bright-red dress?

Why did I assign myself the task that is beyond my abilities?

Did I invent my lover's lover or is he or she real? Ought I to care?

But what if the bell rings and I go down the stairs again and instead of the white-haired woman or man in the bright-red dress my lover's lover is standing there? And what if I bring my lover's lover into the house and sit him or her down in the brown leather club chair and provide him or her with a drink and begin to explain that the task I have undertaken is hopelessly, hopelessly beyond my abilities? And what if my lover's lover listens with the utmost consideration, nodding and smiling and patting my wrist at intervals as one does with a nervous client, if one is a lawyer or doctor, and then abruptly offers me a new strategy: Why not do *this*? And what if, thinking over the new strategy proposed by my lover's lover, I recognize that yes, *this* is the solution which has evaded me for these many months? And what if, recognizing that my lover's lover has found the solution which has evaded me for these many months, I suddenly begin spitting blood, dark red against the blue of my blue work shirt? What then?

For is it not the case that even with the solution in hand, the task will remain beyond my abilities?

And where is my daughter? What is my daughter thinking at this moment? Is my daughter, at this moment, being knocked off her bicycle by a truck with the words HACHARD & CIE painted on its sides? Or is she, rather, in a photographer's studio, sitting for a portrait I have requested? Or has she already done so, and will, today, the bell ring and the mailman bring a large stiff brown envelope stamped PHOTO DO NOT BEND?

HACHARD & CIE?

PHOTO DO NOT BEND?

If I am outraged and there is no basis in law or equity for my outrage nor redress in law or equity for my outrage, am I to decide that my outrage is wholly inappropriate? If I observe myself carefully, using the techniques of introspection most favored by society, and decide, after such observation, that my outrage is not wholly inappropriate but perhaps partially inappropriate, what can I do with my (partially appropriate) outrage? What is there to do with it but deliver it to my lover or my lover's lover or to the task that is beyond my abilities, or to embrace instead the proposition that, after all, things are not so bad? Which is not true?

If I embrace the proposition that, after all, things are not so bad, which is not true, then have I not also embraced a hundred other propositions, kin to the first in that they are also not true? That the Lord is my shepherd, for example?

But what if I decide not to be outraged but to be, instead, calm and sensible? Calm and sensible and adult? And mature? What if I decide to send my daughter stamps for her stamp collection and funny postcards and birthday and Christmas packages and to visit her at the times stated in the agreement? And what if I assign myself simpler, easier tasks, tasks which are well within my powers? And what if I decide that my lover has no other lover (disregarding the matchbooks, the explanations that do not explain, the discrepancies of time and place), and what if I inform my doctor fully and precisely about my case, supplying all relevant details (especially the shameful)? And what if I am able to redefine my errors as positive adjustments to a state of affairs requiring positive adjustments? And what if the operator does *not* break into my telephone conversation, any conversation, and say, "I'm sorry, this is the operator, I have an emergency message for 679-9819"?

Will others aid in the deception?

Will others unveil the deception?

"TWELFTH: Except for the obligations, promises and agreements herein set forth and to be performed by the husband and wife respectively, and for rights, obligations and causes of action arising out of or under this agreement, all of which are expressly reserved, the husband and wife each hereby, for himself or herself and for his or her legal representatives, forever releases and discharges the other, and the heirs and legal representatives of the other, from any and all debts, sums of money, accounts, contracts, claims, cause or causes of action, suits, dues, reckonings, bills, specialties, covenants, controversies, agreements, promises, variances, trespasses, damages, judgments, extents, executions, and demands, whatsoever, in law or in equity, which he or she had, or has or hereafter can, shall or may have, by reason of any matter, from the beginning of the world to the execution of this agreement."

The painters are here. They are painting the apartment. One gallon of paint to eight gallons of benzine. From the beginning of the world to the execution of this agreement. Where is my daughter? I am asking for a carrot to put in the stone soup. The villagers are hostile.

Basil From Her Garden

A: In the dream, my father was playing the piano, a Beethoven something, in a large concert hall that was filled with people. I was in the audience and I was reading a book. I suddenly realized that this was the wrong thing to do when my father was performing, so I sat up and paid attention. He was playing very well, I thought. Suddenly the conductor stopped the performance and began to sing a passage for my father, a passage that my father had evidently botched. My father listened attentively, smiling at the conductor.

Q: Does your father play? In actuality?

A: Not a note.

Q: Did the conductor resemble anyone you know?

A: He looked a bit like Althea. The same cheekbones and the same chin.

Q: Who is Althea?

A: Someone I know.

Q: What do you do, after work, in the evenings or on weekends?

A: Just ordinary things.

Q: No special interests?

A: I'm very interested in bow-hunting. These new bows they have now, what they call a compound bow. Also, I'm a member of the

Galapagos Society, we work for the environment, it's really a very effective—

Q: And what else?

A: Well, adultery. I would say that's how I spend most of my free time. In adultery.

Q: You mean regular adultery.

A: Yes. Sleeping with people to whom one is not legally bound.

Q: These are women.

A: Invariably.

Q: And so that's what you do, in the evenings or on weekends.

A: I had this kind of strange experience. Today is Saturday, right? I called up this haircutter that I go to, her name is Ruth, and asked for an appointment. I needed a haircut. So she says she has openings at ten, ten-thirty, eleven, eleven-thirty, twelve, twelve-thirty—On a Saturday. Do you think the world knows something I don't know?

Q: It's possible.

A: What if she stabs me in the ear with the scissors?

Q: Unlikely, I would think.

A: Well, she's a good soul. She's had several husbands. They've all been master sergeants, in the Army. She seems to gravitate toward N.C.O. Clubs. Have you noticed all these little black bugs flying around here? I don't know where they come from.

Q: They're very small, they're like gnats.

A: They come in clouds, then they go away.

A: I sometimes think of myself as a person who, you know what I mean, could have done something else, it doesn't matter what particularly. Just something else. I saw an ad in the Sunday paper for the C.I.A., a recruiting ad, maybe a quarter of a page, and I suddenly thought, It might be interesting to do that. Even though I've always been opposed to the C.I.A., when they were trying to bring Cuba down, the stuff with Lumumba in Africa, the stuff in Central America . . . Then here is this ad, perfectly straightforward, "where your career is America's strength" or something like that, "aptitude for learning a foreign language is a plus" or something like that. I've always been good at languages, and I'm sitting there thinking about how my résumé might look to them, starting completely over in something completely new, changing the very sort of person I am, and there was an attraction, a definite attraction. Of course the maximum age was thirty-five. I guess they want them more malleable.

Q: So, in the evenings or on weekends—

A: Not every night or every weekend. I mean, this depends on the circumstances. Sometimes my wife and I go to dinner with people, or watch television—

Q: But in the main—

A: It's not that often. It's once in a while.

Q: Adultery is a sin.

A: It is classified as a sin, yes. Absolutely.

Q: The Seventh Commandment says—

A: I know what it says. I was raised on the Seventh Commandment. But.

Q: But what?

A: The Seventh Commandment is wrong.

Q: It's wrong?

A: Some outfits call it the Sixth and others the Seventh. It's wrong.

Q: The whole Commandment?

A: I don't know how it happened, whether it's a mistranslation from the Aramaic or whatever, it may not even have been Aramaic, I don't know, I certainly do not pretend to scholarship in this area, but my sense of the matter is the Seventh Commandment is an error.

Q: Well if that was true it would change quite a lot of things, wouldn't it?

A: Take the pressure off, a bit.

Q: Have you told your wife?

A: Yes, Grete knows.

Q: How'd she take it?

A: Well, she *liked* the Seventh Commandment. You could reason that it was in her interest to support the Seventh Commandment for the preservation of the family unit and this sort of thing but to reason that way is, I would say, to take an extremely narrow view of Grete, of what she thinks. She's not predictable. She once told me that she didn't want me, she wanted a suite of husbands, ten or twenty—

Q: What did you say?

A: I said, Go to it.

Q: Well, how does it make you feel? Adultery?

A: There's a certain amount of guilt attached. I feel guilty. But I feel guilty even without adultery. I exist in a morass of guilt. There's maybe a little additional wallop of guilt but I already feel so guilty that I hardly notice it.

Q: Where does all this guilt come from? The extra-adulterous guilt?

A: I keep wondering if, say, there is intelligent life on other planets, the scientists argue that something like two percent of the other planets have the conditions, the physical conditions, to support life in the way it happened here, did Christ visit each and every planet, go through the same routine, the Agony in the Garden, the Crucifixion, and so on . . . And these guys on these other planets, these lifeforms, maybe they look like boll weevils or something, on a much larger scale of course, were they told that they couldn't go to bed with other attractive six-foot boll weevils arrayed in silver and gold and with little squirts of Opium behind the ears? Doesn't make sense. But of course our human understanding is imperfect.

Q: You haven't answered me. This general guilt—

A: Yes, that's the interesting thing. I hazard that it is not guilt so much as it is inadequacy. I feel that everything is being nibbled away, because I can't *get it right*—

Q: Would you like to be able to fly?

A: It's crossed my mind.

Q: Myself, I think about being just sort of a regular person, one who worries about cancer a lot, every little thing a prediction of cancer, no I don't want to go for my every-two-years checkup because what if they find something? I wonder what will kill me and when it will happen, and I wonder about my parents, who are still alive, and what will happen to them. This seems to be to me a proper set of things to worry about. Last things.

A: I don't think God gives a snap about adultery. This is just an opinion, of course.

Q: So how do you, how shall I put it, pursue—

A: You think about this staggering concept, the mind of God, and then you think He's sitting around worrying about this guy and this woman at the Beechnut Travelodge? I think not.

Q: Well He doesn't have to think about every particular instance, He just sort of laid out the general principles—

A: He also created creatures who, with a single powerful glance—

Q: The eyes burn.

A: They do.

Q: The heart leaps.

A: Like a terrapin.

Q: Stupid youth returns.

A: Like hockey sticks falling out of a long-shut closet.

Q: Do you play?

A: I did. Many years ago.

Q: Who is Althea?

A: Someone I know.

Q: We're basically talking about Althea.

A: Yes. I thought you understood that.

Q: We're not talking about wholesale—

A: Oh Lord no. Who has the strength?

Q: What's she like?

A: She's I guess you'd say a little on the boring side. To the innocent eye.

Q: She appears to be a contained, controlled person, free of raging internal fires.

A: But my eye is not innocent. To the already corrupted eye, she's—

Q: I don't want to question you too closely on this. I don't want to strain your powers of—

A: Well, no, I don't mind talking about it. It fell on me like a ton of bricks. I was walking in the park one day.

Q: Which park?

A: That big park over by—

Q: Yeah, I know the one.

A: This woman was sitting there.

Q: They sit in parks a lot, I've noticed that. Especially when they're angry. The solitary bench. Shoulders raised, legs kicking—

A: I've crossed both major oceans by ship—the Pacific twice, on troopships, the Atlantic once, on a passenger liner. You stand out there, at the rail, at dusk, and the sea is limitless, water in every direction, never-ending, you think *water forever*, the movement of the ship seems slow but also seems inexorable, you feel you will be moving this way forever, the Pacific is about seventy million square miles, about one-third of the earth's surface, the ship might be making twenty knots, I'm eating oranges because that's all I can keep down, twelve days of it with thousands of young soldiers all around, half of them seasick—On the Queen Mary, in tourist class, we got rather good food, there was a guy assigned to our table who had known Paderewski, the great pianist who was also Prime Minister of Poland, he talked about Paderewski for four days, an ocean of anecdotes—

Q: When I was first married, when I was twenty, I didn't know where the clitoris was. I didn't know there was such a thing. Shouldn't somebody have told me?

A: Perhaps your wife?

Q: Of course, she was too shy. In those days people didn't go around saying, This is the clitoris and this is what its proper function is and this is what you can do to help out. I finally found it. In a book.

A: German?

Q: Dutch.

A: A dead bear in a blue dress, face down on the kitchen floor. I trip over it, in the dark, when I get up at 2 A.M. to see if there's anything to eat in the refrigerator. It's an architectural problem, marriage. If we could live in separate houses, and visit each other when we felt particularly gay—It would be expensive, yes. But as it is she has to endure me in all my worst manifestations, early in the morning and late at night and in the nutsy obsessed noontimes. When I wake up from my nap you don't *get* the laughing cavalier, you get a rank pigfooted belching blunderer. I knew this one guy who built a wall down the middle of his apartment. An impenetrable wall. He had a very big apartment. It worked out very well. Concrete block, basically, with fibre-glass insulation on top of that and sheetrock on top of that—

Q: What about coveting your neighbor's wife?

A: Well on one side there are no wives, strictly speaking, there are two floors and two male couples, all very nice people. On the other side, Bill and Rachel have a whole house. I like Rachel but I don't covet her. I could covet her, she's covetable, quite lovely and spirited, but in point of fact our relationship is that of neighborliness. I jump-start her car when her battery is dead, she gives me basil from her garden, she's got acres of basil, not literally acres but—Anyhow, I don't think that's much of a problem, coveting your neighbor's wife. Just speaking administratively, I don't see why there's an entire Commandment devoted to it. It's a mental exercise, coveting. To covet is not necessarily to take action.

Q: I covet my neighbor's leaf blower. It has this neat Vari-Flo deal that lets you—

A: I can see that.

Q: I am feverishly interested in these questions.

Q: Ethics has always been where my heart is.

Q: Moral precepting stings the dull mind into attentiveness.

Q: I'm only a bit depressed, only a bit.

Q: A new arrangement of ideas, based upon the best thinking, would produce a more humane moral order, which we need.

Q: Apple honey, disposed upon the sexual parts, is not an index of decadence. Decadence itself is not as bad as it's been painted.

Q: That he watched his father play the piano when his father could not play the piano and that he was reading a book while his father played the piano in a very large hall before a very large audience only means that he finds his roots, as it were, untrustworthy. The father imagined as a root. That's not unusual.

Q: As for myself, I am content with too little, I know this about myself and I do not commend myself for it and perhaps one day I shall be able to change myself into a hungrier being. Probably not.

Q: The leaf blower, for example.

A: I see Althea now and then, not often enough. We sigh together in a particular bar, it's almost always empty. She tells me about her kids and I tell her about my kids. I obey the Commandments, the sensible ones. Where they don't know what they're talking about I ignore them. I keep thinking about the story of the two old women in church listening to the priest discoursing on the dynamics of the married state. At the end of the sermon one turns to the other and says, "I wish I knew as little about it as he does."

Q: He critiques us, we critique Him. Does Grete also engage in dalliance?

A: How quaint you are. I think she has friends whom she sees now and then.

Q: How does that make you feel?

A: I wish her well.

Q: What's in your wallet?

A: The usual. Credit cards, pictures of the children, driver's license, forty dollars in cash, Amex receipts—

Q: I sometimes imagine that I am in Pest Control. I have a small white truck with a red diamond-shaped emblem on the door and a white jumpsuit with the same emblem on the breast pocket. I park the truck in front of a subscriber's neat three-hundred-thousand-dollar home, extract the silver canister of deadly pest killer from the back of the truck, and walk up the brick sidewalk to the house's front door. Chimes ring, the door swings open, a young wife in jeans and a pink flannel shirt worn outside the jeans is standing there. "Pest Control," I say. She smiles at me, I smile back and move past her into the house, into the handsomely appointed kitchen. The canister is suspended by a sling from my right shoulder, and, pumping the mechanism occasionally with my right hand, I point the nozzle of the hose at the baseboards and begin to spray. I spray alongside the refrigerator, alongside the gas range, under the sink, and behind the kitchen table. Next, I move to the bathrooms, pumping and spraying. The young wife is in another room, waiting for me to finish. I walk into the main sitting room and spray discreetly behind the largest pieces of furniture, an oak sideboard, a red plush Victorian couch, and along the inside of the fireplace. I do the study, spraying the Columbia Encyclopedia, he's been looking up the Seven Years' War, 1756–63, yellow highlighting there, and behind the forty-five-inch RCA television. The master bedroom requires just touches, short bursts in her closet which must avoid the two dozen pairs of shoes there and in his closet which contains six to eight long guns in canvas cases. Finally I spray the laundry room with its big white washer and dryer, and behind the folding table stacked with sheets and towels already folded. Who folds? I surmise that she folds. Unless one of the older children, pressed into service, folds. In my experience they are unlikely to fold. Maybe the au pair. Finished, I tear a properly made out receipt from my receipt book and present it to the young wife. She scribbles her name in the appropriate space and hands it back to me. The house now stinks quite palpably but I know and she knows that the stench will dissipate in two to four hours. The young wife escorts me to the door, and, in parting, pins a silver medal on my chest and kisses me on both cheeks. Pest Control!

A: Yes, one could fit in in that way. It's finally a matter, perhaps, of fit. Appropriateness. Fit in a stately or sometimes hectic dance with nonfit. What we have to worry about.

Q: It seems to me that we have quite a great deal to worry about. Does the radish worry about itself in this way? Yet the radish is a living thing. Until it's cooked.

A: Grete is mad for radishes, can't get enough. I like frozen Mexican dinners, Patio, I have them for breakfast, the freezer is stacked with them—

Q: Transcendence is possible.

A: Yes.

Q: Is it possible?

A: Not out of the question.

Q: Is it really possible?

A: Yes. Believe me.

Paradise Before the Egg

He's not potent more than forty-two percent of the time."

"Maybe we could feed him nourishing broths."

"They say that vitamin E is good for that."

"That's what I hear too."

"I don't think you can give somebody too much of any particular vitamin. The body takes what it needs and rejects the rest. I read about it."

"It's because he's so old."

"I don't think so. I read about this guy who was ninety-three and still was fathering children when he was ninety-three."

"Perhaps at long intervals after he had been carefully fed with vitamin E and nourishing broths."

"Maybe we should offer stimulating photographs."

"Of what?"

"Potentially arousing scenes."

"You mean the photographs would be more arousing than we are?"

"Well I don't know how their minds work."

"Maybe we should offer him potentially arousing scenes that are not photographs."

"You mean like real life."

"That's what I mean."

"Consisting of what?"

"I don't know. I'd have to look in some books."

"He's doing the best he can."

"That's your opinion."

"I think he works quite hard at it, spends hours and hours."

"I just think we've gotten ourselves into a fundamentally false position here, I don't blame the poor bastard, it's just more than the male mechanism is equipped to do."

"I saw this guy in a movie once. I couldn't believe it."

"They have these special guys they use for those movies, they're not what you usually run into. They're specialists."

"We don't want to stress him beyond his capacity or have him go mad or something."

"He shows no signs of going mad."

"He's raveling his clothes. Plucking at threads."

"I just think that means he doesn't have very good clothes. His clothes have a lot of loose ends and it's natural, I think, when you see a loose end to pluck at it."

"Has he made a will?"

"That's an evil thought, has he anything to will?"

"Beats me. I wouldn't take it if he did."

"Sure you would."

"How old is he actually?"

"He says he's fifty-three."

"He does appreciate what he's given."

"As well he should; he's in hog heaven, objectively speaking."

Veronica is bouncing on her trampoline. Dore is reading *Flowers for Algernon*. Simon is in bed with Anne.

"How does it make you feel with us in here and them out there?" she asks.

"Nervous."

"We're very tolerant."

"I see that. What's that wham-wham-wham noise?"

"Veronica."

"Is she making obscene comment?"

"She's just mindless when she gets on the trampoline. She can go for hours. She thinks she's got a problem with her rump. I don't think there's a problem but she thinks there's a problem."

"Makes me nervous."

"Everything makes you nervous."

"True."

"Is this a male fantasy for you? This situation?"

"It's not fantasy, is it?"

"It has the structure of a male fantasy."

"The dumbest possible way to look at it."

"Well, screw you."

"Our purpose here, I thought."

"Where did you go to college? Was it Harvard?"

"No it wasn't Harvard."

"Lots of people didn't go to Harvard."

"There's just not enough Harvard."

"Maybe we could start a branch. In Florida or somewhere."

"They probably don't feel the urgency."

"What are you going to do after we leave?" she asks.

"Go back to work, I guess."

"I wish I could do something."

"Work is God's best invention. Keeps you all seized up and interested."

Simon wanted very much to be a hearty, optimistic American, like the President, but on the other hand did not trust hearty, optimistic Americans, like the President. He had considered the possibility that the President, when not in public, was not really hearty and optimistic but rather a gloomy, obsessed man with a profound fear of the potentially disastrous processes in which he was enmeshed, no more sanguine than the Fisher King. He did not really believe this to be the case. He himself had settled for being a competent, sometimes inventive architect with a tragic sense of brick. Brick was his favorite material as the fortress was the architectural metaphor that he had, more and more, to resist. To force himself into freshness, he thought about bamboo.

Getting old, Simon. Not so limber, dear friend, time for the bone factory? The little blue van. Your hands are covered with tiny pepperoni. Your knees predict your face. Your back stabs you, on the left side, twice a day. The soul's shrinking to a microdot. We're ordering your rocking chair, size 42. Would you like something in southern pine? Loblolly? Send the women away. They're too good for you. Also, not good for you. Are you King Solomon? Your kingdom a scant 259,200 square inches. Annual tearfall, 3¼ inches. You feedeth among the lilies, Simon. There are garter snakes among the lilies, Simon, garter belts too. Your garden is overcultivated, it needs weeds. How's your skiwear, Simon? Done any demolition derbies lately? You run the mile in, what, a year and a half? We're sending you an electric treadmill, a solid-steel barbell curl bar, a digital pedometer. Use them. And send the women away.

When he asked himself what he was doing in a bare elegant almost unfurnished New York apartment with three young and beautiful women, Simon had to admit he *did not know* what he was doing. He was, he supposed, listening. These women were taciturn as cowboys, spoke only to the immediate question, probably did not know in which century the Second World War had taken place. No, too hard; it was, rather, that what they knew was so wildly various, ragout of Spinoza and Cyndi Lauper with a William Buckley sherbet floating in the middle of it. He'd come in one evening to find all three of them kneeling on the dining-room table with their asses pointing at him. Obviously he was supposed to strip off his gentlemanly khakis and attend to all three at once, just as obviously an impossibility. He had placed a friendly hand on each *cul* in turn and said, "O.K., guys, you've had your fun, now get back to the barracks. Out, out, out," he'd shouted, and they'd scattered, giggling. One night on his back in bed he'd had six breasts to suck, swaying above him, he was poor tattered Romulus. When they couldn't get a part of him they'd play with each other.

Dore likes to scold people. When anyone in the house does anything that does not meet her specifications for appropriate behavior, Dore scolds.

"Simon you're not supposed to talk to Anne like that."

"Like what?"

"You were condescending."

"In what way?"

"O.K., she never heard of the Marshall Plan. You don't have to explain it to her. In that way."

"Was I pompous?"

"Not more than usual. It was in that incredulous look. Like you couldn't believe that somebody'd never heard of the Marshall Plan."

"It was a big deal, historically."

"*Simon you are twice as old as we are.*"

"That does not absolve you of the necessity of knowing your own history."

"That's pompous. That's truly pompous. That's just what I'm talking about. And another thing."

"Oh Lord, what?"

"When you made that joke about George Gershwin and his lovely wife, Ira."

"Well?"

"Anne didn't know it was a joke. You can't make jokes that are based on people not knowing things. It's not fair. It's demeaning to women."

"Why to women?"

"Women don't pay attention to silly things like that. All that detail. And there's one more thing."

"Which is?

"You should take the laundry sometimes. Just because we're women doesn't mean that we have to take the laundry all the time."

"O.K. Good point."

"Also I met this interesting guy there last time. He's a professional whistler."

In hog heaven the hogs wait in line for more heaven. No not right, no waiting in line, it's unheavenly, unhogly. The celestial sty is quilted in kale, beloved of hogs. A male hog walks up to a female hog, says, "Want to get something going?" She is repulsed by his language, says, "Bro, unless you can phrase that better, you're chilly forever." No, that's not right, this is hog heaven, they fall into each other's trotters, nothing can be done wrong here, nothing wrong can be done . . .

In the mornings, large figures shrouded in terry cloth lurch back and forth between the several bedrooms and the single bathroom. Dore runs, in the mornings, picks up breakfast at the market on the way back, fresh Italian rolls, green garlicked *Kräuterbutter*, a quarter pound of breast of veal. She has become the manager of breakfast, takes pride in varying the fare, fine cheeses one day, a robust kidney stew the next, blueberry crepes and then chicken-fried steak with beaten biscuits. "This breaded burlap," Veronica says, "nicely done, but what are you, trying to kill us, or what?"

"Try more pepper."

Still in her sweats, she washes the dishes and stows them away, then settles down with the "Business Day" section of the *Times*, REVCO GETS $1.16 BILLION BUY-OUT BID, TROUBLED FARM BANKS TO GET REGULATORY AID, JAPANESE SETBACK ON CHIP PRICES. Scratching a bare foot with one hand, flipping pages with the other. Then she showers, dips into MTV (shoulder to shoulder with Anne for fifteen minutes). Then she's off to the New School for her Tuesday class, Investment Strategies for the Eighties.

"How'd you get in?" Simon asks.

"I'm auditing," she says. "I go early and get a seat. The class is so big they never take roll."

"You getting anything out of it?"

"You can't play unless you have something to play with. Still, it's educational."

After class, her nap. She throws herself on her bed and is dead to the world for an hour and a half, wearing only spun-sugar V-shaped briefs by Olga. Simon stares, on occasion, at the beautiful body at rest, facedown on the bed. What miracles of bawdiness it can perform without thinking, the operator quite unaware. In sleep, she scratches her belly. He feels the urge to sit on the edge of the bed (hurl himself into the bed), but does not. At night, she either puts herself together for Fizz or reads Dickens. She's bought four Dickens novels in worn Everyman editions at the Strand and is moving through them methodically. "The thing about Dickens is," she tells him, "he knew the value of a pound when you didn't have one. All his people are scrambling for money."

"So?" Simon says.

"I identify with that."

Late at night she sits with Simon drinking a Dos Equis and listening to Horace Silver.

"You're the mother of these guys," he says.

"I'm not. Last among equals."

"Veronica's a handful."

"She's her own person. I admire her. She's the smartest."

"How long have you three known each other?"

Dore giggles. "We all worked for a retail outlet in Denver. It was called Frederick's of Hollywood of Denver. It had nothing to do with the real Frederick's of Hollywood."

"Is that clothes?"

"Yes. Clothes."

What if they all lived happily ever after together? An unlikely prospect. What was there in his brain that forbade such felicity? *Too much*, his brain said, but the brain was a fair-to-middling brain at best, the glucose that kept it marching, metabolized crème brûlée, was present, but there was not enough vinegar in this brain, it lacked vinegar.

What was there to do with these women? He'd send them to MIT, make architects of them! Women were coming into the profession in increasing numbers. The group could chat happily about mullions, in the evening by the fireside; tiring of mullions, turn to cladding; wearying of cladding, attack with relish the problems of blast-cleaned pressure-washed gun-applied polymer-cement-coated steel. *Quel* happiness!

Someone would get pregnant, everyone would get pregnant. At seventy he'd be dealing with Pampers and new teeth. The new children would be named Susannah, Clarice, and Buck. He'd stroll out on the lawn, in the twilight, and throw the football at Buck. The football would rocket about two feet, then head for the greensward. The pitiful little child would say, "Kain't anybody here play this game?"

Lightning. Four o'clock in the afternoon. The women are in the kitchen, enjoying the display in the big windows.

Anne says, "What are we going to do about this bozo?"

"What's to do?" Veronica asks.

"He hasn't hurt anything. Yet," says Dore.

"He's been very circumspect."

"I think too circumspect."

"I think he thinks he's doing the right thing."

"He uses too much butter when he cooks. He's making pasta, he throws half a stick of butter in just before he serves it."

"Butter makes everything taste better."

"He looks around to see if anyone's watching before he throws it in. Then he whips it around in there real quick. Hoping it will melt before anybody sees it."

"It's just an effort to raise the level. That kind of shows I think an effort to raise the level of life, that's not too terrible. Typically American."

A majestic crash. They jump.

"That was a biggie."

"Not too bad."

"But what of us? What are we going to do?"

"Bide our time."

"I like that expression."

"Have you ever hung out with an architect before?"

"I knew this guy, he was a contractor, he contracted Port-O-Sans."

"What are they?"

"Moveable outhouses."

"Good Lord this man is old."

"Fifty-three. Old enough to be our father."

"Yet he has a certain spirit."

"He's indifferent."

"I don't think he's indifferent. He fucks well enough. Not the best I've ever seen."

"He can't tell us apart."

"Oh I don't think that's true. He asked me when my birthday was."

"What'd you tell him?"

"I told him. July 3."

"Well what does that prove?"

"He's thoughtful. He can tell one from another. He's interested in us as individuals."

"Maybe it's just a façade. Maybe he just knows what to do to make us think he cares about us as individuals and is doing it."

"Why would he do that? If he cares about us as individuals?"

"Because he likes us to have the feeling that he cares about us as individuals? Because it makes things more warm?"

"Well if he wants to make things more warm I'd say that was something in his favor."

"Yes but you have to make a distinction between making things seem a certain way and having them really be a certain way."

"Well even if he's only interested in making things seem a certain way that means he's not indifferent. To the degree that he makes the effort."

"That's true."

"But maybe, on the other hand, he really cares. About us as individuals."

"How would we know?"

The three women looked for jobs but were turned down by Bendel's, Bergdorf's, Bloomingdale's, Lord & Taylor, Charles Jourdan, Ungaro,

Altman's, Saks, Macy's. They tried all the modeling agencies, starting with Ford and working their way down the list. Simon designed
and had printed the composites for them and they left these at every
ad agency of any size in the city. They applied for substitute-teacher
positions but found this a closed shop, they needed New York State
credentials, which they didn't have. In a moment of desperation
they filed applications for the fire department but were told they
were so far down on the list they had no reasonable hope of consideration before 1999, when they would be too old to begin training.

Anne and Veronica are fighting.

"Stupid bitch!"

"Asshole!"

"C'mon, guys," Simon says. "What's the deal?"

"She's a motherfucker and a dumb motherfucker," Anne says.

"Look who's talking," Veronica says, jumping out of Anne's
reach. "Miss Slut of 1986."

"What's this about? What's the issue?"

"Simon you're so fucking reasonable," Veronica says, sitting
down on the couch.

"I say, what's going on?"

"She got us a job," Anne says.

"Terrific," says Simon. "What's the job?"

"Convention. The National Sprinkler Association. At the Ameri-
cana. We have to stand under these things and get sprinkled. I won't
do it."

"What if they gave us raincoats?"

"It's not raincoats they want to see."

"What if I said transparent plastic raincoats?"

"I might do it with transparent plastic raincoats."

"I'll call the guy and see what he says. It's two hundred each."

"Raincoats and body stockings."

"No thrill in body stockings."

"Let them use their vile imaginations."

"I just feel like a body."

"What in God's name do you think they want?"

"I know, I know."

"Look at it this way," Simon says. "A body is a gift. A great body is a great gift."

"All I need. A Unitarian minister."

"You don't have to take the job."

"We don't have any money."

"You want me to make a little pile of money and burn it right here on the floor? There's enough money around. Take it easy. Wait until you find something you want."

"We're concubines."

"You can make everything sound as terrible as you want," Simon says. "I'm going to bed."

"Who with?"

Simon's wife's lawyer's letter arrives and outlines her demands: She wants full custody of the child, the Pine Street house, both cars, $65,000 a year in alimony, child support at a level consonant with the child's previous style of life, 50 percent of all retirement funds, IRA, Keogh, and the firm's, 50 percent of his partnership interest in the firm in perpetuity, and 50 percent of all odds and ends of stocks, bonds, cash, and real property not subsumable under one of the previous rubrics. The client has been severely damaged in all ways by Simon's desertion and the years of fiendish abuse that had preceded it, the letter suggests.

"What are you going to do?" Veronica asks.

"Give it to her, I guess."

"Were you really that bad?"

"He may be overstating it a bit."

The professional whistler's wife calls and says that if the resident bitches and tarts don't keep their hands off her husband she will cause a tragic happenstance.

"She sounds a little pissed," Anne says.

"These housewives," says Veronica. "I guess you can't blame them they don't have the latitude."

Dore says, "Let her come around, her ass is grass."

"Simon is passive."

"I don't this he's so passive; he grasps you very tightly. I think the quality of the embrace is important."

"I think he's more active than passive. I'm still sore. I don't call that passive."

"He's slender."

"You call that slender?

"I except the paunch."

"He can go maybe eighteen times in a good month."

"That's depressing."

"I think it's depressing."

"We pretend to be O.K."

"I'm fine. I'm really fine."

"I was fine. Spent a lot of time on it, buffing the heels with one of those rocks they sell in the drugstore, oiling the carcass with precious oils—then I found out. How they exploit us and reduce us to nothing. Mere knitters."

"How'd you find out?"

"Read it in a feminist text."

"I heard they're not gonna let us read any more books."

"Where'd you hear that?"

"Just around. On the Rialto."

"Maybe it would be better for us so we wouldn't be exacerbated."

"You're like one of those people who lay down the flag in the dirt before it's time."

"Well that's what you say you fool."

"I want the car of my dreams."

"What is it?"

"Camaro."

"You're like one of those people who have really shitty dreams, know what I mean? Really shitty dreams."

"How can you say that?"

"I played in a band once."

"What was your instrument?"

"Tambourine."

"Can't get a union card for tambourine."

"My knee all black-and-blue, I banged my tambourine on it. First the elbow, then the knee."

"I saw a beautiful ass. In a picture. It was white and was walking away from the camera. She was holding hands with a man. He was naked too. It was a beautiful picture."

"How'd that make you feel?"

"Inferior."

"Well that's what you say you idiot."

"I'd like to light up a child's life, I apologize I was wrong."

"Yes you were wrong."

"But I still think what I think."

"It's hard to get a scrape when you want to light up a child's life."

"I've done it three times."

"Leaves you heavy of heart."

"It does."

Simon was a way station, a bed and breakfast, a youth hostel, a staging area, a C-141 with the jumpers of the 82nd Airborne lined up at the door. There was no place in the world for these women whom he loved, no good place. They could join the underemployed half-crazed demipoor, or they could be wives, those were the choices. The universities offered another path but one they were not likely to take. The universities were something Simon believed in (of course! he was a beneficiary), but there was among the women an animus toward the process that would probably never be overcome, not only impatience but a real loathing, whose source he did not really understand. Veronica told him that she had flunked freshman English three times. "How in the world do you do that?" he asked. "Comma splices," she said. "Also, every time I wrote down something I thought, the small-section teacher said that it was banal. It probably was banal." Simon found what the women had to say anything but banal, instead edged and immediate. Maybe nothing that could be rendered in a five-hundred-word theme, one bright notion and 450 words of hay. Or psychology: *Harlow, rhesus monkeys, raisins, reward.* People did master this stuff, more or less, and emerged more or less enriched thereby. *Compare and contrast extrinsic and intrinsic motivation, giving examples of each.* Father-beaten young women considering extrinsic and intrinsic motivation. "We all went through this," he told them, and Dore said, "Yeah, and you smart guys did the Vietnam War." Simon had opposed the Vietnam War in all possible ways short of self-immolation but could not deny that it was a war constructed by people who had labored through Psychology I, II, III, and IV and Main Currents of Western Thought. "But, dummy, it's the only thing you've got," he said. "Your best idea." "I have the highest respect for education," she said. "The highest. I'd be just as dreary when I came out as when I want in."

Veronica comes into his room looking very gloomy.

"We have to talk," she says. She's wearing a rather sedate dark-blue nightgown, one he hasn't seen before.

"What's the matter?

"Dore. She's falling apart."

"In what way?"

"She's lost her joy of life."

"I hadn't noticed."

"She tries to hide it from you."

"Maybe it's just temporary."

"I've never seen her like this. She's been reading terrible books. Books about how terrible men are and how they've kept us down."

"That should make her feel better, not worse. I mean, knowing the causes."

"Don't need your cheapo irony, Simon. She's very upset."

"What do you want me to do?"

"Talk to her."

"What can I say? I agree with half that stuff and think the other half is garbage."

"Well it's not for you to decide, is it? Whenever we say something you don't like you say we're hysterical or crazy."

"Me?"

"Men in general."

"Have I ever said you were hysterical or crazy?"

"Probably you didn't want to stir us up. Probably you were think-ing it and were just too tactful to say it."

"Are you sure it's Dore who's got this problem?"

"She's been lending us the books. What else do we have to do with our time?"

"So you're all upset."

"The truth shall make you free."

"What makes you think this stuff is the truth?"

"Thirty-five percent of all American women aren't allowed to talk at dinner parties. Think about that."

"How do you know?"

"It's in a book."

Veronica's trampoline is leaning against the wall and Veronica is throwing books at it to see how far they will bounce. *Buddenbrooks* in a paper edition bounces a good twelve feet. Dore is painting her legs red, with a two-inch brush and a big jar into which she has crumbled bright-red Easter-egg glazes. Anne is threatening to cut off her long dark hair. She stands poised, a hank in one hand, scissors in the other, daring anyone to interfere. "Anybody messes with me gets the scissors in the medulla." Simon senses unrest.

A terrible night. Simon is in bed by 10:00, taking a Scotch for company. Anne and Dore are now watching television. Veronica is out somewhere. About 10:30 Anne comes into the room, strips, and gets into bed with him.

"I'm cold," she says.

He turns her on her stomach and begins to stroke her back, gently. A very sculptural waist, narrowing suddenly under the rib cage and then the hipbones flaring.

When Anne goes back to her own bed, at 2:00, Dore appears in the doorway.

"Are you used up?" she asks.

"Probably." Dore climbs into bed, clumsily, peels off her jeans and bikini pants, retaining the tank top she's cut raggedly around the neck in the style of the moment.

"I'm sad and depressed," she says. "I feel useless. All I do is sit around and watch MTV."

"What do you want to do?

"Something. But I don't know what."

He struggles around the bed and begins to kiss the inside of her thighs. "This is a terrible night."

"Why?"

"You guys aren't solving your problems. I can't help you very much." His hands are splayed out over her back, moving up and down, over the shoulders and down to the splendid buttocks. Thinking of buttercups and butterflies and flying buttresses and butts of malmsey.

"Veronica has a rash," she says, coming up for air.

"What kind of rash?"

"Dark red. Looks like a wine stain."

"Where is it?"

"You'll see."

Veronica walks in. "What is taking place here?" she asks, in a voice like thunder.

Simon thinks about Paradise. On the great throne, a naked young woman, her back to the viewer. Simon looks around for Onan, doesn't see him. Onan didn't make it to Paradise? Seems unfair. Great deal of marble about, he notices, shades of rose and terracotta; Paradise seems to have been designed by Edward Durell Stone. Science had worked out a way to cremate human remains, reduce the ashes to the size of a bouillon cube, and fire the product into space in a rocket, solving the Forest Lawn dilemma. Simon had once done a sketch problem on tomb sculpture, for his sophomore Visual Awareness course. No more tomb sculpture.

Was he in love with these women? Yes, he was, however stupid that might be. He was in love with Anne, Veronica, and Dore. "I understand a divided heart," his wife had said to him once. The women would soon be gone. The best thing he could do was to listen to them.

"I've had twenty-six years' practice in standing up. I can do it," Anne says.

She's wearing sweat pants with a dark-gray crew-neck sweater and medium-gray Reeboks. She's been drinking tequila and she's terribly drunk.

"I want to tell you something."

"What?"

"You think we're dumb bunnies."

"What makes you think that?"

"Your attitude."

Simon's been reading *Audubon Action*, "Arizona Dam Project Faces New Challenge."

"What's my attitude?"

"I see fatigue and disgust."

"Sweetie, that's not true."

"Don't call me Sweetie."

Some days they were angry with him, some days they were angry with each other. Four people, many possibilities. Each person could be angry at any given point with one, two, or three others, or angry at the self. Two people could be angry at a third, three people at a fourth. He reached forty-nine possibilities before his math expired.

Their movement through the world required young men, a class to which he did not belong. Simon liked young men, within reasonable limits, and approved, in general, of the idea of young men and young women sleeping together in joyous disregard of history, economics, building codes. Let them have their four hundred square feet. Veronica liked garage apartments. Perhaps the young men would do well in the world, attend the new branch of Harvard Business in Gainesville, market a black-bean soup that would rage through Miami like rabies or a voice attenuator capable of turning crackers into lisping Brits, and end up with seven thousand square feet in Paris on the Ile de la Cité. Young men smelled good, by and large, almost as good as babies.

Simon constructs a white plaster egg eight feet tall and positions it in the sitting room. The women are watching, sitting on the gray couch. He smashes the egg with an iron-headed maul. Inside are three naked young men. Their names are Harry.

Three

I presented myself to the husband. He was an impressive figure in his brown velvet smoking jacket frogged (an ornamental fastening for the front of a coat consisting of a button and a loop through which it passes) with real frogs. I was wearing full dress with a red sash on which all thirty-four of my merit badges were displayed.

"Let there be no misunderstanding," I said. "I am here to ask for the hand in marriage of your wife."

He accepted this news calmly. He handed me a brandy in a brandy glass.

"I see you have Penmanship," he said regarding my sash. "Nothing gives one a better opinion of oneself than Penmanship."

"I also have Reverie," I said, pointing to Reverie.

"As to what you propose," the husband went on, "the girl is too young. Much, much too young. Too young and too beautiful. But a girl. Practically a maid if we are thinking of life experience."

"I love her," I said. "I want to make that clear. I love her, as that term is understood by me. Her perfections—"

"Yes, yes, that's all very well," the husband said, knocking back a bit of the brandy. "To be sure. An attractive match, from some points of view." He looked at his swords, which were crossed on the wall above the fireplace. "You are young and vigorous. I know your

96

family of old. Good people. Your income is acceptable. Your prospects bright. You have delicacy of feeling. You are not bad-looking,
aside from the scar."

"That was Counterinsurgency," I said pointing to the Counterinsurgency on my sash.

"Yes," the husband said, quieting a frog with his stroking fingers.
"You are a fine fellow, as fellows go. But—"

"I faint a good deal," I said. "In fairness I must tell you that faint-
ing is something I do a lot. Even now—"

"Yes," the husband said, "that often happens, with you younger
men. But may I point out that the lady, or rather the girl, whose hand
you seek has already made other arrangements?"

"I am aware of that and do not consider it an insurmountable
obstacle. You see I have Surmounting." I pointed to same, on my
sash.

"Let me top you up," the husband said and did so from his
decanter which bore a small silver plaque on a silver chain reading
Gift of the Mongolian People's Republic.

"You perhaps think I am not right. For Marie-Helene," he
continued.

I made "no no no" noises.

"It is true that I am a man of a certain temperament," he said.
"But *not right!* Marie-Helene doesn't think so. Only this morning
she was remarking upon my muscle tone."

He ripped open his smoking jacket to display the naked muscle
tone beneath. I had to admit it. This was good skin, clear, smooth,
rosy in color.

"Also there is my superb singing voice," the husband said.

He sang then some of Satie's furniture music. There was no gain-
saying the fact that he had a superb singing voice.

"Sir," I said, during a crack in the singing, "she loves me."

The husband left off singing.

"Well *of course!*" he said enthusiastically. "Who in the world
would doubt it? I expected it. Why not? How else? People meet
people and sweet music fills the air, as the poet Schade puts it. Of
course Schade is not my favorite poet."

"Your favorite poet is—"

"Neither here nor there," the husband announced. "No, I am afraid I cannot give you my blessing. You understand that there is nothing I would rather give you than my blessing. But my blessing, in this case, must be withheld. I know that this is something of a disappointment for you, brash successful young riser that you are. I know that you have pictured yourself rising, with Marie-Helene on your arm as it were, to heights. Well, what can I tell you? Into each life some rain must fall. My favorite poet, if I may parenthesize, is the Mills Brothers."

"Longfellow," I corrected him coldly. "'The Rainy Day' 1842. Stanza 3." I have a merit badge in Coldness, of which I am ashamed.

"Will you have a look at her?" the husband asked. "To make more keen the agony of bereftness?"

"Yes," I said, for every glimpse was gold.

The husband yanked upon a bellpull.

Presently Marie-Helene glided into the room. Then she glided into the room again.

"You have two!" I cried.

"Yes," the husband said, "beauties, aren't they."

They were beauties, it was a fact.

"This is Marie-Helene," the husband said, pointing to the one on the right, "and this is Helene-Marie," pointing to the one on the left. My love curtsied prettily twice, and went to sit upon a sofa.

"Two is a beautiful number," the husband said, "don't you think?"

"But if you have two—"

"I know what you are thinking," the husband said. "You reason like the child you are. If I have two, then I could easily give you one. That would be fair. Everything would then be just ducky." The husband moved very close to me. "You are a fool!" he said. "A child! They are *mine!*"

I remembered then that I had a merit badge in Contention.

We contended, the husband and I, for a brief time. I was bested. The weapons were cultural allusions.

He said: "Violette Leduc!"

I said: "Lightnin' Hopkins!"

He said: "Moses ben Maimon!"

I said: "Morse Peckham!"

He said: "Howlin' Wolf!"

I said: "Jurgen Becker!"

He said: "Myles na Gopaleen!"

I fainted.

When I revived I found his face very close to mine. "Listen!" he hissed. "I know that you already have a wife. I have seen her on the boulevards. She is very beautiful. *Give her to me!*"

"But," I said, shrinking, "then I would have none! No wife at all! Wifeless!"

"Three!" he shrieked, bending over me. "Three, three, three!"

Up, Aloft in the Air

1.

Buck saw now that the situation between Nancy and himself was considerably more serious than he had imagined. She exhibited unmistakable signs of a leaning in his direction. The leaning was acute, sometimes he thought she would fall, sometimes he thought she would not fall, sometimes he didn't care, and in every way tried to prove himself the man that he was. It meant dressing in unusual clothes and the breaking of old habits. But how could he shatter her dreams after all they had endured together? after all they had jointly seen and done since first identifying Cleveland as Cleveland? "Nancy," he said, "I'm too old. I'm not nice. There is my son to consider, Peter." Her hand touched the area between her breasts where hung a decoration, dating he estimated from the World War I period—that famous period!

The turbojet, their "ship," landed on its wheels. Buck wondered about the wheels. Why didn't they shear off when the aircraft landed so hard with a sound like thunder? Many had wondered before him. Wondering was part of the history of lighter-than-air-ness, you fool. It was Nancy herself, standing behind him in the exit line, who had suggested that they dance on the landing strip. "To establish rapport with the terrain," she said with her distant coolness, made more intense by the hot glare of the Edward pie vendors and customs trees. They danced the comb, the merengue, the *dolce far niente*. It was glorious there on the strip, amid air rich with the incredible vitality of jet fuel and the sensate music of exhaust. Twilight was lowered onto the landing pattern, a twilight such as has never graced Cleveland before, or since. Then broken, heartless laughter and the hurried trip to the hotel.

"I understand," Nancy said. And looking at her dispassionately, Buck conjectured that she *did* understand, unscrupulous as that may sound. *Probably,* he considered, *I convinced her against my will.* The man from Southern Rhodesia cornered him in the dangerous hotel elevator. "Do you think you have the right to hold opinions which differ from those of President Kennedy?" he asked. "The President of your land?" But the party made up for all that, or most of it, in a curious way. The baby on the floor, Saul, seemed enjoyable, perhaps more than his wont. *Or my wont,* Buck thought, *who knows!* A Ray Charles record spun in the gigantic salad bowl. Buck danced the frisson with the painter's wife Perpetua (although Nancy was alone, back at the hotel). "I am named," Perpetua said, "after the famous typeface designed by the famous English designer, Eric Gill, in an earlier part of our century." "Yes," Buck said calmly, "I know that face." She told him softly the history of her affair with her husband, Saul Senior. Sensuously, they covered the ground. And then two ruly police gentleman entered the room, with the guests blanching, and lettuce and romaine and radishes too flying for the exits, which were choked with grass.

Bravery was everywhere, but not here tonight, for the gods were whistling up their mandarin sleeves in the yellow realms where such matters are decided, for good or ill. Pathetic in his servile graciousness, Saul explained what he could while the guests played telephone games in crimson anterooms. The policemen, the flower of the Cleveland Force, accepted a drink and danced ancient police dances of custody and enforcement. Magically the music crept back under the perforated Guam doors; it was a scene to make your heart cry. "That Perpetua," Saul complained, "why is she treating me like this? Why are the lamps turned low and why have the notes I sent her been returned unopened, covered with red Postage Due stamps?" But Buck had, in all seriousness, hurried away.

The aircraft were calling him, their indelible flight plans whispered his name. He laid his cheek against the riveted flank of a bold 707. "*In case of orange and blue flames,*" he wrote on a wing, "*disengage yourself from the aircraft by chopping a hole in its bottom if necessary. Do not be swayed by the carpet; it is camel and very thin. I suggest that you be alarmed, because the situation is very alarming. You are up in the air perhaps 35,000 feet, with orange and blue flames on the outside and a ragged hole in the floorboards. What will you do?*" And now, Nancy. He held out his arms. She came to him.

"Yes."

"Aren't we?"

"Yes."

"It doesn't matter."

"Not to you. But to me . . ."

"I'm wasting our time."

"The others?"

"I felt ashamed."

"It's being here, in Cleveland."

They returned together in a hired automobile. Three parking lots were filled with overflow crowds in an ugly mood. I am tired, so very tired. The man from Southern Rhodesia addressed the bellmen, who listened to his hateful words and thought of other things. "But, then," Buck said, but then Nancy held a finger on his lips.

"You appear to me so superior, so elevated above all other men," she said, "I contemplate you with such a strange mixture of humility, admiration, revenge, love, and pride that very little superstition would be necessary to make me worship you as a superior being."

"Yes," Buck said, for a foreign sculptor, a Bavarian doubtless, was singing "You Can Take Your Love and Shove It Up Your Heart," covered though he was with stone dust and grog. The crowd roared at the accompanists plying the exotic instruments of Cleveland, the dolor, the mangle, the bim. Strum swiftly, fingers! The butlers did not hesitate for a minute. "History will absolve me," Buck reflected, and he took the hand offered him with its enormous sapphires glowing like a garage. Then Perpetua danced up to him, her great amazing brown eyelashes beckoning. "Where is Nancy?" she asked, and before he could reply, continued her account of the great love of her existence, her relationship with her husband, Saul. "He's funny and fine," she said, "and good and evil. In fact there is so much of him to tell you about, I can hardly get it all out before curfew. Do you mind?"

The din of dancing in Cleveland was now such that many people who did not know the plan were affronted. "This is an affront to Cleveland, this damn din!" one man said; and grog flowed ever more fiercely. The Secretary of State for Erotic Affairs flew in from Washington, the nation's capital, to see for himself at firsthand, and the man from Southern Rhodesia had no recourse. He lurked into the Cleveland Air Terminal. "Can I have a ticket for Miami?" he asked the dancing ticket clerk at the Delta Airlines counter hopelessly. "Nothing to Miami this year," the clerk countered. "How can I talk to him in this madness?" Nancy asked herself. "How can the white bird of hope bless our clouded past and future with all this noise? How? How? How? How? How?"

But Saul waved in time, from the porch of Parking Lot Two. He was wearing his belt dangerously low on his hips. "There is copulation everywhere," he shouted, fanning his neck, "because of the dancing! Yes, it's true!" And so it was, incredibly enough. Affection was running riot under the reprehensible scarlet sky. We were all afraid. "Incredible, incredible," Buck said to himself. "Even by those of whom you would not have expected it!" Perpetua glimmered at his ear. "Even by those," she insinuated, "of whom you would have expected . . . nothing." For a moment . . .

"Nancy," Buck exclaimed, "you are just about the nicest damn girl in Cleveland!"

"What about your wife in Texas?" Nancy asked.

"She is very nice too," Buck said, "as a matter of fact the more I think of it, the more I believe that nice girls like you and Hérodiade are what make life worth living. I wish there were more of them in America so that every man could have at least five."

"Five?"

"Yes, five."

"We will never agree on this figure," Nancy said.

2.

The rubbery smell of Akron, sister city of Lahore, Pakistan, lay like the flameout of all our hopes over the plateau that evening.

When his aircraft was forced down at the Akron Airpark by the lapse of the port engines, which of course he had been expecting, Buck said: "But this, this . . . is Akron!" And it was Akron, sultry, molecular, crowded with inhabitants who held tiny transistor radios next to their tiny ears. A wave of ingratitude overcame him. "Bum, bum," he said. He plumbed its heart. The citizens of Akron, after their hours at the plant, wrapped themselves in ill-designed love triangles which never contained less than four persons of varying degrees of birth, high and low and mediocre. Beautiful Ohio! with your transistorized citizens and contempt for geometry, we loved you in the evening by the fireside waiting for our wife to nap so we could slip out and see our two girls, Manfred and Bella!

The first telephone call he received in his rum raisin hotel room, Charles, was from the Akron Welcome Service.

"Welcome! new human being! to Akron! Hello?"

"Hello."

"Are you in love with any of the inhabitants of Akron yet?"

"I just came from the airport."

"If not, or even if so, we want to invite you to the big get-acquainted party of the College Graduates' Club tonight at 8:30 P.M."

"Do I have to be a college graduate?"

"No but you have to wear a coat and tie. Of course they are available at the door. What color pants are you wearing?"

Buck walked the resilient streets of Akron. His head was aflame with conflicting ideas. Suddenly he was arrested by a shrill cry. From the top of the Zimmer Building, one of the noblest buildings in

Akron, a group of Akron lovers consummated a four-handed suicide leap. *The air!* Buck thought as he watched the tiny figures falling, *this is certainly an air-minded country, America! But I must make myself useful.* He entered a bunshop and purchased a sweet green bun, and dallied with the sweet green girl there, calling her "poppet" and "funicular." Then out into the street again to lean against the warm green façade of the Zimmer Building and watch the workmen scrubbing the crimson sidewalk.

"Can you point me the way to the Akron slums, workman?"

"My name is not 'workman.' My name is 'Pat.'"

"Well, 'Pat,' which way?"

"I would be most happy to orient you, slumwise, were it not for the fact that slumlife in Akron has been dealt away with by municipal progressiveness. The municipality has caused to be erected, where slumlife once flourished, immense quadratic inventions which now house former slumwife and former slumspouse alike. These incredibly beautiful structures are over that way."

"Thanks, 'Pat.'"

At the housing development, which was gauche and grand, Buck came upon a man urinating in the elevator, next to a man breaking windows in the broom closet. "What are you fellows doing there!" Buck cried aloud. "We are expressing our rage at this fine new building!" the men exclaimed. "Oh that this day had never formulated! We are going to call it Ruesday, that's how we feel about it, by gar!" Buck stood in a wash of incomprehension and doubt. "You mean there is rage in Akron, the home of quadratic love?" "There is quadratic rage also," the men said, "Akron *is* rage from a certain point of view." Angel food covered the floor in neat squares. And what could be wrong with that? Everything?

"What is the point of view there, to which you refer?" Buck asked dumbly. *"The point of view of the poor people of Akron,"* those honest yeomen chanted, "or, as the city fathers prefer it, the underdeveloped people of Akron." And in their eyes, there was a strange light. "Do you know what the name of this housing development is?" "What?" Buck asked. "Sherwood Forest," the men said, "isn't that disgusting?"

The men invited Buck to sup with their girls, Heidi, Eleanor, George, Purple, Ann-Marie, and Los. In the tree, starlings fretted and died, but below everything was glass. Harold poured the wine of the region, a light Cheer, into the forgotten napery. And the great horse of evening trod over the immense scene once and for all. We examined our consciences. Many a tiny sin was rooted out that night, to make room for a greater one. It was "hello" and "yes" and "yes, yes" through the sacerdotal hours, from one to eight. Heidi held a pencil between her teeth. "Do you like pencil games?" she asked. Something lurked behind the veil of her eyes. "Not . . . especially," Buck said. "I . . ."

But a parade headed by a battalion of warm and lovely girls from the Akron Welcome Service elected this tense moment to come dancing by, with bands blazing and hideous floats in praise of rubber goods expanding in every direction. The rubber batons of the girls bent in the afterglow of events. "It is impossible to discuss serious ideas during a parade," the Akron Communists said to Buck, and they slipped away to continue expressing their rage in another part of the Forest.

"Goodbye!" Buck said. "Goodbye! I won't forget . . ."

The Welcome Service girls looked very *bravura* in their brief white-and-gold Welcome Service uniforms which displayed a fine amount of "leg." *Look at all that "leg" glittering there!* Buck said to himself, and followed the parade all the way to Toledo.

3.

"Ingarden dear," Buck said to the pretty wife of the mayor of Toledo, who was reading a copy of *Infrequent Love* magazine, "where are the poets of Toledo? Where do they hang out?" He showered her with gifts. She rose and moved mysteriously into the bedroom, to see if Henry were sleeping. "There is only one," she said, "the old poet of the city Constantine Cavity." A frost of emotion clouded her fuzz-colored lenses. "He operates a juju drugstore in the oldest section of the city and never goes anywhere except to make one of his rare and beautiful appearances." "Constantine Cavity!" Buck exclaimed, "even in Texas where I come from we have heard of this fine poet. You must take me to see him at once." Abandoning Henry to his fate (and it was a bitter one!) Buck and Ingarden rushed off hysterically to the drugstore of Constantine Cavity, Buck inventing as they rolled something graceful to say to this old poet, the forerunner so to speak of poetry in America.

Was there fondness in our eyes? We could not tell. Cadenzas of documents stained the Western Alliance, already, perhaps, prejudiced beyond the power of prayer to redeem it. "Do you think there is too much hair on my neck? here?" Ingarden asked Buck. But before he could answer she said: "Oh shut up!" She knew that Mrs. Lutch, whose interest in the pastor was only feigned, would find the American way if anyone could.

At Constantine Cavity's drugstore a meeting of the Toledo Medical Society was being held, in consequence of which Buck did not get to utter his opening words which were to have been: "Cavity, here we are!" A pity, but call the roll! See, or rather hear, who is present, and who is not! Present were

Dr. Caligari
Dr. Frank
Dr. Pepper
Dr. Scholl
Dr. Frankenthaler
Dr. Mabuse
Dr. Grabow
Dr. Melmoth
Dr. Weil
Dr. Modesto
Dr. Fu Manchu
Dr. Wellington
Dr. Watson
Dr. Brown
Dr. Rococo
Dr. Dolittle
Dr. Alvarez
Dr. Spoke
Dr. Hutch

Dr. Spain
Dr. Malone
Dr. Kline
Dr. Casey
Dr. No
Dr. Regatta
Dr. Il y a
Dr. Baderman
Dr. Aveni

and other doctors. The air was stuffy here, comrades, for the doctors were considering (yes!) a resolution of censure against the beloved old poet. An end to this badinage and wit! Let us be grave. It was claimed that Cavity had dispensed . . . but who can quarrel with Love Root, rightly used? It has saved many a lip. The prosecution was in the able hands of Dr. Kline, who invented the heart, and Dr. Spain, after whom Spain is named some believe. Their godlike figures towered over the tiny poet.

Kline advances.

Cavity rises to his height, which is not great.

Ingarden holds her breath.

Spain fades, back, back . . .

A handout from Spain to Kline.

Buck is down.

A luau?

The poet opens . . .

No! No! Get back!

". . . and if that way is long, and leads around by the reactor, and down in the valley, and up the garden path, leave here, I say, to heaven. For science has its reasons that reason knows not of," Cavity finished. And it was done.

"Hell!" said one doctor, and the others shuffled morosely around the drugstore inspecting the strange wares that were being vended there. It was clear that no resolution of censure could possibly . . . But of course not! What were we thinking of?

Cavity himself seemed pleased at the outcome of the proceedings. He recited to Buck and Ingarden his long love poems entitled

"In the Blue of Evening," "Long Ago and Far Away," "Who?" and "Homage to W. C. Williams." The feet of the visitors danced against the sawdust floor of the juju drugstore to the compelling rhythms of the poet's poems. A rime of happiness whitened on the surface of their two faces. "Even in Texas," Buck whispered, "where things are very exciting, there is nothing like the old face of Constantine Cavity. Are you true?"

"Oh I wish things were other."

"You do?"

"There are such a lot of fine people in the world I wish I was one of them!"

"You are, you are!"

"Not essentially. Not inwardly."

"You're very authentic I think."

"That's all right in Cleveland, where authenticity is the thing, but here . . ."

"Kiss me please."

"Again?"

4.

The parachutes of the other passengers snapped and crackled in the darkness all around him. There had been a malfunction in the afterburner and the pilot decided to "ditch." The whole thing was very unfortunate. "What is your life-style, Cincinnati?" Buck asked the recumbent jewel glittering below him like an old bucket of industrial diamonds. "Have you the boldness of Cleveland? the anguish of Akron? the torpor of Toledo? What is your posture, Cincinnati?" Frostily the silent city approached his feet.

Upon making contact with Cincinnati Buck and such of the other passengers of the ill-fated flight 309 had survived the "drop" proceeded to a hotel.

"Is that a flask of grog you have there?"

"Yes it is grog as it happens."

"That's wonderful."

Warmed by the grog which set his blood racing, Buck went to his room and threw himself on his bed. "Oh!" he said suddenly, "I must be in the wrong room!" The girl in the bed stirred sleepily. "Is that you Harvey?" she asked. "Where have you been all this time?" "No, it's Buck," Buck said to the girl, who looked very pretty in her blue flannel nightshirt drawn up about her kneecaps on which there were red lines. "I must be in the wrong room I'm afraid," he repeated. "Buck, get out of this room immediately!" the girl said coldly. "My name is Stephanie and if my friend Harvey finds you here there'll be an unpleasant scene."

"What are you doing tomorrow?" Buck asked.

Having made a "date" with Stephanie for the morning at 10 A.M., Buck slipped off to an innocent sleep in his own bed.

Morning in Cincinnati! The glorious cold Cincinnati sunlight fell indiscriminately around the city, here and there, warming almost no one. Stephanie de Moulpied was wearing an ice-blue wool suit in which she looked very cold and beautiful and starved. "Tell me about your Cincinnati life," Buck said, "the quality of it, that's what I'm interested in." "My life here is very aristocratic," Stephanie said, "polo, canned peaches, *Liaisons Dangéreuses*, and so on, because I am a member of an old Cincinnati family. However it's not much 'fun' which is why I made this 10 A.M. date with you, exciting stranger from the sky!" "I'm really from Texas," Buck said, "but I've been having a little trouble with airplanes on this trip. I don't really trust them too much. I'm not sure they're trustworthy." "Who is trustworthy after all?" Stephanie said with a cold sigh, looking blue. "Are you blue Stephanie?" Buck asked. "Am I blue?" Stephanie wondered. In the silence that followed, she counted her friends and relationships.

"Is there any noteworthy artistic activity in this town?"

"Like what do you mean?"

Buck then kissed Stephanie in a taxicab as a way of dissipating the blueness that was such a feature of her face. "Are all the girls in Cincinnati like you?" "All the *first-class* girls are like me," Stephanie said, "but there are some other girls whom I won't mention."

A faint sound of . . . A wave of . . . Dense clouds of . . . Heavily the immense weight of . . . Thin strands of . . .

Dr. Hesperidian had fallen into the little pool in vanPelt Ryan's garden (of course!) and everyone was pulling him out. Strangers met and fell in love over the problem of getting a grip on Dr. Hesperidian. A steel band played arias from *Wozzeck*. He lay just below the surface, a rime of algae whitening his cheekbones. He seemed to be . . . "Not *that* way," Buck said reaching for the belt buckle. "*This* way." The crowd fell back among the pines.

"You seem to be a nice young man, young man," vanPelt Ryan said, "although we have many of these of our own now since the General Electric plant came to town. Are you in computerization?"

Buck remembered the endearing red lines on Stephanie de Moulpied's knees.

"I'd rather not answer that question," he said honestly, "but if there's some other question you'd like me to answer . . ."

vanPelt turned away sadly. The steel band played "Red Boy Blues," "That's All," "Gigantic Blues," "Muggles," "Coolin'," and "Edward." Although each player was maimed in a different way . . . but the affair becomes, one fears, too personal. The band got a nice sound. Hookers of grog thickened on the table placed there for that purpose. "I grow less, rather than more, intimately involved with human beings as I move through world life," Buck thought, "is that my fault? Is it a fault?" The musicians rendered the extremely romantic ballads "I Didn't Know What Time It was," "Scratch Me," and "Misty." The grim forever adumbrated in recent issues of *Mind* pressed down, down . . . Where *is* Stephanie de Moulpied? No one could tell him, and in truth, he did not want to know. It is not he who asks this question, it is Mrs. Lutch. She glides down her glide path, sinuously, she is falling, she bursts into flame, her last words: "Tell them . . . when they crash . . . turn off . . . the ignition."

Bone Bubbles

bins black and green seventh eighth rehearsal pings a bit fussy at times fair scattering grand and exciting world of his fabrication topple out against surface irregularities fragilization of the gut constitutive misrecognitions of the ego most mature artist then in Regina loops of chain into a box several feet away Hiltons and Ritzes fault-tracing forty whacks active enthusiasm old cell is darker and they use the "Don't Know" category less often than younger people I am glad to be here and intend to do what I can to remain mangle stools tables bases and pedestals without my tree, which gives me rest hot pipe stacked-up cellos spend the semi-private parts of their lives wailing before 1908 had himself photographed with a number of very attractive young girls breasts like ballrooms and orchestras (as in English factories) social eminence Dutch sailors' eyes subsequently destroyed many of these works

distrusted musicians a bending position something I've thought about where their eyes were located cob hidden revolving spotlights slew the eunuch who had done me many kindnesses gourd polished by lips think of a sun-dried photograph tattoo myself attractively because (we) they are part of a process killed our horse free shoes for life at St. Regis established a church shaved beards formation of the ego missed one or more regiments of this army, with its commanders forever on the enclosure system for 250,000 people occasions a shuddering blutwurst tentoonstellingsagenda quietly studying his pocket watch dimness and wandering of the eyes pin down the quality immoderate laughter reverie tense bent steel largely greenish limbs streaks of blood leaping motions pudding crawling along horizontally eight-inch wood beads "burlesque" the Mountain girl comes flying to the door points to crowd drink your hair will grow again

strange reactions scattered black satin pulp hitched up her skirts for a look but he forgot to sigh world power ambiguous orders dipstick sweating or beaded with fine, amber colors disabled servant standing in the center of the frame dead tulips convulsions lasting more than three hours arrested for having no ticket hinges of the body so cough spit feel slight pains local or general heat read flags on naval vessels I gave water away married but they can't live together packing the air the soul of the sleeper was enlarged preposterously jabber Bols in five colors gold stars baby girls white-key music praising his skill loading him with protestations of gratitude what was behind their ugly fences? changing the names of certain people against their will theatre machinery posters of the period plans to dub the dialogue common prickers witch finders the girl holds out her hands to the young man but unfortunately over these past few years

hand or wrist man who rushes forward her body the largest element in the composition vegetables with which she refused to dance people embracing or falling bats popular with professional players benefit for working men between the buttocks I have not yet got the clue and points to herself shoal called the Gabble pausing only to defecate in their incomparable lakes hurled abuse behind the stone wall good smooth she falls to the right in pain, holding the Viennese master tightly partial relief conspiring priests a pill made of bread let's all go down to the plaza partly with his hands discharged a shower of arrows trying to find the opening cries when taken to a museum sane love invitation of the national committee white, gray, or purple ballet the jury nods triumphant contemporaries engineering decisions plump ladycow waiting in the car superb perfs from odd recruited volunteers floor redefined as bed

double dekko balcony of a government building series of closeups of the food gold thread long thin room pamper recent connection steroid perverse cults which have all but replaced Christianity ten filthiest cases men and women with strong convictions lottery breakdown fat arenas that seat a million people young Etruscans had little to say flaps (may be gelded nanny in the original) great plash shining milk at that moment I was perfectly happy puffed and nimble big muscles national friendship social entities bad sketches wonder woman skirt worn-out debauchees who had drained the cup of sensuality to its dregs we know their names creeper bigger than the one the telephone company killed pastures for the expiring cattle this famous charlatan Miko fading back into the vast practice, or method after image other examples could be substituted for the examples which they give us happily the people dance about

shoots Pierre pieces of literature genuine love stumps cantering toward the fine morning half-zip theme of his own choosing ramp shotgun illuminations informal arrangements botulism theories of design raving first sketches thought to be unsatisfactory geological accidents and return ant bulb lacing shoe brave though circumcised crawled all over the dingbat howling inadequate paper hard squeeze long series of closeups authors of the period wet leg breakfast dip snacks and banquets believing he was a child greatness of Finnish achievement 10/150 simple news elaborated sorrow gentle roll of ships Tillie gasped laughing and swayed and August was terrible consented to smear the doors and houses of Milan with a pestiferous salve daughter green ladies looking out of the picture plane forced feeding then responsible technicians hanging garbage unreasonable ideas more to do our views remain substantially the same today

then I went to a wedding and when it was my turn to kick the bride kicked her with commercial photographers snails keep our garden

private Bittermarka now sitting in the airplane hearing a lot of tape
trouser and skirt racks undone Europeans don't bother dried Bibb
exchange of interests primary moves accompanied by a lion raw
November in the black series extra simultaneous decisions big
drum bleeding of the nose royal and ancient good-humored areas
Elephanta how large the statues and ruins are! married the barber
Lamb of God gouty subjects forgot their pains red and blue paper
ice Bernard with a hive of bees virile the train scraped some people
onto the tracks intact sections of streets *bozzetti* shaped his work
livingrooms of subsequent civilizations specific borrowings leer
snug cover bucks and does having held high federal office split raising and lowering of her skirt like an elevator hairy children made a
ballad on the incident

yellow faces let's slip over to the foot of that tree to avoid getting crushed future of English drama water bomb checkered lilies
expensive thrill magazine whispered results a pleasant walk on
this surface blowhole boxes of green ladies blackguardism presses
handkerchief to mouth I found your name in a book commercial
undertakings news and weather bruised or cut document party
zone explosions below the line they had a hard time in Italy convinced that he had seen something remarkable modelled its radia-
tor on the Parthenon cringes diddled statistics bloc voting if there
were no such affinity between atoms it would be impossible for
love to appear "higher up" hobbies sitting on some lumber protest
against what they thought wrong sick whips of the baby on his left
shoulder half-forgotten events far-fetched positions drift of error
cloth cap or biretta figuratively speaking trembling we never forget
anything

weeping map intense activity din it would be better if we just piled
all the stones on the floor crumpled paper wheels out of alignment
prints rescued from the inferno beggars writing my article streaked
with raisins kept putting things into his mouth foxing pages divided
hearts something stuck in the gum a humanizing influence ichor
didn't they tell you list of objects which have their own saucy life

remedy sighted bats reflection of light from garbage cans spirit of the army wispy and diffuse King Lud giving the dog a bad name various itches I thought of firing in the air invisible armatures for piles of felt record of irregularities in a white trench coat aesthetic experience bleeding nails Moscow rehearsals torn and then pasted together in long strips but these have never been very successful black ball Clichy junks crowded with long purplish tubers yanked up from the ground in my black suit, my colored tie

halfway houses navel jelly four Italian architects said shrewd things about her mother lines drawn around the page many-colored oysters flush cameramen senses a desire for change large sheets of flat glass great disputations that he had lately held against all comers gunboat enterprise fatal laxity elegant sawhorses red snout mothering blur from the Sorbonne state ceremonies quaking hare but a glance at the bathtub discouraged her free cookbooks ancient deposits the humiliation of the wedding tiny hero so boring that he couldn't finish it and I am with you! three or more immense sponges by the petrol pump pink chiffon spikes interpenetrating diamonds enormous weather-like forces no relief smear tangle of solutions without problems enemies of vision discussions of the good life (mostly blacks and Puerto Ricans) somber triumph presents a picture of fingertip sensuality borrowed money no aperture had been provided

free offer last gesture smooth man of position purely cinematic vice slap and tickle zippered wallpaper two beautiful heavy books, boxed hears noise goes to window 220 treasures from 11 centuries fixer great and stupefying *Ring* minimum of three if it hadn't been for Y. I would never have gotten my lump local white Democrats gospel seven camera tilts to the balconies filled with joyous people young maidens tape after his brain is formed keep your checks in a safe place modern research sank to her knees on 35 mm color slides thermal machines from a chemical company in Pittsburgh handsome pelt illuminates the entire fluxus at one stroke body shirt spends all his time at the console wrong discard with the most careful and well-considered utilization of all my powers doll houses fastened to the wall photo face blade the world enigmatized skat will pull away the carpet age big tiger these conditions reverse themselves

childish memories of climbing up parents or nurses hollow objects sexual activity doleful cries critical moments abstract wit barges logical facades limping brides young dramatists acquainted with the sleeper plastic light first German edition speech blunder knobkerry imagined that the body was walking through fire during the cotton crisis complained of being misunderstood by the other banged belly duties toward women military service punishment for economic reasons rut prepared regularly two bottles, a blue one and a white one the doctor and his instrument bulbous summit representatives shouting theory golden calf special precautions and I cannot resist citing zeal in the cause against abuses wherever he found them classic critic masculine hysteria attacked by Goethe unsalted caviar member of my household anal opening which is the duke? which is the horse? which? we sat down and wept

poet's slurs extra rations business on 96th Street blueprints of uncompleted projects drunk and naked too malphony down at the old boathouse dark little birds astonishing propositions drummed out of the circle I'll insult him Scotch student rags and bones sunspots spoiled the hash keen satisfaction honors and gifts fit to burst the blue the white hoarse glee caught her knee in her hands with a click tonic night favorite wine well-known bumbler look at his head the bomb is here gulls twins rinse the seven of them appealing tot of rum she rises looks at him mysteriously fades into the closet fades out of the closet again double meaning arms tighten weak with relief silence throwing down the letters her wedding hat lackey slakes thirst nervously puts mask to face back door of the morgue new raincoat and draws away laughing bit of dogfish seated on a green stone bench baked this meat loaf

bad language mutilated Miss Rice I was sorry black coat with longish skirtlike Maxwell's initiative failed the narrator's position is

clear province of religion falling wine barrels tapped or bugged
clattering intensely human document wedding in the long border
that stretched from the Horse Guards' barracks to women in slacks
addressed envelopes I wanted to tell you something pages perforated
for easy song removal challengingly real issues in gerontology there
is but one moment in which the beautiful human being is beautiful cut flowers in rows and rows women reformers watching from
balconies gentle way with materials awarded a medal office visit
monkey's parade my ignorance which I do not wish to disguise blue
pants she turns, smiling bitterly in her tin beard aren't you being
overly emotional about it? discovering reasons hungry actors scars
upon the trunk or face of the sculpture the decisions of 1848

love tap the glass is one and three-sixteenth inches thick laminated
with plastic top stop a bullet from almost any sidearm indifferent
office cleaners smudge views of the acrobat ordered the girl to get up
and dress herself dream of the dandy leaves and their veins modern
soft skin a car drives up a policeman jumps out tinkling sackcloth
provocative back controlled nausea whimpering forms pardonable
in that they trump irresistible to any faithful mind hybrid tissue zut
powerful story of a half-naked girl caught between two emotions
two wavy sheets of steel food towers in Turin a collection of dirks
who is that very sick man? age-old eating habits crowd celebrating
the matter with him is that he is crazy Paul and Barnabas preaching
a bunch of extras going by sketch and final version automatic pump
salad holder taking the French shoe tired lines to be taken literally
no sexual relations with them

The Big Broadcast of 1938

H aving acquired in exchange for an old house that had been theirs, his and hers, a radio or more properly radio *station,* Blooms-bury could now play "The Star-Spangled Banner," which he had always admired immoderately, on account of its finality, as often as he liked. It meant, to him, that everything was finished. Therefore he played it daily, 60 times between 6 and 10 A.M., 120 times between 12 noon and 7 P.M., and the whole night long except when, as was sometimes the case, he was talking.

Bloomsbury's radio talks were of two kinds, called the first and the second kind. The first consisted of singling out, for special notice, from among all the others, some particular word in the English language, and repeating it in a monotonous voice for as much as fifteen minutes, or a quarter-hour. The word thus singled out might be any word, the word *nevertheless* for example. "Neverthe-less," Bloomsbury said into the microphone, "nevertheless, nev-ertheless, nevertheless, nevertheless, nevertheless, nevertheless, nevertheless." After this exposure to the glare of public inspection the word would frequently disclose new properties, unsuspected qualities, although that was far from Bloomsbury's intention. His intention, insofar as he may be said to have had one, was simply to put something "on the air."

The second kind of radio talk which Bloomsbury provided was the *commercial announcement.*

The Bloomsbury announcements were perhaps not too similar to other announcements broadcast during this period by other broadcasters. They were dissimilar chiefly in that they were addressed not to the mass of men but of course to her, she with whom he had lived in the house that was gone (traded for the radio). Frequently he would begin somewhat in this vein:

"Well, old girl" (he began), "here we are, me speaking into the tube, you lying on your back most likely, giving an ear, I don't doubt. Swell of you to tune me in. I remember the time you went walking without your shoes, what an evening! You were wearing, I recall, your dove-gray silk, with a flower hat, and you picked your way down the boulevard as daintily as a real lady. There were chestnuts on the ground, I believe; you complained that they felt like rocks under your feet. I got down on my hands and knees and crawled in front of you, sweeping the chestnuts into the gutter with my hand. What an evening! You said I looked absurd, and a gentleman who was passing in the other direction, I remember he wore yellow spats with yellow shoes, smiled. The lady accompanying him reached out to me on my head, but he grasped her arm and prevented her, and the knees of my trousers tore on a broken place in the pavement.

"Afterwards you treated me to a raspberry ice, calling for a saucer, which you placed daintily, at your feet. I still recall the coolness, after the hot work on the boulevard, and the way the raspberry stained my muzzle. I put my face in your hand, and your little glove came away pink and sticky, sticky and pink. We were comfortable there, in the ice cream parlor, we were pretty as a picture! Man and wife!

"When we got home, that evening, the street lights were just coming on, the insects were just coming out. And you said that next time, if there were a next time, you would wear your shoes. Even if it killed you, you said. And I said I would always be there to sweep away the chestnuts, whatever happened, even if nothing happened. And you said most likely that was right. I always *had* been there, you said. Swell of you to notice that. I thought at the time that there was probably no one more swell than you in the whole world, anywhere. And I wanted to tell you, but did not.

"And then, when it was dark, we had our evening quarrel. A very ordinary one, I believe. The subject, which had been announced by you at breakfast and posted on the notice board, was *Smallness in the Human Male*. You argued that it was willfulness on my part, whereas I argued that it was lack of proper nourishment during my young years. I lost, as was right of course, and you said I couldn't have any supper. I had, you said, already gorged myself on raspberry ice. I had, you said, ruined a good glove with my ardor, and a decent pair of trousers too. And I said, but it was for the love of you! and you said, hush! or there'll be no breakfast either. And I said, but love makes the world go! and you said, or lunch tomorrow either. And I said, but we were everything to each other once! And you said, or supper tomorrow night.

"But perhaps, I said, a little toffee? Ruin your teeth then for all I care, you said, and put some pieces of toffee in my bed. And thus we went happily to sleep. Man and wife! Was there ever anything, old skin, like the old days?"

Immediately following this commercial announcement, or an announcement much like this, Bloomsbury would play "The Star-Spangled banner" 80 or 100 times, for the finality of it.

When he interrogated himself about the matter, about how it felt to operate a radio of his own, Bloomsbury told himself the absolute truth, that it felt fine. He broadcast during this period not only some of his favorite words, such as the words *assimilate, alleviate, authenticate, ameliorate,* and quantities of his favorite music (he was particularly fond of that part, toward the end, that went: da-da, da da da da da da da-a), but also a series of commercial announcements of great power and poignancy, and persuasiveness. Nevertheless he felt, although he managed to conceal it from himself for a space, somewhat futile. For there had been no response from her (she who figured, as both subject and object, in the commercial announcements, and had once, before it had been traded for the radio, lived in the house).

A commercial announcement of the period of this feeling was:

"On that remarkable day, that day unlike any other, that day, if you will pardon me, of days, on that old day from the old days when we were, as they say, young, we walked if you will forgive the extravagance *hand in hand* into a theater where there was a film playing. Do you remember? We sat in the upper balcony and smoke from below, where there were people smoking, rose and we, if you will excuse the digression, smelled of it. It smelled, and I or we thought it remarkable at the time, like the twentieth century. Which was after all our century, none other.

"We were there you and I because we hadn't rooms and there were no parks and we hadn't automobiles and there were no beaches, for making love or anything else. *Ergo,* if you will condone the anachronism, we were forced into the balcony, to the topmost row, from which we had a tilty view of the silver screen. Or would have had had we not you and I been engaged in pawing and pushing, pushing and pawing. On my part at least, if not on yours.

"The first thing I knew I was inside your shirt with my hand and I found there something very lovely and, as they say, desirable. It belonged to you. I did not know, then, what to do with it, therefore I simply (simply!) held it in my hand, it was, as the saying goes, soft and warm. If you can believe it. Meanwhile down below in the pit events were taking place, whether these were such as the people in the pit had paid for, I did not and do not know. Nor did or do, wherever you are, you. After a time I was in fact distracted, I still held it in my hand but I was looking elsewhere.

"You then said into my ear, get on with it, can't you?

"I then said into your ear, I'm watching the picture.

"At this speech of mine you were moved to withdraw it from my hand, I understood, it was a punishment. Having withdrawn it you began, for lack of anything better, to watch the picture also. We watched the picture together, and although this was a kind of intimacy, the other kind had been lost. Nevertheless it had been there once, I consoled myself with that. But I felt, I felt, I felt (I think) that you were, as they say, angry. And to that row of the balcony, we, you and I, never returned."

After this announcement was broadcast Bloomsbury himself felt called upon to weep a little, and did, but not "on the air."

He was in fact weeping quietly in the control room, where were kept the microphone, the console, the turntables, and the hotplate, with "The Star-Spangled Banner" playing bravely and a piece of buttered toast in his hand, when he saw in the glass that connected the control room with the other room, which had been a reception room or foyer, a girl or woman of indeterminate age dressed in a long bright red linen duster.

The girl or woman removed her duster, underneath she was wearing black toreador pants, an orange sweater, and harlequin glasses. Bloomsbury immediately stepped out into the reception room or foyer in order to view her more closely, he regarded her, she regarded him, after a time there was conversation.

"You're looking at me!" she said.

"Oh, yes," he said. "Right. I certainly am."

"Why?"

"It's something I do," he said. "It's my you might say *métier*."

"*Milieu*," she said.

"*Métier*," Bloomsbury said. "If you don't mind."

"I don't often get looked at as a matter of fact."

"Because you are not very good-looking," Bloomsbury said.

"Oh I say."

"Glasses are discouraging," he said.

"Even harlequin glasses?"

"Especially harlequin glasses."

"Oh," she said.

"But you have a grand behind," he said.

"Also a lively sense of humor," she said.

"Lively," he said. "Whatever possessed you to use that word?"

"I thought you might like it," she said.

"No," he said. "Definitely not."

"Do you think you ought to stand around and look at girls?" she asked.

"Oh, yes," Bloomsbury said. "I think it's indicated."

"*Indicated,*" she cried. "What do you mean, *indicated!*"

"Tell me about your early life," Bloomsbury said.

"To begin with I was president of the Conrad Veidt fan club," she began. "That was in, oh, I don't remember the year. His magnetism and personality got me. His voice and gestures fascinated me. I hated him, feared him, loved him. When he died it seemed to me a vital part of my imagination died too."

"I didn't mean necessarily in such detail," he said.

"My world of dreams was bare!"

"Fan club prexies are invariably homely," Bloomsbury said.

"*Plain,*" she suggested. "I prefer the word plain. Do you want to see a picture of Conrad Veidt?"

"I would be greatly interested," Bloomsbury said (although this was not the truth).

The girl or woman then retrieved from her purse, where it had apparently remained for some time, perhaps even years, a page from a magazine. It bore a photograph of Conrad Veidt who looked at one and the same instant handsome and sinister. There was moreover printing on the photograph which said: *If CONRAD VEIDT offered you a cigarette, it would be a DE REZKE—of course!*

"Very affecting," Bloomsbury said.

"I never actually met Mr. Veidt," the girl (or woman) said. "It wasn't that sort of club. I mean we weren't in actual communication with the star. There was a Joan Crawford fan club, and *those* people now, *they* were in actual communication. When they wanted a remembrance . . ."

"A remembrance?"

"Such as Kleenex that had been used by the star, for instance, with lipstick on it, or fingernail clippings, or a stocking, or a hair from the star's horse's tail or mane . . ."

"Tail or mane?"

"The star naturally, *noblesse oblige,* forwarded that object to them."

"I see," Bloomsbury said.

"Do you look at a lot of girls?"

"Not a *lot*," he said, "but quite a number."

"Is it fun?"

"Not *fun*," he said, "but better than nothing."

"Do you have affairs?"

"Not *affairs*," he said, "but sometimes a little flutter."

"Well," she said, "I have feelings too."

"I think it's very possible," he said. "A great big girl like you."

This remark however seemed to offend her, she turned on her heel and left the room. Bloomsbury himself felt moved by this meeting, which was in fact the first contact he had enjoyed with a human being, of any description, since the beginning of the period of his proprietorship of the radio, and even before. He immediately returned to the control room and introduced a new commercial announcement.

"I remember" (he enunciated), "the quarrel about the ice cubes, that was a beauty! That was one worth . . . remembering. You had posted on the notice board the subject *Refrigeration*, and I worried about it all day long, and wondered. Clever minx! I recalled at length that I had complained, once, because ice cubes were not *frozen*. But were in fact unfrozen! watery! useless! I had said that there *weren't enough ice cubes*, whereas you had said there were *more than enough*.

"You said that I was a fool, an idiot, an imbecile, a stupid!, that the machine in your kitchen which you had procured and caused to be placed there was without doubt and on immaculate authority the most accomplished machine of its kind known to those who knew about machines of its kind, that among its attributes was the attribute of conceiving containing and at the moment of need whelping a fine number of ice cubes so that no matter how grave the demand, how vast the occasion, how indifferent or even hostile the climate, how inept or even treacherous the operator, how brief or even nonexistent the lapse between genesis and parturition, between the wish and the fact, ice cubes in multiples of sufficient would present themselves. Well, I said, perhaps.

"Oh! how you boggled at that word *perhaps*. How you sweated, old girl, and cursed. Your chest heaved, if I may say so, and your eyes (your eyes!) flashed. You said we would, by damn, *count* the damn ice cubes. As we, subsequently, did.

"How I enjoyed, although I concealed it from you, the counting! You were, as they say, magisterial. There were I observed twelve rows of three, or three of twelve, in each of four trays. But this way of counting was not your way of counting. You chose, and I admired your choice, the explicitness and *implicitness* of it, to run water over the trays so that the cubes, loosened, fell into the salad bowl, having previously turned the trays, and thus the cubes, bottoms up, so that the latter would fall, when water was upon the former, in the former direction. That these matters were so commendably arranged I took to be, and even now take to be, a demonstration of your fundamental decency, and good sense.

"But you reckoned wrong, when it came to that. You were never a reckoner. You reckoned that there were in the bowl one hundred forty-four cubes, taking each cube, individually, from the bowl and placing it, individually, in the sink, bearing in mind meanwhile the total that could be obtained by simple multiplication of the spaces in the trays. Thus having it, in this as in other matters, both ways! However you failed on this as on other occasions to consider the imponderables, in this instance the fact that I, unobserved by you, had put three of the cubes into my drink! Which I then drank! And that one had missed the bowl entirely and fallen into the sink! And melted once and for all! These events precluded sadly enough the number of cubes in the bowl adding up to a number corresponding to the number of spaces in the trays, proving also that *there is no justice!*

"What a defeat for you! What a victory for me! It was my first victory, I fear I went quite out of my head. I dragged you to the floor, among the ice cubes, which you had flung there in pique and chagrin, and forced you, with results that I considered then, and consider now, to have been 'first rate.' I thought I detected in you . . ."

But he could not continue this announcement, from a surfeit of emotion.

The girl or woman, who had become a sort of follower of the

radio, made a practice during this period of sleeping in the former reception room underneath the piano, which being a grand provided ample shelter. When she wished to traffic with Bloomsbury she would tap on the glass separating them with one finger, at other times she would, with her hands, make motions.

A typical conversation of the period when the girl (or woman) was sleeping in the foyer was this:

"Tell me about your early life," she said.

"I was, in a sense, an All-American Boy," Bloomsbury replied.

"In what sense?"

"In the sense that I married," he said.

"Was it love?"

"It was love but it was only temporary."

"It didn't go on forever?"

"For less than decade. As a matter of fact."

"But while it did go on . . ."

"It filled me with a somber and paradoxical joy."

"Coo!" she said. "It doesn't sound very American to me."

"*Coo*," he said. "What kind of an expression is that?"

"I heard it in a movie," she said. "A Conrad Veidt movie."

"Well," he said, "it's distracting."

This conversation was felt by Bloomsbury to be not very satisfactory, however he bided his time, having if the truth were known no alternative. The word *matriculate* had engaged his attention, he pronounced it into the microphone for what seemed to him a period longer than normal, that is to say, in excess of a quarter-hour. He wondered whether or not to regard this as significant.

It was a fact that Bloomsbury, who had thought himself dispassionate (thus the words, the music, the slow turning over in his brain of events in the lives of him and her), was beginning to feel, at this time, disturbed. This was attributable perhaps to the effect, on him, of his radio talks, and also perhaps to the presence of the "fan," or listener, in the reception room. Or possibly it was something else entirely. In any case this disturbance was reflected, beyond a doubt, in the announcements made by him in the days that, inevitably, followed.

One of these was:

"The details of our housekeeping, yours and mine. The scuff under the bed, the fug in the corners. I would, if I could, sigh to remember them. You planted prickly pear in the parlor floor, and when guests came . . . Oh, you were a one! You veiled yourself from me, there were parts I could have and parts I couldn't have. And the rules would change, I remember, in the middle of the game, I could never be sure which parts were allowed and which not. Some days I couldn't have anything at all. Is it remarkable, then, that there has never been another? Except for a few? Who don't count?

"There has, I don't doubt, never been anything like it. The bed, your mother's bed, brought to our union with your mother in it, she lay like sword between us. I had the gall to ask what you were thinking. It was one of those wonderful days of impenetrable silence. Well, I said, and the child? Up the child, you said, 'twasn't what I wanted anyway. What then did you want? I asked, and the child cried, its worst forebodings confirmed. Pish, you said, nothing you could supply. Maybe, I said. Not bloody likely, you said. And where is it (the child) now? Gone, I don't doubt, away.

"Are you with me, old bush?

"Are you tuned in?

"A man came, in a hat. In the hat was a little feather, and in addition to the hat and the feather there was a satchel. Jack, this is my husband, you said. And took him into the bedroom, and turned the key in the lock. What are you doing in there? I said, the door being locked, you and he together on the inside, me alone on the outside. Go away and mind your own silly business, you said, from behind the door. Yes, Jack said (from behind the door), go away and don't be bothering people with things on their minds. Insensitive brute! you said, and Jack said, filthy cad! Some people, you said, and Jack said, the cheek of the thing. I watched at the door until nightfall, but could hear no more words, only sounds of a curious nature, such as grunts and moans, and sighs. Upon hearing these (through the door which was, as I say, locked), I immediately rushed to the attic to obtain our copy of *Ideal Marriage*, by Th. H. Van De Velde, M.D., to determine whether this situation was treated of therein. But it was not. I therefore abandoned the book and returned to my station outside the door, which remained (and indeed why not?) shut.

"At length the door opened, your mother emerged, looking as they say 'put out.' But she had always taken your part as opposed to my part, therefore she said only that I was a common sneak. But, I said, what of those who even now sit in the bed? laughing and joking? Don't try to teach thy grandmother to chew coal, she said. I then became, if you can believe it, melancholy. Could not we two skins, you and me, climb and cling for all the days that were left? Which were not, after all, so very many days? Without the interpolation of such as Jack? And, no doubt, others yet to come?"

After completing this announcement and placing "The Star-Spangled Banner" on the turntable, and a cup of soup on the hotplate, Bloomsbury observed that the girl in the reception room was making motions with her hands, the burden of which was, that she wanted to speak to him.

"Next to Mr. Veidt my favorite star was Carmen Lambrosa," she said. "What is more, I am said to resemble her in some aspects."

"Which?" Bloomsbury said with interest. "Which aspects?"

"It was said of Carmen Lambrosa that had she just lived a little longer, and not died from alcohol, she would have been the top box office money-maker in the British Cameroons. Where such as she and me are appreciated."

"The top box office money-maker for what year?"

"The year is not important," she said. "What is important is the appreciation."

"I would say you favored her," Bloomsbury observed, "had I some knowledge of her peculiarities."

"Do I impress you?"

"In what way?"

"As a possible partner? Sexually I mean?"

"I haven't considered it," he said, "heretofore."

"They say I'm sexy," she noted.

"I don't doubt it," he said. "I mean it's plausible."

"I am yours," she said, "if you want me."

"Yes," he said, "there's the difficulty, making up my mind."

"You have only," she said, "to make the slightest gesture of acquiescence, such as a nod, a word, a cough, a cry, a kick, a crook, a giggle, a grin."

"Probably I would not enjoy it," he said, "now."

"Shall I take off my clothes?" she asked, making motions as if to do so.

With a single stride, such as he had often seen practiced in the films, Bloomsbury was "at her side."

"Martha," he said, "old skin, why can't you let the old days die? That were then days of anger, passion, and dignity, but are now, in the light of present standards, practices, and attitudes, days that are done?"

Upon these words from him, she began to weep. "You looked interested at first," she said (through her tears).

"It was kind of you to try it," he said. "Thoughtful. As a matter of fact, you were most appealing. Tempting, even. I was fooled for whole moments at a time. You look well in bullfighter pants."

"Thank you," she said. "You said I had a grand behind. You said that at least."

"And so you do."

"You can't forget," she asked, "about Dudley?"

"Dudley?"

"Dudley who was my possible lover," she said.

"Before or after Jack?"

"Dudley who in fact broke up our *ménage*," she said, looking at him expectantly.

"Well," he said, "I suppose."

"Tell me about joy again."

"There was some joy," Bloomsbury said. "I can't deny it."

"Was it really like you said? Somber and paradoxical?"

"It was all of that," he said gallantly, "then."

"Then!" she said.

There was a moment of silence during which they listened, thoughtfully, to "The Star-Spangled Banner" playing softly in the other room behind them.

"Then we are, as they say, through?" she asked. "There is no hope for us?"

"None," he said. "That I know of."

"You've found somebody you like better?"

"It's not that," he said. "That has nothing to do with it."

"Balls," she said. "I know you and your letchy ways."

"Goodbye," Bloomsbury said, and returned to the control room, locking the door behind him.

He then resumed broadcasting, with perhaps a tremor but no slackening in his resolve not to flog, as the expression runs, a dead horse. However the electric company, which had not been paid from the first to the last, refused at length to supply further current for the radio, in consequence of which the broadcasts, both words and music, ceased. That was the end of this period of Bloomsbury's, as they say, life.

This Newspaper Here

Again today the little girl come along come along dancing doggedly with her knitting needle steel-blue knitting needle. She knows I can't get up out of this chair theoretically and sticks me, here and there, just to make me yell, nice little girl from down the block somewhere. Once I corrected her sharply saying "don't for God's sake what pleasure is there hearing me scream like this?" She was wearing a blue Death of Beethoven printed dress and white shoes which mama had whited for her that day before noon so white were they (shoes). I judged her to be eleven. The knitting needle in the long thrust and hold position she said "torment is the answer old pappy man it's torment that is the game's name that I'm learning about under laboratory conditions. Torment is the proper study of children of my age, class, and median income, and *you* don't matter in any case you're through dirty old man can't even get out of rotten old chair." Summed me up she did in those words which I would much rather not have heard so prettily put as they were nevertheless. I hate it here in this chair in this house warm and green with Social Security. Do you know how little it is? The little girl jabbed again hitting the thin thigh that time and said "we know *exactly* how little it is and even that is money down the drain why don't you die damn you dirty old man what are you contributing?" Then

I explained about this newspaper here sprinkled with rare lies and photographs incorrectly captioned accumulated along a lifetime of disappointments and some fun. I boasted saying "one knows just where nerves cluster under the skin, how to pinch them so citizens jump as in dreams when opened suddenly a door and there see two flagrantly . . ." But I realize then her dreams are drawn in ways which differ so that we cannot read them together. I threw then jam jar (black currant) catching her nicely on kneecap and she ran howling but if they come to object I have jab marks in extenuation. Nice little girl from down the block somewhere.

The reason I like to read this newspaper here the one in my hand, is because I like what it says. It is my favorite. I would be pleased really quite if you could read it. But you can't. But some can. It comes in the mail. I give it to a fellow some time back, put it in his hand and said "take a look." He took a look took a look but he couldn't see anything strawdinary along this newspaper here, couldn't see it. And he says "so what?" Of course I once was in this business myself making newspapers in the depression. We had fun then. This fellow I give it to take a look some time back he that said "so what" is well educated reads good travels far drinks deep gin mostly talks to dolphins click click click click. A professor of ethnology at the University of California at Davis. Not in fine a dullard in any sense but he couldn't see anything strawdinary along this newspaper here. I said look there page 2 the amusing story of the plain girl fair where the plain girls come to vend their wares but he said "on *my* page 2 this newspaper here talk about the EEC." Then I took it from his hand and showed him with my finger the plain girl fair story. Then he commences to read aloud from under my finger there some singsong about the EEC. So I infer that he is one who can't. So I let the matter drop.

I went to see the plain girl fair out Route 22 figuring I could get one if I just put on a kind face. This newspaper here had advertising the aspidistra store not far away by car where I went then and bought one to carry along. At the plain girl fair they were standing in sudden-death décolletage and brown arms everywhere. As you passed along into the tent after paying your dollar fifty carrying your aspidistra a blinding flash of some hundred contact lenses came. And a quality of dental work to shame the VA Hospital it was so fine. One fell in love temporarily with all this hard work and money spent just to please to improve. I was sad my dolphin friend was not there to see. I took one by the hand and said "come with me I will buy you a lobster." My real face behind my kind face smiling. And the other girls on their pedestals waved and said "goodbye Marie." And they also said "have a nice lobster," and Marie waved back and said "bonne chance!" We motored to the lobster place over to Barwick, then danced by the light of the moon for a bit. And then to my hay where I tickled the naked soles of feet with a piece of it and admired her gestures of marvellous gaucherie. In my mind.

Of course I once was in this business myself making newspapers in the depression. So I know some little some about it, both the back room and the front room. If you got in the makeups' way they'd yell "dime waitin' on a nickel." But this here and now newspaper I say a thing of great formal beauty. Sometimes on dull days the compositors play which makes paragraphs like

(!) (!) (!) (!) (!) (!) (!) (!) (!) (!) (!) (!) (!)
* *
? / ? / ? / ? / ? / ? / ? / ? / ? / ? / ? / ? / ? /
o : o : o : o : o : o : o : o : o : o : o : o : o
? / ? / ? / ? / ? / ? / ? / ? / ? / ? / ? / ? / ? /
* *
(!) (!) (!) (!) (!) (!) (!) (!) (!) (!) (!) (!) (!)

refreshing as rocks in this newspaper here. And then you come along a page solid bright aching orange sometimes and parts printed in alien languages and invisible inks. This newspaper here fly away fly away through the mails to names from the telephone book. Have you seen my library of telephone books I keep in the kitchen with names from Greater Memphis Utica Key West Toledo Santa Barbara St. Paul Juneau Missoula Tacoma and every which where. It goes third class because I print HOTELS-MOTELS NEED TRAINED MEN AND WOMEN AMAZING FREE OFFER on the wrapper. As a disguise.

Then a learned man come to call saying "this with the news-paper is not kosher you know that." He had several degrees in Police Engineering and the like and his tiny gun dwelt in his armpit like the growling described by Defoe in *Journal of the Plague Year*. I judged him to be with some one of the governments. Not overfond of him in my house but I said in a friendly way "can I see it." He took out the tiny black gun and held it in his hand, then slapped me up against the head with it in a friendly way. He coughed and looked at the bottle of worrywine sitting on the table on the newspaper saying "and we can hear the presses in the basement with sensitive secret recording devices." And finally he said sighing "we know it's you why don't you simply take a few months off, try Florida or Banff which is said to swing at this season of the year and we'll pay everything." I told him smiling I didn't get the reference. He was almost crying it seemed to me saying "you know it excites the people stirs them up exacerbates hopes we thought laid to rest generations ago." He nodded to agree with himself laying soft hands around the windpipe of the gramophone automatically feeling for counter-bugs down its throat saying "we don't understand what it is you're after. If you don't like our war you don't have to come to it, too old anyway you used-up old poop." Then he slapped me up alongside the head couple more times with his exquisite politesse kicking my toothpick scale model of Heinrich von Kleist in blue velvet to splinters on the way out.

Can you imagine some fellow waking at dawn in Toledo looking at his red alarm clock and then thinking with wonder of a picture drawn in this newspaper here by my friend Golo. When we were in Paris Golo was a famous one because he drew with his thumbs in black paint which was not then done yet much on brown paper and it made people stop. Now Golo has altered his name because he is wanted. Still he sends me drawings on secular subjects from here and there, when they irritate me I put them in. It is true that I dislike their war and have pointed out that the very postage stamps shimmer with dangerous ideological radiation. They hated that. I run coupons to clip offering Magnificent Butterfly Wing Portraits Send Photo, Transistorized Personal Sun Tanner, How to Develop

135

a He-Man Voice, Darling Pet Monkey Show It Affection and Enjoy Its Company, British Shoes for Gentlemen, Live Seahorses $1 Each, Why Be Bald, Electric Roses Never Fade or Wither, Hotels-Motels Need Trained Men and Women. And I keep the money.

But what else can I do? Making this newspaper here I hold a pre-requisite to eluding death which is looking for me don't you know. Girl with knitting needle simply sent to soften me up, a probing action as it were. My newspaper warms at the edges fade in fade out a tissue of hints whispers glimpses uncertainties, zoom in zoom out. I considered in an editorial the idea that the world is an error on the part of God, one of the earliest and finest heresies, they hated that. Ringle from the telephone "what do you mean the world is a roar on the part of god," which pleased me. I said "madam is your name Marie if so I will dangle your health in verymerrywine this very eve blast me if I will not." She said into the telephone "dirty old man." Who ha who ha. I sit here rock around the clock interviewing Fabian on his plate glass window incident in my mind. Sweet to know your face uncut and unabridged. Who ha who ha dirty old man.

Tales of the Swedish Army

Suddenly, turning a corner, I ran into a unit of the Swedish Army. Their vehicles were parked in orderly rows and filled the street, mostly six-by-sixes and jeeps, an occasional APC, all painted a sand color quite different from the American Army's dark green. To the left of the vehicles, on a big school playground, they had set up two-man tents of the same sand color, and the soldiers, blond red-faced men, lounged about among the tents, making not much noise. It was strange to see them there, I assumed they were on their way to some sort of joint maneuvers with our own troops. But it was strange to see them there.

I began talking to a lieutenant, a young, pleasant man; he showed me a portable chess clock he'd made himself, which was for some reason covered in matchstick bamboo painted purple. I told him I was building an addition to the rear of my house, as a matter of fact I had with me a carpenter's level I'd just bought, and I showed him that. He said he had some free time, and asked if I needed help. I suggested that probably his unit would be moving out fairly soon, but he waved a hand to indicate their departure was not imminent. He seemed genuinely interested in assisting me, so I accepted.

His name was Bengt and he was from Uppsala, I'd been there so we talked about Uppsala, then about Stockholm and Bornholm and

Malmö. I asked him if he knew the work of the Swedish poet Bodil Malmsten; he didn't. My house (not really mine, my sister's, but I lived there and paid rent) wasn't far away, we stood in the garden looking up at the rear windows on the parlor floor, I was putting new ones in. So I climbed the ladder and he began handing me up one of the rather heavy prefab window frames, and my hammer slid from the top of the ladder and fell and smashed into his chess clock, which he'd carefully placed on the ground, against the wall.

I apologized profusely, and Bengt told me not to worry, it didn't matter, but he kept shaking the chess clock and turning it over in his hands, trying to bring it to life. I rushed down the ladder and apologized again, and looked at it myself, both dials were shattered and part of the purple matchstick casing had come off. He said again not to worry, he could fix it, and that we should get on with the job.

After a while Bengt was up on the ladder tacking the new frames to the two-by-fours with sixteen-penny nails. He was very skillful and the work was going quickly; I was standing in the garden steadying the ladder as he was sometimes required to lean out rather far. He slipped and tried to recover, and bashed his face against the wall, and broke his nose.

He stood in the garden holding his nose with both hands, the hands as if clasped in prayer over his nose. I apologized profusely. I ran into the house and got some ice cubes and paper towels and told him I'd take him to the hospital right away but he shook his head and said no, they had doctors of their own. I wanted to do something for him so I took him in and sat him down and cooked him some of my fried chicken, which is rather well-known although the secret isn't much of a secret, just lots of lemon-pepper marinade and then squeezing fresh lemon juice over it just before serving. I could see he was really very discouraged about his nose and I had to keep giving him fresh paper towels but he complimented me very highly on the chicken and gave me a Swedish recipe for chicken stuffed with parsley and butter and stewed, which I wrote down.

Then Bengt told me various things about the Swedish Army. He said that it was a tough army and a sober one, but small; that everybody in the army pretty well knew everybody else, and that they kept their Saab jets in deep caves that had been dug in the mountains, so that if there was a war, nothing could happen to them. He said that the part I'd seen was just his company, there were two more plus a heavy-weapons company bivouacking at various spots in the city, making up a full battalion. He said the soldiers were mostly Lutherans, with a few Presbyterians and Evangelicals, and that drugs were not a problem but that people sometimes overslept, driving the sergeants crazy. He said that the Swedish Army was thought to have the best weapons in the world, and that they kept them very clean. He said that he probably didn't have to name their principal potential enemy, because I knew it already, and that the army-wide favorite musical group was Abba, which could sometimes be seen on American television late at night.

By now the table was full of bloody towels and some blood had gotten on his camouflage suit, which was in three shades of green and brown. Abruptly, with a manly gesture, Bengt informed me that he had fallen in love with my sister. I said that was very curious, in that he had never met her. "That is no difficulty," he said, "I can see by looking around this house what kind of a woman she must be. Very tall, is she not? And red hair, is that not true?" He went on describing my sister, whose name is Catherine, with a disturbing accuracy and increasing enthusiasm, correctly identifying her as a teacher, and furthermore, a teacher of painting. "These are hers," he said, "they must be," and rose to inspect some oils in Kulicke frames on the walls. "I knew it. From these, dear friend, a great deal can be known of the temperament of the painter, his or her essential spirit. I will divorce my wife immediately," he said, "and marry Catherine as soon as it is legally possible." "You're already married!" I said, and he hung his head and admitted yes, that it was so. But in Sweden, he said, many people were married to each other who, for one reason or another, no longer loved each other . . . I said that happened in our own country too, many cases personally known to me, and that if he wished to marry Catherine I would not stand in his way, but would, on the contrary, do everything in my power to further the project. At this moment the bell rang; I answered it and Catherine entered with her new husband, Richard.

I took Bengt back to his unit in a cab, one hand clutching his nose, the other his heart, the remains of his chess clock in his lap. We got there just in time, a review was in progress, the King of Sweden was present, a handsome young man in dress uniform with a silver sword, surrounded by aides similarly clad. A crowd had gathered and Bengt's company paraded by, looking vastly trim and efficient in their polished boots and red berets, and a very pretty little girl came out of the crowd and shyly handed the King a small bouquet of flowers. He bent graciously to accept them, beautiful small yellow roses, and a Rocky Mountain spotted-fever tick leaped from a rose and bit him on the cheek. I was horrified, and the King slapped his cheek and swore that the Swedish Army would never come to visit us again.

And Then

The part of the story that came next was suddenly missing, I couldn't think of it, so I went into the next room and drank a glass of water (my "and then" still hanging in the frangible air) as if this were the most natural thing in the world to do at that point, thinking that I would "make up" something, while in the other room, to put in place of that part of the anecdote that had fallen out of my mind, to keep the light glittering in his cautious eyes. And in truth I was getting a little angry with him now, not fiercely angry but slight *désabusé*, because he had been standing very close to me, closer than I really like people to stand, the rims of his shoes touching the rims of my shoes, our belt buckles not four inches distant, a completely unwarranted impingement upon my personal space. And so I went, as I say, into the next room and drank a glass of water, trying to remember who he was and why I was talking to him, not that he wasn't friendly, if by "friendly" you mean standing aggressively close to people with an attentive air and smiling teeth, that's not what I mean by "friendly," and it was right then that I decided to lie to him, although what I had been telling him previously was true, to the best of my knowledge and belief. But, faced now with this "gap" in the story, I decided to offer him a good-quality lie in place of the part I couldn't remember, a better strategy, I felt, than simply stopping, leaving him with a maimed, not-whole anecdote, violating his basic trust, simple faith, or personhood even, for all I knew. But the lie had to be a good one, because if your lie is badly done it makes everyone feel wretched, liar and lied-to alike plunged into the deepest lackadaisy, and everyone just feels like going into the other room and drinking a glass of water, or whatever is available there, whereas if you can lie really well then get dynamite results, 35 percent report increased intellectual understanding, awareness, insight, 40 percent report more tolerance, acceptance of others, liking for self, 29 percent report they receive more personal and more confidential information from people and that others become more warm and supportive toward them—all in consequence of a finely orchestrated, carefully developed untruth. And while I was thinking about this, counting my options, I noticed that he was a policeman, had in fact a dark-blue uniform, black shoes, a badge, and a gun, a policeman's hat, and I noticed also that my testicles were aching, as they sometimes do if you sit too long in an uncomfortable or strained position, but I had been standing, and then I understood, in a flash, that what he wanted from me was not to hear the "next" part of my story, or anecdote, but that I give my harpsichord to his wife as a present.

Now, my harpsichord has been out of tune for five years, some of the keys don't function, and there are drink rings on top of it where people have set their drinks down carelessly, at parties and the like, still it is mine and I didn't particularly want to give it to his wife, I believe her name is Cynthia, and although I may have drunkenly promised to give it to her in a fit of generosity or inadvertence, or undue respect for the possible pleasures of distant others, still it was and is my harpsichord and what was his wife giving me? I hadn't in mind sexual favors or anything of that kind, I had in mind real property of equivalent value. So I went into the other room and drank a glass of water, or rather vodka, thinking to stall him with the missing "part" of the trivial anecdote I had been telling him, to keep his mind off what he wanted, the harpsichord, but the problem was, what kind of lie would he like? I could tell him about "the time I went to Hyde Park for a drink with the President," but he could look at me and know I was too young to have done that, and then the failed lie would exist between us like a bathtub filled with ruinous impotent nonsense, he would simply seize the harpsichord and make off with it (did I say that he was a sergeant? with three light-blue chevrons sewn to the darker blue of his right and left sleeves?). Who knows the kinds of lies that sergeants like, something that would confirm their already existing life-attitudes, I supposed, and I tried to check back mentally and remember what these last might be, drawing upon my (very slight) knowledge of the sociology of authority, something in the area of child abuse perhaps, if I could fit a child-abuse part to the structure already extant, which I was beginning to forget, something to do with walking at night, if I could spot-weld a child-abuse extension to what was already there, my partial anecdote, that might do the trick.

So I went into the next room and had a glass of something, I think I said, "Excuse me," but maybe I didn't, and it had to be fabrication that would grammatically follow the words "and then" without too much of a seam showing, of course I could always, upon reentering the first room, where the sergeant stood, begin the sentence anew, with some horrific instance of child abuse, of which I have several in the old memory bank, and we could agree that it was terrible, terrible, what people did, and he would forget about the harpsichord, and we could part with mutual regard, generated by the fact (indisputable) that neither of us were child abusers, however much we might have liked to be, having children of our own. Or, to get away from the distasteful subject of hurting children, I might tack, to the flawed corpus of the original anecdote, something about walking at night in the city, a declaration of my own lack of leftness—there's not a radical bone in my body, all I want is ease and bliss, not a thing in this world do I desire other than ease and bliss, I think he might empathize with that (did I mention that he had the flap on his holster unbuttoned and his left hand resting on the butt of his weapon, and the rim of his black shoes touching the rim of my brown boots?). That might ring a bell.

Or I could, as if struck by a sudden thought, ask him if he was a "real" policeman. He would probably answer truthfully. He would probably say either, "Yes, I am a real policeman," or, "No, I am not a real policeman." A third possibility: "What do you mean by 'real,' in this instance?" Because even among policemen who are "real," that is, bona fide, duly appointed officers of the law, there are degrees of realness and vivacity, they say of one another, "Fred's a *real* policeman," or announce a finding contrary to this finding, I don't know this of my own knowledge but am extrapolating from my knowledge (very slight) of the cant of other professions. But if I asked him this question, as a dodge or subterfuge to cover up the fact of the missing "part" of the original, extremely uninteresting, anecdote, there would be an excellent chance that he would take umbrage, and that his colleagues (did I neglect to say that there are two of his colleagues, in uniform, holding on to the handles of their bicycles, standing behind him, stalwartly, in the other room, and that he himself, the sergeant, is holding on to the handle of his bicycle, stalwartly, with the hand that is not resting on the butt of his .38, teak-handled I believe, from the brief glance that I snuck at it, when I was in the other room?) would take umbrage also. Goals incapable of attainment have driven many a man to despair, but despair is easier to get to than that—one need merely look out of the window, for example. But what we are trying to do is get away from despair and over to ease and bliss, and that can never be attained with three policemen, with bicycles, standing alertly in your other room. They can, as we know, make our lives miserable than they are already if we arouse their ire, which must be kept slumbering, by telling them stories, for example, such as the story of the four bears, known to us all from childhood (although not everyone knows about the fourth bear) and it is clear that *they can't lay their bicycles down* and sit, which would be the normal thing, no, they must stand there at more-or-less parade rest, some department ruling that I don't know about, but of course it irritates them, it even irritates me, and I am not standing there holding up a bicycle, I am in the other room having a glass of beef broth with a twist of lemon, perhaps you don't believe me about the policemen but there they are, pictures lie but words don't, unless one is lying on purpose, with an end in view, such as to get three policemen with bicycles out of your other room while retaining your harpsichord (probably the departmental regulations state that the bicycles must never be laid down in a civilian space, such as my other room, probably the sergeant brought his colleagues to help him haul away the harpsichord, which has three legs, and although the sight of three policemen on bicycles, each holding aloft one leg of a harpsichord, rolling smoothly through the garment district, might seem ludicrous to you, who knows how it seems to them? entirely right and proper, no doubt) which he, the sergeant, considers I promised to his wife as a wedding present, and it is true that I was at the wedding, but only to raise my voice and object when the minister came to that part of the ceremony where he routinely asks for objections, "*Yes!*" I shouted, "*she's my mother! And although she is a widow, and legally free, she belongs to me in dreams!*" but I was quickly hushed up by a quartet of plainclothesmen, and the ceremony proceeded. But what is the good of a mother if she is another man's wife, as they mostly are, and not around in the morning to fix your buckwheat cakes or Rice Krispies, as the case may be, and in the evening to argue with you about your vegetables, and in the middle of the day to iron your shirts and clean up your rooms, and at all times to provide intimations of ease and bliss (however misleading and ill-founded), but instead insists on hauling your harpsichord away (did I note that Mother, too, is in the other room, with the three policemen, she is standing with the top half of her bent over the instrument, her arms around it, at its widest point—the keyboard end)? So, standing with the glass in my hand, the glass of herb tea with sour cream in it, I wondered what kind of useful prosthesis I could attach to the original anecdote I was telling all these people in my other room—those who seem so satisfied with their tableau, the three peelers posing with their bicycles, my mother hugging the harpsichord with a mother's strangle—what kind of "and then" I could contrive which might satisfy all the particulars of the case, which might redeliver to me my mother, retain to me my harpsichord, and rid me of these others, in their uniforms.

I could tell them the story of the (indeterminate number of) bears, twisting it a bit to fit my deeper designs, so that the fourth bear enters (from left) and says, "I don't care who's been sleeping in my bed just so long as it is not a sergeant of police," and the fifth bear comes in (from right) and says, "Harpsichords wither and warp when their soundboards are exposed to the stress of bicycle transport," and the sixth bear strides right down to the footlights, center stage (from a hole in the back of the theater, or a hole in the back of the anecdote), and says, "Dearly beloved upholders, enforcers, rush, rush away and enter six-year bicycle race that is even now awaiting the starter's gun at the corner of Elsewhere and Not-Here," and the seventh bear descends from the flies on a nylon rope and cries, "*Mother! Come home!*" and the eighth bear—

But bears are not the answer. Bears are for children. Why am I thinking about bears when I should be thinking about some horribly beautiful "way out" of this tense scene, which has reduced me to a rag, just contemplating it here in the other room with this glass of chicken livers *flambé* in my hand—

Wait.

I will reenter the first room, cheerfully, confidently, even gaily, and throw chicken livers *flambé* all over the predicament, the flaming chicken livers clinging like incindergel to Mother, policemen, bicycles, harpsichord, and my file of the *National Review* from its founding to the present time. That will "open up" the situation successfully. I will resolve these contradictions with flaming chicken parts and then sing the song of how I contrived the ruin of my anaconda.

Can We Talk

I went to the bank to get my money for the day. And they had painted it yellow. Under cover of night, I shrewdly supposed. With white plaster letters saying CREDIT DEPARTMENT. And a row of new vice-presidents. But I have resources of my own, I said. Sulphur deposits in Texas and a great humming factory off the coast of Kansas. Where we make little things.

Thinking what about artichokes for lunch? Pleased to be in this yellow bank at 11:30 in the morning. A black man cashing his check in a Vassar College sweatshirt. A blue policeman with a St. Christopher pinned to his gunbelt. Thinking I need a little leaf to rest my artichokes upon. The lady stretching my money to make sure none of hers stuck to it.

Fourteenth Street gay with Judy Bond Dresses Are On Strike. When I leaned out of your high window in my shorts, did you really think I had hurting to destruction in mind? I was imagining a loudspeaker-and-leaflet unit that would give me your undivided attention.

When I leaned out of your high window in my shorts, did you think *why me?*

Into his bank I thought I saw my friend Kenneth go. To get his money for the day. Loitering outside in my painted shoes. Considering my prospects. A question of buying new underwear or going to the laundromat. And when I put a nickel in the soap machine it barks.

When I leaned out of your high window in my shorts, were you nervous because you had just me? I said: Your eyes have not been surpassed.

The artichokes in their glass jar from the artichoke heart of the world, Castroville, Calif. I asked the man for a leaf. Just one, I said. We don't sell them in ones, he said. Can we negotiate, I asked. Breathing his disgust he tucked a green leaf into my yellow vest with his brown hands.

When I asked why you didn't marry Harry you said it was because he didn't like you. Then I told you how I cheated the Thai lieutenant who was my best friend then.

Posing with my leaf against a plastic paper plate. Hoping cordially that my friend Victor's making money in his building. Then the artichokes one by one. Yes, you said, this is the part they call Turtle Bay.

Coffee wondering what my end would be. Thinking of my friend Roger killed in the crash of a Link Trainer at Randolph Field in '43. Or was it breakbone fever at Walter Reed.

Then out into the street again and uptown for my fencing lesson. Stopping on the way to give the underwear man a ten. Because he looked about to bark.

When I reached to touch your breast you said you had a cold. I believed you. I made more popcorn.

Thinking of my friend Max who looks like white bread. A brisk bout with my head in a wire cage. The Slash Waltz from "The Mark of Zorro." And in the shower a ten for Max, because his were the best two out of three. He put it in his lacy shoe. With his watch and his application to the Colorado School of Mines.

In the shower I refrained from speaking of you to anyone.

The store where I buy news buttoned up tight. Because the owners are in the mountains. Where I would surely be had I not decided to make us miserable.

I said: I seem to have lost all my manuscripts, in which my theory is proved not once but again and again and again, and now when people who don't believe a vertical monorail to Venus is possible shout at me, I have nothing to say. You peered into my gloom.

My friend Herman's house. Where I tickle the bell. It is me. Invited to put a vacuum cleaner together. The parts on the floor in alphabetical order. Herman away, making money. I hug his wife Agnes. A beautiful girl. And when no one hugs her tightly, her eyes fill.

When I asked you if you had a private income, you said something intelligent but I forget what. The skin scaling off my back from the week at the beach. Where I lay without knowing you.

Discussing the real estate game, Agnes and I. Into this game I may someday go, I said. Building cheap and renting dear. With a doorman to front for me. Tons of money in it, I said.

When my falling event was postponed, were you disappointed? Did you experience a disillusionment-event?

Hunted for a *Post*. To lean upon in the black hours ahead. And composed a brochure to lure folk into my new building. Titled "The Human Heart In Conflict With Itself." Promising 24-hour incineration. And other features.

Dancing on my parquet floor in my parquet shorts. To Mahler.

After you sent me home you came down in your elevator to be kissed. You knew I would be sitting on the steps.

Hiding Man

Enter expecting to find the place empty (I. A. L. Burligame walks through any open door). But it is not, there is a man sitting halfway down the right side, heavy, Negro, well dressed, dark glasses. Decide after moment's thought that if he is hostile, will flee through door marked EXIT (no bulb behind EXIT sign, no certainty that it leads anywhere). The film is in progress, title *Attack of the Puppet People*. Previously observed films at same theater, *Cool and the Crazy, She Gods of Shark Reef, Night of the Blood Beast, Diary of a High School Bride*. All superior examples of genre, tending toward suggested offscreen rapes, obscene tortures: man with huge pliers advancing on disheveled beauty, cut to girl's face, to pliers, to man's face, to girl, scream, blackout.

"It's better when the place is full," observes Negro, lifting voice slightly to carry over Pinocchio noises from puppet people. Voice pleasant, eyes behind glasses sinister? Choice of responses: anger, agreement, indifference, pique, shame, scholarly dispute. Keep eye on EXIT, what about boy in lobby, what was kite for? "Of course it's never *been* full." Apparently there is going to be a conversation. "Not all these years. As a matter of fact, you're the first one to come in, ever."

"People don't always tell the truth."

Let him chew that. Boy in lobby wore T-shirt, printed thereon, OUR LADY OF THE SORROWS. Where glimpsed before? Possible agent of the conspiracy, in the pay of the Organization, duties: lying, spying, tapping wires, setting fires, civil disorders. Seat myself on opposite side of theater from Negro and observe film. Screen torn from top to bottom, a large rent, faces and parts of gestures fall off into the void. Hard-pressed U. S. Army, Honest John, Hound Dog, Wowser notwithstanding, psychological warfare and nerve gas notwithstanding, falls back at onrush of puppet people. Young lieutenant defends Army nurse (uniform in rags, tasty thigh, lovely breast) from sexual intent of splinter men.

"Don't you know the place is closed?" calls friend in friendly tone. "Didn't you see the sign?"

"The picture is on. And you're here."

Signs after all mean everyone, if there are to be exceptions let them be listed: soldiers, sailors, airmen, children with kites, dogs under suitable restraint, distressed gentlefolk, people who promise not to peek. Well-dressed Negroes behind dark glasses in closed theaters, the attempt to scrape acquaintance, the helpful friend with the friendly word, note of menace as in *Dragstrip Riot*, as in *Terror from the Year 5000*. Child's play, amateur night, with whom do they think they have to deal?

"The silly thing just keeps running," alleges friend. "That's what's so fascinating. Continuous performances since 1944. Just keeps rolling along." Tilts head back, laughs theatrically. "It wasn't even any good then, for chrissake."

"Why do you keep coming back?"

"I don't think that's an interesting question."

Friend looks bland, studies film. Fires have started in many areas, the music is demure. I entrust myself to these places advisedly, there are risks but so also are there risks in crossing streets, opening doors, looking strangers in the eye. Man cannot live without placing himself naked before circumstance, as in warfare, under the sea, jet planes, women. Flight is always available, concealment is always possible.

"What I *meant* was," continues friend, animated now, smiling and gesturing, "other theaters. When they're full, you get lost in the crowd. Here, if anybody came in, they'd spot you in a minute. But *most* people, they believe the sign."

I. A. L. Burligame walks through any open door, private homes, public gatherings, stores with detectives wearing hats, meetings of Sons and Daughters of I Will Arise, but should I boast? Keep moving, counterpunching, examination of motives reveals appeal of dark places has nothing to do with circumstance. But because I feel warmer. The intimation was, *most* people do what they are told, NO LOITERING, NO PARKING BETWEEN 8 A.M. AND 5 P.M., KEEP OFF THE GRASS, CLOSED FOR REPAIRS KEEP OUT. Negro moves two seats closer, lowers voice confidentially.

"Of course it's no concern of mine . . ." Face appears gentle, interested as with old screw in *Girl on Death Row*, aerialist-cum-strangler in *Circus of Horrors*. "Of course I couldn't care less. But frankly, I feel a certain want of seriousness."

"I am absolutely serious."

On the other hand, perhaps antagonist is purely, simply what he pretends to be: well-dressed Negro with dark glasses in closed theater. But where then is the wienie? What happens to the twist? All of life is rooted in contradiction, movement in direction of self, two spaces, diagonally, argues hidden threat, there must be room for irony.

"Then what are you doing *here*!" Friend sits back in sliding seat with air of having clinched argument. "Surely you don't imagine *this* is a suitable place?"

"It looked good, from the outside. And there's no one here but you."

"Ah, but I *am* here. What do you know about me? Nothing, absolutely nothing. I could be anybody."

"So could I be anybody. And I notice that you too keep an eye on the door."

"Thus, we are problematic for each other." Said smoothly, with consciousness of power. "Name's Bane, by the way." Lights pipe, with flourishes and affectations. "Not my real one, of course."

"Of course." Pipe signal to confederates posted in balcony,

behind arras, under EXIT signs? Or is all this dumb show merely incidental, concealing vain heart, empty brain? On screen famous scientist has proposed measures to contain puppet people, involving mutant termites thrown against their flank. The country is in a panic, Wall Street has fallen, the President looks grave. And what of young informer in lobby, what is his relevance, who corrupted wearer of T-shirt, holder of kite?

"I'm a dealer in notions," friend volunteers. "Dancing dolls, learn handwriting analysis by mail, secrets of eternal life, coins and stamps, amaze your friends, pagan rites, abandoned, thrilling, fully illustrated worldwide selection of rare daggers, gurkhas, stilettos, bowies, hunting, throwing."

"And what are you doing here?"

"Like you," he avers. "Watching the picture. Just dropped in."

We resume viewing. Role of Bane obscure, possible motives in igniting conversation: (1) Agent of the conspiracy, (2) Fellow sufferer in the underground, (3) Engaged in counterespionage, (4) Talent scout for Police Informers School, (5) Market research for makers of *Attack of the Puppet People*, (6) Plain nosy bastard unconnected with any of the foregoing. Decide hypotheses (1), (2), and (6) most tenable, if (6), however, simple snubs should have done the job, as administered in remark "People don't always tell the truth." Also discourse has hidden pattern, too curious, too knowledgeable in sociology of concealment. Cover story thin, who confines himself to rare daggers, gurkhas, bowies, hunting, throwing in this day and age when large-scale fraud is possible to even the most inept operator, as in government wheat, television, uranium, systems development, public relations? Also disguise is commonplace, why a *Negro*, why a Negro in *dark glasses*, why sitting in the dark? Now he pretends fascination with events on screen, he says it has been playing since 1944, whereas I know to my certain knowledge that last week it was *She Gods of Shark Reef*, before that *Night of the Blood Beast*, *Diary of a High School Bride*, *Cool and the Crazy*. Coming: *Reform School Girl* on double bill with *Invasion of the Saucer Men*. Why lie? or is he attempting to suggest the mutability of time? Odor of sweetness from somewhere, flowers growing in cracks of floor, underneath the seats? Possible verbena, possible gladiolus, iris, phlox. Can't identify at this distance, what does he want? Now he looks sincere, making face involves removing glasses (his eyes burn in the dark), wrinkling forehead, drawing down corners of mouth, he does it very well.

"Tell me exactly what it is you hide from," he drops, the *Enola Gay* on final leg of notorious mission.

Bomb fails to fire, Burligame reacts not. Face the image of careless gaiety, in his own atrocious phrase, couldn't care less. Bane now addresses task *con amore,* it is clear that he is a professional, but sent by whom? In these times everything is very difficult, the lines of demarcation are not clear.

"Look," pleads he, moving two spaces nearer, whispering, "I know you're hiding, you know you're hiding, I will make a confession, I too am hiding. We have discovered each other, we are mutually embarrassed, we watch the exits, we listen for the sound of rough voices, the sound of betrayal. Why not confide in me, why not make common cause, every day is a little longer, sometimes I think my hearing is gone, sometimes my eyes close without instruction. Two can watch better than one, I will even tell you my real name."

Possible emotions in the face of blatant sincerity: repugnance, withdrawal, joy, flight, camaraderie, denounce him to the authorities (there are still authorities). And yet, is this not circumstance before which the naked Burligame might dangle, is this not real life, risk, and danger, as in *Voodoo Woman,* as in *Creature from the Black Lagoon!*

Bane continues, "My real name (how can I say it?) is Adrian Hipkiss, it is this among other things I flee. Can you imagine being named Adrian Hipkiss, the snickers, the jokes, the contumely, it was insupportable. There were other items, in 1944 I mailed a letter in which I didn't say what I meant, I moved the next day, it was New Year's Eve and all the moving men were drunk, they broke a leg on the piano. For fear it would return to accuse me. My life since has been one mask after another, Watford, Watkins, Watley, Watlow, Watson, Watt, now identity is gone, blown away, who am I, who knows?"

Bane-Hipkiss begins to sob, cooling system switches on, city life a texture of mysterious noises, starting and stopping, starting and stopping, we win control of the physical environment only at the expense of the auditory, what if one were sensitive, what if one flinched in the dark? Mutant termites devouring puppet people at a great rate, decorations for the scientists, tasty nurse for young lieutenant, they will end it with a joke if possible, meaning: it was not real after all. Cheating exists on every level, the attempt to deny what the eye reveals, what the mind knows to be true. Bane-Hipkiss strains credulity, a pig in a poke, if not (6) or (1) am I prepared to deal with (2)? Shall there be solidarity? But weeping is beyond toleration, unnatural, it should be reserved for great occasions, the telegram in the depths of the night, rail disasters, earthquakes, war.

"I hide from the priests" (my voice curiously tentative, fluting), "when I was the tallest boy in the eighth grade at Our Lady of the Sorrows they wanted me to go out for basketball, I would not, Father Blau the athletic priest said I avoided wholesome sport to seek out occasions of sin, in addition to the sin of pride, in addition to various other sins carefully enumerated before an interested group of my contemporaries."

Bane-Hipkiss brightens, ceases sobbing, meanwhile film begins again, puppet people move once more against U. S. Army, they are invincible, Honest John is a joke, Hound Dog malfunctions, Wowser detonates on launching pad, flower smell stronger and sweeter, are they really growing underneath our feet, is time in truth passing?

"Father Blau took his revenge in the confessional, he insisted on knowing everything. And there was so much to know. Because I no longer believed as I was supposed to believe. Or believed too much, indiscriminately. To one who has always been overly susceptible to slogans they should never have said: *You can change the world.* I suggested to my confessor that certain aspects of the ritual compared unfavorably with the resurrection scene in *Bride of Frankenstein.* He was shocked."

Bane-Hipkiss pales, he himself is shocked.

"But because he had, as it were, a vested interest in me, he sought to make clear the error of my ways. I did not invite this interest, it embarrassed me, I had other things on my mind. Was it my fault that in all that undernourished parish only I had secreted sufficient hormones, had chewed thoroughly enough the soup and chips that were our daily fare, to push head and hand in close proximity to the basket?"

"You could have faked a sprained ankle," Bane-Hipkiss says reasonably.

"That was unfortunately only the beginning. One day in the midst of a good Act of Contrition, Father Blau officiating with pious malice, I leaped from the box and sprinted down the aisle, never to return. Running past people doing the Stations of the Cross, past the tiny Negro lady, somebody's maid, our only black parishioner, who always sat in the very last row with a handkerchief over her head. Leaving Father Blau, unregenerate, with the sorry residue of our weekly encounter: impure thoughts, anger, dirty words, disobedience."

Bane-Hipkiss travels two seats nearer (why two at a time?), there is an edge to his voice. "Impure thoughts?"

"My impure thoughts were of a particularly detailed and graphic kind, involving at that time principally Nedda Ann Bush who lived two doors down the street from us and was handsomely developed. Under whose windows I crouched on many long nights awaiting revelations of beauty, the light being just right between the bureau and the window. Being rewarded on several occasions, namely 3 May 1942 with a glimpse of famous bust, 18 October 1943, a particularly chill evening, transfer of pants from person to clothes hamper, coupled with three minutes' subsequent exposure in state of nature. Before she thought to turn out the light."

"Extraordinary!" Bane-Hipkiss exhales noisily. It is clear that confession is doing him good in some obscure way. "But surely this priest extended some sort of spiritual consolation, counsel . . ."

"He once offered me part of a Baby Ruth."

"This was a mark of favor?"

"He wanted me to grow. It was in his own interest. His eye was on the All-City title."

"But it was an act of kindness."

"That was before I told him I wasn't going out. In the dark box with sliding panels, faces behind screen as in *Bighouse Baby*, as in *Mysterious House of Usher*, he gave me only steadfast refusal to understand these preoccupations, wholly natural and good interests in female parts however illicitly pursued, as under window. Coupled with skilled questioning intended to bring forth every final detail, including self-abuse and compulsive overconsumption of Baby Ruths, Mars Bars, Butterfingers, significance of which in terms of sexual self-aggrandizement was first pointed out to me by this good and holy man."

Bane-Hipkiss looks disturbed, why not? it is a disturbing story, there are things in this world that disgust, life is not all Vistavision and Thunderbirds, even Mars Bars have hidden significance, dangerous to plumb. The eradication of risk is the work of women's organizations and foundations, few of us, alas, can be great sinners.

"Became therefore a convinced anticlerical. No longer loved God, cringed at words 'My son,' fled blackrobes wherever they appeared, pronounced anathemas where appropriate, blasphemed, wrote dirty limericks involving rhymes for 'nunnery,' was in fine totally alienated. Then it became clear that this game was not so one-sided as had at first appeared, that there was a pursuit."

"Ah . . ."

"This was revealed to me by a renegade Brother of the Holy Sepulcher, a not overbright man but good in secret recesses of heart, who had been employed for eight years as cook in bishop's palace. He alleged that on wall of bishop's study was map, placed there were pins representing those in the diocese whose souls were at issue."

"Good God!" expletes Bane-Hipkiss, is there a faint flavor here of . . .

"It is kept rigorously up-to-date by the coadjutor, a rather political man. As are, in my experience, most church functionaries just under episcopal rank. Paradoxically, the bishop himself is a saint."

Bane-Hipkiss looks incredulous. "You still believe in saints?"

"I believe in saints,

"Holy water,

"Poor boxes,

"Ashes on Ash Wednesday,
"Lilies on Easter Sunday,
"Crèches, censers, choirs,
"Albs, Bibles, miters, martyrs,
"Little red lights,
"Ladies of the Altar Society,
"Knights of Columbus,
"Cassocks and cruets,
"Dispensations and indulgences,
"The efficacy of prayer,
"Right Reverends and Very Reverends,
"Tabernacles, monstrances,
"Bells ringing, people singing,
"Wine and bread,
"Sisters, Brothers, Fathers,
"The right of sanctuary,
"The primacy of the papacy,
"Bulls and concordats,
"The Index, the Last Judgment,
"Heaven and Hell,
"I believe it all. It's impossible not to believe. That's what makes things so difficult."
"But then . . ."
"It was basketball I didn't believe in."
But there is more, it was the first ritual which discovered to me the possibility of other rituals, other celebrations, for instance, *Blood of Dracula, Amazing Colossal Man, It Conquered the World*. Can Bane-Hipkiss absorb this nice theological point, that one believes what one can, follows that vision which most brilliantly exalts and vilifies the world? Alone in the dark one surrenders to *Amazing Colossal Man* all hope, all desire, meanwhile the bishop sends out his patrols, the canny old priests, the nuns on simple errands in stately pairs, I remember the year everyone wore black, what dodging into doorways, what obscene haste in crossing streets!

Bane-Hipkiss blushes, looks awkward, shuffles feet, opens mouth to speak.

"I have a confession."

"Confess," I urge, "feel free."

"I was sent here."

Under their noses or in Tibet, they have agents even in the lamaseries.

"That reminds me of something," I state, but Bane-Hipkiss rises, raises hand to head, commands: "Look!" As Burligame shrinks he *strips away his skin.* Clever Bane-Hipkiss, now he has me, I sit gapemouthed, he stands grinning with skin draped like dead dishrag over paw, he is white! I pretend imperturbability. "That reminds me, regarding the point I was making earlier, the film we are viewing is an interesting example . . ."

But he interrupts.

"Your position, while heretical, has its points," he states, "but on the other hand we cannot allow the integrity of our operation to be placed in question, willy-nilly, by people with funny ideas. Father Blau was wrong, we get some lemons just like any other group. On the other hand if every one of our people takes it into his head to flee us, who will be saved? You might start a trend. It was necessary to use this" (holds up falseface guiltily) "to get close to you, it was for the health of your soul."

Barefaced Bane-Hipkiss rattles on, has Burligame at last been taken, must he give himself up? There is still the sign marked EXIT, into the john, up on the stool, out through the window. "I am empowered to use force," he imparts, frowning.

"Regarding the point I was making earlier," I state, "or beginning to make, the film we are watching is itself a ritual, many people view such films and refuse to understand what they are saying, consider the . . ."

"At present I have more pressing business," he says, "will you come quietly?"

"No," I affirm, "pay attention to the picture, it is trying to tell you something, revelation is not so frequent in these times that one can afford to diddle it away."

"I must warn you," he replies, "that to a man filled with zeal nothing is proscribed. Zeal," he states proudly, "is my middle name."

"I will not stir."

"You must."

Now Bane-Hipkiss moves lightly on little priest's feet, sidewise through rows of seats, a cunning smile on face now revealed as hierarchical, hands clasped innocently in front of him to demonstrate purity of intent. Strange high howling noises, as in *Night of the Blood Beast*, fearful reddish cast to sky, as in *It Conquered the World*, where do they come from? The sweetness from beneath the seats is overpowering, I attempted to warn him but he would not hear, slip the case from jacket pocket, join needle to deadly body of instrument, crouch in readiness. Bane-Hipkiss advances, eyes clamped shut in mystical ecstasy, I grasp him by the throat, plunge needle into neck, his eyes bulge, his face collapses, he subsides quivering into a lump among the seats, in a moment he will begin barking like a dog.

Most people haven't the wit to be afraid, most view television, smoke cigars, fondle wives, have children, vote, plant gladiolus, iris, phlox, never confront *Screaming Skull, Teenage Werewolf, Beast with a Thousand Eyes*, no conception of what lies beneath the surface, no faith in any manifestation not certified by hierarchy. Who is safe with *Teenage Werewolf* abroad, with streets under sway of *Beast with a Thousand Eyes*? People think these things are jokes, but they are wrong, it is dangerous to ignore a vision, consider Bane-Hipkiss, he has begun to bark.

The Reference

"**W**arp."

"In the character?"

"He warp *ever' which way.*"

"You don't think we should consider him then."

"My friend Shel McPartland whom I have known deeply and intimately and too well for more than twenty years, is, sir, a brilliant O.K. engineer-master builder-cum-city and state planner. He'll plan your whole cotton-pickin' *state* for you, if you don't watch him. Right down to the flowers on the sideboard in the governor's mansion. He'll choose marginalia."

"I sir am not familiar sir with that particular bloom sir."

"Didn't think you would be, you bein' from Arkansas and therefore likely less than literate. You *are* from Arkansas State Planning Commission, are you not?"

"I am one of it. Mr. McPartland gave you as a reference."

"Well sir let me tell you sir that my friend Shel McPartland who has incautiously put me down as a reference has a wide-ranging knowledge of all modern techniques, theories, dodges, orthodoxies, heresies, new and old innovations, and scams of all kinds. The only thing about him is, he warp."

"Sir, it is not necessary to use dialect when being telephone-called from the state of Arkansas."

"Different folk I talk to in different ways. I got to keep myself interested."

"I understand that. Leaving aside the question of warp for a minute: let me ask you this: Is Mr. McPartland what you would call a hard worker?"

"Hard, but warp. He sort of goes off in his own direction."

"Not a team player."

"Very much a team player. You get your own team out there, and he'll play it, and *beat* it, all by his own self."

"Does he fiddle with women?"

"No. He has too much love and respect for women. He has so much love and respect for women that he has nothing to do with them. At all."

"You said earlier that you wouldn't trust him to salt a mine shaft with silver dollars."

"Well sir that was before I fully understood the nature of your interest. I thought maybe you were thinking of going into *business* with him. Or some other damn-fool thing of that sort. Now that I understand that it's a government gig . . . You folks don't go around salting mine shafts with silver dollars, do you?"

"No sir, that work comes under the competence of the Arkansas Board of Earth Resources."

"So, not to worry."

"But it doesn't sound very likely if I may say so Mr. Cockburn sir that Mr. McPartland would neatly infit with our outfit. Which must of necessity as I'm sure you're hip to sir concern itself mostly with the mundanities."

"McPartland is sublime with the mundanities."

"Truly?"

"You should see him tying his shoes. Tying other people's shoes. He's good at inking-in. *Excellent* at erasing. One of the great erasers of our time. Plotting graphs. Figuring use-densities. Diddling flow charts. Inflating statistics. Issuing modestly deceptive reports.

Chairing and charming. Dowsing for foundation funds. Only a fool and a simpleton sir would let Mr. McPartland slip through his fingers."

"But before you twigged to the fact sir that your role was that of a referencer, you signaled grave and serious doubts."

"I have them still. I told you he was warp and he *is* warp. I am attempting dear friend to give you Mr. McPartland in the round. The whole man. The gravamen and the true gen. When we reference it up, here in the shop, we don't stint. Your interrobang meets our galgenspiel. We do good work."

"But is he reliable?"

"Reliability sir is much overrated. He is inspired. What does this lick pay, by the way?"

"In the low forties with perks."

"The perks include?"

"Arkansas sir. Chauffered VW to and from place of employment. Crab gumbo in the cafeteria every Tuesday. Ruffles and flourishes played on the Muzak upon entry and exit from building. Crab gumbo in the cafeteria every Thursday. Sabbaticals every second, third, and fifth year. Ox stoptions."

"The latter term is not known to me."

"Holder of the post is entitled to stop a runmad ox in the main street of Little Rock every Saturday at high noon, preventing thereby the mashing to strawberry yogurt of one small child furnished by management. Photograph of said act to appear in the local blats the following Sunday, along with awarding of medal by the mayor. On TV."

"Does the population never tire of this heroicidal behavior?"

"It's bread and circuitry in the modern world, sir, and no place in that world is more modern than Arkansas."

"Wherefrom do you get your crabs?"

"From our great sister state of Lose-e-anna, whereat the best world-class eating crabs hang out."

"The McPartland is a gumbohead from way back, this must be known to you from your other investigations."

"The organization is not to be tweedled with. Shelbaby's partialities will be catered to, if and when. Now I got a bunch more questions here. Like, is he good?"

"Good don't come close. One need only point to his accomplishment *in re* the sewer system of Detroit, Mich. By the sewage of Detroit I sat down and wept, from pure stunned admiration."

"Is he fake?"

"Not more than anybody else. He has facades but who does not?"

"Does he know the blue lines?"

"*Excellent* with the blue lines."

"Does he know the old songs?"

"He'll crack your heart with the old songs."

"Does he have the right moves?"

"People all over America are sitting in darkened projection rooms right this minute, studying McPartland moves."

"What's this dude look like?"

"Handsome as the dawn. If you can imagine a bald dawn."

"You mean he's old?"

"Naw, man, he's young. A boy of forty-five, just like the rest of us. The thing is, he thinks so hard he done burned all the hair off his head. His head overheats."

"Is that a danger to standers-by?"

"Not if they exercise due caution. Don't stand too close."

"Maybe he's too fine for us."

"I don't think so. He's got a certain common-as-dirt quality. That's right under his laser-sharp M.I.T. quality."

"He sounds maybe a shade too rich for our blood. For us folk here in the downhome heartland."

"Lemme see, Arkansas, that's one of them newer states, right? Down there at the bottom edge? Right along with New Mexico and Florida and such as that?"

"Mr. Cockburn sir, are you jiving me?"

"Would I jive you?"

"Just for the record, how would you describe your personal relation to Mr. McPartland?"

"Oh I think 'blood enemy' might do it. Might come close. At the same time, I am forced to acknowledge merit. In whatever obscene form it chooses to take. McPartland worked on the kiss of death, did you know that? When he was young. Never did get it perfected but the theoretical studies were elegant, elegant. He's what you might call a engineer's engineer. He designed the artichoke that is all heart. You pay a bit of a premium for it but you don't have to do all that peeling."

"Some people like the peeling. The leaf-by-leaf unveiling."

"Well, some people like to bang their heads against stone walls, don't they? Some people like to sleep with their sisters. Some people like to put on suits and ties and go sit in a concert hall and listen to the New York Philharmonic *Orchestra* for God's sake. Some people—"

"Is this part of his warp?"

"It's related to his warp. The warp to power."

"Any other glaring defects or lesions of the usual that you'd like to touch upon—"

"I think not. Now you, I perceive, have got this bad situation down there in the great state of Arkansas. Your population is exploding. It's mobile. You got people moving freely about, colliding and colluding, pairing off just as they please and exploding the population some more, lollygagging and sailboating and making leather moccasins from kits and God knows what all. And enjoying free speech and voting their heads off and vetoing bond issues carefully thought up and packaged and rigged by the Arkansas State Planning Commission. And general helter-skeltering around under the gross equity of the democratic system. Is that the position, sir?"

"Worse. Arkansas is, at present, pure planarchy."

"I intuited as much. And you need someone who can get the troops back on the track or tracks. Give them multifamily dwellings, green belts, dayrooms, grog rations, and pleasure stamps. Return the great state of Arkansas to its originary tidiness. Exert a plenipotentiary beneficence while remaining a masked marvel. Whose very existence is known only to the choice few."

"Exactly right. Can McPartland do it?"

"Sitting on his hands. Will you go to fifty?"

"Fervently and with pleasure, sir. It's little enough for such a treasure."

"I take 10 percent off the top, sir."

"And can I send you as well, sir, a crate of armadillo steak, sugar-cured, courtesy of the A.S.P.C.? It's a dream of beauty, sir, this picture that you've limned."

"Not a dream, sir, not a dream. Engineers, sir, never sleep, and dream only in the daytime."

Edwards, Amelia

melia Edwards was washing the dishes when she noticed that a dish that she had already washed had a tiny piece of spinach stuck to the back of it.

I am not washing these dishes well, she thought. I am not washing these dishes as well as I used to wash them.

Mrs. Edwards stopped washing the dishes, even though half of them remain unwashed in the sink. She dried her arms on a paper towel and went into the bedroom. She sat down on the bed. Then she stood up again and looked at the bed.

The bedspread had been placed on the bed in a somewhat sloppy manner. She thought: I am not making the bed as well as I used to.

She sat down on the bed again and stared at the floor. Then her eyes moved to the corner of the room near the closet. In the corner, in the place where the two walls met, there was a gray dustball the size of an egg.

I have not vacuumed this room correctly, she thought. Is it because I am thirty-eight now?

No. Thirty-eight is young, relatively.

I am young and vigorous. George is handsome and well paid. We are going to Hawaii in June.

I wonder if I should have a drink?

Mrs. Edwards went out to the kitchen and looked at the vodka bottle.

Then she looked at the plate with the bit of spinach stuck to the back. She scratched the spinach from the plate with her fingernail. She poured some vodka into a glass. She went to the refrigerator to get some ice cubes, but when she opened the door to the freezing compartment it came off in her hands.

Mrs. Edwards regarded the door to the freezing compartment, a rectangular piece of white plastic.

The door to the freezing compartment has come off, she thought.

She placed it on the floor next to the refrigerator. Then she moved a tray of ice cubes from the freezing compartment and made herself a vodka-tonic. The telephone rang. Mrs. Edwards did not answer it. She was sitting on the bed looking at her vodka-tonic. The telephone rang eleven times.

Perhaps I should listen to some music?

Mrs. Edwards arose and walked into the living room. She found an Angel record. "Don Giovanni Highlights," with Eberhard Wächter, Joan Sutherland, and Elisabeth Schwarzkopf. She placed the record on the turntable and switched on the amplifier. Then she sat down and listened to the music.

She remembered something she had read in the newspaper:

GIRL, 8, FOUND SLAIN

Mrs. Edwards drank some of her vodka-tonic. Then she noticed that something was wrong with the music. The turntable was slow. The music was dragging.

She got up and lifted the arm of the turntable to see if there was anything the matter with the needle. She scratched the needle with her finger. A scratching noise came out of the speakers. Behind the cabinet on which the turntable sat—between the back of the cabinet and the wall—there was a pair of black socks.

Black socks, she thought.

Mrs. Edwards turned off the amplifier and carried the black socks to the closet. She placed them in the dirty clothes hamper.

Take clothes to laundromat, she thought.

Then she went into the kitchen and made herself another vodka-tonic.

Which she did not drink. She placed the second vodka-tonic on the small table beside the big chair in the living room and looked at it.

I used to put lime juice in my vodka-tonics, she thought. Now I just put in the vodka and the tonic, and the ice. When did I stop putting in the lime juice? I remember buying limes, slicing limes, squeezing limes . . .

If we had had children, I could have interested myself in the problems of children.

I once won a prize for whistling with crackers in my mouth, she remembered. I whistled best. At a birthday party. When I was eight.

The telephone rang again. Mrs. Edwards did not answer it. Because she was afraid it was the Telephone Company calling about the telephone bill. The Telephone Company had already called once about the telephone bill. She had told the woman from the Telephone Company that she would send a check right away but had not done so.

The telephone bill is one hundred and twelve dollars, she thought.

I can pay it on the fifteenth. Or I can send them a check and forget to sign it. I have not done that for a long time. Probably that would work, at this time.

Mrs. Edwards drank some of the second vodka-tonic.

Do I not put the lime juice in because of the war? she wondered. The incredible war? Is that why I don't put the lime juice in?

Behind her—that is, behind the chair in which she was sitting—a large picture fell off the wall. There was a sound of glass breaking.

Mrs. Edwards did not turn around to look.

I never liked that picture. George liked that picture. Our taste in pictures differs. I like Josef Albers. George does not understand what Josef Albers is all about. Only I understand what Josef Albers is all about. Our tastes differ. I have not been courted properly in three years. It is ridiculous to have a reproduction of Marie Laurencin hanging in one's home. In the living room.

Once, I would have refused to have a reproduction of Marie Laurencin hanging in my home.

Not that she is bad. She is not bad at all. She is rather good, if one likes that sort of thing. Once, I would have fought about it. Tooth and nail.

She thought: A long time ago.

She thought: Did I remember to have photostats made, front and back, of the two checks for $16.22 each that the Internal Revenue Service says we didn't send it for the maid's Social Security for the first two quarters of 1970? That we did send? Because I have the cancelled checks?

No, I did not. I must take the check to the photostat place and have the photostats made front and back and then send them with a letter to the Internal Revenue Service.

I will not have another vodka-tonic. Because I have will power.

When I lived in the city I had a dog. I would go out and walk my dog at ten o'clock in the morning. I would see all the other people walking their dogs. We would smile at one another over our dogs.

If I have will power, why don't I take my anti-alcohol pills?

Because I would rather drink.

Marie Laurencin had a good time. In life. Relatively. 1885–1956.

Am I a standard-issue American alcoholic housewife? Assembled by many hands, like a Rambler, like a Princess telephone?

But there is my love for the work of Josef Albers.

But perhaps every one of us has a wrinkle—kink would not be too strong a word—which enables us to think of ourselves as . . . Marginal differentiation, as they call it in George's business.

Three years.

Mrs. Edwards looked at her fingernails. There was a time, she thought, when I cared about my cuticles.

Mrs. Edwards thought about Duke Ellington. She knew everything about Ellington there was to know. She thought about Johnny Hodges, Harry Carney, Ivie Anderson, Tricky Sam Nanton, Ray

Nance the fiddler, Jimmy Blanton. She thought especially hard about Barney Bigard. She thought about "Transblucency," "What Am I Here For?," and "East St. Louis Too-dle-oo." This music had made her happy, when she was young.

But the turntable—

I have done something wrong, she thought.

At this point, the water, which had been accumulating for many days, walked up the stairs from the basement and presented itself in the living room.

Living room, Amelia thought. What does that mean?

There is water on the floor of the *living room.*

Chagall is soft, she thought. All those floating lovers. Kissing above the rooftops. He has radically misperceived the problem.

The telephone rang but Mrs. Edwards did not answer it, because she knew the caller was a professional woman-terrorizer who was not very good at it: too tentative. She had talked to him before. His name was Fred.

I do not want to talk to Fred today.

Mrs. Edwards looked at herself and noticed that she had forgotten to put any clothes on. When she had gotten up, after George had left for the office. She was not wearing any clothes.

Then she went into the kitchen and washed the rest of the dishes. Very well, very well indeed. Very carefully. Nobody could object to the way she washed them, nobody in the whole world.

Marie, Marie, Hold On Tight

enry Mackie, Edward Asher, and Howard Ettle braved a rain-storm to demonstrate against the human condition on Wednes-day, April 26 (and Marie, you should have used waterproof paint; the signs were a mess after half an hour). They began at St. John the Precursor on 69th Street at 1:30 P.M. picketing with signs bearing the slogans MAN DIES!/ THE BODY IS DISGUST!/ COGITO ERGO NOTHING!/ ABANDON LOVE! and handing out announcements of Henry Mackie's lecture at the Playmor Lanes the next evening. There was much interest among bystanders in the vicinity of the church. A man who said his name was William Rochester came up to give encouragement: *"That's the way!"* he said. At about 1:50 a fat, richly dressed beadle emerged from the church to dispute our right to picket. He had dewlaps which shook unpleasantly and, I am sorry to say, did not look like a good man.

"All right," he said, "now *move* on, you have to *move along, you can't* picket us!" He said that the church had never been picketed, that it could not be picketed without its permission, that it owned the sidewalk, and that he was going to call the police. Henry Mackie, Edward Asher, and Howard Ettle had already obtained police per-mission for the demonstration through a fortunate bit of foresight; and we confirmed this by showing him our slip that we had obtained at Police Headquarters. The beadle was intensely irritated at this and stormed back inside the church to report to someone higher up. Henry Mackie said, "Well, get ready for the lightning bolt," and Edward Asher and Howard Ettle laughed.

Interest in the demonstration among walkers on 69th Street increased and a number of people accepted our leaflet and began to ask the pickets questions such as "What do you mean?" and "Were you young men raised in the church?" The pickets replied to these questions quietly but firmly and in as much detail as casual passers-by could be expected to be interested in. Some of the walkers made taunting remarks—"Cogito ergo your ass" is one I remember—but the demeanor of the pickets was exemplary at all times, even later when things began, as Henry Mackie put it, "to get a little rough." (Marie, you would have been proud of us.) People who care about the rights of pickets should realize that these rights are threatened mostly not by the police, who generally do not molest you if you go through the appropriate bureaucratic procedures such as getting a permit, but by individuals who come up to you and try to pull your sign out of your hands or, in one case, spit at you. The man who did the latter was, surprisingly, very well dressed. What could be happening with an individual like that? He didn't even ask questions as to the nature or purpose of the demonstration, just spat and walked away. He didn't say a word. We wondered about him.

At about 2 P.M. a very high-up official in a black clerical suit emerged from the church and asked us if we had ever heard of Kierkegaard. It was raining on him just as it was on the pickets but he didn't seem to mind. "This demonstration displays a Kierke-gaardian spirit which I understand," he said, and then requested that we transfer our operations to some other place. Henry Mackie had a very interesting discussion of about ten minutes' duration with this official during which photographs were taken by the *New York Post, Newsweek,* and CBS Television whom Henry Mackie had alerted prior to the demonstration. The photographers made the churchman a little nervous but you have to hand it to him, he maintained his phony attitude of polite interest almost to the last. He said several rather bromidic things like "The human condition is the *given*, it's what we do with it that counts" and "The body is simply the temple wherein the soul dwells" which Henry Mackie countered with his famous question "*Why does it have to be that way?*" which has dumbfounded so many orthodox religionists and thinkers and with which he first won us (the other pickets) to his banner in the first place.

"*Why?*" the churchman exclaimed. It was clear that he was radically taken aback. "Because it *is* that way. You have to deal with what is. With reality."

"But why does it *have* to be that way?" Henry Mackie repeated, which is the technique of the question, which used in this way is unanswerable. A blush of anger and frustration crossed the churchman's features (it probably didn't register on your TV screen, Marie, but I was there, I saw it—it was beautiful).

"The human condition is a fundamental datum," the cleric stated. "It is immutable, fixed, and changeless. To say otherwise..."

"Precisely," Henry Mackie said, "why it must be challenged."

"But," the cleric said, "it is God's will."

"Yes," Henry Mackie said significantly.

The churchman then retired into his church, muttering and shaking his head. The rain had damaged our signs somewhat but the slogans were still legible and we had extra signs cached in Edward Asher's car anyway. A number of innocents crossed the picket line to worship including several who looked as if they might be from the FBI. The pickets had realized in laying their plans the danger that they might be taken for Communists. This eventuality was provided for by the mimeographed leaflets which carefully explained that the pickets were not Communists and cited Edward Asher's and Howard Ettle's Army service including Asher's Commendation Ribbon. "We, as you, are law-abiding American citizens who support the Constitution and pay taxes," the leaflet says. "We are simply opposed to the ruthless way in which the human condition has been imposed on organisms which have done nothing to deserve it and are unable to escape it. *Why does it have to be that way?*" The leaflet goes on to discuss, in simple language, the various unfortunate aspects of the human condition including death, unseemly and degrading bodily functions, limitations on human understanding, and the chimera of love. The leaflet concludes with the section headed "What Is To Be Done?" which Henry Mackie says is a famous revolutionary catchword and which outlines, in clear, simple language, Henry Mackie's program for the reification of the human condition from the ground up.

A Negro lady came up, took one of the leaflets, read it carefully, and then said: "They look like Communists to *me!*" Edward Asher commented that no matter how clearly things were explained to the people, the people always wanted to believe you were a Communist. He said that when he demonstrated once in Miami against vivisection of helpless animals he was accused of being a Nazi Communist which was, he explained, a contradiction in terms. He said ladies were usually the worst.

By then the large crowd that had gathered when the television men came had drifted away. The pickets therefore shifted the site of the demonstration to Rockefeller Plaza in Rockefeller Center via Edward Asher's car. Here were many people loafing, digesting lunch etc. and we used the spare signs which had new messages including

WHY ARE YOU STANDING
WHERE ARE YOU STANDING?
THE SOUL IS NOT!
NO MORE
ART
CULTURE
LOVE
REMEMBER YOU ARE DUST!

The rain had stopped and the flowers smelled marvelously fine. The pickets took up positions near a restaurant (I wish you'd been there, Marie, because it reminded me of something, something you said that night we went to Bloomingdale's and bought your new

175

cerise-colored bathing suit: "The color a new baby has," you said, and the flowers were like that, some of them). People with cameras hanging around their necks took pictures of us as if they had never seen a demonstration before. The pickets remarked among themselves that it was funny to think of the tourists with pictures of us demonstrating in their scrapbooks in California, Iowa, Michigan, people we didn't know and who didn't know us or care anything about the demonstration or, for that matter, the human condition itself, in which they were so steeped that they couldn't stand off, and look at it, and know it for what it was. "It's a paradigmatic situation," Henry Mackie said, "exemplifying the distance between the potential knowers holding a commonsense view of the world and what is to be known, which escapes them as they pursue existences."

At this time (2:45 P.M.) the demonstrators were approached by a group of youths between the ages I would say of sixteen and twenty-one. They were dressed in hood jackets, T-shirts, tight pants etc., and were very obviously delinquents from bad environments and broken homes where they had received no love. They ringed the pickets in a threatening manner. There were about seven of them. The leader (and Marie, he wasn't the oldest; he was younger than some of them, tall, with a peculiar face, blank and intelligent at the same time) walked around looking at our signs with exaggerated curiosity. "What are you guys," he said finally, "some kind of creeps or something?"

Henry Mackie replied quietly that the pickets were American citizens pursuing their right to demonstrate peaceably under the Constitution.

The leader looked at Henry Mackie. "You're flits, you guys, huh?" he said. He then snatched a handful of leaflets out of Edward Asher's hands, and when Edward Asher attempted to recover them, danced away out of reach while two others stood in Asher's way. "What do you flits think you're doin'?" he said. "What *is* this shit?"

"You haven't got any right . . ." Henry Mackie started to say, but the leader of the youths moved very close to him then.

"What do you mean, you don't believe in God?" he said. The other ones moved in closer too.

"That is not the question," Henry Mackie said. "Belief or non-belief is not at issue. The situation remains the same whether you believe or not. The human condition is . . ."

"Listen," the leader said, "I thought all you guys went to church every day. Now you tell me that flits don't believe in God. You putting me on?"

Henry Mackie repeated that belief was not involved, and said that it was, rather, a question of man helpless in the grip of a definition of himself that he had not drawn, that could not be altered by human action, and that was in fundamental conflict with every human notion of what should obtain. The pickets were simply subjecting this state of affairs to a radical questioning, he said.

"You're putting me on," the youth said, and attempted to kick Henry Mackie in the groin, but Mackie turned away in time. However the other youths then jumped the pickets, right in the middle of Rockefeller Center. Henry Mackie was thrown to the pavement and kicked repeatedly in the head, Edward Asher's coat was ripped off his back and he sustained many blows in the kidneys and elsewhere, and Howard Ettle was given a broken rib by a youth called "Cutter" who shoved him against a wall and smashed him viciously even though bystanders tried to interfere (a few of them). All this happened in a very short space of time. The pickets' signs were broken and smashed, and their leaflets scattered everywhere. A policeman summoned by bystanders tried to catch the youths but they got away through the lobby of the Associated Press building and he returned empty-handed. Medical aid was summoned for the pickets. Photos were taken.

"Senseless violence," Edward Asher said later. "They didn't understand that . . ."

"On the contrary," Henry Mackie said, "they understand everything better than anybody."

The next evening, at 8 P.M. Henry Mackie delivered his lecture in the upstairs meeting room at the Playmor Lanes, as had been announced in the leaflet. The crowd was very small but attentive and interested. Henry Mackie had his head bandaged in a white bandage. He delivered his lecture titled "What Is To Be Done?" with good diction and enunciation, and in a strong voice. He was very eloquent. And eloquence, Henry Mackie says, is really all any of us can hope for.

Pages from the Annual Report

William Elderly Baskerville posed with the ink bottle in his hand. A lovely robust drop trembled on the lip; with a smooth slight movement of the wrist, he heaved it over the edge. It made a satisfying smash on the letterhead between his feet. Reaching, he picked the paper up and folded it in half. "Mislike me not for my complexion," he murmured, and looked around the room. De Vinne was watching him. William Elderly Baskerville blinked twice. "Voyeur!" he spat. He ran his thumb up the edge of the paper. What terrors, monsters, troglodytes, and conflagrations lay inside? He threw the paper away; it lay curling in his wastebasket.

From their window one could see the dismal underside of an identical building, sometimes with faces pressed against the glass. William Elderly Baskerville spent a good deal of his time looking out the window, making faces for the people in the other building. De Vinne did not approve. He refused to look out the window at all. "Why?" William Elderly Baskerville asked suddenly. De Vinne pretended to start. "Why what?" Baskerville played with his paperknife; for a moment, he was a Borgia. "Why have they cast us here, and left us?"

De Vinne reached for his own paperknife, defensively. He was younger, heavy, and worried. He also refused to take off his coat in the office. Executives wore their jackets at all times; his was a light green tweed. "Be damned if I know," he said.

Baskerville dangled the knife like a jewel before his own bedazzled eyes. "I was pleased, once. I saw a horse burn to the ground."

"A horse?"

"The eyes lit up with an interior light."

"Did he scream?"

"It was a chocolate horse in my mother's skillet. We had hot chocolate."

"You aim to shock."

"I only like things a little more exciting than they are."

De Vinne was . . . tolerable. On occasion, he showed real promise. And after thirteen years, why not? Or had it been that long? Perhaps only since January. William Elderly Baskerville ran a hand through what he firmly believed was full white hair. The gray of the sky outside their window never changed; it was difficult to tell the time. Was he thirty-one or fifty? On the wall behind him a sign said BLINK.

The girl from the mimeograph room barged through the door backward trailing a supermarket basket filled with paper. She looked uneasily from one to the other, then smiled at Baskerville: he was the handsomer. De Vinne, enraged, stood up and hurled his knife across the room. It clattered to the floor a foot from the wire basket: the girl screamed with real terror. "Put it over there, Cynthia," De Vinne said kindly. He helped her empty the basket onto a long table where stacks and stacks of identical paper already sat. She shrank from him as much as possible. One of the stacks began to teeter and slip off the edge; they piled the rest on the floor. Other piles drifted against the walls on three sides of the room, some of them four feet tall.

"Cynthia," Baskerville said. He employed his best Harvard Business manner. "Before you go, one thing. Are you ready to divulge the whereabouts of your headquarters?"

"Mr. Baskerville, I can't. I told you a hundred times. They'll kill me if I tell."

"But Cynthia," he said kindly, reasonably. "Look at it from our point of view. Look at this room. DID YOU EVER SEE ANYTHING LIKE IT?" he shouted. "What in the name of God do you expect us to do?"

De Vinne interposed a soothing hand. "You know we have to consider everything carefully. These things take time. Meanwhile, we're being pressed to death by your people. By the people you represent."

"Let her go," William Elderly Baskerville said suddenly. "What is she? A transient, just passing through. Get yourself out of here, scab," he said. "Get back to headquarters. And you can tell them from us . . ." He paused, looking at De Vinne. "What can she tell them from us?"

"Let's just send them the knife. A declaration of war." He formally tendered the paperknife, as if surrendering a sword.

The girl fled, bumping and clanging down the hall. "We probably shouldn't have done that," Baskerville said. "There'll be repercussions." He moved to the window. "What kind of day is it?" De Vinne asked. He sat slumped in his chair, toying with a rubber stamp that printed his initials H.D.V. He printed them several times on the telephone book. Baskerville pressed his face to the glass and squinted upward, to the bit of sky between the two buildings. "The same kind," he said moodily. "Look for yourself."

"You know I have a fear of heights."

"Have you got any paper clips?"

"More than I can possibly use. Have a thousand."

"Two will do. What time is it?"

"Almost lunch."

A rat appeared on one of the piles of paper on the floor, looked at them, and scuttled along the wall. "Game!" De Vinne cried, and ran delightedly to the supply closet, where he pulled an ancient crossbow from an upper shelf. Winding it with difficulty, he laid a feathered bolt in place. "Where is it?" His face was flushed with unnatural exertion.

"I think it's under the watercooler. Here, give me the bow. Let me shoot."

"No," De Vinne held the weapon high above his head, "no, no, no." He danced out of reach. "It's mine, I found it." The thing went off with a shivering clang, shattering the great globe of the watercooler. Dank green growths cascaded over the floor. De Vinne quietly put the crossbow back on its shelf.

"It's an outmoded weapon," Baskerville said. "Don't reproach yourself."

"There was something in my eye," De Vinne said, rubbing.

"Usually you're better."

"Usually IT stands still."

"I hope it didn't drown."

William Elderly Baskerville sat with his feet on the desk, watching the telephone. Sooner or later it would ring. He was not discouraged by the fact that it never had, in all the years or months he had been watching it. In the meantime, there were diversions. De Vinne wasn't a bad fellow, really, although he was young and a Christian Scientist. Baskerville stared at his collection of Rorschachs, taped on the wall behind him. There were hundreds of them: bats and shattered golfballs, broken butterflies and carnivorous leemings and amphibious bandicoots, falling angels and whirling circus tents. With practice he could look at them and see nothing at all.

Palatino the office boy looked in the door. He was an old man of retirement age, or close to it, with a twisted foot. "Do you want to know what I heard about your guys?" he said, leering. "Do you want to know? What's it worth to you?"

"A thousand paper clips," De Vinne said.

"Skin of a drowned rat," Baskerville countered.

"A genuine antique crossbow in excellent condition."

"A cloot on the snoot."

"William, don't be unkind." De Vinne turned. "He's only trying to be helpful. Aren't you, you filthy mother?" He grabbed the old man by the shoulders and shook him furiously, then pushed him back out the door.

Palatino jumped. There was someone behind him. It was Miss Angel Craw, a beautiful Negress who was the floor maid. She was singing "Bringing In The Sheaves" in a lovely dark contralto. "They're going to flood this place and wash you all away," the old man shrilled. "They're going to hook the fire hoses up to the transoms. You'll be drowned! You'll be drowned!" He laughed insanely and pinched Miss Angel Craw; with a quick gesture, she shoved the end of her mop up under his chin. He howled and ran.

"Did he mean it?" De Vinne looked worried. "Does he know something?"

"A born turncoat. He might."

"Do you think maybe they're not satisfied? With our work?"

"How would they know? We never send anything *out*. Everything comes *in*. How could they possibly know?"

"Maybe we haven't complained enough."

"Maybe we haven't complained in the *right way*."

"We'd better cover ourselves. First we'll draw up formal complaint. Then we'll seal the transoms."

"After all these years," Baskerville mused. "Not satisfied with *our* work." Miss Angel Craw mopped the floor in the background, singing softly. Her mop swished through little puddles of water and broken glass. "When I retired, they said I was the best man they ever had on this job. The best."

"We're not so young anymore." De Vinne answered. "We're thirty-one. But alert for our age."

"It's a flagrant example of . . . What shall I say in the complaint?"

"Let me think." De Vinne began pacing, lifting his feet delicately to avoid the waves from Miss Angel Craw's mop. "Say: When in the course of human events it becomes necessary . . . No, that won't do. We don't want to *petition*. We want to *demand*."

"You can't *demand* if you have nothing to bargain with. Use your head. We need hostages." They both looked at Miss Angel Craw, who gave them a seductive smile. William Elderly Baskerville took her by the hand. She posed prettily as Pocahontas. "Won't do," Baskerville said, shaking his head, "she's under age." Miss Angel Craw looked hurt. She returned to her mopping.

"I never had any children," De Vinne said.

"I don't see the relevance."

"I didn't expect you to."

"You're not helping."

"I know what you're thinking."

"You don't."

"I do. You're ready to give them *me*."

"It never occurred . . ."

"It's written all over your face."

"Not even for a moment."

"After all these years."

"Would you mind?"

"Judas!"

There was a crash in the supply closet. Miss Angel Craw had locked herself in. They rushed to the door, pulling and jerking on it. It refused to move. "Are you all right?" De Vinne called. Miss Angel Craw could be heard singing behind the door. "She's all right," Baskerville said testily. "Concentrate on the problem." They both sat down at their desks in a businesslike way. "We forgot lunch," De Vinne said.

"It's dull here," he went on. "I think I'll look out the window."

"Be careful. Remember your affliction."

"I'm tired. I'm tired and I'm overworked." He was working himself into a rage; Baskerville knew the signs. The strain of their assignment was telling on him. He was, after all, a young man, comparatively inexperienced. You had to make allowances. William Elderly Baskerville felt tolerant and fatherly. From the abundant supply on the floor he chose several pieces of paper and fashioned an elaborate Valentine heart, inscribing it, with many flourishes, with the words "Thirty-Five Years, In Grateful Memory." He placed it wordlessly on his partner's desk. De Vinne began to cry.

"You never answered my question," Baskerville said gently.

"What question?" De Vinne's face was hidden behind his hands.

"Why have we been thrown here, and abandoned?"

"It was a rhetorical question."

"Then *I* didn't answer it. But you try, first."

"To do our work."

"But what precisely *is* our work?"

"It has something to do with all this." De Vinne indicated the paper strewn all over the room. His interest was reviving; he wiped his tear-streaked face. "There is an organization, somewhere," he began, patiently, "and it sends us the, uh, material, and we . . ."

"And we?"

"We *act* on it.

"When?"

"I thought *you* knew."

"Maybe I do. But aren't you getting impatient?"

"I bloody well am."

"I don't blame you."

"I was rabid the first couple of months. Or years. But you said to wait. You seemed to know what you were doing."

"You're very kind."

"Do you?"

"It's well you ask."

"I'm trying to be efficient. God knows." De Vinne brushed some lint from his green tweed jacket. "But it's trying, with you being mysterious and Lord knows what going on outside . . ." He began to look tearful again.

"Henry," Baskerville said quietly.

"Yes?"

"You've noticed the paper?"

"*Noticed* it! My God, we're drowning in it. You yourself told Cynthia . . ."

"You've noticed that there's nothing on it?"

"Yes."

"And you know that in a model of the typical clerical or administrative function, we would initial it and send it forward?"

"Typically, we would."

"But we don't."

"We don't."

"We *contain* it."

"I don't see . . ."

"When I first came, Harry Garamond, he was in charge then, took me aside and told me that although what we did here might seem foolish to me at first, that I would eventually get the idea. I'd understand, he said. And he was right. But it took some time."

"And the idea was . . ." De Vinne leaned forward eagerly.

"That we were to be a bottleneck. That everything was to stop here. Although there might be pressures from outside."

"But . . ."

"Both pro and con."

"I'm confused."

"I regret it."

"Get to the point. What *is* this stuff?" De Vinne kicked a pile of paper; it flowed over the adjoining floorspace in a snowy wave.

"The substance of human lives."

"This . . . waste?"

"Of hundreds of lives. Of real men in real rooms."

"But what has it to do with *us?*"

"Our task is to know it for what it is."

"You're very helpful."

"It's a terrible responsibility."

"So . . ."

"In a sense, we hold together the meaningless lives of hundreds and hundreds of people."

"How?"

"You're aware that there's nothing on the paper?"

"Yes."

Baskerville masked a smile. "Not everybody is."

"I don't believe it."

"Think of the sense of being needed and necessary, of achievement and authority, of promotion and advancement."

"It's not clear."

"Examine your conscience."

"Must I?"

"If you want to know."

"Good God."

"This is the truth of all offices. Of all organizations."

"What would they do . . . if they knew?"

"There would be corpses hanging from lampposts, I suppose. Or other places. The stockmarket would explode in a marvel of fission. Blood would run in the gutters. The price of eggs would go up. *I* don't know."

"But why has our own organization turned on us?"

"Because it knows we're thinking. It's painful for everybody. Revolution is not a polite word."

"And if we let it go?"

"It's best not to think about it."

"We're finks, then."

"Only in a sense."

"Isn't there anything to be said for us?"

"We do our job."

"I'm sick."

"You weren't prepared."

De Vinne sat down. For a long moment he thought heavily, then brightened.

"But what about General Dynamics?"

"I hardly see why they should be an exception."

"What about 'Better Things for Better Living Through Chemistry'?"

"Do parades make you weak inside?"

"I'm *already* weak inside."

"Let Miss Angel Craw out of the closet."

De Vinne took a key out of his pocket and unlocked the door. Miss Angel Craw stumbled out of the closet, coughing. She began mopping again. Baskerville and De Vinne sat down at their desks once more.

A little rough on the kid, William Elderly Baskerville thought. And it isn't even true. Still, it *might* be true. He gazed affectionately at his favorite inkblot, in which he could sometimes see William Howard Taft. He had had a horror of veracity ever since, as a little boy, he had been punished for owning up manfully to a shattered aquarium in his father's study. Truth is punishment, he thought.

De Vinne was still mulling the problem. "We've been here all our lives," he began, but Baskerville motioned for him to stop.

"I hear something."

They concentrated, their hands clenched before them on the desktops. There was a faint sighing sound in the corridors outside, as of giant snakes inching toward them "The hoses," De Vinne hissed. "They're bringing up the hoses." He sprang to the closet and armed himself with the crossbow. "Get ready to open the door."

William Elderly Baskerville gripped the doorknob; De Vinne cranked the crossbow; Miss Angel Craw cowered in the rear. "Now!" said De Vinne. Baskerville jerked open the door and his partner let fly. There was a short, high scream down the corridor. The slithering noises stopped. Baskerville slammed the door and leaned against it. "Good work!" he said congratulatorily. "Make every shot count. We shall sell dearly."

But there were no more noises. They waited for a quarter of an hour, while Miss Angel Craw fixed tea on a hotplate, but nothing disturbed the holy quiet. At length De Vinne looked up hopefully. "What about Container Corporation of America?"

"You want me to tell you that everything's going to be all right?"

"Yes."

"Everything's going to be . . . interminable."

"What about the Army?"

"It's winning."

"What about the President?"

"Dick Tracy will be reelected."

"What about psychoanalysis?"

"I love it."

"WHAT ABOUT LOVE?"

"WHAT ABOUT IT?"

Miss Angel Craw looked distressed. The tea wasn't very good, but all helped themselves to seconds. Baskerville gazed into his wastebasket. It was an interesting moral question. De Vinne had gone at once to the heart of it, but he, William Elderly Baskerville, had difficulty feeling that the problem was real. His analyst had said, once, that one had to remember in order to forget. It was the kind of riddle that confused him; Dr. Rococo had been a kindly man with a weak chin. Irreducible, irrefragable, irrefrangible, irrefutable. Incontrovertible. He was tired of games. Miss Angel Craw was smearing pink lipstick on already brilliant lips.

There was a ker-umphf! in the middle distance, as of a howitzer firing, then a peculiar high whine, as of an artillery shell in transit. "Hit it!" De Vinne screamed. "They've got us bracketed!" Baskerville cowered under his desk. The shell came through the roof in a shower of plaster and fragments of concrete, exploding harmlessly with a bright blue flash. At the same time a high discordant voice came booming into the room, mechanically amplified. "Good afternoon, Americans," it said, with the intonation of an Oriental villain of some recent war. "How foolish of you it is to hold out in there," the voice whined sourly. "Our forces are preparing even now to destroy you. This is your last chance, Americans."

"My God," exclaimed De Vinne, who had previous military experience, "it's a loudspeaker and leaflet unit." They scrambled around on the floor amid scraps of poorly printed broadsides. "Listen to this," Baskerville said. He read: "*Documentary Evidence Revives Hope for Younger Vitality and New Smoothness in Any Woman's Skin.* From Mrs. J. B.D.—Case=546-1 (Age, 41): 'After using ULTI-MATE for three weeks, my skin has taken on a new glow, a radiant look for the first time in years.'" The two men looked at each other. Baskerville read another: "*Our* blend of Dacron and cotton is utterly different from ordinary wash and wear shirts. Single-needle stitching, extra-long tails. Go to the stores that keep up the great tradition. Or you can write to . . ."

"Unspeakable." De Vinne wiped his sweating palms. The loudspeaker was now playing "Pennsylvania 65000." Miss Angel Craw sat on the floor, fascinatedly reading the ads from the leaflet shell. "I don't like the way things are going," he said.

"No more do I," replied Baskerville.

"Where did we go wrong?"

"Perhaps in our choice of regimentals . . ."

"It may have something to do with religion . . ."

"Perhaps we should have joined a union . . ."

"If only I'd not cheated that waiter . . ."

"They say there's a danger of socialism . . ."

"But I only had seventy-five cents."

"Although most of us are non-political . . ."

"How was I to know he was the Man in Charge?"

"Who?"

'The waiter."

"You were in the Army. What will they do next?"

"Probably try to flank us. Although I was only a mail clerk."

"We're skirting the problem."

"I say attack."

"You mean the paper?"

"Shouldn't we?"

"You have a feeling for it?"

"*About* it."

"That we should . . ."

"Yes."

"You and I . . ."

"Yes."

"Manipulate in some way . . ."

"The paper, yes."

"You feel, in sum . . ."

"LET'S GET ON WITH IT." De Vinne suddenly realized that he was shouting, and turned his face to the wall.

"You're overwrought."

"Perhaps. A bit."

"I'll call Personnel."

"The telephones don't work."

"They never have. But I thought I'd make the gesture. Have you ever used your sick leave?"

"Repeatedly. To excess."

"Then you can't be sick."

"I'm willing to try."

"You want to dispose of the paper."

"Of our work. Our operation."

"I agree in principle . . ."

"You do?"

"And I would suggest we begin at once," Baskerville finished grandly.

"How do we go about it?"

"We INITIAL it . . ."

"And then?"

"Forward it through channels to . . ."

"To?"

"Just *forward* it."

"Through channels. It's not a bad idea."

"It's the best so far."

"The letter drop would do."

"The letter drop would be *excellent*."

"They'd have to be folded."

"Miss Angel Craw would help."

"But if we put them in the letter drop . . ."

"Yes?"

"They'd go *everywhere*."

"Do you have a better idea?"

"Give me a moment."

De Vinne was a good sort, Baskerville decided. Queer, but a good heart. These strange enthusiasms, they must be put down to youth. Wasted on the young. De Vinne was pacing furiously now. Baskerville noted the fevered brow, the distressed fluttering of the hands; an odd affection coursed through him. We're all in this together, he thought with satisfaction. Hang together or all hang separately. All for one and . . . all for one. Nothing to lose but our chains. Mysteriously, the air conditioners coughed into action. Tear gas?

"There's the wastebaskets," De Vinne said. "We could start fires in the wastebaskets."

"You refer, of course, to the moral issue."

"Well. We can hardly ignore it."

"The slaughter. The rapine."

"You can't make an omelette."

"I know. Without breaking eggs."

"And there are those people outside."

"They've been strangely quiet."

"They're waiting for us to decide."

"We could examine our consciences again."

"Oh, ignoble!"

"Chauvinist!"

"Charlatan!"

"Weakling!"

"Fascist!"

"Pig!"

"This is unseemly."

"It postpones a decision."

"When it gets about . . ."

"We'll be heroes of the revolution."

"Our pictures will hang in the schoolrooms."

"Egotist!" Baskerville spat. "Cult of personality!"

"And you?" De Vinne advanced threateningly.

A man in a policeman's uniform, carrying a stuffed club, burst into the room. De Vinne, shooting from the hip, transfixed him with a crossbow bolt. "Well done!" cried Miss Angel Craw, who had climbed to the top of a filing cabinet. It was the first time she had spoken. The policeman sagged to the floor, where he lay in a pool of ink. "Quickly!" Baskerville cried. Their eyes met in silent agreement. Feverishly they began to initial the strange documents.

The Bed

roblem: A new bed for an old wife.

Not that she's old in point of fact. Old? No. She's young, beautiful, quick, kind. Intelligent, gay, thoughtful, distinguished. Nine lines in *Who's Who*, a professorship at Brown, a *hacienda* outside Oaxaca. But now she's back in town, and needs a bed. I promised.

What's old is our affair. It degenerated into marriage and declined from there. And Sam and Margaret came along, and God knows who. She needs a bed. I promised. Why? I'll be damned if I can tell. We were tight once, it's true. We thought about each other and left the others out. That passes, as I'm sure you've heard, but something's always left, a bit of business left undone, lawyer's texts, children, pewter, friends, joint tax returns for some as yet unaudited year— a trace of frisky residue.

There's a bed in the basement, maybe I could award her it. Been there since '67, when we acquired the "new" bed. Has it rotted? Probably. Can't plant her in a mulch pile. Old wife sleeping in rotted bed. Ha-ha. Necroded ticking injuring the sense of smell. Ha-ha. Sluglike yellowish things-with-no-name emerging from the mattress. Ha-ha. Malicious bastard, am I not? But malice too is a mode of feeling. Bent, to be sure, but feeling still.

Nip down to the basement, inspect the bed. It's stacked against a wall somewhere. Can't find the light. Bang leg on tricycle, bang again on busted rocking chair, again on cast-iron walrus left over from someone's failed off-off-Broadway bow. Who covered the floor with blown fuses? I've got a neck to break.

The light at last, and, under a couple of hundred square feet of tattered wallboard, the bed.

Someone's been nailing nails into the bed.

Someone's been stabbing the bed with ice picks.

Someone's been sloshing the bed with acid.

Someone's been tearing at the bed's entrails.

Somebody put out a contract on the bed.

The bed's dead.

I remember my dream of Tuesday night. I was in a gigantic bed, a bed big as a football field. I was bicycling on the surface. Pursued by fires and clowns. Behind me on the right, raging fires, and on the left, vicious clowns in packs. I pedaled as hard as I could. Is there no end to this bedevilment? Is there no off-ramp to this bed? At the same time I was reading *The New York Times Guide to Dining Out in New York*, third edition. Xavier's, I noticed, now had three stars. Honoria and I thought we'd invented the place, the waiters knew us well, smiled, gave us good tables, asked how we'd been. Fine, we said, and Charlie, how are you? Charlie was fine too. A blend of gin and fineness over everything, tables, chairs, the future and the past, the *bollito misto*. The fires and clowns were joined by avalanches and sword-swallowers, all getting close. The bicycle's chain blew. I woke up.

Just a friendly little anxiety dream. A bit of bedlam to help one through the night.

Where did we buy the "new" bed? In which I have my nightly Late, Late Shows? At Bloomingdale's? We bounced together, Honoria and I, among a sea of bare natty Beautyrests. Did we remove our shoes? I think not, just dangled them over the edge. Did we show the salesman what we could do, if we really put our minds to it? How we could get entangled, legs and arms and heads and such, in the most peculiar knots, and then puzzle our way out again? I don't think so.

He would have had a stroke, popped off then and there. We bought the bed. There was a warranty on it, not us.

Tonight, she telephoned.

"Did you get it?"

"Did I get what?"

"The bed."

"Oh, the bed."

"Well, did you?"

"Ah—not yet."

"Why not?"

"Well, I've been busy. Doing things."

"But what about the bed?"

"I told you I'd take care of it."

"Yes, but when? It's been a week."

"I went to Toronto."

"I know. For two days. How is it that you can do everything in the world but take care of one tiny detail like getting a bed for my new apartment?"

"Some people can get their own beds for their new apartments."

"Yes, but that's not the point, is it? You promised."

"That was in the first flush of good feeling and warmth. When you said you were coming back to town. I wanted to be helpful."

"Now you don't have any good feeling and warmth?"

"I'm full of good feeling and warmth. Brimming. How's Sam?"

"He's getting tired of sleeping on the couch. It's not big enough for both of us."

"My heart cries out for him. Tell him so."

"All I can say is, you bedder get a move on, buddy."

"Don't take that tone with me. I'm doing the very bedst I can."

She's seeing Sam now, that's a little strange. She didn't seem to dig him, early on.

Sam. What's he look like? Like a villain, like a villain. Hair like an oil spill; mustache, a twist of carbon paper; high white lineless forehead; black tights and doublet; dagger clasped in treacherous right hand; sneaks when he's not slithering . . .

No. That's incompletely true. What's he look like? Just like the rest of us. Jeans, turtleneck, beard, smile with one (1) chipped tooth, good with children, backward in his taxes, a degree in education, he's a B. Ed. How then a villain? Because he attempted to seduce Honoria, and failed. We were failing too, I needed him. I did the best I could, poured him large drinks and left the two of them alone for hours, days—I had, I must admit, another fish to fry, a dainty little slippery little eel from Reykjavik, one of Icelandic's finest. We were failing, Honoria and I, we'd wake up and not even kiss. So Sam seemed plausible, a way out, a transitional figure as it were. It didn't work. Honoria wouldn't have him. Told me he was "too nice." And he came with the very best references too. Charlotte doted, Francine couldn't get enough, Mary Jo chased him through Penn Station with the great whirling loop of her lariat, causing talk—but Honoria said no. This is a marriage, she said, you're not getting out without due misery. She was right. All that's behind us now. I wish she hadn't thrown the turntable on the floor, a $400 B & O—but all that's behind us now. And Sam's been reconsidered.

I saw this morning that the building at the end of the street's been sold. It stood empty for years, an architectural anomaly, three-storied, brick, but most of all, triangular. The street comes to a point there, and prospective buyers must have boggled at the angles. I judge the owners have decided to let morality go hang and sold to a *ménage à trois*. They'll need a triple bed, customized too, to fit those odd corners. I can see them with protractor and Skilsaw, getting the thing just right. Then sweeping up the bedcrumbs.

She telephones again.

"It doesn't have to be the best bed in the world. Any old bed will do. Sam's bitching all night long."

"For you, dear friend, I'll take every pain. Not less than the best. We're checking now in Indonesia, a rare albino bed's been sighted there . . ."

"Tom, this isn't funny. I slept in the bathtub last night."

"You're too long for the bathtub."

"Do you want Sam to do it?"

Do I want Sam to do it?

"No. I'll do it."

"Then *do it.*"

Why does this business bother me? I jumped ship long ago. What mix of memory and perversity ties me to this lady still? Is it true that furniture music is the sweetest music, that purchasing the towels, the cups and saucers, the wastebaskets and wine racks is what it's all about? That cables spliced from plant food, paint samples, throw rugs, and wire whisks maintain an underground connection? The thought is sinful, still I think it.

In the morning comes a letter:

Dear Tom,
It is clear that you understand nothing. Once I thought you
sensitive and fine, but you are not sensitive. No one who was
sensitive could persistently misunderstand my sleep needs
as you do, and always have. Surely the great number of sleep
aids you have seen me employ in the days when we were
cohabitating—the mask, the record of sea sounds, the electric
back scratcher—would have suggested special needs even to
the dimmest brain. And as I know that the words "dimmest
brain" do not accurately describe you, I can only conclude that
it is your malice that makes you throw obstacles in the path of
my happiness like this. Tear yourself away from your own tiny
concerns for a moment (are you still seeing that skinny fishlike
Icelandic, girl, Margaret?) and try to focus upon mine. Malice
is not nourishing for long. You will choke on it if you persist in
this path. Why don't you want me to get a solid eight hours a
night, with the companion of my choice? I implore you to come
to your senses, and bedraggle yourself to one of our fine local
department stores immediately. You have, after all, promised.
     Love,
     Honoria

I have, after all, promised. But not to suffer abuse. In the heat of the moment, I fire off my own brief:

Dear Honoria,
Listen, baby, are you trying to make yourself something that
you are not? Like a bloody martyr? That is not necessary, dear
Honoria. We already love you, in the past tense—not only me
but all the other members of your former community, Paul,

Jacques, Ramona, etc. There is a danger in mythologizing the self-image, especially the image of the self as put-upon, outraged, bedreft. This simply does not square with the facts. Take a little care to be careful of the sensibilities and psychic determinants of the Other—the person to whom you are speaking, that is to say, me. Just as the white snow on the ground is loved and applauded by everyone, but would be derided if it pretended to be vanilla ice cream, so the human persona can stand only so much artificial enhancement, for instance by lies. Instant gratification is not as good as that gratification which comes dropping slow, over the sere seasons. Picture yourself a withered crone of eighty, at the warm hearthside, or at least close to the thermostat, and surrounded by withered grandchildren and friends, to whom your integrity has been a rock, these sixty years. And picture to yourself the alternative: a Honoria similarly withered, but cuffed and spat upon, and hurled into the gutter, candy bar wrappers and crushed aluminum beer cans being dropped on your head by uncaring strangers, simply because you have visualized yourself as something you were not, some kind of heroic figure, a Jeanne d'Arc of the bedroom, who will not be satisfied until she exacts from the whole male world the tribute of a lustrous king-or-queen-sized bed? I am a former husband, remember? Not much can be expected of me.

> In extremis,
> Tom

But these letters are not serious. We are playing with one another. So I'll buy a bloody bed. I know how it's done. I've been there before. When I was young and easy under the apple boughs, in all the Bloomingdales' they knew my name. There! The thing's accomplished. And now the problem of transport, from my portal to her portal. The U-Haul place is giving me a busy signal. Must be mounds of people moving beds today. We'll form a caravan like bedouins and wind our ways to diverse addresses. Will my bicycle be equal to the task? I'm sick. A fever. I should be put to bed. Or laid to rest. Don't joke. One lays a ghost, that's routine enough, I've entertained a shade myself a time or two. There were bold bed-springing moments, I don't deny it, but lastly it was . . . ghostly.

The Bed

I posed as a good man, wise, supporting, ardent, sucked her in, had a better schtick than Sam's (remember Sam?), her routine was also nicely done, we were content for quite a while, not long enough, it's ended, I was right and wrong, she taught me what she'd majored in, a lovely Romance tongue, we visited the country and when I'd walk into a drugstore and ask for razor blades, they'd give me sanitary napkins. Tom! Your malice has run wild. That's not the way I feel at all. The bell is ringing. United Parcel's here, two men and a mattress. I wish you well, dear bedlamite, I really do—sleep, lust, luck, impostures new.

The Discovery

I 'm depressed," Kate said.

Boots became worried. "Did I say something wrong?"

"You don't know *how* to say anything wrong."

"What?"

"The thing about you is, you're dull."

"I'm dull?"

There was a silence. Then Fog said: "Anybody want to go over to Springs to the rodeo?"

"Me?" Boots said. "Dull?"

The Judge got up and went over and sat down next to Kate.

"Now Kate, you oughtn't to be goin' round callin' Boots dull to his face. That's probably goin' to make him feel bad. I know you didn't mean it, really, and Boots knows it too, but he's gonna feel bad anyhow—"

"How 'bout the rodeo, over at Springs?" Fog asked again.

The Judge gazed sternly at his friend, Fog.

"—he's gonna feel bad, anyhow," the Judge continued, "just thinkin' you *mighta* meant it. So why don't you just tell him you didn't mean it."

"I did mean it."

"Aw come on, Katie. I know you mean what you say, but why

make trouble? You can mean what you say, but why not say something else? On a nice day like this?"

The dry and lifeless air continued parching the concrete-like ground.

"It's not a nice day."

The Judge looked around. Then he said: "By God, Katie, you're right! It's a terrible day." Then he took a careful look at Boots, his son.

"I guess you think I'm dull, too, is that right, Pa?" Boots said with a disarming laugh.

"Well . . ."

Boots raised himself to his feet. He looked cool and unruffled, with just a hint of something in his eyes.

"So," he said. "So that's the way it is. So that's the way you, my own father, really feel about me. Well, it's a fine time to be sayin' something about it, wouldn't you say? In front of company and all?"

"Now don't get down on your old man," Fog said hastily. "Let's go to the rodeo."

"Fog—"

"He don't mean nothin' by it," Fog said. "He was just tryin' to tell the truth."

"Oh," Boots said. "He don't mean nothin' by it. He don't mean nothin' by it. Well, it seems to me I just been hearin' a lot talk about people meanin' what they say. I am going to assume the Judge here means what he says."

"Yes," the Judge said. "I mean it."

"Yes," Kate said, "you have many fine qualities, Boots."

"See? He means it. My own father thinks I'm dull. And Katie thinks I'm dull. What about you, Fog? You want to make it unanimous?"

"Well Boots you are pretty doggone dull to my way of thinking. But nobody holds it against you. You got a lot of fine characteristics. Can't everybody be Johnny Carson."

"Yes, there are lots duller than you, Boots," Kate said. "Harvey Brush, for example. Now that number is *really* dull."

"You're comparin' *me* with *Harvey Brush!*"

"Well I said he was worse, didn't I?"

"Good God."

"Why don't you go inside and read your letters from that girl in Brussels?" Kate suggested.

"*She* doesn't think I'm dull."

"Probably she don't understand English too good neither," the Judge said. "Now go on inside and read your mail or whatever. We just want to sit silently out here for a while."

"Goodbye."

After Boots had gone inside the Judge said: "My son."

"It is pretty terrible, Judge," Kate said.

"It's awful," Fog agreed.

"Well, it's not a hanging offense," the Judge said. "Maybe we can teach him some jokes or something."

"I've got to get back in the truck now," said Kate. "Judge, you have my deepest sympathy. If I can think of anything to do, I'll let you know."

"Thanks, Kate. It's always a pleasure to see you and be with you, wherever you are. *You* are never dull."

"I know that, Judge. Well, I'll see you later."

"O.K. Kate," said Fog. "Goodbye. Drive carefully."

"Goodbye Fog. Yes, I'll be careful."

"See you around, Kate."

"O.K., Judge. Goodbye, Fog."

"So long, Kate."

"See you. You know I can't marry that boy now, Judge. Knowing what I know."

"I understand, Kate. I wouldn't expect you to. I'll just have to dig up somebody else."

"It's going to be hard."

"Well, it's not going to be easy."

"So long, Kate," said Fog.

"O.K., goodbye. Be good."

"Yes," said Fog. "I'll try."

"'Bye now, Judge."

"O.K., Katie."

"Wonder how come I never noticed it before?"

"Well don't *dwell* on it, Kate. See you in town."

"O.K., *adios.*"

"Goodbye, Kate."

"It's terrible but we've got it into focus now, haven't we?"

"I'm afraid we do."

"I sure would like to be of help, Judge."

"I know you would, Katie, and I appreciate it. I just don't see what can be done about it, right off."

"It's just his nature, probably."

"You're probably right. *I* was never dull."

"I know you weren't, Judge. Nobody blames you."

"Well, it's a problem."

"Quite a thorny one. But he'll be O.K., Judge. He's a good boy, basically."

"I know that, Kate. Well, we'll just have to wrestle with it."

"O.K., Judge. I'll see you later, O.K.?"

"Right."

"Behave yourself, Fog."

"Right, Katie."

"I'll see y'all. Bye-bye."

"Goodbye, Kate."

"You all right, Judge?"

"I'm fine, Katie. Just a little taken aback by what we've found out here today."

"Oh. O.K. Well, take care of yourself. You too, Fog."

"I will, Kate."

"O.K. See you two."

"Goodbye, Kate."

"You sure you don't want to come into town with me? I'll make you some tamale pie."

"That's O.K. Kate we got lots of stuff to eat right here."

"Oh. O.K. 'Bye."

The truck moved off into the dust.

"Look!" said the Judge. "She's waving."

"Wave back to her," Fog said.

"I am," said the Judge. "Look, I'm waving."

"I see it," said Fog. "Can she see you?"

"Maybe if I stand up," the Judge said. "Do you think she can see me now?"

"Not if she's watchin' the road."

"She's too young for us," the Judge said. He stopped waving.

"Depends on how you look at it," said Fog. "You want to go on over to the rodeo now?"

"I don't want to go to no rodeo," said the Judge. "All that youth."

You Are Cordially Invited

I am cordially invited. I have nothing else to do. So I go. Men and women standing on a terrace holding drinks. The date is Thursday, the twenty-fourth of May. The time, 6:32 P.M. The quality of the air, acceptable. Similarly the quality of the whiskey. A ferocious vivacity amidst the green-painted iron garden furniture. A kind of harvest festival. A publisher's cow has calved, and we are celebrating that. The host's barns bursting with cocktail onions and potato chips. At the finish we will fall many floors to the street, where we will all join hands and dance around a taxi. The boldest dancer making it into the cab with a bruising hip check to the lady on his left.

I am spoken to by the lady on my left—a very old lady, seventy if she's a day.

"Hey!" she says. "Wake up!"

"I beg your pardon?"

"You were exhibiting the gaze vacant. Dangerous in a man your age."

She has a beautiful smile and her eyes are very bright. "*Things are not that bad!*" she says.

"They're not?"

"Listen! I have something to tell you. There is a new eight-cent

U.S. postage stamp honoring Copernicus, the great astronomer. Copernicus is wearing a fur-trimmed robe and looks, on the stamp, struck dumb with terror. Can you explain this?"

"No," I say, for I cannot.

"Of course you can't," she says with satisfaction. "That is a minus. But I can give you a plus. Listen! The membership rolls of the New York Architectural League for the year 1912 list a Franz Kafka. Kafka was born in 1883. Could he have been moonlighting as an architect in New York in 1912? If so, which buildings are his? Have any survived? Have you wondered about that?"

I shake my head.

"*We* are wondering for you," she says. "We wonder well. We wonder *efficiently* and *constructively*. We are *on your side*. I have to sit down, my legs are killing me. There's a bench in the corner."

I am led to the bench and seated there. She does not stop talking.

"Listen!" she says. "We bring you hope. Your head hurts but we know that your head hurts and we are working on it. Everybody's head hurts. Our organization is on top of the situation, not in the sense that we have it licked but in the sense that we can see the outlines." During all this she has been feeling me, shoulder, elbow, back of the neck, as one feels a child who has been lost but now is found.

"My name is Cornelia," she says, knocking back a good fifty percent of her drink. "Pay attention. This is very important. I saw, on Saturday the twelfth, a young woman walking confidently. I immediately wondered: What does it mean to walk confidently? How is it possible? The good news I bring you is that *I have seen it done*. [Emphatic squeeze of kneecap here.] And our people are now hacking away at the problems of analysis, replication, quantification. *You, too, may someday walk confidently*."

"Are all your people, uh . . ."

"Old ladies?" she says maliciously. "Damn right. Old ladies are solid gold, young trooper, and don't ever forget it. Listen! On Thursday the tenth I saw a woman wearing platinum I.U.D. earrings on behalf of Zero Population Growth. This joyous sight, a definite plus, was of course balanced by the news that attack cats are now being trained for the defense of small households in Queens. But—"

"Where do you get your funding?"

Cornelia looks, for a moment, a little glum. Then she takes hold of my belt buckle, a firm grasp, and continues.

"Our work is proceeding under great handicaps. The feds don't like to give money to bunches of old ladies not under the umbrella of an officially certified O.K. institution—Harvard, for example. We flirted for a while with M.I.T., where there is a certain openness of mind, but finally the trustees got cold feet. Old *men*," she hisses. "Sale of homemade lemonade from a card table on the sidewalk outside the office netted $67.50 for the quarter. But was probably counterproductive in terms of staff hours lost. You didn't by any chance write this abomination, did you?" she asks, holding up a copy of the book we are theoretically celebrating.

"No."

"I'm pleased," she says. "I will give you two pieces of advice. Always talk to the oldest lady at the party—then you will have the best time. And when you wake up at three o'clock in the morning, never light a cigarette, because if you do you will think about your crimes for the next two hours. Those are the only two pieces of advice I ever give anybody and they are both solid gold."

"Thank you," I say. I notice across the room a nymph talking to an editor. The nymph appears to be naked to the waist and, from the waist down, clothed in the purest gossamer.

"You can get me another drink," Cornelia says, "and have a closer look at that quite beautiful girl while doing so. You don't drink enough. Make it quick."

I fetch us two more of the same, not neglecting to take another look at the girl, who is in fact quite beautiful.

"Now, my colleague Anne-Marie," Cornelia says, slapping me on the thigh a few times in a rough fatherly way, "is eighty. She's working on the falling sickness—trying to find out what can be done with nets of words. She's using words of two kinds: words made out of various polymers (du Pont is cooperating) and magic words. For the last, she's testing a group of forty burglars, all volunteers from the Tombs."

"What are they like?"

"Extremely interesting people. Alert, intelligent. They wouldn't be burglars if they could be something else, they say. When you ask them what they'd rather be, they say rich. I think that's extremely sensible. What do you do?"

I tell her.

"Well," she says, "don't feel bad. As Jules Renard said, no matter how much care an author takes to write as few books as possible, there will be people who haven't heard of some of them. But listen!" she goes on, kneading my ankle. "I am delighted to report that terror inspired by organized religion is diminishing everywhere. I ask you to notice that the new opium of the people is opium, and I think that's quite a hopeful development. At least the thing is what it is, not something disguised as something else. On the other hand, pain-dependent sexual behavior is increasing, and political torture has reached new international highs. We are working on everything, from the trauma of opening the front door to the unbearable consequences of being loved. We offer hope. If the federal money doesn't come through we'll just add Kool-Aid and possibly peanut-butter cookies to the line. Set out more card tables. And before I release you to pursue your lubricious way across the party, I want you to join me in a toast."

"Of course. To what?"

"Our noble predecessors," Cornelia says, raising her glass, her eyes positively brimming with benevolent malice. "Whose valiant efforts. Without which. Their heads were, you know, *green* and their hands were blue and they went to sea in a sieve."

The Viennese Opera Ball

I do not like to see an elegant pair of forceps! Blundell stated. Let the instrument look what it is, a formidable weapon! *Arte, non vi* (art, not strength) may be usefully engraved upon one blade; and *Care perineo* (take care of the perineum) on the other. His companion replied: The test of a doctor's prognostic acumen is to determine the time to give up medicinal and dietetic measures and empty the uterus, and overhesitancy to do this is condemnable, even though honorable . . . I do not mean that we should perform therapeutic abortion with a light spirit. On the contrary, I am slow to adopt it and always have proper consultation. If on the other hand a bear kills a man, someone said, the Croches immediately organize a hunt, capture a bear, kill it, eat its heart, and throw out the rest of the meat; they save the skin, which with the head of the beast serves as a shroud for the dead man. Among the Voguls the nearest relative was required to seek revenge. The Goldi have the same custom in regard to the tiger; they kill him and bury him with this little speech: *Now we are even, you have killed one of ours, we have killed one of yours. Now let us live in peace. Don't disturb us again, or we will kill you.* Carola Mitt, brown-haired, brown-eyed and just nineteen was born in Berlin (real name: Mittenstein), left Germany five years ago. In her senior year at the Convent of the Sacred Heart in Greenwich, Conn., Carola went to the Viennese Opera Ball at the Waldorf-Astoria, was spotted by a *Glamour* editor.

I mean, the doctor resumed, we should study each patient thoroughly and empty the uterus before she has retinitis; before jaundice has shown that there is marked liver damage; before she has polyneuritis; before she has toxic myocarditis; before her brain is degenerated, *et al.*—and it can be done. Meyer Davis played for the Viennese Opera Ball. Copperplate printers, said a man, deliver Society Printing in neat, stylish boxes. They are compelled to slipsheet the work with tissue paper, an expense the letterpress printer may avoid, if careful. Boxes, covered with enameled paper for cards and all kinds of Society Printing, are on sale to carry the correct sizes. No matter how excellent your work and quality may be, women who know the correct practice will not be satisfied unless the packages are as neat as those sent out by the copperplate printers. The devil is not as wicked as people believe, and neither is an Albanian. (Carola Mitt soon dropped her plans to be a painter, made $60 an hour under the lights, appeared on the covers of *Vogue, Harper's Bazaar, Mademoiselle* and *Glamour*, shared a Greenwich Village apartment with another girl, yearned to get married and live in California. But that was later.)

The *Glamour* editor said: Take Dolores Wettach. Dolores Wettach is lush, Lorenesque, and doubly foreign (her father is Swiss, her mother Swedish); she moved at the age of five from Switzerland to Flushing, N.Y., where her father set up a mink ranch. Now about twenty-four ("You learn not to be too accurate"), Dolores was elected Miss Vermont in the 1956 Miss Universe contest, graduated in 1957 from the University of Vermont with a B.S. in nursing. Now makes $60 an hour. While Dolores Wettach was working as a nurse at Manhattan's Doctors Hospital, a sharp-eyed photographer saw beyond her heavy Oxfords, asked her to pose. Dying remarks: Oliver Goldsmith, 1728–74, British poet, playwright and novelist, was asked: Is your mind at ease? He replied: No, it is not, and died. Hegel: Only one man ever understood me. And he didn't understand me. Hart Crane, 1899–1932, poet, as he jumped into the sea: Goodbye, everybody! Tons of people came to the Viennese Opera

Ball. At noon, the first doctor said, on January 31, 1943, while walking, the patient was seized with sudden severe abdominal pain and profuse vaginal bleeding. She was admitted to the hospital at 1 P.M. in a state of exsanguination. She presented a tender, rigid abdomen and uterus. Blood pressure 110/60. Pulse rate 110—thready. Fetal heart not heard. Patient was given intravenous blood at once. The membranes were ruptured artificially and a Spanish windlass was applied. Labor progressed rapidly. At 6 P.M., a five-pound stillborn infant was delivered by low forceps. Hemorrhage persisted following delivery in spite of hypodermic Pituitrin, intravenous ergotrate, and firm uterine packing. Blood transfusion had been maintained continuously. At 9 P.M. a laparotomy was done, and a Couvelaire uterus with tubes and ovaries was removed by supracervical hysterectomy. The close adherence of the tubes and ovaries to the fundus necessitated their removal. Patient stood surgery well. A total of 2000 c.c. of whole blood and 1500 c.c. of whole plasma had been administered. Convalescence was satisfactory, and the patient was dismissed on the fourteenth postoperative day. Waiters with drinks circulated among the ball-goers.

Carola Mitt met Isabella Albonico at the Viennese Opera Ball. Isabella Albonico, Italian by temperament as well as by birth (twenty-four years ago, in Florence), began modeling in Europe when she was fifteen, arrived in New York four years ago. Brown-haired and brown-eyed, she has had covers on *Vogue, Harper's Bazaar,* and *Life,* makes $60 an hour, and has won, she says, "a reputation for being allergic to being pummeled around under the lights. Nobody touches me." I entirely endorse these opinions, said a man standing nearby, and would only add that the wife can do much to avert that fatal marital *ennui* by independent interests which she persuades him to share. For instance, an interesting book, or journey, or lecture or concert, experienced, enjoyed, and described by her, with sympathy and humor, may often be a talisman to divert his mind from work and worry, and all the irritations arising therefrom. But, of course, he, on his side, must be able to appreciate her appreciation and her conversation. The stimuli to the penile nerves may differ in degrees of intensity and shades of quality; and there are corresponding diversities in the sensations of pleasure they bestow. It is of much importance in determining these sensations whether the stimuli are localized mainly in the frenulum preputti or the posterior rim of the glans. *Art* rather than *sheer force* should prevail. (There is an authentic case on record in which the attendant braced himself and pulled so hard that, when the forceps slipped off, he fell out of an open window onto the street below and sustained a skull fracture, while the patient remained undelivered.) The Jumbo Tree, 254 feet high, is named from the odd-shaped growths at the base resembling the heads of an elephant, a monkey, and a bison. Isabella told Carola that she "would like most of all to be a movie star," had just returned from Hollywood, where she played a small part ("but opposite Cary Grant") in *That Touch of Mink* and a larger one in an all-Italian film, *Smog.* Besides English and Italian, Isabella speaks French and Spanish, hates big groups. What kind of big groups? Carola asked. *This* kind, Isabella said, waving her hand to indicate the Viennese Opera Ball.

Smog is an interesting name, Carola said. In the empty expanses of Islamabad, the new capital that Pakistan plans to erect in the cool foothills of the Himalayas, the first buildings scheduled to go up are a cluster of airy structures designed by famed U.S. architect Edward Stone. Set in a cloistered water garden, the biggest of Stone's buildings will house Pakistan's first nuclear reactor—one of the largest sales made by New York's American Machine & Foundry Co. Fifteen years ago, AMF was a company with only a handful of products (cigarette, baking, and stitching machines) and annual sales of about $12,000,000. Today, with 42 plants and 19 research facilities scattered across 17 countries, AMF turns out products ranging from remote-controlled toy airplanes to ICBM launching systems. Thanks to AMF's determined pursuit of diversification and growth products, its 1960 sales were $361 million, its earnings $24 million. And in the glum opening months of 1961, the company's sales and earnings hit new first-quarter highs. AMF's expansion is the work of slow-spoken, low-pressured Chairman Morehead Patterson, 64, who took over the company in 1943 from his father, Rufus L. Patterson, inventor of the first automated tobacco machine. After World War II,

The Viennese Opera Ball

Morehead Patterson decided that the company had to grow or die. Searching for new products, he turned up a crude prototype of an automatic bowling-pin setter. To get the necessary cash to develop the intricate gadget, Patterson swapped off AMF stock to acquire eight small companies with fast-selling products. The Pinspotter, perfected and put on the market in 1951, helped to turn bowling into the most popular U.S. competitive sport. Despite keen competition from the Brunswick Corp., AMF has remained the world's largest maker of automatic pin setters. With 68,000 machines already on lease in the U.S. (for an average annual gross of $68 million), AMF last week got a $3,000,000 contract to equip a new chain of bowling centers in the East. Is there another Pinspotter in AMF's future? Chairman Patterson cautiously admits to the hope that perhaps the firm's intensive research into purifying brackish and fouled water might produce another product breakthrough. "Companies, like people," says Patterson, "get arteriosclerosis. My job is to see that AMF doesn't." Morehead Patterson did not attend the Viennese Opera Ball.

Carola Mitt said: Among other things, I mean the ego; it is also the symbol, in *astronomy*, for the inclination of an orbit to the ecliptic; in *chemistry*, for iodine; in *physics*, for the density of current, the intensity of magnetization, or the moment of inertia; in *logic*, for a particular affirmative proposition. Lester Lannin also played for the Viennese Opera Ball. Nonsense! said a huge man wearing the Double Eagle of St. Puce, what about sailing, salesmen, salt, sanitation, Santa Claus, saws, scales, schools, screws, sealing wax, secretaries, sects, selling, the Seven Wonders, sewerage, sewing machines, sheep, sheet metal, shells, shipbuilding, shipwrecks, shoemaking, shopping, shower baths, sieges, signboards, silverware, sinning, skating, skeletons, skeleton *keys*, sketching, skiing, skulls, skyscrapers, sleep, smoking, smugglers, Socialism, soft drinks, soothsaying, sorcery, space travel, spectacles, spelling, sports, squirrels, steamboats, steel, stereopticons, the Stock Exchange, stomachs, stores, storms, stoves, streetcars, strikes, submarines, subways, suicide, sundials, sunstroke, superstition, surgery, surveying, sweat, and syphilis! It is one of McCormack's proudest boasts,

Carola heard over her lovely white shoulder, that he has never once missed having dinner with his wife in their forty-one years of married life. She remembered Knocko at the Evacuation Day parade, and Baudelaire's famous remark. Mortality is the final evaluator of methods. An important goal is an intact sphincter. The greater prematurity, the more generous should be the episiotomy. Yes said Leon Jaroff, Detroit Bureau Chief for *Time,* at the Thomas Elementary School on warm spring afternoons I could look from my classroom into the open doors of the Packard plant. Ideal foster parents are mature people who are not necessarily well off, but who have a good marriage and who love and understand children. The ninth day of the ninth month is the festival of the chrysanthemum (Kiku No Sekku), when *sake* made from the chrysanthemum is drunk. Kiku Jido, a court youth, having inadvertently touched with his foot the pillow of the emperor, was banished to a distant isle, where, it is said, he was nourished by the dew of the chrysanthemums which abounded there. Becoming a hermit, he lived for a thousand years. Husbands have been known to look at their wives with new eyes, Laura La Plante thought to herself. Within the plane of each individual work—experienced apart from a series—he presents one with a similar set of one-at-a-time experiences each contained within its own compartment, and read in a certain order, up or down or across. Far off at Barlow Ranger Station, as the dawn was breaking, Bart slept dreamlessly at last. *Peridermium coloradense* on spruce *(Picea)* has long been considered conspecific with *Melampsorella caryophyllacearum* Schroet., which alternates between fir *(Abies)* and *Caryophylaceae.* Evidence that these rusts are identical consists largely of inoculation results of Weit and Hubert (1, 2), but these have never been fully confirmed. Take Dorothea McGowan, the *Glamour* editor said. Dorothea McGowan is the exception in the new crop: she speaks only English and was born in Brooklyn. Her premodeling life took her as far from home as Staten Island, where she finished her freshman year at Notre Dame College before taking a summer job modeling $2.98 house dresses. A few months later, her first photographic try at a cover made *Vogue;* this year she set some kind of a record by appearing on four *Vogue* covers in a row (nobody but her mother or agent could have told that it was the same girl). Twenty-year-old Dorothea ("My middle initial is E, and Dorothy sounded so ordinary") makes $60 an hour, has her own apartment in New York, studies French at Manhattan's French Institute twice a week ("so that when my dream of living in Paris comes true, I'll be ready for it"). Dorothea has been sent, all expenses paid, to be photographed in front of the great architectural monuments of Europe, among Middle East bazaars and under Caribbean palms. She is absolutely infatuated with the idea of being paid to travel. I never saw so many autumn flowers as grow in the woods and sheep-walks of Maryland. But I confess, I scarcely knew a single name: Let no one visit America without first having studied botany.

Carola was thrilled by all the interesting conversations at the Viennese Opera Ball. The Foundation is undertaking a comprehensive analytical study of the economic and social positions of the artist and of his institutions in the United States. In part this will serve as a basis for future policy decisions and program activities. The contemplated study will also be important outside the Foundation. The climate of the arts today, discussion in the field reveals, is complex and various. Pack my box with Title Shaded Litho. Pack my box with Boston Breton Extra Condensed. Pack my box with Clearface Heavy. (C) Brasol, 261–285; Buck 212–221; Carr, *D*, 281–301; Collins, 76–82; Curle, 176–224; A. G. Dostoevsky, *D Portrayed by His Wife*, 268–269; F. Dostoevsky, *Letters and Reminiscences*, 241–242, 247, 251–252; F. Dostoevsky, *New D Letters*, 79–102; Freud, *passim*; Gibian, "D's Use of Russian Folklore," *passim*; Hesse—see; Hromadka, 45–50; Ivanov, 142–166 and *passim*; King, 22–29; Lavrin, *D and His Creation*, 114–142; Lavrin, *D: A Study*, 119–146; Lavrin, "D and Tolstoy," 189–195; Lloyd, 275–290; McCune, *passim*; Mackiewicz, 183–191; Matlaw, 221–225; Maugham, 203–208; Maurina, 147–153, 198–203, 205–210, 218–221; Meier–Graefe, 288–377; Muchnic, *Intro* . . ., 165–172; Mueller, 193–200; Murry, 203–259; Passage, 162–174; Roe, 20–25, 41–51, 68–91, 100–110; Roubiczek, 237–244, 252–260, 266–271; Sachs, 241–246; Scott, 204–209; Simmons, 263–279 and *passim*; Slonim, *Epic* . . ., 289–293 and *passim*; Soloviev, 195–202; Strakosch, *passim*; Troyat, 395–416; Tymms,

99–103; Warner, 80–101; Colin Wilson, 178–201; Yarmolinsky, *D, His Life and Art*, 355–361 and *passim;* Zander, 15–30, 63–95, 119–137. Carola said: What a wonderful ball! The width of the black band varies according to relationship. For a widow's card a band of about one-third inch (No. 5) during the first year of widowhood, diminishing about one-sixteenth inch each six months thereafter. On a widower's card one-quarter inch (No. 3) is the widest, diminishing gradually from time to time. For other relatives, the band may vary from the thickness of No. 3 to that of the "Italian." No. 5 band is now considered excessive, but among the Latin races is held to be moderate, and if preferred, is entirely correct. To administer the agreement and facilitate the attainment of its ends, a Committee on Trade Policy and Payments will be set up with all member countries represented. The judicial form contemplated in the agreement is that of a free trade zone to be transformed gradually into a customs union. As Emile Myerson has said, *"L'homme fait de la métaphysique comme il respire, sans le vouloir et surtout sans s'en douter la plupart du temps."* No woman is worth more than 24 cattle, Pamela Odede B.A.'s father said. With this album Abbey Lincoln's stature as one of the great jazz singers of our time is confirmed, Laura La Plante said. Widely used for motors, power tools, lighting, TV, etc. Generator output: 3500 watts, 115/230 volt, 60 cy., AC, continuous duty. Max. 230 V capacitor motor, loaded on starting—1/2 hp; unloaded on starting—2 hp. Control box mounts starting switch, duplex 115 V receptacle for standard or 3-conductor grounding plugs, tandem 230 V grounding receptacles, and wing nut battery terminals. More than six hundred different kinds of forceps have been invented. Let's not talk about the lion, she said. Wilson looked over at her without smiling and now she smiled at him. This process uses a Lincoln submerged arc welding head to run both inside and outside beads automatically. The rate of progress during the first stage will determine the program to be followed in the second stage. The *Glamour* editor whose name was Tutti Beale "moved in." What's your name girl? she said coolly. Carola Mitt, Carola Mitt said. The Viennese Opera Ball continued.

Belief

A group of senior citizens on a bench in Washington Square Park in New York City. There were two female senior citizens and two male senior citizens.

"Rabbit, rabbit, rabbit, rabbit," one of the women said suddenly. She turned her head to each of the four corners of an imaginary room as she did so.

The other senior citizens stared at her.

"Why did you do that?" one of the men asked.

"It's the first of the month. If you say 'rabbit' four times, once to each corner of the room, or the space that you are in, on the first of the month before you eat lunch, then you will be loved in that month."

Some angry black people walked by carrying steel-band instruments and bunches of flowers.

"I don't think that's true," the second woman senior citizen said. "I never heard it before and I've heard everything."

"I think it's probably just an old wives' tale," one of the men said. The other male senior citizen cracked up.

"Shall we discuss *old men?*" the first woman asked the second woman.

The two men looked at the sky to make sure all of our country's satellites were in the right places.

"What about your daughter the nun?" the second woman, whose name was Elise, asked the first, whose name was Kate. "You haven't heard from her?"

"My daughter the nun," Kate said, " you wouldn't believe."

"Where is she?" Elise asked. "Georgia or somewhere, you told me but I forgot. Going to school you said."

"She's getting her master's," Kate said, "they send them. She's a rambling wreck from Georgia Tech. I was going down to visit at Thanksgiving."

"But you didn't."

"I called her and said I was coming and she said but Thanksgiving Day is the game. So I said the game, the game, O.K. I'll go to the game, I don't mind going to the game, get me a ticket. And she said but Mother I'm in the flash card section. My daughter the nun."

"They're different now," Elise said, "you're lucky she's not keeping company with one of those priests with his hair in a pigtail."

"Who can tell?" said Kate. "I'd be the last to know."

One of the men leaned around his partner and asked: "Well, is it working? Are you loved?"

"There was another thing we used to do," Kate said calmly. "You and your girl friend each wrote the names of three boys on three slips of paper, on the first day of the month. The names of three boys you wanted to ask you to go out with them. Then your girl friend held the three slips of paper in her cupped hands and you closed your eyes and picked—"

"I don't believe it," said the second male senior citizen, whose name was Jerome.

"You closed your eyes and picked one and put it in your shoe. And you did the same for her. And then that boy would come around. It always worked. Invariably."

"I don't believe it," Jerome said again. " I don't believe in things like that and never have. I don't believe in magic and I don't believe in superstition. I don't believe in Judaism, Christianity, or Eastern thought. None of 'em. I didn't believe in the First World War even though I was a child in the First World War and you'll go a long way before you find somebody who didn't believe in the First World War. That was a very popular war, where I lived. I didn't believe in the Second World War either and I was in it."

"How could you be in it if you didn't believe in it?" Elise asked.

"My views were not consulted," Jerome said. "They didn't ask me, they told me. But I still had my inner belief, which was that I didn't believe in it. I was in the MPs. I rose through the ranks. I was a provost marshal, at the end. I once shook down an entire battalion of Seabees, six hundred men."

"What is 'shook down'?"

"That's when you and your people go through their foot lockers and sea bags and personal belongings looking for stuff they shouldn't have."

"What shouldn't they have?"

"Black market stuff. Booze. Dope. Government property. Unauthorized weapons." He paused. "What else didn't I believe in? I didn't believe in the atom bomb but I was wrong about that. The unions."

"You were wrong about that too," said the other man, Frank. "I was a linotype operator when I was nineteen and I was a linotype operator until I was sixty and let me tell you, mister, if we hadn't had the union all we would have got was nickels and dimes. Nickels and dimes. Period. So don't say anything against the trade union movement while I'm sitting here, because I know what I'm talking about. You don't."

"I didn't believe in the unions and I didn't believe in the government whether Republican or Democrat," Jerome said. "And I didn't believe in—"

"The I.T.U. is considered a very good union," Elise said. "I once went with a man in the I.T.U. He was a composing-room foreman and his name was Harry Foreman, that was a coincidence, and he made very good money. We went to Luchow's a lot. He liked German food."

"Did you believe in the international Communist conspiracy?" Frank asked Jerome.

"Nope."

"You can't read," Frank said, "you're blind."

"Maybe."

"I haven't decided about whether there is an international Communist conspiracy," Elise said. "I'm still thinking about it."

"What's to think about?" Frank asked. "There was Czechoslovakia. Czechoslovakia says it all."

Some street people walked past the group of senior citizens but decided that the senior citizens weren't worth asking for small change. The decision was plain on their faces.

"When I was a girl, a little girl, I had to go into my father's bar to get the butter," Kate said. "My father had a bar in Brooklyn. The icebox was in the bar. The only icebox. My mother sent me downstairs to get the butter. All the men turned and looked at me as I entered the bar."

"But your father bounded out from behind the bar and got you the butter meanwhile looking sternly at all the other people in the bar to keep them from looking at you," Elise suggested.

"No," Kate said "He was on his ass most of the time. What they say about bartenders not drinking is not true."

"Also I didn't believe in the League of Nations," Jerome said. "Furthermore," he said, giving Kate a meaningful glance, "I didn't believe women should be given the vote."

Kate gazed at Jerome's coat, which was old, at his shirt, old, then at his pants, which were quite old, and at his shoes, which were new.

"Do you have prostate trouble?" she asked.

"Yes," Jerome said, with a startled look. "Of course. Why?"

"Good," Kate said. "I don't believe in prostate trouble. I don't believe there is such a thing as a prostate."

She gave him generous and loving smile.

"You mean to tell me that if you put the piece of paper with the boy's name on it in your shoe on the first day of the month he *invariably* came around?" Elise asked Kate.

"Invariably," Kate said. "Without fail. Worked every time."

"Goddamn," Elise said. "Wish I'd known that."

Belief

"There was one thing I believed," Jerome said.

"What?"

"It's religious."

"What is it?"

"My pal the rabbi told me, he's dead now. He said it was a Hasidic writing."

"So?" said Elise. "So, so, so?"

"It is forbidden to grow old."

The old people thought about this for a while, on the bench.

"It's good," Kate said. "I could do without the irony."

"Me too," Elise said. "I could do without the irony."

"Maybe it's not so good?" Jerome asked. "What do you think?"

"No," Kate said. "It's good." She gazed about her at the new life sprouting in sandboxes and jungle gyms. "Wish I had some kids to yell at."

Wrack

Cold here in the garden.
> — You were complaining about the sun.
> —But when it goes behind a cloud—
> —Well, you can't have everything.
—The flowers are beautiful.
—Indeed.
—Consoling to have the flowers.
—Half-way consoled already.
—And these Japanese rocks—
—Artfully placed, most artfully.
—You must admit, a great consolation.
—And Social Security.
—A great consolation.
—And philosophy. Futhermore.
—I read a book. Just the other day.
—Sexuality, too.
—They have books about it. I read one.
—We'll to the woods no more. I assume.
—Where there's a will there's a way. That's what my mother always said.
> —I wonder if it's true.

Wrack

—I think not.

—Well, you're driving me crazy.

—Well you're driving me crazy too. Know what I mean?

—Going to snap one of these days.

—If you were a Japanese master you wouldn't snap. Those guys never snapped. Some of them were ninety.

—Well, you can't have everything.

—Cold, here in the garden.

—Caw caw caw caw.

—You want to sing that song.

—Can't remember how it goes.

—Getting farther and farther away from life.

—How do you feel about that?

—Guilty but less guilty than I should.

—Can you fine-tune that for me?

—Not yet I want to think about it.

—Well, I have to muck out the stable and buff up the silver.

—They trust you with the silver?

—Of course. I have their trust.

—You enjoy their trust.

—Absolutely.

—Well we still haven't decided what color to paint the trucks.

—I said blue.

—Surely not your last word on the subject.

—I have some swatches. If you'd care to take a gander.

—Not now. This sun is blistering.

—New skin. You're going to complain?

—Thank the Lord for all small favors.

—The kid ever come to see you?

—Did for a while. Then stopped.

—How does that make you feel?

—Oh, I don't blame him.

—Well, you can't have everything.

—That's true. What's the time?

—Looks to be about one.

—Where's your watch?

—Hocked it.

—What'd you get?

—Twelve-fifty.

—God, aren't these flowers beautiful!

—Only three of them. But each remarkable, of its kind.

—What are they?

—Some kind of Japanese dealies I don't know.

—Lazing in the garden. This is really most luxurious.

—Listening to the radio. "Elmer's Tune."

—I don't like it when they let girls talk on the radio.

—Never used to have them. Now they're everywhere.

—You can't really say too much. These days.

—Doesn't that make you nervous? Girls talking on the radio?

—I liked H. V. Kaltenborn. He's long gone.

—What'd you do yesterday?

—Took a walk. In the wild trees.

—They spend a lot of time worrying about where to park their cars. Glad I don't have one.

—Haven't eaten anything except some rice, this morning. Cooked it with chicken broth.

—This place is cold, no getting around it.

—Forgot to buy soap, forgot to buy coffee—

—All right. The hollowed-out book containing the single Swedish municipal bond in the amount of fifty thousand Swedish crowns is not yours. We've established that. Let's go on.

—It was never mine. Or it might have been mine, once. Perhaps it belonged to my former wife. I said I wasn't sure. She was fond of hiding things in hollowed-out books.

—We want not the shadow of a doubt. We want to be absolutely certain.

—I appreciate it. She had gray eyes. Gray with a touch of violet.

—Yes. Now, are these your doors?

—Yes. I think so. Are they on spring hinges? Do they swing?

—They swing in either direction. Spring hinges. Wood slats.

—She did things with her eyebrows. Painted them gold. You had the gray eyes with a touch of violet, and the gold eyebrows. Yes, the doors must be mine. I seem to remember her bursting through them. In one of the several rages of a summer's day.

—When?

—It must have been some time ago. Some years. I don't know what they're doing here. It strikes me they were in another house. Not this house. I mean it's kind of cloudy.

—But they're here.

—She sometimes threw something through the doorway before bursting through the doorway herself. Acid, on one occasion.

—But the doors are here. They're yours.

—Yes. They seem to be. I mean, I'm not arguing with you. On the other hand, they're not something I want to remember, particularly. They have sort of an unpleasant aura around them, for some reason. I would have avoided them, left to myself.

—I don't want to distress you. Unnecessarily.

—I know, I know, I know. I'm not blaming you, but it just seems to me that you could have let it go. The doors. I'm sure you didn't mean anything by it, but still—

—I didn't mean anything by it. Well, let's leave the doors, then, and go on to the dish.

—Plate.

—Let's go on to the plate, then.

—Plate, dish, I don't care, it's something of an imposition, you must admit, to have to think about it. Normally I wouldn't think about it.

—It has your name on the back. Engraved on the back.

—Where? Show me.

—Your name. Right there. And the date, 1962.

—I don't want to look. I'll take your word for it. That was twenty years ago. My God. She read R. D. Laing. Aloud, at dinner. Every night. Interrupted only by the telephone. When she answered the telephone, her voice became animated. Charming and animated. Gaiety. Vivacity. Laughter. In contrast to her reading of R. D. Laing. Which could only be described as punitive. O.K., so it's mine. My plate.

—It's a dish. A bonbon dish.

—You mean to say that you think that *I* would own a bonbon dish? A sterling-silver or whatever it is bonbon dish? You're mad.

—The doors were yours. Why not the dish?

—A *bonbon* dish?

—Perhaps she craved bonbons?

—No no no no no. Not so. Sourballs, perhaps.

—Let's move on to the shoe, now. I don't have that much time.

—The shoe is definitely not mine.

—Not yours.

—It's a woman's shoe. It's too small for me. My foot, this foot here, would never in the world fit into that shoe.

—I am not suggesting that the shoe is yours in the sense that you wear or would wear such a shoe. It's obviously a woman's shoe.

—The shoe is in no sense a thing of mine. Although found I admit among my things.

—It's here. An old-fashioned shoe. Eleven buttons.

—There was a vogue for that kind of shoe, some time back, among the young people. It might have belonged to a young person. I sometimes saw young persons.

—With what in mind?

—I fondled them, if they were fondleable.

—Within the limits of the law, of course.

—Certainly. "Young persons" is an elastic term. You think I'm going to mess with jailbait?

—Of course not. Never occurred to me. The shoe has something of the pathetic about it. A wronged quality. Do you think it possible that the shoe may be in some way a *cri de coeur?*

—Not a chance.

—You were wrong about the dish.

—I've never heard a *cri de coeur.*

—You've never heard a *cri de coeur?*

—Perhaps once. When Shirley was with us?

—Who was Shirley?

—The maid. She was studying eschatology. Maiding part-time. She left us for a better post. Perfectly ordinary departure.

—Did she perhaps wear shoes of this type?

—No. Nor was she given to the *cri de coeur*. Except perhaps, once. Death of her flying fish. A cry wrenched from her bosom. Rather like a winged phallus it was, she kept it in a washtub in the basement. One day it was discovered belly-up. She screamed. Then, insisted it be given the Last Rites, buried in a fish cemetery, holy water sprinkled this way and that—

—You fatigue me. Now, about the hundred-pound sack of saccharin.

—Mine. Indubitably mine. I'm forbidden to use sugar. I have a condition.

—I'm delighted to hear it. Not that you have a condition but that the sack is, without doubt, yours.

—Mine. Yes.

—I can't tell you how pleased I am. The inquiry moves. Progress is made. Results are obtained.

—What are you writing there, in your notes?

—That the sack is, beyond a doubt, yours.

—I think it's mine.

—What do you mean, *think?* You stated . . . Is it yours or isn't it?

—I think it's mine. It seems to be.

—Seems!

—I just remembered, I put sugar in my coffee. At breakfast.

—Are you sure it wasn't saccharin?

—White powder of some kind . . .

—There is a difference in texture . . .

—No, I remember, it was definitely sugar. Granulated. So the sack of saccharin is definitely not mine.

—Nothing is yours.

—Some things are mine, but the sack is not mine, the shoe is not mine, the bonbon dish is not mine, and the doors are not mine.

—You admitted the doors.

—Not wholeheartedly.

—You said, I have it right here, written down, "Yes, they must be mine."

—Sometimes we hugged. Lengthily. Heart to heart, the one trying to pull the other into the upright other . . .

—I have it right here. Written down. "Yes, they must be mine."

—I withdraw that.

—You can't withdraw it. I've written it down.

—Nevertheless I withdraw it. It's inadmissible. It was coerced.

—You feel coerced?

—All that business about "dish" rather than "plate"—

—That was a point of fact, it was, in fact, a dish.

—You have a hectoring tone. I don't like to be hectored. You came here with something in mind. You had made an a priori decision.

—That's a little ridiculous when you consider that I have, personally, nothing to gain. Either way. Whichever way it goes.

—Promotion, advancement . . .

—We don't operate that way. That has nothing to do with it. I don't want to discuss this any further. Let's go on to the dressing gown. Is the dressing gown yours?

—Maybe.

—Yes or no?

—My business. Leave it at "maybe."

—I am entitled to a good, solid, answer. Is the dressing gown yours?

—Maybe.

—Please.

—Maybe maybe maybe maybe.

—You exhaust me. In this context, the word "maybe" is unacceptable.

—A perfectly possible answer. People use it every day.

—Unacceptable. What happened to her?

—She made a lot of money. Opened a Palais de Glace, or skating rink. Read R. D. Laing to the skaters over the PA system meanwhile supplementing her income by lecturing over the country as a spokesperson for the unborn.

—The gold eyebrows, still?

—The gold eyebrows and the gray-with-violet eyes. On television, very often.

—In the beginning, you don't know.

—That's true.

—Just one more thing: The two mattresses surrounding the single slice of salami. Are they yours?

—I get hungry. In the night.

—The struggle is admirable. Useless, but admirable. Your struggle.

—Cold, here in the garden.

—You're too old, that's all it is, think nothing of it. Don't give it a thought.

—I haven't agreed to that. Did I agree to that?

—No, I must say you resisted. Admirably, resisted.

—I did resist. Would you allow "valiantly"?

—No no no no. Come come come.

—"Wholeheartedly"?

—Yes, O.K., what do I care?

—*Wholeheartedly*, then.

—Yes.

—*Wholeheartedly.*

—We still haven't decided what color to paint the trucks.

—Yes. How about blue?

The Question Party

"Y es, Maria, we will give the party on next Thursday night and I have an agreeable surprise in contemplation for all our old friends who may be here." The pleasant air about Mrs. Teach as she entered the parlor where her daughter was seated betokened the presence of something on her mind that gave her great satisfaction. The daughter had been importuning her mother for a party which after due deliberation she had decided to give and to make the evening more entertaining she had determined to introduce a new feature which she thought would create some excitement in the circle of her acquaintances and afford them the means of much amusement. She had just hit upon the plan before entering the room and the smile of satisfaction upon her face was noticed by her daughter.

"Shall we, Mother? I am so glad!" she answered. "But what is it you are preparing for our friends? Are you going to sing?"

"No, Miss, I ain't going to do no such foolish thing! And, for your quizzing, you shall not know what it is until the evening of the party!"

"Now, Mother, that is too bad. You are too hardhearted. You know the extent of woman's curiosity and yet you will not gratify me. Are you going to introduce a new polka?"

"There is no use in your questioning; I shall not tell you anything about it, so you may as well save your breath."

"Do you intend showing your album quilt?" perseveringly inquired Maria.

"Now do not provoke me to cancel my promise by your pertinacity. I tell you as a punishment for quizzing your mother you shall not know until Thursday next what it is."

"Morning or evening, Mother?"

"Evening, Miss. So no more questions but get about writing your invitations."

Maria proceeded to the bookcase and taking from it her notepaper and envelopes commenced writing.

Eight o'clock on the evening of the party. The first who were ushered into the parlor were Mrs. Jawart and her two daughters, who were always the first at the reunions. The younger Miss Jawart was somewhere out of her teens, and the elder, although her face was profusely bedecked with curls—the original owner of which, being dead, had no further use for them—could not conceal that she was much older than she wished to be considered. Mr. and Mrs. White came next, the lady somewhat pompous in her manner, and the gentleman quite so. An interest in a canal boat had placed him, in his own view, among shipping merchants, and some of his acquaintances broadly hinted that if he were cut up in small pieces and retailed out for starch, he would be fulfilling his destiny. The two Misses Jennings and brother came next. These young ladies, the one eighteen and the other twenty, seemed somewhat disappointed, when they entered the room, at the absence of some of their young beaux, whom they expected to find there; this feeling was dispelled in a few moments, when a matched pair of the latter presented themselves.

Mr. Lynch, a bachelor of fifty, was the next to claim the attention of the company. He was a short, thickset man, with a small pair of whiskers that curled up on his cheekbones as if endeavoring to cultivate an acquaintance with his eyes. A few gray hairs in them, overlooked by the owner—his attention to them was exemplary—had been, in his toilet for the evening, elbowed, as it were, by the others to the fore, possibly to attract the attention of a few of the same color which peeped from behind the false hair of Miss Jawart A standing collar formed a semi-wall around his neck, and shoes of the brightest polish graced his feet. At about half past nine, then, all the guests had assembled, filling comfortably both parlors and rendering the place vocal with their animated conversation.

The company had been engaged some time in singing when there was a call for a polka. In a few moments partners were selected and everyone was hopscotching through the figures at a lively rate, reminding one strongly of a group in a state of advanced intoxication. The mind of Maria suddenly became abstracted to such an extent by thoughts of the surprise that her mother had promised that she forgot her time and the dancers were compelled to stop and reprove her jokingly for her remissness. Just at that moment Mrs. Teach's voice could be heard, above the general din of laughter and music, calling for everyone, without exception, to come into the front parlor as she had something to show them which she thought would amuse. In her haste to get into the room Maria almost knocked one of the Misses Jennings over.

The company after much confusion being seated, Mrs. Teach took from the center table a handsome marble card basket containing a pack of plain, gilt-edged cards and explained that she had prepared an innocent and entertaining amusement for them which she hoped would prove interesting.

"Maria," she continued, "will you pass around this basket, my dear, and let each one of the company select from it one of the cards?"

Maria did as her mother requested.

"I shall propose a question," said Mrs. Teach, "to which each one must write an answer on the card they have. Which cards shall be placed in this vase on the pedestal behind me. After they are all deposited I will draw them out singly and will read them aloud. There is to be no mark upon the response by which its author may be known."

There was a general mustering of pencils at this announcement and an evident curiosity was immediately raised in regard to the subject which would be propounded.

"As there is a majority of ladies here, I shall propose for the first question: What is a bachelor?"

For the space of a quarter of an hour the pencils of the company made desperate attacks upon the faces of the cards which left them covered over with black lines. The last answer written and deposited in the vase, Mrs. Teach, with a smile, commenced the task of reading them aloud.

"*A target for fair hands to shoot at,*" she read.

A general laugh greeted this response.

"I beg of you, ladies," said Mr. Lynch, "not to shoot too close to me, but I know that my prayer is to no avail since your arrows are already in that vase."

The second card was drawn forth.

"*Any icy peak, on the mountain of humanity, that the sun of woman's love has never melted,*" read Mrs. Teach.

"Then I will nip you with my frost," said Mr. Lynch, putting his arms playfully around one of the Misses Jennings.

"How do you know it was my answer?" she cried, releasing herself from him.

"I read it in your face this moment," he replied.

"Then we must turn our faces from you, or we shall all betray ourselves, if you are such an excellent face reader," said the elder Miss Jawart.

"I beg you, do not!" exclaimed Mr. Lynch. "For that would deprive me of much pleasure."

"*An old maid's forlorn hope,*" said Mrs. Teach, reading the next response, the aptness of which was felt by all—yet a sense of propriety restrained any acknowledgment of this. Another card was instantly drawn to divert attention from it, and to relieve Miss Jawart from her unpleasant dilemma.

"*A fox longing for the grapes he pronounces sour.*"

"Now I really do object!" said Mr. Lynch. "I could never find it in my heart to pronounce any lady sour."

"Heart, indeed! This is the first time I ever knew you to acknowledge the possession of such an article," Mrs. Teach quickly replied.

"There you do me wrong, for, see! I have one now which you gave me," said Mr. Lynch, taking from his pocket a handsomely worked velvet heart. "And observe, there are as many pins in it as you are endeavoring to plant thorns in its partner here," he went on, placing his hand over that part of his coat which covered the real article.

The laugh was turned on Mrs. Teach and she drew forth another card.

"*A creature whose miseries might be pitied had he not the remedy within his reach.*"

"It must be you, Miss Bookly," said Mr. Lynch, "as you are sitting closest to me."

"I did not write it," said Miss Bookly. "And besides, Miss Jennings was sitting closest to you before she moved away after you put your arms around her."

"That is true," he said with a mock sigh.

Another card terminated the conversation on that subject.

"*Just like Mr. Lynch.*"

The merriment of the company knew no bounds at this answer. Mr. Lynch joined the rest with great zeal, and in a few moments exclaimed, "Well! I really do think you are making me a target to shoot at tonight. It is well for you that I am good-natured, else I might retaliate with some formulations of my own."

This is really a dumb game, thought Maria.

Mrs. Teach dipped into the vase for the next card.

"*One who boasts of liberty but sighs for the slavery he condemns.*"

"That would be acute," Mr. Lynch said thoughtfully, "had I ever boasted. But I recall no such occasion. There is, in fact, a kind of shame and horror attached to the bachelor state—an odium combined with a tedium. Sleeping with strumpets is not the liveliest business in the world, I assure you."

"What are they like, really?" asked Miss Bookly.

"Some are choice, some are not," said Mr. Lynch.

"For heaven's sakes, man, be silent!" exclaimed Mr. White.

"A bit of fresh, as the expression runs," said Mr. Lynch, "can—"

Mr. White drew forth his pistol and shot Mr. Lynch dead with it.

"Good Lord! He is dead!" cried Mrs. Teach.

Dr. Balfour knelt over the body. "Yes, he is dead," he said. All assisted the Doctor in placing the carcass on the sofa.

"There is but one more card in the vase," said Mrs. Teach, peering into the article in question. "Dare we look at it?"

"Yes, yes," was the answer, in a subdued murmur.

"I sincerely hope that it may be a favorable one," said Mrs. Teach, "for I fear we have dealt harshly with our late friend tonight."

The last card was drawn from the vase. Mrs. Teach examined it closely on both sides and then proclaimed, "*Blank!*"

"A prophecy," said the younger Miss Jennings. "Who could have foreseen what was to happen?"

"It was not a matter of foreknowledge," said Maria. "The card is mine. I couldn't think of anything to write."

"Well," said Mrs. Teach, "I am not entirely satisfied with my little experiment this evening, and so shall leave it to another to choose the entertainment for our next."

"Not at all," said Mr. White. "The evening, despite its sad but necessary consequences, has been most delightful. I can't recall when more interesting things have been said or done, in all the years of my residence in this city. And as I shall have the pleasure of giving the next party, I shall most certainly adopt your little experiment, as you call it."

"What will the question be?" asked Miss Jawart.

"Something dangerous," said Mr. White, with a twinkle.

"Parties are always dangerous," said Miss Jawart.

"I am inviting Geronimo, chief of the Apache Indians, who happens to be in town," said Mr. White.

"That will make it all the more dangerous," said Mrs. Teach, "as I am told that he is extremely cruel to his enemies."

"He is extremely cruel to *everyone*," said Mr. White.

Yes, it was an agreeable party after all, Maria thought. My mother is not dumb. My mother is surprisingly intelligent. It was wrong of me to think ill of her. Now no one will ever know that Mr. Lynch was the man who—How strange is justice! How artful woman!

Author's note: This piece is an *objet trouvé.* It was originally published in *Godey's Lady's Book* in 1850, under the byline of a Hickory Broom. I have cut it and added some three dozen lines.

Manfred

O ut for a walk I was, wanted to clear my head, I'd been drinking the night before, tequila mostly, a bit of lime juice, one lime per bottle, or four limes in all, by the end of the evening. I was feeling poorly. I had asked for help with the tequila, but no one came, all sent regrets, busy elsewhere, prior engagement, don't go out after dark anymore, that sort of thing, allergic to rats, that sort of thing. I could not blame them. My brother sent regrets, from his room behind the kitchen, stuffy bastard, nose in a book probably, or playing his drums, the jackass, fraternity is not among his talents.

So I wandered out, in the cool of the morning, fell down a time or two, that was to be expected, reached the whorehouse district without other difficulty but they'd all gone to bed, banged my head on a door or two but no one answered, that was to be expected, it was 7 or thereabouts, fresh, cool, and golden. And I said why not the graveyard? and could think of no compelling contrary argument, and went there, and tumbled into an open grave, and broke a leg.

It was a new grave, having been readied the previous day for a 10 A.M. ceremonial, I say 10 A.M. because that was the hour at which they discovered me. They fished me out and took me in a van to a hospital where a young man cut straight up my trouser leg with shears, not knowing I suppose that I had no other trousers, and then did the necessary with the plaster and canvas or whatever it is, and hung the finished product from a sort of slingshot affair above the bed. Double spiral break, he said, very nasty, and asked the date of my birth and what authority I belonged to, city, county, state or federal, and I told him, as best as I could remember. And thus I found myself, for three months and ten days, at the mercy of my brother Manfred, for whom pig is perhaps too soft, or sweet, a word.

Manfred sits in his room behind the kitchen, calculating, humming, cabalistic summing, watching N.F.L. football or playing his drums: interests passed on by our father, but to which in the genetic scheme of things, thank God, I inherited a recessive genotype.

Father, a first cousin twice removed of B. Spinoza, inherited his interest in the gematria* from the Hebraic side of the family and his reductivist inclination from his great-nephew A. Reinhardt, the painter. Father spent his entire life summing up the written word and oral information of the Western World, assigning a numerical equivalent to each letter of the alphabet according to its position: A=1, B=2, C=3, D=4, E=5, F=6, G=7, H=8, I=9, J=10, K=11, L=12, M=13, N=14, O=15, P=16, Q=17, R=18, S=19, T=20, U=21, V=22, W=23, X=24, Y=25, Z=26. In so doing he could spell out any word numerically and add it to reach the sum, the essence, the heart of the word. Adding the sum of each word to the heart of the next (an addiction inherited from his granduncle R. Descartes), Father would reduce the glib, the banal, the genius, the truth, the beauty in fiction and nonfiction of the Western World to one final number, to be grasped by all of Occidental mankind instantly and at once. Sums that were prime were entered into a double-entry profit ledger as they were deemed prophetic.

To the end Father summed. Giving up the ghost, as it were, dying so to speak, on the penultimate page of St. Matthew's "Gospel According To." Manfred took up the mantle having the genotype of an adder but the phenotype of a pig. He completed Father's last summation, a number that boggles the mind, but alas, not prime.

---

* Gematria (n., Heb.): A cabalistic method of interpretation of the Hebrew scriptures based upon the numerical value of the letters in the words.

Manfred

Manfred works night and day interpreting numbers, searching for the additional meanings in lists of numerals, reversing the paternal process; translating random and not so random numbers into language. He believes this to be more humanistic and humane, forgetting there is more to a person than his shoe size, blood pressure, diastolic and systolic, weight, age, and blood count. His interest in N.F.L. football has nothing to do with being one of the boys or hail fellow well met, but instead is an obsessive need to decode the lineup on the line of scrimmage. He mutters to himself, "There's more to N.F.L. football than fun and games."

Nothing misses his porcine eyes and calculating mind. He notices immediately that the 57 on the can of pork and beans is incorrect as far as PORK AND BEANS $(16 + 15 + 18 + 11 + 1 + 14 + 4 + 2 + 5 + 1 + 14 + 19)$ is concerned, it being equal to 120, whereas 57 equals PEACHES $(16 + 5 + 1 + 3 + 8 + 5 + 19)$, AFOOT $(1 + 6 + 15 + 15 + 20)$, DEMIGOD $(4 + 5 + 13 + 9 + 7 + 15 + 4)$, and FUNGI $(6 + 21 + 14 + 7 + 9)$, none of which is in the can.

Unable to move without aid, a captive in my brother's room, abused and bemused by morphemes and phonemes, by "Science and Sanity," Manfred pontificates on general semantics (a trait inherited from his close friend A. Korzybski). He tells me, "We are handicapped in the knowledge of our language by being born into it . . ." He says, "The meaning of meanings, in a given case, in a given individual, at a given moment represents composite, affective psychological configurations of all relations pertaining to the case, colored by past experiences, state of health, mood of the moment and other contingencies . . ." He says, ". . . Only in mathematics do we find a language of similar structure . . . the importance of mathematics considered as a language becomes of fundamental significance for the theory of sanity . . ." Fraternity is not among his talents.

And so I spent all of February and March and April and ten days in May of this leap year deprived of comfort, companionship, and conversation. For one hundred days and nights hurting and healing. All things being equal 100 equals USELESS $(21 + 19 + 5 + 12 + 5 + 19 + 19)$, and so it was.

A Man

A fireman woke up one morning to find that his left hand was gone.

My left hand! he thought.

Then he thought: This is going to be damned inconvenient.

The fireman cursed for a while. "God damn it! Jesus, Mary, and Joseph! God damn it to Hell! Bloody Hell! Dumb ass! Christ Almighty! Son of a bitch!"

But the stump is not bad-looking, he reflected. A neat separation. Not offensive to the eye.

He got out of bed and took a shower. Washing his right side, which he customarily did with his left hand, was difficult. It was also difficult to dry himself with one hand. Usually he took a large brown towel in both hands and zipped it back and forth across his back. But he discovered that one cannot zip a towel with one hand. One can only flop a towel with one hand.

Putting on socks with one hand is not easy. Shaving, however, presented no particular problems.

At the firehouse nobody said anything about the hand. Firemen are famously tactful and kind to each other. Harvey read *The New York Times* until there was an alarm. Then he put on his rubber coat

240

and boots and climbed up on the engine in his regular place, second from left, in the back.

"No," the captain said.

"What do you mean, 'No'?"

"You can't go to the fire," the captain said. "You don't have any left hand."

"I can cradle the hose in my arms as one would a baby and pull it in the right direction!"

"Get down off there, Harvey. We're in a hurry."

Harvey stood in the empty firehouse.

My livelihood is threatened! he thought.

My livelihood!

And it wasn't even an on-the-job injury. It was, rather, a "mysterious occurrence." No compensation!

He sat down in a chair. He placed his fireman's hat on top of *The New York Times.*

I must face this problem intelligently. But what is intelligently? Prosthesis? Prosthetic device concealed under black glove? A green glove? A blue glove? The cops wear white gloves on traffic duty. But a man would be a fool to wear a white glove to a fire. A brown suede driving glove from Abercrombie—the Stirling Moss model? Probably there is such a thing in the world.

He got up and went to the place in the firehouse where the whiskey was hidden and had a shot, neat.

He thought: Why don't we buy better whiskey for the firehouse? This stuff tastes like creosote.

A twelve-year-old girl who hung around the firehouse a lot entered at this moment.

"Harvey," she said. "How come you aren't out on the run with the rest of the men?"

Harvey waved his stump in the air.

"What's with the hand?" the girl asked. "I mean, where is it?"

"It fell off, or something, last night, while I was sleeping."

"What do you mean, *fell off?* Was it in bed with you when you woke up? Or on the floor? Or under the bed?"

"It was just . . . missing."

"Man, that's *strange*," the girl said. "God, I mean that's *weird*. It gives me a funny feeling. Let's talk about something else." Then she paused. "Is there anything I can do? I could go out on your runs with you. Function as your extra hand, as it were." There was a look of childish eagerness in her eyes.

The fireman thought: This child is childish. But a good kid.

"Thank you, Elaine," he said. "But it wouldn't work. There'd be union problems and stuff." Delicately he avoided mentioning that she was a twelve-year-old girl.

"I've been studying the Civil Service exam for fire lieutenant," Elaine said, producing a study guide to the Civil Service examination for fire lieutenant published by Arco Publishing Co. "I know it backwards and forwards. Ask me anything. Just dip in anywhere and ask me anything. At random. I know the answers."

"Elaine," Harvey said, "would you mind letting me alone for a little while? I have to think about something."

Silently the little girl withdrew.

A hook? Harvey wondered.

The next day at the firehouse Harvey was playing chess with his friend Nick Ceci. He consciously made all his moves with his new artificial hand in its black glove. Every time Harvey moved, a lot of the pieces fell off the board. Nick said nothing. He just picked up the pieces off the floor and put them back in their proper places. The alarm bell rang.

Harvey climbed up on the back of the engine, second from left.

"Get down off there, Harvey. For God's sake," the captain said. "This is a serious business we're in, firefighting. Quit screwing around."

"But I have this new hand!"

"Yes, but it's no good," the captain replied. "I don't want to hurt your feelings, Harvey, but that hand is just a piece of junk."

"I paid two hundred and twelve bucks for it!"

"You got taken," the captain said. "I cannot risk the safety of my men on a possibly fallible plastic-and-metal hand which looks to me unsound and junky. I must use my best judgment. That is why I am captain, because I have good judgment. Now will you get your ass down from there and let us get out of here?"

Harvey hung up his rubber coat and went home to Staten Island. He spent some time looking at a picture of his mother, who was dead. In the picture his mother was reading a book.

I am a finished fireman, he thought. But yet, a human being, I have courage, resiliency—even hope. I will remold myself into something new, by reading a lot of books. I will miss firehouse life, but I know that other lives are possible—useful work in a number of lines, socially desirable activities contributing to the health of the society . . .

The fireman told himself a lot more garbage of this nature.

Then he told himself some true things:

(1) Women do not like men with one hand as much as they like men with two hands.

(2) His fake hand was a piece of expensive junk, like a gold jeweled bird that could open its mouth and sing, and also tell the time.

(3) He had only $213.09 in the bank, after having paid for the hand.

(4) God had taken his hand away for a reason, because God never does anything mindlessly, appearance notwithstanding.

(5) God's action *in re* the hand could only be regarded as punitive. It could hardly be regarded as a reward or congratulations.

(6) Therefore he, Harvey Samaras, either had done something wrong or, more specifically, *been* something wrong.

(7) His mother was dead. His father was dead. All his grandmothers and grandfathers were dead, as were his uncles, aunts, and cousins.

(8) He had never had the guts to marry anybody, although Sheila had wanted to get married.

(9) No children were his.

(10) Reading a lot of books would solve nothing.

(11) As he had grown older he had become less brave. That time at the P.S. 411 fire . . .

(12) In essence, he had failed to improve. He had failed to become a better man.

(13) There were mitigating circumstances—his very poor education, for example.

(14) Having a gold jeweled bird that could open its mouth and sing and also tell the time was in no sense as good as having an ordinary left hand.

(15) He did not know what he had done wrong. But he knew that a better man would have, somehow, done better.

(16) But how?

(17) How does that arise, that condition of being a better man?

(18) Reading a lot of books?

(19) But to be honest, he did not want to be a better man. All he wanted to do was drink and listen to music.

(20) He did not love anybody, really.

(21) No one loved him, particularly. Nick Ceci was friendly but probably that was just his nature, to be friendly.

(22) We are all replaceable parts, like a bashed-in fender on a Maverick. His left hand was a replaceable part of an organism that was itself replaceable.

(23) His death, his own death, would not be noticed by the world, would not make the slightest difference to the world.

(24) He would live anyhow.

(25) Poorly.

Heather

This it?"

"That's it."

The twins, Hilda and Heidi, have had a baby.

Sam is in shock. How did this happen?

True, he's been sleeping with them both.

"Baby's crying," says Hilda.

"'*Course* it's crying," said Heidi. "Got no credit cards, can't speak French, don't know where its next meal is comin' from, I'd cry too."

Sam pokes the bundle with a knuckle.

"Appears to be some kind of foot down here."

"A good foot," says Hilda. "Made it myself."

"She did the feet," Heidi says, "I did the elbows."

"C'mon, guys," says Sam, "ease up, ease up."

The baby's in a clear plastic bin atop a rolling cart placed between their beds. Why do the nurses giggle constantly as they bring trays, offer pills?

Sam's been away for months. They did this behind his back, as it were.

The baby is a handsome article with light brown hair and one ear that folds forward when she turns her head against the pillow. He's allowed to hold her.

He's brought the twins pâte, spinach quiche, beer, and wine.

"Well," he says, "what are we going to do now? I mean practically speaking?"

"When you were in North Dakota for all that time," Hilda says, "we thought of you."

"Yeah," says Heidi. "Barbecued, mostly."

"It was an intolerable situation," he says. When they nurse the baby, handing her from bed to bed, he notices that both have breasts bursting with milk. "But what are we going to *do* about this? I mean we got to regularize this thing in some way, is the way I see it."

"The wages of sin," Hilda says, "are doubt, confusion, fear, and paternity suits, plural."

"Come off it," he says. "You guys knew what you were doing." They've named the baby Heather. He was not consulted. He takes a swig of red wine from a Styrofoam cup. "Like where are we going to live, for example?"

"We and Heather," Hilda says, "will live t' home, like always. Where you live will depend entirely on how you act."

"How I act? What am I supposed to do?"

"The right thing," says Heidi.

"Which one?"

"Both."

"That's against the *law*."

"Little late in the day for ethical musings, ain't it?" says Heidi.

They're both musicians, Heidi a violinist, Hilda a flutist.

"Them that sows wild oats has got to bale the barley," Hilda says.

"O.K., you got fast mouths, this we knew already," Sam says. "The question is, Smart Asses, which of you is the actual producer? Which one did the work?"

"Us did it," the twins say together. "We."

"I did the ears, footprints, and organs of generation," says Hilda, "buddy let me tell you it was not easy. Gettin' all those whorly lines on the footprints just exactly right, took me nine fuckin' months."

"I did the hair, the chin, and the joints," says Heidi. "You notice she's got a lot of flex in those joints. We do good work around here. We don't let nothin' out of the shop less it's just 'zackly right.'"

"Whoo boy," says Hilda, "you bein' off reconstructing North Dakota and all, you missed a lot. You missed morning sickness, evening sickness, and high-noon sickness. You ain't been pullin' your weight, Donor."

"I remind you," says Sam, "that putting old Hilda in old Heidi's bed was not my idea."

"Got to have some fun in the world," says Heidi, and Hilda says, "Mother always taught us to share."

"So you've told me." The baby's staring at him.

"She did the medulla and the bad habits, I did the thyroid and the family resemblances," Hilda says. "Doesn't she look a bit like Uncle Hamish?"

"That the one hung for stamp theft?"

"Now come on," says Hilda, "don't be bitter."

"We're just funnin' you," Heidi says.

"Well," says Sam, "I'll marry somebody, but I'll be Goddamned if I'll marry *everybody*."

"One potato, two potato," Hilda says, "who do you love best?" She really wants to know the answer. She sits up in bed.

Heidi reaches for a Tab that's close to hand.

"You mean you want to know who I love best," Sam says. "Like more than the other one."

"That's the question, Daddy," says Heidi.

"Well," he says, "old Heidi is the really good-looking one, of course."

"The hell you say," says Heidi.

"But on the other hand, old Hilda is the most fun to roll around in bed with. There's just no doubt about it."

"*You pig!*" says Hilda.

He's grinning. They begin to giggle. The truth is, he loves them both, adores them both, that's why he fled to Fargo.

"We-all are going to have to leave town, you know that," he says. "I don't want any damn scandal."

"Prepare the caravan," says Hilda. "Hitch up the oxen."

"You kids think you can get work in Missoula, Montana?"

"What's the population?" asks Heidi.

"Maybe eighty-five thousand."

"We need a semi-pro symphony and at least the possibility of chamber music," Hilda says. "Check it out."

He lingers in the door.

"Tomorrow I wouldn't mind a little chili," Heidi says. She looks at her sister. "Can we eat chili?"

"This ain't right," he says. "You know that."

"We got the Blue Cross, the Red Cross, and the Star-Spangled Banner," Heidi says. "What can go wrong?"

Pandemonium

The unfortunate thing—

We learned to our chagrin that the annual games had been scheduled for the dates we had picked, with great care, for our event. Because the stars in the heavens had to dispose themselves in a certain peculiar alignment to assure the success of our project, changing the dates was impossible. We applied for relief to the sponsors of the games, but were met with a stony indifference. "Go fly a kite," they told us.

I wondered about my colleague. Wondered about his wisdom.

Doubt was not confined to any one person. Doubt was, I may say, general.

He was, and is, incorrigible. This was not the first time I had lent myself to his schemes.

I am, I do admit, fertile.

"The time in Panama—"

"The time in Paraguay—"

"But this event, having a religious character, will I submit, redeem the rest."

"He was persuaded that this event, having a religious character, would redeem the rest, sorry string of failures, farces, and calamities that had marked our history together."

"An event of such glamour and such radiance, just on the secular level even—"

"Redemption. Within our grasp."

"The ecstasy of the crowds."

"Fervor extending in every direction like a beneficent effluvium . . ."

"Blessed outflow of invisible vapor or imponderable radiation . . ."

"It was to be our first event of the year. Much thought had gone into the planning of it."

"We hoped not only to entertain, but also to instruct."

"But also to entertain. 'Production values' were never far from our minds."

"The plans were drawn on vellum."

"Twelve bloody dollars a sheet."

"I have always made my plans on vellum. If one begins to cut corners at the conceptual stage, all that follows is inevitably compromised."

"We established a subcommittee to deal with the rubber-glove salesmen who were passionate in their importunities. Sales of rubber gloves nation-wide, they said, were up four hundred percent. Why then did we not buy?"

"Semaphore and shared memory were to be the second and third principal means of communication between the 'center' and the massing hordes. Straight talk was to be the first."

"Do you think she'll really do it?"

"In no mythology anywhere does Eve refuse the apple. Our Eve would, so to say, return the apple. This was to be the first event of the event."

"Our Eve's real name was Eve."

"We sought unity. To have a real Eve appear as Eve was an advantage."

"A slight advantage."

"We thought it an advantage."

"Our Eve was, by training, an architectural draughtswoman."

"Sparkling black lines on the crispy vellum."

"Difficult to hold an argument firmly in mind while also worrying about tent pegs and the quality of the lemonade. Thus the need for a script to ensure that the higher urgencies were not neglected."

"Desperate for approbation, desperate."

"He was desperate for approbation, myself less so but still, one might say, hungry, the various blows life had showered upon me during my forty-six years of ill-considered fecklessness and ruth now . . . worn . . . faltering . . ."

"Courage."

"What?"

"Courage."

"What?"

"White chocolate."

"Then Eve informed me that she was pregnant. But, I said, you can't be. I'm too old."

"Far, far too old."

"She had been using she told me now one of the new devices. It failed."

"The oldest person in my rather wide acquaintanceship. I usually prefer youth. I made an exception, for you."

"And it was much appreciated, it was like a new lease on life. I bought a new necktie, then another. The first clashed. With itself."

"The photographer Nadar was said to know ten thousand people in Paris alone. Many of them young."

"Youth. A hoot and a half."

"For thou art Pan, thou Bacchus art, and Shepherd of bright stars!"

"I had given her a personal adornment allowance. Anything in the world she wanted so long as it was made of hair."

"They're doing some great things with hair nowadays, elephant hair, fish hair—"

"We made mistakes."

"Brilliant mistakes, frequently, of the kind only the most gifted among us can achieve."

"A light rain was threatening but did not fall."

"I gave her a bouquet, scarletina, diptherium, phthisis, sweet megrims, purple mange—"

"We were going to kill somebody right in front of them, and then bring him back to life, the regular Corn God routine, I suppose, but enlivened with certain aesthetic touches no one had ever envisioned before—"

I wondered about my colleague. Was he, perhaps, skewed in the brain?

A Picture History of the War

Kellerman, gigantic with gin, runs through the park at noon with his naked father slung under one arm. Old Kellerman covers himself with both hands and howls in the tearing wind, although sometimes he sings in the bursting sunlight. Where there is tearing wind he howls, and where there is bursting sunlight he sings. The park is empty except for a pair of young mothers in greatcoats who stand, pressed together in a rapturous embrace, near the fountain. "What are those mothers doing there," cries the general, "near the fountain?" "That is love," replies the son, "which is found everywhere, healing and beautiful." "Oh what a desire I have," cries the general, "that there might happen some great dispute among nations, some great anger, so that I might be myself again!" "Think of the wrack," replies the son. "Empty saddles, boots reversed in the stirrups, tasteful eulogies—" "I want to tell you something!" shrieks the general. "On the field where this battle was fought, I saw a very wonderful thing which the natives pointed out to me!"

On the night of the sixteenth, Wellington lingered until three in the morning in Brussels at the Duchess of Richmond's ball, sitting in the front row. "Showing himself very cheerful," according to Müffling. Then with Müffling he set out for the windmill at Brye, where they found Marshal Blücher and his staff. Kellerman, followed by the young mothers, runs out of the park and into a bar.

"Eh, hello, Mado. A Beaujolais."

"Eh, hello, Tris-Tris," the barmaid replies. She is wiping the zinc with a dirty handkerchief. "A Beaujolais?"

"Cut the sentimentality, Mado," Kellerman says. "A Beaujolais. Listen, if anybody asks for me—"

"You haven't been in."

"Thanks, Mado. You're a good sort."

Kellerman knocks back the Beaujolais, tucks his naked father under his arm, and runs out the door.

"You were rude with that woman!" the general cries. "What is the rationale?"

"It's a convention," Kellerman replies. The Belgian regiments had been tampered with. In the melee, I was almost instantly disabled in both arms, losing first my sword, and then my reins, and followed by a few men, who were presently cut down, no quarter being asked, allowed, or given, I was carried along by my horse, till, receiving a blow from a sabre, I fell senseless on my face to the ground. Kellerman runs, reading an essay by Paul Goodman in *Commentary*. His eye, caught by a line in the last paragraph ("In a viable constitution, every excess of power should structurally generate its own antidote"), has wandered back up the column of type to see what is being talked about ("I have discussed the matter with Mr. and Mrs. Beck of the Living Theatre and we agree that the following methods are tolerable").

"What's that?" calls the first mother. "On the bench there, covered with the overcoat?"

"That's my father," Kellerman replies courteously. "My dad."

"Isn't he cold?"

"Are you cold?"

"He looks cold to me!" exclaims the one in the red wrapper. "They're funny-looking, aren't they, when they get that old? They look like radishes."

"Something like radishes," Kellerman agrees. "Dirty in the vicinity of the roots, if that's what you mean."

"What does he do?" asks the one in the blue boots. "Or, rather, what did he do when he was of an age?"

Kellerman falls to his knees in front of the bench. "Bless me, Father, for I have sinned. I committed endoarchy two times, melanicity four times, encropatomy seven times, and preprocity with igneous intent, pretolemicity, and overt cranialism once each."

"Within how long a period?"

"Since Monday."

"Did you enjoy it?"

"Which?"

"Any of it."

"Some of it. Melanicity in the afternoon promotes a kind of limited joy."

"Have you left anything out?"

"A great deal." On the field where this battle was fought I saw a very wonderful thing which the natives pointed out to me. The bones of the slain lie scattered upon the field in two lots, those of the Persians in one place by themselves, those of the Egyptians in another place apart from them. If, then, you strike the Persian skulls, even with a pebble, they are so weak, that you break a hole in them; but the Egyptian skulls are so strong, that you may smite them with a stone and you will scarcely break them in.

"Oh what a desire I have," cried the general, "that my son would, like me, jump out of airplanes into aggressor terrain and find farmers with pitchforks poised to fork him as he drifts into the trees! And the farmer's dog, used for chivying sheep usually—how is it possible that I have a son who does not know the farmer's dog? And then calling out in the night to find the others, voices in the night, it's incredibly romantic. I gave him a D-ring for a teething toy and threw him up in the air, higher than any two-year-old had ever been, and put him on the mantel, and said, 'Jump, you little bastard,' and he jumped, and I caught him—this when I was only a captain and chairman of the Machine Gun Committee at Benning. He had expensive green-gold grenadiers from F.A.O. Schwarz and a garrote I made myself from the E flat on his mother's piano. Firefights at dusk on the back lawn at Leonard Wood. Superior numbers in the shower room. Give them a little more grape, Captain Gregg, under the autumnal moon."

"Now, Agnes, don't start crying! We better go see Uncle René all together right away, and he'll explain anything you need to know."

"Interesting point of view," the ladies remarked. "Does he know anything about skin?"

"Everything."

Touched by the wind, the general howls.

"He was a jumping general," Kellerman explains to the ladies, "who jumped out of airplanes with his men to fall on the aggressor rear with sudden surprise and great hurt to that rear. He jumped in Sicily with the One-Oh-Bloody-One Airborne. The German cemetery at Pomezia has 27,400 graves," Kellerman declares. "What could he have been thinking of, on the way down? Compare if you will the scene with the scene at the battle of Borodino, at the battle of Arbela, at the battle of Metaurus, at the battle of Châlons, at the battle of Pultowa, at the battle of Valmy—"

"Eh, hello, Mado. A Beaujolais."

"Eh, hello, Tris-Tris. A Beaujolais?"

"Listen, Mado, if anybody asks for me—"

"You haven't been in."

"Bless me, Father, for I have sinned. I wanted to say a certain thing to a certain man, a certain true thing that had crept into my head. I opened my head, at the place provided, and proceeded to pronounce the true thing that lay languishing there—that is, proceeded to propel that trueness, that felicitous trularity, from its place inside my head out into world life. The certain man stood waiting to receive it. His face reflected an eager acceptingness. Everything was right. I propelled, using my mind, my mouth, all my muscles. I propelled. I propelled and propelled. I felt that trularity inside my head moving slowly through the passage provided (stained like the caves of Lascaux with garlic, antihistamines, Berlioz, a history, a history) toward its début on the world stage. Past my teeth, with their little brown sweaters knitted of gin and cigar smoke, toward its leap to critical scrutiny. Past my lips, with their tendency to flake away in cold weather—

"Father, I have a few questions to ask you. Just a few questions about things that have been bothering me lately." In the melee, I was almost instantly disabled in both arms. Losing first my sword, and then my reins. And followed by a few men, who were presently cut down, no quarter being asked, allowed, or given, I was carried along by my horse, till—"Who is fit for marriage? What is the art of love? What physical or mental ailments can be hereditary? What is the best age for marriage? Should marriage be postponed until the husband alone can support a family? Should a person who is sterile marry? What is sterility? How do the male reproductive organs work? Is a human egg like a bird's? What is a false pregnancy? What is artificial insemination? What happens if the sex glands are removed? In the male? In the female? Is it possible to tell if a person is emotionally fit for marriage? Why are premarital medical examinations important? What is natural childbirth? What is the best size for a family? Can interfaith marriages be successful? Can a couple know in advance if they can have children? Are there any physical standards to follow in choosing a mate? How soon after conception can a woman tell if she is pregnant? What is the special function of the sex hormones? What are the causes of barrenness? How reliable are the various contraceptive devices? If near relatives marry will their children be abnormal? Do the first sex experiences have a really important bearing upon marital adjustment? Can impotence be cured? Can the sex of a child be predicted? How often should intercourse be practiced? How long should it last? Should you turn out the lights? Should music be played? Is our culture sick? Is a human egg like a bird's?"

Kellerman stops at the ginstore. "We can't use any of those," the ginstoreman says. "Those whatever-it-ises you've got under your arm there."

"That's my dad," Kellerman says. "Formerly known as the Hammer of Thor. Now in reduced circumstances."

"I thought it was radishes," the ginstoreman says. "A bunch of radishes."

Kellerman kneels on the floor of the ginstore. "Bless me, Father, for I have sinned. That one was venial. But in respect to mortal sins, I would announce the following sins. Their mortalaciousness will not disappoint, is in fact so patent, so demonstrable, that the meanest confessor would, with a shy wave of the hand, accept and forgive them, in the manner of a customs inspector running his hand generously, forgivingly around the inside of a Valpak presented by a pretty girl."

"What do *you* do?" the mothers ask. "You yourself."

"I'm a bridge expert," Kellerman says kindly. "The father of a book on the subject, *Greater Bridge,* which attempts to make complex the simple, so that we will not be bored. A Bible of bridge, if you take my meaning. Some of our boys carried it in the pockets over their hearts during the war. As they dropped through the air. Singing 'Johnny Got a Zero.'" All deliriously pretty and sexy mothers in brawny Chanel tweeds. Black-and-white hound's-tooth checks, say; black-and-white silk Paisley blouses; gleaming little pairs of white kidskin gloves. Very correct hang to the jackets. Short skirts with a clochelike slide over the hip, lots of action at the hemline—couldn't be better. Café-ed mouths, shiny orange-brown cheeks, ribbons of green enamel eye makeup. Mrs. Subways.

"I'm cold," old Kellerman says.

"Cold," the ladies remark, pointing.

Kellerman pulls out his flask. "Winter gin," he says, "it absumeth the geniture."

"Say something professional," the ladies request.

"♠6 ♥KQJ94 ♦AK85 ♣KQ2," Kellerman says.

On the third, Hood's main army was in the neighborhood of Lost Mountain. Stewart's Corps was sent to strike the railway north of Marietta and to capture, if possible, Allatoona. Stewart, on the morning of the fifth, rejoined Hood, having destroyed two small posts on the railroad and having left French's division to capture Allatoona and destroy the Etowah Bridge. The Army of the Cumberland led the pursuit, and on the evening of the fourth it was bivouacking at the foot of Kenesaw Mountain. "And many others," Kellerman says. "Just as steamy and sordid as that one. Each sin preserved in amber in the vaults of the Library of Congress, under the management of the Registrar of Copyrights."

"With all the sticky details?"

"Rife with public hair," Kellerman says, "just to give you a whiff of the sordidness possible since the perfection of modern high-speed offset lithography."

"O sin," exclaims the general from his bench, "in which fear and guilt encrandulate (or are encrandulated by) each other to mess up the real world of objects with a film of nastiness and dirt, how well I understand you! Standing there! How well I understand your fundamental motifs! How ill I understand my fundamental motifs! Why are objects preferable to parables? How did I get so old so suddenly? In what circumstances is confusion a virtue? Why have I never heard of Yusef Lateef? (1) On flute, Lateef creates a completely distinctive sound—sensitive, haunting, but filled with a firm and passionate strength unequalled among jazz flutists. (2) On tenor saxophone, Yusef is again thoroughly and excitingly individual, combining brilliantly modern conception with a big, deep, compellingly full-throated tone. (3) The oboe, as played by Lateef, undergoes a startling transformation into a valid jazz instrument, wailing with a rich and fervently funky blues quality. (4) What is 'wailing'? What is 'funky'? Why does language subvert me, subvert my seniority, my medals, my oldness, whenever it gets a chance? What does language have against me—me that has been good to it, respecting its little peculiarities and nicilosities, for sixty years? (5) What do 'years' have against me? Why have they stuck stones in my kidneys, devaluated my tumulosity, retracted my hair? (6) Where does 'hair' go when it dies?"

Kellerman is eating one of his fifty-two-cent lunches: a 4½ oz. can of Sells Liver Pâté (thirty-one cents) and a box of Nabisco Saltines (twenty-one cents), washed down with the last third of a bottle of leftover Chablis. He lifts the curiously ugly orange wineglass, one of four (the fourth destroyed in the dishwasher) sent to Noëlie at Christmas by her Oregon aunt. He is reading an essay by Paul Goodman in *Commentary*. His eye, caught by a line in the last paragraph ("In a viable constitution, every excess of power should structurally generate its own antidote"), has wandered back up the page to see what is being talked about ("I have discussed the matter with

Mr. and Mrs. Beck of the Living Theatre and we agree that the following methods are tolerable"). He nicks the little hump of pâté
with the sharp edge of a Saltine. He congratulates himself on the
economical elegance of the meal. Gregg meantime has attacked Fitzhugh Lee on the Louisa Courthouse road and has driven him back
some distance, pursuing until nightfall. Near one of the hedges of
the Hougoumont farm, without even a drummer to beat the *rappel,*
we succeeded in rallying under the enemy's fire 300 men; I made a
villager act as our guide, and bound him by his arm to my stirrup.

Kellerman stands before a chalkboard with a long wooden pointer
in his hand. The general has been folded into a schoolchild's desk,
sitting in the front row. On the board, in chalk, there is a diagram-
matic sketch of a suit of armor. Kellerman points.

"A.: *Palette.*"

"Palette," the old man repeats.

"Covers the shoulder joint," Kellerman says.

"The armpit?" the old man suggests.

"The shoulder joint," Kellerman says.

"Are you certain?"

"Absolutely."

The general writes in his tablet.

Kellerman points. "B.: *Breastplate.*"

His father scribbles.

"Covers the—"

"Breast," old Kellerman says.

"Chest," Kellerman says.

"Mustard plaster," the old man says. "Trying to break up the clog
in your little lung. Your mother and I. All through the night. Tears
in her eyes. The doctor forty miles away."

"C.: *Tasset.*"

"Semolina pudding you wanted, 'No,' I said. 'Later,' I said. 'Bad
for the gut,' I said. You cried and cried."

"*Tasset,*" Kellerman repeats. "For the upper thigh. Suspended
from the waistplate by straps."

"Strap. Ah, strap!"

"D.: *Cuisse.*"

"I was good with the strap. Fast, but careful. Not too much, not too little. Calculating the angles, wind velocity, air-spring density, time of day. My windup a perfect hyperbolic paraboloid."

"Covers the thigh proper," Kellerman says. "Fastened by means of—"

"Strap," the general says, with satisfaction. "Unpleasant duty. When in the course of human events it becomes necessary—"

"*You loved it!*" Kellerman says, shouting.

The Belgian regiments had been tampered with. In the melee, I was almost instantly disabled in both arms, losing first my sword, and then my reins, and followed by a few men, who were presently cut down, no quarter being asked, allowed, or given, I was carried along by my horse, till, receiving a blow from a sabre, I fell senseless on my face to the ground. Germany was unspeakably silly. Technically, I was a radar operator on the guidance system. It was a rotten job. Ten hours a day of solid boredom. I did get one trip to the wild Hebrides for the annual firing of the missile (it's called a Corporal). Confidentially, it doesn't work worth a damn. We have a saying: Its effective range is thirty-five feet—its length. If it falls on you, it can be lethal. "There are worms in words!" the general cries. "The worms in words are, like Mexican jumping beans, agitated by the warmth of the mouth."

"Flaming gel," Kellerman says. "You were fond of flaming gel."

"Not overfond," the general replies. "Not like some of them."

"What's that you have there, under you arm?" asks the bookstoreman.

"The Black Knight," Kellerman says. "I want one of those Histomaps of Evolution that you have in the window there, showing the swelling of the unsegmented worms—flatworms, ribbon worms, arrow worms, wheelworms, spring heads, and so forth."

"Worms in words," the general repeats, "agitated by the warmth of the mouth."

"I'm not accepting any more blame, Papa," Kellerman says finally. "Blame wouldn't melt in my . . ." He hands round the pâté. "I love playing with mugged-up cards," Kellerman says, to the nearest mother. She is wearing a slim sand-tweed coat with two rows of gilt buttons and carrying a matchbook that says (black lettering, rose-blush ground) "VD Is On the Rise In New York City." "The four of fans, the twelve of wands, the deuce of kidneys, the Jack of Brutes. And shaved decks and readers of various kinds, they make the game worthy of the name." And it was true that his wife pulled one hair out of his sleeping head each night, but what if she decided upon two, or five, or even eleven?

Of those who remained and fought, none were so rudely handled as the Chians, who displayed prodigies of valor, and disdained to play the part of cowards. The order and harmony of the universe, what a beautiful idea! He was obsessed by a vision of beauty—the shimmering, golden Temple, more fascinating than a woman, more eternal than love. And because he was ugly, evil, impotent, he determined someday to possess it . . . by destruction. He had used the word incorrectly. He had mispronounced the word. He had misspelled the word. It was the wrong word.

"Eh, hello, Mado. A Beaujolais."

"Eh, hello, Tris-Tris. A Beaujolais?"

Kellerman runs down the avenue, among the cars, in and out. There are sirens, there is a fire. The huge pieces of apparatus clog the streets. Hoses are run this way and that. Hundreds of firemen stand about, looking at each other, asking each other questions. Kellerman runs. There is a fire somewhere, but the firemen do not know where it is. They stand, gigantic in their black slickers, yellow-lined, their black hats covering the back of the neck, holding shovels. The street is full of firemen, gigantic, standing there. Kellerman runs up to a group of firemen, who look at him with frightened eyes. He begins asking them questions. "Should a person who is sterile marry? What is sterility? What is a false pregnancy? How do the male reproductive organs work? What is natural childbirth? Can a couple know in advance if they can have children? Can impotence be cured? What are the causes of barrenness? Is a human egg like a bird's?"

The Police Band

I t was kind of the department to think up the Police Band. The original impulse, I believe, was creative and humanitarian. A better way of doing things. Unpleasant, bloody things required by the line of duty. Even if it didn't work out.

The Commissioner (the old Commissioner, not the one they have now) brought us up the river from Detroit. Where our members had been, typically, working the Sho Bar two nights a week. Sometimes the Glass Crutch. Friday and Saturday. And the rest of the time wandering the streets disguised as postal employees. Bitten by dogs and burdened with third-class mail.

What are our duties? we asked at the interview. Your duties are to wail, the Commissioner said. That only. We admired our new dark-blue uniforms as we came up the river in canoes like Indians. We plan to use you in certain situations, certain tense situations, to alleviate tensions, the Commissioner said. I can visualize great success with this new method. And would you play "Entropy." He was pale, with a bad liver.

We are subtle, the Commissioner said, never forget that. Subtlety is what has previously been lacking in our line. Some of the old ones, the Commissioner said, all they know is the club. He took a little pill from a little box and swallowed it with his Scotch.

When we got to town we looked at those Steve Canyon recruiting posters and wondered if we resembled them. Henry Wang, the bass man, looks like a Chinese Steve Canyon, right? The other cops were friendly in a suspicious way. They liked to hear us wail, however.

The Police Band is a very sensitive highly trained and ruggedly anti-Communist unit whose efficacy will be demonstrated in due time, the Commissioner said to the Mayor (the old Mayor). The Mayor took a little pill from a little box and said, We'll see. He could tell we were musicians because we were holding our instruments, right? Emptying spit valves, giving the horn that little shake. Or coming in at letter E with some sly emotion stolen from another life.

The old Commissioner's idea was essentially that if there was a disturbance on the city's streets—some ethnic group cutting up some other ethnic group on a warm August evening—the Police Band would be sent in. The handsome dark-green band bus arriving with sirens singing, red lights whirling. Hard-pressed men on the beat in their white hats raising a grateful cheer. We stream out of the vehicle holding our instruments at high port. A skirmish line fronting the angry crowd. And play "Perdido." The crowd washed with new and true emotion. Startled, they listen. Our emotion stronger than their emotion. A triumph of art over good sense.

That was the idea. The old Commissioner's *musical* ideas were not very interesting, because after all he was a cop, right? But his police ideas were interesting.

We had drills. Poured out of that mother-loving bus onto vacant lots holding our instruments at high port like John Wayne. Felt we were heroes already. Playing "Perdido," "Stumblin'," "Gin Song," "Feebles." Laving the terrain with emotion stolen from old busted-up loves, broken marriages, the needle, economic deprivation. A few old ladies leaning out of high windows. Our emotion washing rusty Rheingold cans and parts of old doors.

This city is too much! We'd be walking down the street talking about our techniques and we'd see out of our eyes a woman standing in the gutter screaming to herself about what we could not imagine. A drunk trying to strangle a dog somebody'd left leashed to a parking meter. The drunk and the dog screaming at each other. This city is too much!

We had drills and drills. It is true that the best musicians come from Detroit but there is something here that you have to get in your playing and that is simply the scream. We got that. The Commissioner, a sixty-three-year-old hippie with no doubt many graft qualities and unpleasant qualities, nevertheless understood that. When we'd play "ugly," he understood that. He understood the rising expectations of the world's peoples also. That our black members didn't feel like toting junk mail around Detroit forever until the ends of their lives. For some strange reason.

He said one of our functions would be to be sent out to play in places where people were trembling with fear inside their houses, right? To inspirit them in difficult times. This was the plan. We set up in the street. Henry Wang grabs hold of his instrument. He has a four-bar lead-in all by himself. Then the whole group. The iron shutters raised a few inches. Shorty Alanio holding his horn at his characteristic angle (sideways). The reeds dropping lacy little fill-ins behind him. We're cooking. The crowd roars.

The Police Band was an idea of a very romantic kind. The Police Band was an idea that didn't work. When they retired the old Commissioner (our Commissioner), who it turned out had a little drug problem of his own, they didn't let us even drill anymore. We have never been used. His idea was a romantic idea, they said (right?), which was not adequate to the rage currently around in the world. Rage must be met with rage, they said. (Not in so many words.) We sit around the precinct houses, under the filthy lights, talking about our techniques. But I thought it might be good if you knew that the Department still has us. We have a good group. We still have emotion to be used. We're still here.

The Sea of Hesitation

I f Jackson had pressed McClellan in White Oak Swamp," Francesca said. "If Longstreet had proceeded vigorously on the first day at Second Manassas. If we had had the forty thousand pairs of shoes we needed when we entered Maryland. If Bloss had not found the envelope containing the two cigars and the copy of Lee's Secret Order No. 191 at Frederick. If the pneumonia had not taken Jackson. If Ewell had secured possession of Cemetery Heights on the first day of Gettysburg. If Pickett's charge . . . If Early's march into the Valley . . . If we had had sufficient food for our troops at Petersburg. If our attack on Fort Stedman had succeeded. If Pickett and Fitzhugh Lee had not indulged in a shad bake at Five Forks. If there had been stores and provisions as promised at Amelia Court House. If Ewell had not been captured at Saylor's Creek together with sixteen artillery pieces and four hundred wagons. If Lee had understood Lincoln—his mind, his larger intentions. If there had been a degree of competence in our civilian administration equal to that exhibited by the military. Then, perhaps, matters would have been brought to a happier conclusion."

"Yes," I said.

Francesca is slightly obsessed. But one must let people talk about what they want to talk about. One must let people do what they want to do.

This morning in the mail I received an abusive letter from a woman in Prague.

Dear Greasy Thomas:
You cannot understand what a pig you are. You are a pig, you idiot. You think you understand things but there is nothing you understand, nothing, idiot pig-swine. You have not wisdom and you have no discretion and nothing can be done without wisdom and discretion. How did a pig-cretin like yourself ever wriggle into life? Why do you exist still, vulgar swine? If you don't think I'm going to inform the government of your inappropriate continued existence, a stain on the country's face . . . You can expect Federal Marshals in clouds very soon, cretin-hideous-swine, and I will laugh as they haul you away in their green vans, ugly toad. You know nothing about anything, garbage-face, and the idea that you would dare "think" for others (I know you are not capable of "feeling") is so wildly outrageous that I would laugh out loud if I were not sick of your importunate posturing, egregious fraud-pig. You are not even an honest pig which is at least of some use in the world, you are rather an ocean of pig-dip poisoning everything you touch. I do not like you at all.
     Love,
     Jinka

I read the letter twice. She is certainly angry. But one must let people do what they want to do.

I work for the City. In the Human Effort Administration. My work consists of processing applications. People apply for all sorts of things. I approve all applications and buck them upwards, where they are usually disapproved. Upstairs they do not agree with me, that people should not be permitted to do what they want to do. Upstairs they have different ideas. But "different ideas" are welcomed, in my particular cosmos.

Before I worked for the City I was interested in changing behavior. I thought behavior could be changed. I had a B.A. in psychology, was working on an M.A. I was into sensory deprivation. I did sensory deprivation studies for a while at McGill and later at Princeton.

At McGill we inhabited the basement of Taub Hall, believed to be the first building in the world devoted exclusively to the study of hatred. But we were not studying hatred, we were doing black-box work and the hatred people kindly lent us their basement. I was in charge of the less intelligent subjects (the subjects were divided into less intelligent and more intelligent). I spent two years in the basement of Taub Hall and learned many interesting things.

The temperature of the head does not decrease in sleep. The temperature of the rest of the body does.

There I sat for weeks on end monitoring subjects who had half Ping-Pong balls taped over their eyes and a white-noise generator at 40db singing in their ears. I volunteered as a subject and, gratified at being assigned to the "more intelligent" group, spent many many hours in the black-box with half Ping-Pong balls taped over my eyes and the white-noise generator emitting its obliterating whine/ whisper. Although I had some intricate Type 4 hallucinations, nothing much else happened to me. Except . . . I began to wonder if behavior *should be* changed. That there was "behavior" at all seemed to me a small miracle.

I pondered going on to stress theory, wherein one investigates the ways in which the stressed individual reacts to stress, but decided suddenly to do something else instead. I decided to take a job with the Human Effort Administration and to try, insofar as possible, to let people do what they want to do.

I am aware that my work is, in many ways, meaningless.

A call from Honor, my ex-wife. I've promised her a bed for her new apartment.

"Did you get it?"

"Not yet."

"Why not?"

"I've been busy. Doing things."

"But what about the bed?"

"I told you I'd take care of it."

"Yes but when?"

"Some people can get their own beds for their new apartments."

"But that's not the point. You promised."

"That was in the first flush of good feeling and warmth. When you said you were coming back to town."

"Now you don't have any good feeling and warmth?"

"Full of it. Brimming. How's Sam?"

"He's getting tired of sleeping on the couch. It's not big enough for both of us."

"My heart cries out for him."

She's seeing Sam now, that's a little strange. She didn't seem to take to him, early on.

Sam. What's he like? Like a villain. Hair like an oil spill, mustache like a twist of carbon paper, high white lineless forehead, black tights and doublet, dagger clasped in treacherous right hand, sneaks when he's not slithering . . .

No. That's incompletely true. Sam's just like the rest of us: jeans, turtleneck, beard, smile with one chipped tooth, good with children, backward in his taxes, a degree in education, a B. Ed. And he came with the very best references too, Charlotte doted, Francine couldn't get enough, Mary Jo chased him through Grand Central with the great whirling loop of her lariat, causing talk—But Honor couldn't really see him, in the beginning. She's reconsidered. I wish she hadn't thrown the turntable on the floor, a $600 B & O, but all that's behind us now.

I saw this morning that the building at the end of the street's been sold. It stood empty for years, an architectural anomaly, three-storied, brick, but most of all, triangular. Two streets come together in a point there, and prospective buyers must have boggled at the angles. I judged that the owners decided to let morality go and sold to a *ménage à trios*. They'll need a triple bed, customized to fit those odd corners. I can see them with protractor and Skilsaw, getting the thing just right. Then sweeping up the bedcrumbs.

She telephones again.

"It doesn't have to be the best bed in the world. Any old bed will do. Sam's bitching all night long."

"For you, dear friend, I'll take every pain. We're checking now in Indonesia, a rare albino bed's been sighted there . . ."

"Tom, this isn't funny. I slept in the bathtub last night."

"You're too long for the bathtub."

"Do you want Sam to do it?

Do I want Sam to do it?

"No. I'll do it."

"Then *do* it."

We were content for quite a while, she taught me what she'd majored in, a lovely Romance tongue, we visited the country and when I'd ask in a pharmacy for a razor they'd give me rosewater. I'm teasing her, and she me. She wants Sam. That's good.

Francesca was reading to me.

"This is the note Lee wrote," she said. "Listen. 'No one is more aware than myself of my inability for the duties of my position. I cannot even accomplish what I myself desire. How can I fulfill the expectations of others? In addition I sensibly feel the growing failure of my bodily strength. I have not yet recovered from the attack I experienced the past spring. I am becoming more and more incapable of exertion, and am thus prevented from making the personal examinations and giving the personal supervision to the operations in the field which I feel to be necessary. I am so dull making use of the eyes of others I am frequently misled. Everything, therefore, points to the advantages to be derived from a new commander. A younger and abler man than myself can readily be obtained. I know that he will have as gallant and brave an army as ever existed to second his efforts, and it would be the happiest day of my life to see at its head a worthy . . .'"

Francesca stopped reading.

"That was *Robert E. Lee*," she said.

"Yes," I said.

"The leader of all the armies of the Confederacy," she said.

"I know."

"I wanted him to win. So much."

"I understand."

"But he did not."

"I have read about it."

Francesca has Confederate-gray eyes which reflect, mostly, a life-long contemplation of the nobility of Lee's great horse, Traveller. I left Francesca and walked in the park, where I am afraid to walk, after dark. One must let people do what they want to do, but what if they want to slap you upside the head with a Stillson wrench and take the credit cards out of your pockets? A problem.

The poor are getting poorer. I saw a poor man and asked him if he had any money.

"Money?" he said. "Money thinks I died a long time ago."

We have moved from the Age of Anxiety to the Age of Fear. This is of course progress, psychologically speaking. I intend no irony.

Another letter from Jinka.

Undear Thomas:
The notion that only man is vile must have been invented to describe you, vile friend. I cannot contain the revulsion that whelms in me at the sight of your name, in the Prague telephone book, from your time in Prague. I have scratched it out of my copy, and scratched it out of all the copies I could get my hands on, in telephone booths everywhere. This symbolic removal of you from the telephone booths of our ancient city should not escape your notice, stinking meat. You have been erased and the anointment of the sick, formerly known as Extreme Unction, also as the Last Rites, is what I have in mind for you, soon. Whatever you are doing, stop it, drear pig. The insult to consciousness afforded by your project, whatever it is, cannot be suffered gladly, and I for one do not intend to so suffer. I have measures not yet in the books, and will take them. What I have in mind is not shallots and fresh rosemary, gutless wonder, and your continued association with that ridiculously thin Robert E. Lee girl has not raised you in my esteem, not a bit. One if by land and two if by sea, and it will be sudden, I promise you. Be afraid.

   Cordially,
   Jinka

I put this letter with the others, clipped together with a paper clip. How good writing such letters must make her feel!

Wittgenstein was I think wrong when he said that about that which we do not know, we should not speak. He closed by fiat a great amusement park, there. Nothing gives me more pleasure than speaking about that which I do not know. I am not sure whether my ideas about various matters are correct or incorrect, but speak about them I must.

I decided to call my brother in San Francisco. He is a copy editor on the *San Francisco Chronicle* (although he was trained as a biologist—he is doing what he wants to do, more or less). Because we are both from the South our conversations tend to be conducted in jiveass dialect.

"Hey," I said.

"Hey," he said.

"What's happening? You got any girl copy boys on that newspaper yet?"

"Man," Paul said, "we got not only girl copy boys we got *topless* girl copy boys. We gonna hire us a reporter next week. They promised us."

"That's wonderful," I said. "How are you feeling?"

"I'm depressed."

"Is it specific or nonspecific?"

"Well," Paul said, "I have to read the paper a lot. I'm ready to drop the bomb. On us."

One must let people do what they want to do. Fortunately my brother has little to say about when and where the bomb will be dropped.

My other friend is Catherine. Catherine, like Francesca, is hung up on the past. She is persuaded that in an earlier existence she was Balzac's mistress (one of Balzac's mistresses).

"I endured Honoré's grandness," she said, "because it was spurious. Spurious grandness I understand very well. What I could not understand was his hankering for greatness."

"But he *was* great," I said.

"I was impatient with all those artists, sitting around, hankering for greatness. Of course Honoré was great. But he didn't know, at the time, for sure. Or he did and he didn't. There were moments of doubt, depression."

"As is natural."

"The seeking after greatness," said Catherine, "is a sickness, in my opinion. It is like greed, only greed has better results. Greed can at least bring you a fine house on a grand avenue, and strawberries for breakfast, in a rich cream, and servants to beat, when they do not behave. I *prefer* greed. Honoré was greedy, in a reasonable way, but what he was mostly interested in was greatness. I was stuck with greatness."

"Yes," I said.

"You," Catherine said, "are neither great nor greedy."

"One must let people be—" I began.

"Yes," Catherine said, "that sounds good, on the surface, but thinking it through—" She finished her espresso, placed the little cup precisely on the little saucer. "Take me out," she said. "Take me to a library."

We went to a library and spent a pleasant afternoon there.

Francesca was stroking the brown back of a large spayed cat—the one that doesn't like me.

"Lee was not without his faults," she said. "Not for a moment would I have you believe that he was faultless."

"What was his principal fault?"

"Losing," she said.

I went to the Art Cinema and saw a Swedish film about a man living alone on an island. Somebody was killing a great many sheep on the island and the hero, a hermit, was suspected. There were a great many shots of sheep with their throats cut, red blood on the white snow, glimpses. The hermit fixed a car for a woman whose car had broken down. They went to bed together. There were flashbacks having to do with the woman's former husband, a man in a wheelchair.

273

It was determined that somebody else, not the hermit, had been killing the sheep. The film ended with a car crash in which the woman was killed. Whiteout.

Should great film artists be allowed to do what they want to do?

Catherine is working on her translation of the complete works of Balzac. Honoré, she insists, has never been properly translated. She will devote her life to the task, she says. Actually I have looked at some pages of her *Louis Lambert* and they seem to me significantly worse than the version I read in college. I think of Balzac in the great statue by Rodin, holding his erect (possibly overstated) cock in both hands under his cloak of bronze. An inspiration.

When I was in the black box, during my SD days, there was nothing I wanted to do. I didn't even want to get out. Or perhaps there was one thing I wanted to do: Sit in the box with the half Ping-Pong balls taped over my eyes and the white-noise generator standing in for the sirens of Ulysses (himself an early SD subject) and permit the Senator Investigator (Dr. Colcross, the one with the bad leg) to do what *he* wanted to do.

Is this will-lessness, finally? Abulia, as we call it in the trade? I don't think so.

I pursue Possibility. That's something.

There is no moment that exceeds in beauty that moment when one looks at a woman and finds that she is looking at you in the same way that you are looking at her. The moment in which she bestows that look that says, "Proceed with your evil plan, sumbitch." The initial smash on glance. Then, the drawing near. This takes a long time, it seems like months, although only minutes pass, in fact. Languor is the word that describes this part of the process. Your persona floats toward her persona, over the Sea of Hesitation. Many weeks pass before they meet, but the weeks are days, or seconds. Still, everything is decided. You have slept together in the glance.

She takes your arm and you leave the newsstand, walking very close together, so that your side brushes her side lightly. Desire is here a very strong factor, because you are weak with it, and the woman is too, if she has any sense at all (but of course she is a sensible woman, and brilliant and witty and hungry as well). So, on the side-walk outside the newsstand, you stand for a moment thinking about where to go, at eleven o'clock in the morning, and here it is, in the sunlight, that you take the first good look at her, and she at you, to see if either one has any hideous blemish that has been over-looked, in the first rush of good feeling. There are none. None. No blemishes (except those spiritual blemishes that will be discovered later, after extended acquaintance, and which none of us are with-out, but which are now latent? dormant? in any case, not visible on the surface, at this time). Everything is fine. And so, with renewed confidence, you being to walk, and to seek a place where you might sit down, and have a drink, and talk a bit, and fall into each other's eyes, temporarily, and find some pretzels, and have what is called a conversation, and tell each other what you think is true about the world, and speak of the strange places where each of you has been (Surinam, in her case, where she bought the belt she is wearing, Lima in your case, where you contracted telegraph fever), and make arrangements for your next meeting (both of you drinking Scotch and water, at eleven in the morning, and you warm to her because of her willingness to leave her natural mid-morning track, for you), and make, as I say, arrangements for your next meeting, which must be this very night! or you both will die—

There is no particular point to any of this behavior. Or: This behavior is only behavior which has point. Or: There is some point to this behavior but this behavior is not the only behavior which has point. Which is true? Truth is greatly overrated, volition where it exists must be protected, wanting itself can be obliterated, some people have forgotten how to want.

The Mothball Fleet

It was early morning, just after dawn, in fact. The mothball fleet was sailing down the Hudson. Grayish-brown shrouds making odd shapes at various points on the superstructures. I counted forty destroyers, four light cruisers, two heavy cruisers, and a carrier. A fog lay upon the river.

I went aboard as the fleet reached the Narrows. I noticed a pair of jeans floating on the surface of the water, stiff with paint. I abandoned my small outboard and jumped for the ladder of the dead destroyer.

There was no one on deck. All of the gun mounts and some pieces of special equipment were coated with a sort of plastic webbing, which had a slightly repellent feeling when touched. I watched my empty Pacemaker bobbing in the heavy wake of the fleet. I called out. "Hello! Hello!"

Behind us, the vessels were disposed in fleet formation—the carrier in the center, the two heavy cruisers before and behind her, the destroyer screen correctly placed in relation to the cruisers, or as much so as the width of the channel would allow. We were making, I judged, ten to twelve knots.

There was no other traffic on the water; this I thought strange.

It was now about 6:30; the fog was breaking up, a little. I decided to climb to the bridge. I entered the wheelhouse; there was no one at the wheel. I took the wheel in my hands, tried to turn it a point or two, experimentally; it was locked in place.

A man entered from the chartroom behind me. He immediately walked over to me and removed my hands from the wheel.

He wore a uniform, but it seemed more a steward's or barman's dress than a naval officer's. His face was not unimpressive: dark hair carefully brushed, a strong nose, good mouth and chin. I judged him to be in his late fifties. He re-entered the chartroom. I followed him.

"May I ask where this . . ."

"Mothball fleet," he supplied.

"—is bound?"

He did not answer my question. He was looking at a chart.

"If it's a matter of sealed orders or something . . ."

"No no," he said, without looking up. "Nothing like that." Then he said, "A bit careless with your little boat, aren't you?"

This made me angry. "Not normally. On the contrary. But something—"

"Of course," he said. "You were anticipated. Why d'you think that ladder wasn't secured?"

I thought about this for a moment. I decided to shift the ground of the conversation slightly.

"Are there crews aboard the other ships?"

"No," he said. I felt however that he had appreciated my shrewdness in guessing that there were no crews aboard the other ships.

"Radio?" I asked. "Remote control or something?"

"Something like that," he said.

The forty destroyers, four light cruisers, two heavy cruisers, and the carrier were moving in perfect formation toward the open sea. The sight was a magnificent one. I had been in the Navy—two years as a supply officer in New London, principally.

"Is this a test of some kind?" I asked. "New equipment or—"

"You're afraid that we'll be used for target practice? Hardly." He seemed momentarily amused.

"No. But ship movements on this scale—"

"It was difficult," he said. He then walked out of the chartroom and seated himself in one of the swivel chairs on posts in front of the bridge windows. I followed him.

"May I ask your rank?"

"Why not ask my name?"

"All right."

"I am the Admiral."

I looked again at his uniform which suggested no such thing.

"Objectively," he said, smiling slightly.

"My name is—" I began.

"I am not interested in your name," he said. "I am only interested in your behavior. As you can see, I have at my disposal forty-seven brigs, of which the carrier's is the most comfortable. Not that I believe you will behave other than correctly. At the moment, I want you to do this: Go down to the galley and make a pot of coffee. Make sandwiches. You may make one for yourself. Then bring them here." He settled back in his seat and regarded the calm, even sea.

"All right," I said. "Yes."

"You will say: 'Yes, sir,'" he corrected me.

"Yes, sir."

I wandered about the destroyer until I found the galley. I made the coffee and sandwiches and returned with them to the bridge.

The "Admiral" drank his coffee silently. Seabirds made passes at the mast where the radar equipment, I saw, was covered with the same plastic material that enclosed the gun installations.

"What is that stuff used for the mothballing?" I asked.

"It's a polyvinylchloride solution which also contains vinyl acetate," he said. "It's sprayed on and then hardens. If you were to cut it open you'd find inside, around the equipment, four or five small cloth bags containing silicate of soda in crystals, to absorb moisture. A very neat system. It does just what it's supposed to do, keeps the equipment good as new."

He had finished his sandwich. A bit of mustard had soiled the sleeve of his white coat, which had gold epaulets. I thought again that he most resembled not an admiral but a man from whom one would order drinks.

"What is your mission?" I asked, determined not to be outfaced by a man with mustard on his coat.

"To be at sea," he said.

"Only that?"

"Think a bit," he said. "Think first of shipyards. Think of hundreds of thousands of men in shipyards, on both coasts, building these ships. Think of the welders, the pipefitters, the electricians, naval architects, people in the Bureau of the Budget. Think of the launchings, each with its bottle of champagne on a cord of plaited ribbons hurled at the bow by the wife of some high official. Think of the first sailors coming aboard, the sea trials, the captains for whom a particular ship was a first command. Each ship has a history, no ship is without its history. Think of the six-inch guns shaking a particular ship as they were fired, the jets leaving the deck of the carrier at tightly spaced intervals, the maneuvering of the cruisers during this or that engagement, the damage taken. Think of each ship's log faithfully kept over the years, think of the Official Naval History which now runs, I am told, to three hundred some-odd very large volumes.

"And then," he said, "think of each ship moving up the Hudson, or worse, being towed, to a depot in New Jersey where it is covered with this disgusting plastic substance. Think of the years each ship has spent moored next to other ships of its class, painted, yes, at scheduled times, by a crew of painters whose task it is to paint these ships eternally, finished with one and on to the next and back to the first again five years later. Watchmen watching the ships, year in and year out, no doubt knocking off a little copper pipe here and there—"

"The ships were being stockpiled against a possible new national emergency," I said. "What on earth is wrong with that?"

"I was a messman on the *Saratoga*," he said, "when I was sixteen. I lied about my age."

"But what are your intentions?"

"I am taking these ships away from them," he said.

"You are stealing forty-seven ships from the government of the United States?"

"There are also submarines," he said. "Six submarines of the Marlin class."

"But why?"

"Remember that I was, once, in accord with them. Passionately, if I may say so, in accord with them. I did whatever they wished, without thinking, hated their enemies, participated in their crusades, risked my life. Even though I only carried trays and wiped up tables. I heard the singing of the wounded and witnessed the burial of the dead. I believed. Then, over time, I discovered that they were lying. Consistently. With exemplary skill, in a hundred languages. I decided to take the ships. Perhaps they'll notice." He paused. "Now. Do you wish to accompany me, assist me?"

"More than anything."

"Good." He moved the lever of the bridge telegraph to Full Ahead.

Subpoena

And now in the mail a small white Subpoena from the Bureau of Compliance, Citizen Bergman there, he wants me to comply. *We command you that, all business and excuses being laid aside, you and each of you appear and attend . . .* The "We command you" in boldface, and a shiny red seal in the lower left corner. To get my attention.

I thought I had complied. I comply every year, sometimes oftener than necessary. Look at the record. Spotless list of compliances dating back to '48, when I was a pup. What can he mean, this Bergman, finding a freckle on my clean sheet?

I appeared and attended. Attempted to be reasonable. "Look here Bergman what is this business." Read him an essay I'd written about how the State should not muck about in the affairs of its vassals overmuch. Citizen Bergman unamused.

"It appears that you are the owner or proprietor perhaps of a monster going under the name of Charles Evans Hughes?"

"Yes but what has that to do with—"

"Said monster inhabiting quarters at 12 Tryst Lane?"

"That is correct."

"This monster being of humanoid appearance and characteristics,

including ability to locomote, production of speech of a kind, ingestion of viands, and traffic with other beings?"

"Well, 'traffic' is hardly the word. Simple commands he can cope
with. Nothing fancy. Sit. Eat. Speak. Roll over. Beg. That sort of
thing."

"This monster being employed by you in the capacity, friend?"

"Well, employed is not quite right."

"He is remunerated is he not?"

"The odd bit of pocket money."

"On a regular basis."

"See here Bergman it's an allowance. For little things he needs.
Cigarettes and handkerchiefs and the like. Nose drops."

"He is nevertheless in receipt of sums of money from you on a
regular basis?"

"*He is forty-four percent metal, Officer.*"

"The metal content of said monster does not interest the Bureau.
What we are interested in is compliance."

"Wherein have I failed to comply?"

"You have not submitted Form 244 which governs paid companionship, including liaisons with prostitutes and pushing of wheel-
chairs by hired orderlies not provided by the Bureau of Perpetual
Help. You have also failed to remit the Paid Companionship Tax
which amounts to one hundred twenty-two percent of all moneys
changing hands in any direction."

"One hundred twenty-two percent!"

"That is the figure. There is also a penalty for noncompliance.
The penalty is two hundred twelve percent of one hundred twenty-
two percent of five dollars a week figured over five years, which I
believe is the period at issue."

"What about depreciation?"

"Depreciation is not figurable in the case of monsters."

I went home feeling less than sunny.

He had a knowing look that I'd painted myself. One corner of the
mouth curled upward and the other downward, when he smiled.
There was no grave-robbing or anything of that sort. Plastic and

metal did very nicely. You can get the most amazing things in drug-stores. Fingernails and eyelashes and such. The actual construction was a matter of weeks. I considered sending the plans to *Popular Mechanics*. So that everyone could have one.

He was calm—calm as a hat. Whereas I was nervous as a strobe light, had the shakes, Valium in the morning and whiskey beginning at two o'clock in the afternoon.

Everything was all right with him.

"Crushed in an elevator at the welfare hotel!" someone would say.

"It's a very serious problem," Charles would answer.

When I opened the door, he was sitting in the rocking chair reading *Life*.

"Charles," I said, "they've found out."

"Seventy-seven percent of American high-school students declare that religion is important to them, according to a recent Louis Harris poll," Charles said, rocking gently.

"Charles," I said, "they want money. The Paid Companionship Tax. It's two hundred twelve percent of one hundred twenty-two percent of five dollars a week figured over five years, plus of course the basic one hundred twenty-two percent."

"That's a lot of money," Charles said, smiling. "A pretty penny."

"I can't pay," I said. "It's too much."

"Well," he said, both smiling and rocking, "fine. What are you going to do?"

"Disassemble," I said.

"Interesting," he said, hitching his chair closer to mine, to demonstrate interest. "Where will you begin?"

"With the head, I suppose."

"Wonderful," Charles said. "You'll need the screwdriver, the pliers, and the Skilsaw. I'll fetch them."

He got up to go to the basement. A thought struck him. "Who will take out the garbage?" he asked.

"Me. I'll take it out myself."

He smiled. One corner of his mouth turned upward and the other downward, "Well," he said, "right on."

I called him my friend and thought of him as my friend. In fact I kept him to instruct me in complacency. He sat there, the perfect noncombatant. He ate and drank and slept and awoke and did not change the world. Looking at him I said to myself, "See, it is possible to live in the world and not change the world." He read the newspapers and watched television and heard in the night screams under windows thank God not ours but down the block a bit, and did nothing. Without Charles, without his example, his exemplary quietude, I run the risk of acting, the risk of risk. I must participate, I must leave the house and walk about.

The New Member

The presiding officer noted that there was a man standing outside the window looking in.

The members of the committee looked in the direction of the window and found that the presiding officer's observation was correct: There was a man standing outside the window looking in.

Mr. Macksey moved that the record take note of the fact.

Mr. O'Donoghue seconded. The motion passed.

Mrs. Brown wondered if someone should go out and talk to the man standing outside the window.

Mrs. Mallory suggested that the committee proceed as if the man standing outside the window wasn't there. Maybe he'd go away, she suggested.

Mr. Macksey said that that was an excellent idea and so moved.

Mr. O'Donoghue wondered if the matter required a motion.

The presiding officer ruled that the man standing outside the window looking in did not require a motion.

Ellen West said that she was frightened.

Mr. Birnbaum said there was nothing to be frightened about.

Ellen West said that the man standing outside the window looked larger than a man to her. Maybe it was not human, she said.

Mr. Macksey said that that was nonsense and that it was only just a very large man, probably.

The presiding officer stated that the committee had a number of pressing items on the agenda and wondered if the meeting could go forward.

Not with that thing out there, Ellen West said.

The presiding officer stated that the next order of business was the matter of the Worth girl.

Mr. Birnbaum noted that the Worth girl had been doing very well.

Mrs. Brown said quite a bit better than well, in her opinion.

Mr. O'Donoghue said that the improvement was quite remarkable.

The presiding officer noted that the field in which she, the Worth girl, was working was a very abstruse one and, moreover, one in which very few women had successfully established themselves.

Mrs. Brown said that she had known the girl's mother quite well and that she had been an extremely pleasant person.

Ellen West said that the man was still outside the window and hadn't moved.

Mr. O'Donoghue said that there was, of course, the possibility that the Worth girl was doing too well.

Mr. Birnbaum said there was such a thing as too much too soon.

Mr. Percy inquired as to the girl's age at the present time and was told she was thirty-five. He then said that didn't sound like "too soon" to him.

The presiding officer asked for a motion.

Mr. O'Donoghue moved that the Worth girl be hit by a car.

Mr. Birnbaum seconded.

The presiding officer asked for discussion.

Mrs. Mallory asked if Mr. O'Donoghue meant fatally. Mr. O'Donoghue said he did.

Mr. Percy said he thought that a fatal accident, while consonant with the usual procedures of the committee, was always less interesting than something that left the person alive, so that the person's situation was still, in a way, "open."

Mr. O'Donoghue said that Mr. Percy's well-known liberalism was a constant source of strength and encouragement to every member of the committee, as was Mr. Percy's well-known predictability.

Mrs. Mallory said wouldn't it look like the committee was punishing excellence?

Mr. O'Donoghue said that a concern for how things looked was not and should never be a consideration of the committee.

Ellen West said that she thought the man standing outside the window looking in was listening. She reminded the committee that the committee's deliberations were supposed to be held *in camera*.

The presiding officer said that the man could not hear through the glass of the window.

Ellen West said was he sure?

The presiding officer asked if Ellen West would like to be put on some other committee.

Ellen West said that she only felt safe on this committee.

The presiding officer reminded her that even members of the committee were subject to the decisions of the committee, except of course for the presiding officer.

Ellen West said she realized that and would like to move that the Worth girl fall in love with somebody.

The presiding officer said that there was already a motion before the committee and asked if the committee was ready for a vote. The committee said it was. The motion was voted on and failed, 14-4.

Ellen West moved that the Worth girl fall in love with the man standing outside the window.

Mr. Macksey said you're just trying to get him inside so we can take a look at him.

Ellen West said well, why not, if you're so sure he's harmless.

The presiding officer said that he felt that if the man outside were invited inside, a confusion of zones would result, which would be improper.

Mr. Birnbaum said that it might not be a bad idea if the committee got a little feedback from the people for whom it was responsible, once in a while.

Mrs. Mallory stated that she thought Mr. Birnbaum's idea about feedback was a valuable and intelligent one but that she didn't approve of having such a warm and beautiful human being as the Worth girl fall in love with an unknown quantity with demonstrably peculiar habits, *vide* the window, just to provide feedback to the committee.

Mrs. Brown repeated that she had known the Worth girl's mother.

Mr. Macksey asked if Ellen West intended that the Worth girl's love affair be a happy or an unhappy one.

Ellen West said she would not wish to overdetermine somebody else's love affair.

Mr. O'Donoghue moved that the Worth girl be run over by a snowmobile.

The presiding officer said that O'Donoghue was out of order and also that in his judgment Mr. O'Donoghue was reintroducing a defeated motion in disguised form.

Mr. O'Donoghue said that he could introduce new motions all night long, if he so chose.

Mrs. Brown said that she had to be home by ten to receive a long-distance phone call from her daughter in Oregon.

The presiding officer said that as there was no second, Ellen West's motion about the man outside the window need not be discussed further. He suggested that as there were four additional cases awaiting disposition by the committee he wondered if the case of the Worth girl, which was after all not that urgent, might not be tabled until the next meeting.

Mr. Macksey asked what were the additional cases.

The presiding officer said those of Dr. Benjamin Pierce, Casey McManus, Cynthia Croneis, and Ralph Lorant.

Mr. Percy said that those were not very interesting names. To him.

Mr. Macksey moved that the Worth girl be tabled. Mr. Birnbaum seconded. The motion carried.

Mr. Birnbaum asked if he might have a moment for a general observation bearing on the work of the committee. The presiding officer graciously assented.

Mr. Birnbaum said that he had observed, in the ordinary course of going around taking care of his business and so on, that there were not many pregnant women now. He said that yesterday he had seen an obviously pregnant woman waiting for a bus and had remembered that in the last half year he had seen no others. He said he wondered why this was and whether it wasn't within the purview of the committee that there be more pregnant women, for the general good of the community, to say nothing of the future.

Mrs. Mallory said she knew why it was.

Mr. Birnbaum said why? and Mrs. Mallory smiled enigmatically.

Mr. Birnbaum repeated his question and Mrs. Mallory smiled enigmatically again.

Oh me oh my, said Mr. Birnbaum.

The presiding officer said that Mr. Birnbaum's observations, as amplified in a sense by Mrs. Mallory, were of considerable interest.

He said further that such matters were a legitimate concern of the committee and that if he might be allowed to speak for a moment not as the presiding officer but merely as an ordinary member of the committee he would urge, strongly urge, that Cynthia Croneis become pregnant immediately and that she should have twin boys.

Hear hear, said Mr. Macksey.

How about a boy and a girl? asked Ellen West.

The presiding officer said that would be O.K. with him.

This was moved, seconded, and voted unanimously.

On Mr. Macksey's motion it was decided that Dr. Pierce win fifty thousand dollars in the lottery.

It was pointed out by Mrs. Brown that Dr. Pierce was already quite well fixed, financially.

The presiding officer reminded the members that justice was not a concern of the committee.

On Mr. Percy's motion it was decided that Casey McManus would pass the Graduate Record Examination with a score in the upper 10 percent. On Mr. O'Donoghue's motion it was decided that Ralph Lorant would have his leg broken by having it run over by a snowmobile.

Mr. Birnbaum looked at the window and said he's still out there.

Mr. O'Donoghue said for God's sake, let's have him in.

Mr. Macksey went outside and asked the man in.

The man hesitated in the doorway for a moment.

Mr. Percy said come in, come in, don't be nervous.

The presiding officer added his urgings to Mr. Percy's.

The man left the doorway and stood in the middle of the room.

The presiding officer inquired if the man had, perhaps, a grievance he wished to bring to the attention of the committee.

The man said no, no grievance.

Why then was he standing outside the window looking in? Mr. Macksey asked.

The man said something about just wanting to "be with somebody."

Mr. Percy asked if he had a family, and the man said no.

Are you from around here? asked Mrs. Mallory, and the man shook his head.

Employed? asked Mr. Birnbaum, and the man shook his head.

He wants to be with somebody, Mrs. Mallory said.

Yes, said the presiding officer, I understand that.

It's not unusual, said Mr. Macksey.

Not unusual at all, said Mrs. Brown. She again reminded the members that she had to be home by ten to receive a call from her daughter in Oregon.

Maybe we should make him a member of the committee, said Mr. Percy.

He could give us some feedback, said Mr. Birnbaum. I mean, I would assume that.

Ellen West moved that the man be made a member of the committee. Mr. Birnbaum seconded. The motion was passed, 12-6.

Mr. Percy got up and got a folding chair for the man and pulled it up to the committee table.

The man sat down in the chair and pulled it closer to the table.

All right, he said. The first thing we'll do is, we'll make everybody wear overalls. Gray overalls. Gray overalls with gray T-shirts.

We'll have morning prayers, evening prayers, and lunch prayers. Calisthenics for everyone over the age of four in the 5–7 P.M. time slot. Boutonnieres are forbidden. Nose rings are forbidden. Gatherings of one or more persons are prohibited. On the question of bedtime, I am of two minds.

To London and Rome

D o you know what I want more than anything else? Alison asked.

THERE WAS A
BRIEF PAUSE

What? I said.

A sewing-machine Alison said, with button-hole-making attachments.

THERE WAS A
LONG PAUSE

There are so many things I could do with it, for instance fixing up last year's fall dresses and lots of other things.

THERE WAS A
TREMENDOUS
PAUSE DURING
WHICH I
BOUGHT HER A
NECCHI
SEWING-MACHINE

Wonderful! Alison said sitting at the controls of the Necchi and making buttonholes in a copy of *The New York Times* Sunday Magazine. Her eyes glistened. I had also bought a two-year subscription to *Necchi News* because I could not be sure that her interest would not be held for that long at least.

THERE WAS A
PAUSE BROKEN
ONLY BY THE
HUMMING OF
THE NECCHI

Then I bought her a purple Rolls which we decided to park on the street because our apartment building had no garage. Alison said she absolutely loved the Rolls! and gave me an enthusiastic kiss. I paid for the car with a check drawn on the First City Bank.

THERE WAS AN INTERVAL

Peter Alison said, what do you want to do now?

Oh I don't know I said.

THERE WAS A LONG INTERVAL

Well we can't simply sit around the apartment Allison said so we went to the races at Aqueduct where I bought a race horse that was running well out in front of the others. What a handsome race horse! Alison said delightedly. I paid for the horse with a check on the Capital National Bank.

THERE WAS AN INTERMISSION BETWEEN RACES SO WE WENT AROUND TO THE STABLE AND BOUGHT A HORSE TRAILER

The trailer was attached by means of a trailer hitch, which I bought when it became clear that the trailer could not be hitched up without one, to the back of our new Rolls. The horse's name was Dan and I bought a horse blanket, which he was already wearing but which did not come with him, to keep him warm.

He *is* beautiful Alison said.

A front-runner too I said.

THERE WAS AN INTERVAL OF SEVERAL DAYS. THEN ALISON AND I DROVE THE CAR WITH THE TRAILER UP THE RAMP INTO THE PLANE AND WE FLEW BACK TO MILWAUKEE

After stopping for lunch at Howard Johnson's where we fed Dan some fried clams which he seemed to like very much Alison said: Do you know what we've completely forgotten? I knew that there was something but although I thought hard I could not imagine what it was.

There's no place to keep him in our apartment building! Alison said triumphantly, pointing at Dan. She was of course absolutely right and I hastily bought a large three-story house in Milwaukee's best suburb. To make the house more comfortable I bought a concert grand piano.

ON THE DOORSTEP
OF THE NEW
HOUSE THE PIANO
MOVERS PAUSED
FOR A GLASS
OF COLD WATER

Here are some little matters which you must attend to Alison said, handing me a box of bills. I went through them carefully, noting the amounts and thinking about money.

What in the name of God is this! I cried, holding up a bill for $1,600 from the hardware store.

Garden hose Alison said calmly.

THERE WAS AN
UNCOMFORTABLE
SILENCE

It was clear that I would have to remove some money from the State Bank & Trust and place it in the Municipal National and I did so. The pilot of the airplane which I had bought to fly us to Aqueduct, with his friend the pilot of the larger plane I had bought to fly us back, appeared at the door and asked to be paid. The pilots' names were George and Sam. I paid them and also bought from Sam his flight jacket, which was khaki-colored and pleasant-looking. They smiled and saluted as they left.

Well I said looking around the new house, we'd better call a piano teacher because I understand that without use pianos tend to fall out of tune.

Not only pianos Alison said giving me an excited look.

A SILENCE
FREIGHTED
WITH SEXUAL
SIGNIFICANCE
ENSUED. THEN
WE WENT TO BED
FIRST HOWEVER
ORDERING A PIANO
TEACHER AND A PIANO
TUNER FOR THE
EARLY MORNING

The next day Mr. Washington from the Central National called to report an overdraft of several hundred thousand dollars for which I apologized. Who was that on the telephone? Alison asked. Mr. Washington from the bank I replied. Oh Alison said, what do you want for breakfast? What have you got? I asked. Nothing Alison said, we'll have to go out for breakfast.

So we went down to the drugstore where Alison had many eggs sunny side up and I had buckwheat cakes with sausage. When we got back to the house I noticed that there were no trees surrounding it, which depressed me.

Have you noticed I asked, that there are no trees?

A SILENCE   Yes Alison said, I've noticed.

A PROLONGED   In fact Alison said, the treelessness of
SILENCE   this house almost makes me yearn for our old apartment building.

A TERRIBLE SILENCE   *There* at least one could look at the large plants in the lobby.

ABSOLUTE SILENCE   As soon as we go inside I said, I will call
FOR ONE MINUTE   the tree service and buy some trees.

SHORT SILENCE   *Maples* I said.

Oh Peter what a fine idea Alison said brightly. But who are these people in our livingroom?

SILENTLY WE   Realizing that the men were the piano
REGARDED THE   teacher and the piano tuner we had
TWO MEN WHO   requested, I said: Well did you try the
SAT ON THE SOFA   piano?

Yep the first man said, couldn't make heads or tails out of it.

And you? I asked, turning to the other man.

Beats me he said with a mystified look.

What seems to be the difficulty? I asked.

THERE WAS A   Frankly the piano teacher said, this isn't
SHAMEFACED   my real line of work. *Really* he said, I'm a
SILENCE   jockey.

How about you? I said to his companion.

Oh I'm a bona fide piano tuner all right

the tuner said. It's just that I'm not very good at it. Never was and never will be.

I have a proposition to make I announced. What is your name? I asked, nodding in the direction of the jockey.

Slim he said, and my friend here is Buster.

Well Slim I said, we need a jockey for our race horse, Dan, who will fall out of trim without workouts. And Buster, you can plant the maple trees which I have just ordered for the house.

I settled on a salary of $12,000 a year for Slim and a slightly smaller one for Buster. This accomplished I drove the Rolls over to Courtlandt Street to show it to my mistress, Amelia.

When I knocked at the door of Amelia's apartment she refused to open it. Instead she began practicing scales on her flute. I knocked again and called out: Amelia!

I knocked again but Amelia continued to play. So I sat down on the steps and began to read the newspaper which was lying on the floor, knocking at intervals and at the same time wondering about the psychology of Amelia.

Montgomery Ward I noticed in the newspaper was at 40½. Was Amelia being adamant I considered, because of Alison?

Amelia I said at length (through the door), I want to give you a nice present of around $5,500. Would you like that?

Do you mean it? she said.

Certainly I said.

Can you afford it? she asked doubtfully.

To London and Rome

THE FLUTE OPENED THE DOOR — I have a new Rolls I told her, and took her outside where she admired the car at great length. Then I gave her a check for $5,500 on the Commercial National for which she thanked me. Back in the apartment she gracefully removed her clothes and put the check in a book in the bookcase. She looked very pretty without her clothes, as pretty as ever, and we had a pleasant time for an hour or more. When I left the apartment Amelia said Peter, I think you're a very pleasant person which made me feel very good and on the way home I bought a new gray Dacron suit.

WHEN I GAVE THE SALESMAN A CHECK ON THE MEDICAL NATIONAL HE PAUSED, FROWNED, AND SAID: "THIS IS A NEW BANK ISN'T IT?" — Where have you been? Alison said, I've been waiting lunch for hours. I bought a new suit I said, how do you like it? Very nice Alison said, but hurry I've got to go shopping after lunch. Shopping! I said, I'll go with you!

So we ate a hasty lunch of vichyssoise and ice cream and had Buster drive us in the Rolls to the Federated Department Store where we bought a great many things for the new house and a new horse blanket for Dan.

Do you think we ought to buy uniforms for Buster and Slim? Alison asked and I replied that I thought not, they didn't seem the sort who would enjoy wearing uniforms.

A FROSTY SILENCE — I think they ought to wear uniforms Alison said firmly.

No I said, I think not.

DEAD SILENCE — Uniforms with something on the pocket Alison said. A crest or something.

No.

THERE WAS AN INTERVAL DURING WHICH I SENT A CHECK FOR $500,000 TO THE MUSEUM OF MODERN ART Instead of uniforms I bought Slim a Kaywoodie pipe and some pipe tobacco, and bought Buster a larger sterling silver cowboy belt buckle and a belt to go with it.

Buster was very pleased with his sterling silver belt buckle and said that he thought Slim would be pleased too when he saw the Kaywoodie pipe which had been bought for him. You were right after all Alison whispered to me in the back seat of the Rolls.

Alison decided that she would make a pie for supper, a chocolate pie perhaps, and that we would have Buster and Slim and George and Sam the pilots too if they were in town and not flying. She began looking in her recipe book while I read the *Necchi News* in my favorite armchair.

Then Slim came in from the garage with a worried look. Dan he said is not well.

A STUNNED PAUSE Everyone was thrown into a panic by the thought of Dan's illness and I bought some Kaopectate which Slim however did not believe would be appropriate. The Kaopectate was $0.98 and I paid for it with a check on the Principal National. The delivery boy from the drugstore, whose name was Andrew, suggested that Dan needed a doctor. This seemed sensible so I tipped Andrew with a check on the Manufacturers' Trust and asked him to fetch the very best doctor he could find on such short notice.

WE LOOKED AT ONE ANOTHER IN WORDLESS FEAR Dan was lying on his side in the garage, groaning now and then. His face was a rich gray color and it was clear that if he did not have immediate attention, the worst might be expected.

Peter for God's sake do something for this poor horse! Alison cried.

PAUSING ONLY TO WHIP A FRESH CHECKBOOK FROM THE DESK DRAWER, I BOUGHT A LARGE HOSPITAL NEARBY FOR $1.5 MILLION

We sent Dan over in his trailer with strict instructions that he be given the best of everything. Slim and Buster accompanied him and when Andrew arrived with the doctor I hurried them off to the hospital too. Concern for Dan was uppermost in my mind at that moment.

The telephone rang and Alison answered.

RETURNING TO THE LIVINGROOM, ALISON HESITATED

Then she said: It's some girl, for you.

As I had thought it might be, it was Amelia. I told her about Dan's illness. She was very concerned and asked if I thought it would be appropriate if she went to the hospital.

A MOMENT OF INDECISION FOLLOWED BY A PAINFUL SILENCE

You don't think it would be appropriate Amelia said.

No Amelia I said truthfully, I don't.

Then Amelia said that this indication of her tiny status in all our lives left her with nothing to say.

THE CONVERSATION LAPSED

To cheer her up I said I would visit her again in the near future. This pleased her and the exchange ended on a note of warmth. I knew however that Alison would ask questions and I returned to the living room with some anxiety.

A HIATUS FILLED WITH DOUBT AND SUSPICION

But now the pilots George and Sam rushed in with good news instead. They had gotten word of Dan's illness over the radio they said, and filled with concern had flown straight to the hospital, where they learned that Dan's stomach had been pumped and all was well. Dan was resting easily George and Sam said, and could come home in about a week.

Oh Peter! Alison exclaimed in a pleased way, our ordeal is over. She kissed me with abandon and George and Sam shook hands with each other and with Andrew and Buster and Slim, who had just come in from the hospital. To celebrate we decided that we would all fly to London and Rome on a Viscount jet which I bought for an undisclosed sum and which Sam declared he knew how to fly very well.

The Apology

Sitting on the floor by the window with only part of my face in the window. He'll never come back.

—Of course he will. He'll return, open the gate with one hand, look up and see your face in the window.

—He'll never come back. Not now.

—He'll come back. New lines on his meager visage. Yet with head held high.

—I was unforgivable.

—I would not argue otherwise.

—The black iron gate, difficult to open. Takes two hands. I can see it. It's closed.

—I've had hell with the gate. In winter, without gloves, yanking, late at night, turning my pretty head to see who might be behind me . . .

—That time that guy was after you . . .

—The creep—

—With the chain.

—Naw he wasn't the one with the chain he was the other one. With the cudgel.

—Yes they do seem to be carrying cudgels now, I've noticed that. Big knobby cudgels.

—It's a style, makes a statement, something to do with their sexual . . . I imagine.

—Sitting on the floor by the window with only part of my face in the window, the upper part, face truncated under the eyes by the what do you call it, sill.

—But bathed nevertheless by the heat of the fire, which spreads a pleasing warm tickle across your bare back—

—I was unforgivable.

—I don't disagree.

—He'll never come back.

—Say you're sorry.

—I'm not sorry.

—Genuine sorrow is gold. If you can't do it, fake it.

—I'm not sorry.

—Well screw it. It's six of one and half dozen of the other to me. I don't care.

—What?

—Forgive me I didn't mean that.

—What?

—I just meant you could throw him a bone is all I meant. A note written on pale-blue notepaper, in an unsteady hand. "Dear William, it is one of the greatest regrets of my poor life that—"

—Never.

—He may. He might. It's possible. Your position, there in the window, strongly suggests that the affair has yet some energy unexpended. That the magnetic north of your brain may attract his wavering needle still.

—That's kind of you. Kind.

—Your wan, white back. Your green, bifurcated French jeans. Red lines on your back. Cat hair on your jeans.

—Wait. What is it that makes you spring up so, my heart?

—The gate.

—The sound of the gate. The gate opening.

—Is it he?

—It is not. It is someone.

—Let me look.

—He's standing there.

—I know him. Andy deGroot. Looking up at our window.

—Who's Andy deGroot?

—Guy I know. Melville Fisher Kirkland Leland & deGroot.

—What's he want?

—My devotion. I've disabused him a hundred times, to little avail. If he rings, don't answer. Of course he's more into standing outside and gazing up.

—He looks all right.

—Yes he is all right. That's Andy.

—Powerful forehead on him.

—Yes it is impressive. Stuffed with banana paste.

—Good arms.

—Yes, quite good.

—Looks like he might fly into a rage if crossed.

—He rages constantly.

—We could go out in the street and hit on him, drive him away with blows and imprecations.

—Probably have little or no effect.

—Stick him with the spines of sea urchins.

—Doubt you could penetrate.

—But he's a friend of yours so you say.

—I got no friends babe, no friends, no friends. When you get down to the nut-cutting.

—Go take a poke.

—I don't want to be the first you do it.

—Ah the hell with it. Sitting here with my head hanging in the window, what a way for a grown woman to spend her time.

—Many ways a grown woman can spend her time. Many ways. Lace-making. Feeding the golden carp. Fibonacci numbers.

—Perhaps a new gown, in fawn or taupe. That might be a giggle. Meanwhile, I am planted on this floor. Sitting on the floor by the window with only my great dark eyes visible. My great dark eyes and, in moments of agitation, my great dark nose. Ogled by myriads of citizens bopping down these Chuck's Pizza–plated streets.

—How pale the brow! How pallid the cheek! How chalk the neck! How floury the shoulders! And so on. Say you're sorry.

—I cannot. What's next? Can't sit here all night. I'm nervous. Look on the bright side, maybe he'll go away. He's got a gun stuck in his belt, a belly gun, I saw it. I scraped the oatmeal out of the pot you'll be glad to know. Used the mitt, the black mitt. Throw something at him, a spear or a rock. Open the window first. Spear's in the closet. I can lend you a rock if you don't have a rock. Hurt him. Make him go away. Make the other return. Stir up the fire. Put on some music. Have you no magic? Why do I know you? What are you good for? Why are you here? Fetch me some chocolate? Massage?

—He'll never come back. Until you say it.

—Be damned if I will. Damned a thousand times.

—Then you'll forfeit the sunshine of his poor blasted face forever. You are dumb, if I may say so, dumb, dumb. It's easy. It's like saying thank you. Myself, I shower thanks everywhere. Thank people for their kindness, thank them for their courtesy. Thank them for their thoughtfulness. Thank them for little things they do if they do little things that are kind, courteous, or thoughtful. Thank them for coming to my house and thank them for leaving. Thank them for what they are about to do as well as thank them for what they have already done, thank them in public and then take them aside privately and thank them again. Thank the thankless and thank the already adequately thanked. In fine, let no occasion pass to slip the chill blade of my thanks between the ribs of every human ear.

—Well. I see what you mean.

—Act.

—Andy has bestirred himself.

—What's he doing?

—Sitting. On a garbage can.

—I knew him long ago, and far away.

—Cincinnati.

—Yes. Engaged then in the manufacture of gearshafts. Had quite a nice wife at that period, name of Caledonia. She split. Then another wife, Cecile as I recall, ran away with a gibbon. Then another wife whose name taxes my memory as it cannot be brought to consciousness, think I spilled something on her once, something that stained. She too evaporated. He came here and joined Melville Fisher etc. Fell in love with a secretary. Polly. She had a beaded curtain in front of her office door and burnt incense. Quite exotic, for Melville Fisher. She ended up in the harem of one of those mystics, a mahrooni. Met the old boy once, he grasped my nose and pulled, I felt a great surge of something. Like I was having my nose pulled.

—So that's Andy.

—Yes. What's that sucker doing now?

—He's combing his head. Got him a steel comb, maybe aluminum.

—What's to comb? What's he doing now?

—Adjusting his pants. He's zipping.

—You are aware dear colleague are you not that I cannot abide, cannot abide, even the least wrinkle of vulgarity in social discourse? And that this "zipping" as you call it—

—You are censorious, madame.

—A mere scant shallow preludium, madame, to the remarks I shall bend in your direction should you persist.

—Shall we call the cops?

—And say what?

—Someone's sitting on our garbage can?

—Maybe that's not illegal?

—Oh my God he's got it out in his hands. Oh my god he's pointing his gun at it.

—Oh my God. Shall we call the cops?

—Open the window.

—Open the window?

—Yes open the window.

—O.K. the window's open.

—*William! William, wherever you are!*

—You're going to say you're sorry!

—*William! I'm sorry!*

—Andy's put everything away!

—*William I'm sorry I let my brother hoist you up the mast in that crappy jury-rigged bosun's chair while everybody laughed!*

William I'm sorry I could build better fires than you could! I'm sorry my stack of Christmas cards was always bigger than yours!

—Andy quails. That's good.

—*William I'm sorry you don't ski and I'm sorry about your back and I'm sorry I invented bop jogging which you couldn't do! I'm sorry I loved Antigua! I'm sorry my mind wandered when you talked about the army! I'm sorry I was superior in argument! I'm sorry you slit open my bicycle tires looking for incriminating letters that you didn't find! You'll never find them!*

—Wow babe that's terrific babe. Very terrific.

—*William! I'm sorry I looked at Sam but he was so handsome, so handsome, who could not! I'm sorry I slept with Sam! I'm sorry about the library books! I'm sorry about Pete! I'm sorry I never played the guitar you gave me! William! I'm sorry I married you and I'll never do it again!*

—Wow.

—Was I sorry enough?

—Well Andy's run away howling.

—Was I sorry enough?

—Terrific. Very terrific.

—Yes I feel much better.

—Didn't I tell you?

—You told me.

—Are you O.K.?

—Yes I'm fine. Just a little out of breath.

—Well. What's next? Do a little honky-tonking maybe, hit a few bars?

—We could. If you feel like it. Was I sorry enough?

—No.

Florence Green Is 81

Dinner with Florence Green. The old babe is on a kick tonight: *I want to go to some other country*, she announces. Everyone wonders what this can mean. But Florence says nothing more: no explanation, no elaboration, after a satisfied look around the table bang! she is asleep again. The girl at Florence's right is new here and does not understand. I give her an ingratiating look (a look that says, "There is nothing to worry about, I will explain everything later in the privacy of my quarters Kathleen"). Lentils vegetate in the depths of the fourth principal river of the world, the Ob, in Siberia, 3200 miles. We are talking about Quemoy and Matsu. "It's a matter of leading from strength. What is the strongest possible move on our part? To deny them the islands even though the islands are worthless in themselves." Baskerville, a sophomore at the Famous Writers School in Westport, Connecticut, which he attends with the object of becoming a famous writer, is making his excited notes. The new girl's boobies are like my secretary's knees, very prominent and irritating. Florence began the evening by saying, grandly, "The upstairs bathroom leaks you know." What does Herman Kahn think about Quemoy and Matsu? I can't remember, I can't remember . . .

Oh Baskerville! you silly son of a bitch, how can you become a famous writer without first having worried about your life, is it the *right kind* of life, does it have the right people in it, is it *going well*? Instead you are beglamoured by J. D. Ratcliff. The smallest city in the United States with a population over 100,000 is Santa Ana, California, where 100,350 citizens nestle together in the Balboa blue Pacific evenings worrying about their lives. I am a young man but very brilliant, very ingratiating, I adopt this ingratiating tone because I can't help myself (for fear of boring you). I edit with my left hand a small magazine, very scholarly, very brilliant, called *The Journal of Tension Reduction* (social-psychological studies, learned disputation, letters-to-the-editor, anxiety in rats). Isn't that distasteful? Certainly it is distasteful but if Florence Green takes her money to another country who will pay the printer? answer me that. From an article in *The Journal of Tension Reduction: "One source of concern in the classic encounter between patient and psychoanalyst is the patient's fear of boring the doctor."* The doctor no doubt is also worrying about his life, unfolding with ten minutes between hours to smoke a cigarette in and wash his hands in. Reader, you who have already been told more than you want to know about the River Ob, 3,200 miles long, in Siberia, we have roles to play, thou and I: you are the doctor (washing your hands between hours), and I, I am, I think, the nervous dreary patient. I am free associating, brilliantly, brilliantly, to put you into the problem. Or for fear of boring you: which? *The Journal of Tension Reduction* is concerned with everything from global tensions (drums along the Ob) to interpersonal relations (Baskerville and the new girl). There is, we feel, too much tension in the world, I myself am a perfect example, my stomach is like a clenched fist. Notice the ingratiating tone here? the only way I can relax it, I refer to the stomach, is by introducing quarts of Fleischmann's Gin. Fleischmann's I have found is a magnificent source of tension reduction, I favor the establishment of comfort stations providing free Fleischmann's on every street corner of the city Santa Ana, California, and all other cities. Be serious, can't you?

The new girl is a thin thin sketchy girl with a big chest looming over the gazpacho and black holes around her eyes that are very promising. Surely when she opens her mouth toads will pop out. I am tempted to remove my shirt and show her my trim midsection sporting chiseled abdominals, my superior shoulders and brilliantly developed pectoral-latis-simus tie-in. Jackson called himself a South Carolinian, and his biographer, Amos Kendall, recorded his birthplace as Lancaster County, S.C.; but Parton has published documentary evidence to show that Jackson was born in Union County, N.C., less than a quarter mile from the South Carolina line. Jackson is my great hero even though he had, if contemporary reports are to be believed, lousy lats. I am also a weightlifter and poet and admirer of Jackson and the father of one abortion and four miscarriages; who among you has such a record and no wife? Baskerville's difficulty not only at the Famous Writers School in Westport, Connecticut, but in every part of the world, is that he is slow. "That's a slow boy, that one," his first teacher said. "That boy is what you call *real slow*," his second teacher said. "That's a *slow son of a bitch*," his third teacher said. And they were right, right, entirely correct, still I learned about Andrew Jackson and abortions, many of you walking the streets of Santa Ana, California, and all other cities know nothing about either. *"In such cases the patient sees the doctor as a highly sophisticated consumer of outré material, a connoisseur of exotic behavior. Therefore, he tends to propose himself as more colorful, more eccentric (or more ill) than he really is; or he is witty, or he fantasticates."* You see? Isn't that sensible? In the magazine we run many useful and sensible pieces of this kind, portages through the whirlpool-country of the mind. In the magazine I cannot openly advocate the use of Fleischmann's Gin in tension reduction but I did run an article titled "Alcohol Reconsidered" written by a talented soak of my acquaintance which drew many approving if carefully worded letters from secret drinkers in psychology departments all over this vast, dry, and misunderstood country . . .

"That's a *slow son of a bitch*," his third teacher remarked of him, at a meeting called to discuss the formation of a special program for Inferior Students, in which Baskerville's name had so to speak rushed to the fore. The young Baskerville, shrinking along the beach brushing sand from his dreary Texas eyes, his sad fingers gripping $20 worth of pamphlets secured by post from Joe Weider, "Trainer of Terror Fighters" (are they, Baskerville wondered, like fire fighters?

do they fight terror? or do they, rather, inspire it? the latter his, Baskerville's, impossible goal), was even then incubating plans for his novel *The Children's Army* which he is attending the Famous Writers School to learn how to write. "You will do famously, Baskerville," said the Registrar, the exciting results of Baskerville's Talent Test lying unexamined before him. "Run along now to the Cashier's Office." "I am writing doctor an immense novel to be called *The Children's Army!*" (Why do I think the colored doctor's name, he with his brown hand on the red radishes, is Pamela Hansford Johnson? Why do I think?) Florence Green is a small fat girl eighty-one years old, old with blue legs and very rich. Rock pools deep in the earth, I salute the shrewdness of whoever filled you with Texaco! Texaco breaks my heart, Texaco is particularly poignant. Florence Green who was not always a small fat girl once made a voyage with her husband Mr. Green on the *Graf Zeppelin*. In the grand salon, she remembers, there was a grand piano, the great pianist Mandrake the Magician was also on board but could not be persuaded to play. The Zeppelins could not use helium; the government of this country refused to sell helium to the owners of the Zeppelins. The title of my second book will be I believe *Hydrogen After Lakehurst*. For the first half of the evening we heard about the problem of the upstairs bathroom: "I had a man come out and look at it, and he said it would be two hundred and twenty-five dollars for a new one. I said I didn't want a new one, I just wanted this one fixed." Shall I offer to obtain a new one for Florence, carved out of solid helium? would that be ingratiating? Does she worry about her life? "He said mine was old-fashioned and they didn't make parts for that kind anymore." Now she sleeps untidily at the head of the table, except for her single, mysterious statement, delivered with the soup (*I want to go to some other country!*), she has said nothing about her life whatsoever . . . The diameter of the world at the Poles is 7899.99 miles whereas the diameter of the world at the Equator is 7926.68 miles, mark it and strike it. I am sure the colored man across from me is a doctor, he has a doctor's doctorly air of being needed and necessary. He leans into the conversation as if to say: Just make *me* Secretary of State and then you will see some action. "I'll tell you one thing, there are a hell of a lot of Chinese over there." Surely the very kidneys of wisdom, Florence Green has only one kidney, I have a kidney stone, Baskerville was stoned by the massed faculty of the Famous Writers School upon presentation of his first lesson: he was accused of formalism. It is well known that Florence adores doctors, why didn't I announce myself, in the beginning, from the very first, as a doctor? Then I could say that the money was for a very important research project (use of radioactive tracers in reptiles) with very important ramifications in stomach cancer (the small intestine is very like a reptile). Then I would get the money with much less difficulty, cancer frightens Florence, the money would rain down like fallout in New Mexico. I am a young man but very brilliant, very ingratiating, I edit with my left hand a small magazine called . . . did I explain that? And you *accepted* my explanation? Her name is not really Kathleen, it is Joan Graham, when we were introduced she said, "Oh are you a native of Dallas Mr. Baskerville?" No Joan baby I am a native of Bengazi sent here by the UN to screw your beautiful ass right down into the ground, that is not what I said but what I should have said, it would have been brilliant. When she asked him what he did Baskerville identified himself as an American weightlifter and poet (that is to say: *a man stronger and more eloquent than other men*). "It moves," Mandrake said, pointing to the piano, and although no one else could detect the slightest movement, the force of his personality was so magical that he was not contradicted (the instrument sat in the salon, Florence says, as solidly as Gibraltar in the sea).

The man who has been settling the hash of the mainland Chinese searches the back of his neck, where there is what appears to be a sebaceous cyst (I can clear that up for you; my instrument will be a paper on the theory of games). What if Mandrake *had* played, though, what if he had seated himself before the instrument, raised his hands, and . . . what? The Principal Seas, do you want to hear about the Principal Seas? Florence has been prodded awake; people are beginning to ask questions. If not this country, then what country? Italy? "No," Florence says smiling through her emeralds, "not Italy. I've *been* to Italy. Although Mr. Green was very fond of Italy." "*To bore the doctor is to become, for this patient, a case similar to other cases; the patient strives mightily to establish his uniqueness. This is also, of course, a tactic for evading the psychoanalytic issue."* The first thing the All-American Boy said to Florence Green at the very brink of their acquaintanceship was "It is closing time in the gardens of the West Cyril Connolly." This remark pleased her, it was a pleasing remark, on the strength of this remark Baskerville was invited again, on the second occasion he made a second remark, which was "Before the flowers of friendship faded friendship faded Gertrude Stein." Joan is like one of those marvelous *Vogue* girls, a tease in a half-slip on Mykonos, bare from the belly up on the rocks. "It moves," Mandrake said, and the piano raised itself a few inches, magically, and swayed from side to side in a careful Baldwin dance. "It moves," the other passengers agreed, under the spell of posthypnotic suggestion. "It moves," Joan says, pointing at the gazpacho, which sways from side to side with a secret Heinz trembling movement. I give the soup a serious warning, couched in the strongest possible terms, and Joan grins gratefully not at me but at Pamela Hansford Johnson. The Virgin Islands maybe? "We were there in 1925, Mr. Green had indigestion, I sat up all night with his stomach and the flies, the flies were something you wouldn't believe." They are asking I think the wrong questions, the question is not where but why? "I was reading the other day that the average age of Chiang's enlisted men is thirty-seven. You can't do much with an outfit like that." This is true, I myself am thirty-seven and if Chiang must rely on men of my sort then he might as well kiss the Mainland goodbye. Oh, there is nothing better than intelligent conversation except thrashing about in bed with a naked girl and Egmont Light Italic.

Despite his slowness already remarked upon which perhaps inhibited his ingestion of the splendid curriculum that had been prepared for him, Baskerville never failed to be "promoted," but on the contrary was always "promoted," the reason for this being perhaps that his seat was needed for another child (Baskerville then being classified, in spite of his marked growth and gorgeous potential, as a child). There were some it was true who never thought he would extend himself to six feet, still he learned about Andrew Jackson, helium-hydrogen, and abortions, where are my mother and father now? answer me that. On a circular afternoon in June 1945—it was raining, Florence says, hard enough to fill the Brazen Sea—she was sitting untidily on a chaise in the north bedroom (on the wall of the north bedroom there are twenty identically framed photographs of Florence from eighteen to eighty-one, she was a beauty at eighteen) reading a copy of *Life*. It was the issue containing the first pictures from Buchenwald, she could not look away, she read the text or a little of the text, then she vomited. When she recovered she read the article again, but without understanding it. What did *exterminated* mean? It meant nothing, an eyewitness account mentioned a little girl with one leg thrown alive on top of a truckload of corpses to be burned. Florence was sick. She went immediately to the Greenbrier, a resort in West Virginia. Later she permitted me to tell her about the Principal Seas, the South China, the Yellow, the Andaman, the Sea of Okhotsk. "I spotted you for a weightlifter," Joan says. "But not for a poet," Baskerville replies. "What have you written?" she asks. "Mostly I make remarks," I say. "Remarks are not literature," she says. "Then there's my novel," I say, "it will be twelve years old Tuesday." "Published?" she asks. "Not finished," I say, "however, it's very violent and necessary. It has to do with this Army see, made up of children, young children but I mean really well armed with M-1's, carbines, .30 and .50 caliber machine guns, 105 mortars, recoilless rifles, the whole works. The central figure is the General, who is fifteen. One day the Army appears in the city, in a park, and takes up positions. Then it begins killing the people. Do you understand?" "I don't think I'd like it," Joan says. "I don't like it either," Baskerville says, "but it doesn't make any difference that I don't like it. Mr. Henry James writes fiction as though it were a painful duty Oscar Wilde."

Does Florence worry about her life? "He said mine was old-fashioned and they didn't make parts for that kind any more." Last year Florence tried to join the Peace Corps and when she was refused, telephoned the President to complain. "I have always admired the work of the Andrews Sisters," Joan says. I feel feverish; will you take my temperature doctor? Baskerville that simple preliterate soaks up all the Taylor's New York State malmsey in reach meanwhile wondering about his Grand Design. France? Japan? "Not Japan dear, we had a lovely time there but I wouldn't want to go back now. France is where my little niece is, they have twenty-two acres near Versailles, he's a count and a biochemist, isn't that wonderful?" The others nod, they know what is wonderful. The Principal Seas are wonderful, the Important Lakes of the World are wonderful, the Metric System is wonderful, let us measure something together Florence Green baby. I will trade you a walleyed hectometer for a single golden micron. The table is hushed, like a crowd admiring 300 million dollars. Did I say that Florence has 300 million dollars? Florence Green is eighty-one with blue legs and has 300 million dollars and in 1932 was in love, airily, with a radio announcer named Norman Brokenshire, with his voice. "*Mean*while Edna Cather's husband who takes me to church, he's got a very good job with the Port, I think he does very well, he's her second husband, the first was Pete Duff who got into all that trouble, where was I? Oh yes when Paul called up and said he wouldn't come because of his hernia—you heard about his hernia—John said *he'd* come over and look at it. Mind you I've been using the *down*stairs bathroom all this time." In fact the whole history of Florence's radio listenership is of interest. In fact I have decided to write a paper called "The Whole History of Florence Green's Radio Listenership." Or perhaps, in the seventeenth-century style, "The Whole and True History of Florence Green's Radio Listenership." Or perhaps . . . But I am boring you, I sense it, let me say only that she can still elicit, from her ancient larynx, the special thrilling sound used to introduce Cap-tain Midnight . . . The table is hushed, then, we are all involved in a furious pause, a grand parenthesis (here I will insert a description of Florence's canes. Florence's canes line a special room, the room in which her cane collection is kept. There are hundreds of them: smooth black Fred Astaire canes and rough chewed alpenstocks, blackthorns and quarterstaffs, cudgels and swagger sticks, bamboo and ironwood, maple and slippery elm, canes from Tangier, Maine, Zurich, Panama City, Quebec, Togoland, the Dakotas and Borneo, resting in notched compartments that resemble arm racks in an armory. Everywhere Florence goes, she purchases one or more canes. Some she has made herself, stripping the bark from the green unseasoned wood, drying them carefully, applying layer on layer of a special varnish, then polishing them, endlessly, in the evenings, after dark and dinner) as vast as the Sea of Okhotsk, 590,000 square miles. I was sitting, I remember, in a German restaurant on Lexington, blowing bubbles in my seidel, at the next table there were six Germans, young Germans, they were laughing and talking. At Florence Green's here-and-now table there is a poet named Onward Christian or something whose spectacles have wide silver sidepieces rather than the dull brown horn sidepieces of true poets and weightlifters, and whose poems invariably begin: "Through all my clangorous hours . . ." I am worried about his remarks, are his remarks better than my remarks? We are elected after all on the strength of our glamorous remarks, what is he saying to her? to Joan? what sort of eyewash is he pouring in her ear? I am tempted to walk briskly over and ask to see his honorable discharge from the Famous Writers School. What could be more glamorous or necessary than *The Children's Army*, "An army of youth bearing the standard of truth" as we used to sing in my fourth-grade classroom at Our Lady of the Sorrows under the unforgiving eye of Sister Scholastica who knew how many angels could dance on the head of a pin . . .

Florence I have decided is evading the life-issue. She is proposing herself as more unhappy than she really is. She has in mind making herself more interesting. She is afraid of boring us. She is trying to establish her uniqueness. She does not really want to go away. Does Onward Christian know about the Important Lakes of the World? Terminate services of employees when necessary. I terminate you, brightness that seems to know me. She proceeded by car from Tempel-hof to a hotel in the American zone, registered, dined, sat in a chair in the lobby for a time observing the American lieutenant colonels and their healthy German girls, and then walked out into the street. The first German man she saw was a policeman directing traffic. He wore a uniform. Florence walked out into the traffic island and tugged at his sleeve. He bent politely toward the nice old

American lady. She lifted her cane, the cane of 1927 from Yellowstone, and cracked his head with it. He fell in a heap in the middle of the street. Then Florence Green rushed awkwardly into the plaza with her cane, beating the people there, men and women, indiscriminately, until she was subdued. The Forms of Address, shall I sing to you of the Forms of Address? What Florence did was what Florence did, not more or less, she was returned to this country under restraint on a military plane. "Why do you have the children kill everybody?" "Because everybody has already been killed. Everybody is absolutely dead. You and I and Onward Christian." "You're not very sanguine." "That's true." For an earl's younger son's wife, letters commence: *Madam* ... "We put in the downstairs bathroom when Ead came to visit us. Ead was Mr. Green's sister and she couldn't climb stairs." What about Casablanca? Santa Cruz? Funchal? Málaga? Valletta? Iráklion? Samos? Haifa? Kotor Bay? Dubrovnik? "I want to go to some *other* place," Florence says. "Somewhere where *everything is different*." For the Talent Test a necessary but not a sufficient condition for matriculation at the Famous Writers School Baskerville delivered himself of "Impressions of Akron" which began: "Akron! Akron was full of people walking the streets of Akron carrying little transistor radios which were turned on."

Florence has a Club. The Club meets on Tuesday evenings, at her huge horizontal old multibathroom home on Indiana Boulevard. The Club is a group of men who gather, on these occasions, to recite and hear poems in praise of Florence Green. Before you can be admitted you must compose a poem. The poems begin, usually, somewhat in this vein: "Florence Green is eighty-one/ Nevertheless she's lots of fun ..." Onward Christian's poem began "Through all my clangorous hours ..." Florence carries the poems about with her in her purse, stapled together in an immense, filthy wad. Surely Florence Green is a vastly rich vastly egocentric old-woman nut! Six modifiers modify her into something one can think of as a nut. "But you have not grasped the living reality, the essence!" Husserl exclaims. Nor will I, ever. His examiner (was it J. D. Ratcliff?) said severely: "Baskerville, you blank round, discursiveness is not literature." "The aim of literature," Baskerville replied grandly, "is the creation of a strange object covered with fur which breaks your heart." Joan says: "I have two children." "Why did you do that?" I ask. "I don't know," she says. I am struck by the modesty of her answer. Pamela Hansford Johnson has been listening and his face jumps in what may be described as a wince. "That's a terrible thing to say," he says. And he is right, right, entirely correct, what she has said is the First Terrible Thing. We value each other for our remarks, on the strength of this remark and the one about the Andrews Sisters, love becomes possible. *I* carry in my wallet an eight-paragraph General Order, issued by the adjutant of my young immaculate Army to the troops: "(1) You are in this Army because you wanted to be. So you have to do what the General says. Anybody who doesn't do what the General says will be kicked out of the Army. (2) The purpose of the Army is to do what the General says. (3) The General says that nobody will shoot his weapon unless the General says to. It is important that when the Army opens fire on something everybody does it together. This is very important and anybody who doesn't do it will have his weapon taken away and will be kicked out of the Army. (4) Don't be afraid of the noise when everybody fires. It won't hurt you. (5) Everybody has enough rounds to do what the General wants to do. People who lose their rounds won't get any more. (6) Talking to people who are not in the Army is strictly forbidden. Other people don't understand the Army. (7) This is a serious Army and anybody that laughs will have his weapon taken away and will be kicked out of the Army. (8) What the General wants to do now is, find and destroy the enemy."

I want to go somewhere where everything is different. A simple, perfect idea. The old babe demands nothing less than total otherness. Dinner is over. We place our napkins on our lips. Quemoy and Matsu remain ours, temporarily perhaps; the upstairs bathroom drips away unrepaired; I feel the money drifting, drifting away from me. I am a young man but very brilliant, very ingratiating, I edit . . . but I explained all that. In the dim foyer I slip my hands through the neck of Joan's yellow dress. It is dangerous but it is a way of finding out everything all at once. Then Onward Christian arrives to resume his yellow overcoat. No one has taken Florence seriously, how can anyone with three hundred million dollars be taken seriously? But I know that when I telephone tomorrow, there will be no answer. Iráklion? Samos? Haifa? Kotor Bay? She will be in none of these places but in another place, a place where *everything is different*. Outside it is raining. In my rain-blue Volkswagen I proceed down the rain-black street thinking, for some simple reason, of the Verdi *Requiem*. I begin to drive my tiny car in idiot circles in the street, I begin to sing the first great *Kyrie*.

Tickets

I have decided to form a new group and am now contemplating the membership, the prospective membership, of my new group. My decision was prompted by a situation that arose not long ago vis-à-vis the symphony. We say "the symphony" because there is only one symphony orchestra here, as opposed to other cities where there are several and one must distinguish among them. The situation had to do with an invitation my wife received from Barbet, the artist, to attend the symphony with him on the evening of the ninth of March.

My wife, as it happened, was already planning to attend the performance of the ninth of March with her friend Morton. Barbet had extra tickets and wanted my wife to join his group and was gracious enough to enlarge his invitation to include my wife's friend, Morton. My wife could join his group, Barbet said, and took special pains to make clear that this invitation extended to Morton also. My wife responded, with characteristic warmth, with a counter-invitation, saying that she already had tickets for the ninth of March including extra tickets, that Barbet was most welcome to join her group, the group of my wife and Morton, and that the members of Barbet's group were also most welcome to join my wife's group, the group consisting, at that moment, of herself and Morton. My wife had previously asked me, with the utmost cordiality, if I wished to go to the symphony with her on the ninth of March, despite being fully apprised of my views on the matter of going to the symphony.

I had replied that I did not care to join her at the symphony on the occasion in question, but had inquired, out of politeness, what the program was to be, although my wife is fully aware that my views on the symphony will never change. My views on the symphony are that only the socially malformed would choose to put on a dark suit, a white shirt, a red tie, and so on, black shoes, and so on, and go to the symphony, there to sit pinned between two other people, albeit one of them one's own warm and sweet-smelling wife, for two hours or more, listening to music that may very well exist, in equally knowing and adroit performances, in one's own home, on records. That is to say that such people, the socially malformed (my wife, of course, excepted), go to the symphony out of extramusical need, clear extramusical need. But because of the raging politeness that always obtains between us I asked her what the program was to be on the ninth of March, and she told me that it was to be an all-Laurenti evening.

Laurenti is a composer held in quite high esteem hereabouts, perhaps less so elsewhere but of that I cannot judge, he is attached to the symphony as our composer-in-residence. It was to be, she told me, an all-Laurenti performance with just a bit of Orff by way of curtain-raiser, the conductor of the symphony, Gilley, which he pronounces "Gil-lay," having decided that Orff would make an appropriate, even delicious, curtain-raiser for Laurenti. While I am respectful of Laurenti's tragedy, what is called in some circles Laurenti's tragedy — that he has not a shred of talent of any description—still the prospect of sitting tightly wedged between two other human beings for the length of an all-Laurenti evening would have filled me with dismay had I not been aware that the invitation from my wife was perfectly pro forma. It appears that Gilley is sleeping with Mellow the new first-desk cellist, who sits at the head of the cellos with her golden cornrows, or so it is said at the Opera-Cellar, where I have a drink from time to time, especially often during the rather hectic period when my wife was both chairperson of the Friends of French Art Fandango and head whipper-in for the Detached Retina Bal.

It could be relied upon that Barbet, being an artist, would respond with enthusiasm to the notion of yet another disastrous all-Laurenti evening, possibly with the idea of mocking Laurenti behind his hand, although Barbet, as an artist, would not literally mock Laurenti behind his hand but rather in speech, or ironic speech rotten with wit. Barbet, being an artist of a particular kind, no doubt feels that a mocking attitude is appropriate to an artist of his kind, known not only hereabouts but in much larger cities, cities with two and even three distinct symphony orchestras, not even counting a Youth Symphony or one maintained by the Department of Sanitation. Barbet's reputation rests, not unimpressively, upon his "Cancellation" paintings—or simply "cancellations," in the language of his métier—a form he is believed to have invented and in which he displays his rotten wit along with the usual exhausting manual dexterity. The "cancellations" are paintings in which a rendering of a well-known picture, an Edvard Munch, say, has superimposed on it a smaller, but yet not small, rendering of another but perhaps not so well known picture, an El Lissitzky, say, for example the "Untitled" of 1919–20, a rather geometrical affair of squares and circles, reds and blacks, whose impetuses not only contest, contradict, the impetuses of the Munch, the Scandinavian miserablism of the Munch, but effectively *cancel* it, an action one can see taking place before one's eyes. I must say in his defense (because what Barbet is doing, has been doing all his life as a painter, is fundamentally indefensible), I must say in Barbet's defense that the contestation between the two paintings he has chosen to superimpose, one on the other, is of a very high order, is of substantial visual interest just *as paint,* and that the way the historically unrelated paintings relate to each other *as forms or collections of forms* is a value in addition to the value one awards the destructive act that is the soul of Barbet's painting, as much as the decayed wit displayed in titling these things "Improved Painting #1," "Improved Painting #2," "Improved Painting #19"—all these values must be taken into account in deciding whether or not Barbet should be shot, on the basis of ill will. But because Barbet is one of our few, our very few, genuine artists, we embrace him. This is not to say that the work of many other painters not our own is not similarly indefensible and that they, too, from a strictly construed moral-aesthetic standpoint, should not be shot. There are forty-four examples of Barbet's work in the museum, I refer to our quite grand local museum, in which my wife's family's money has had quite an important role over the years; it can be imagined how much I detest the phrase "provincial museum" but there is no other way of describing the place, which is, of course, quite grand, with its old part done in the classical mode and its new part done in a mode that respects the classical mode to the point of being indistinguishable from the classical mode but is also fresh, new, contemporary, and ironic.

This Morton who has been my wife's friend for ten years at least, who is forever calling her on the telephone so that I have come to recognize his voice although I have never met him—I recognize not only his voice but the characteristic pause before he asks if my wife is there, the freighted pause, I recognize that and say yet, Morton, just a moment, I'll see if she's in—this Morton, on the other hand, is a singer, and thus has no irony. He has, however, a legitimate interest in the symphony, as well as a truly frightening voice, easily recognized, a bass voice of remarkable color and strength, and patina; it is not wrong to add "patina" since this Morton is a man of a certain age, not old in any sense, but not young either, and of course not new to my wife, whose constant companion he has been for the past ten years. Morton does not go to the symphony or to musical occasions of any sort merely to make jokes or scoff behind his hand. And considered in the light of the possible attendance of someone like Morton, a sage and well-tempered listener, even some of Laurenti is perhaps worth hearing, the "Songs" perhaps, which draw from reviewers notices that begin "Among the best, perhaps, of this fluent but uneven composer's efforts are the 'Songs.'" I must tell you that last night I slept with my wife, I use the term "slept with" in the sense of congress, it was four-fifteen in the morning and

I awoke with an itch to sleep with my wife, who was sleeping beside me as she has every night for the past fifteen years or thereabouts. My wife appeared to me to be a young person, that was interesting, I of course have no idea how I appeared to her but she appeared to me to be a young person and together after arduous endeavor we achieved quite sublime heights of sexual communion, such as one does not often achieve, we achieved that, at about four-fifteen in the morning, last night, the children sleeping soundly, the dog awake, she said in the morning, "Good morning, sexy boy."

It is the case that Barbet actively dislikes Morton, whereas Morton is absolutely indifferent to Barbet. Morton acts upon Barbet like a rug that makes you ill, a rug that is your own rug, clean, in good condition, not frayed or stained, but suddenly looking at the rug you are made ill, a wind around the heart, looking at the gray, green, and yellow rug, with its melon-shaped figure, purchased, yes, at Klecksel's, where the very best recent rugs, V'Soke and the like, are to be found (as well as both Klecksel and Jeri, his girlfriend, yes, even Klecksel has a girlfriend, so bounteous/fortunate are the times, even Klecksel has a girlfriend and the two are always at the symphony, or at the opera, or at the ballet, giving one very odd feelings, in that the person who sells you rugs, whom you regard as a rug person, someone who swims into your ken when rugs are an issue, and then swims out again when the issue has been resolved, must also be regarded as part of a social pair on quite another plane, and not just part of a social pair but part of a set of *new lovers*, God help us all), illness ensues. Morton is a very fine singer, a bass with the opera, where he sings Hunding in "Die Walküre," Méphistophélès in "La Damnation de Faust," etc. I find a slightly nasal quality to his singing, but perhaps I am imagining it. He is a handsome fellow, of course, my wife's self-regard would not allow her to be seen out with anyone who is not a handsome fellow. The nose is quite large but there is, I suppose, no necessary connection between the quite large nose and the slightly nasal quality he brings to Hunding or Méphistophélès or Abul in "Der Barbier von Baghdad," the last a role in which his comic flair, what is called in the newspaper his comic flair, is employed to great advantage. I have seen him many times at the opera (which offers something for the eye as opposed to the symphony where one can watch the kettledrums going out of tune) and have found his performances juicy and his comic flair endurable and have chosen him as a member of my new group, an honor he may, of course, decline.

My group will be unlike any existing group, will exist in contradistinction to all existing groups, over against all existing groups, will be in fine an anti-group, given the ethos of our city, the hysterical culture of our city. My new group will contain my wife, that sugarplum, and her friend Morton and a Gypsy girl and a blind man and will take its ethos from the car wash. My new group will march along the boulevards shouting "Let's go! Let's go!" with the enthusiasm of the young men at the car wash who are forever shouting "Let's go! Let's go!" to inspirit their fellows, if there is a moment of quiet at the car wash someone will take up the cry "Let's go! Let's go!" and then others will take up the cry "Let's go! Let's go!" shouting "Let's go! Let's go!" over and over, as long as the car wash washes.

Notes

Flying to America
This story appeared in *The New Yorker*, December 4, 1971, and is a particularly intriguing example of Barthelme's tendency to use and reuse material in various ways. "Flying to America" incorporates material first published in "Notes and Comment" in *The New Yorker* (unsigned, June 13, 1970) and reprinted in *The Teachings of Don B.* (1992) as "Many have remarked . . .". Sections had also been part of "A Film" (*The New Yorker*, September 26, 1970). "A Film" was included in *Sadness* (1972), and then reprinted again in *Forty Stories* (1987) as "The Film." Some sections not used in "A Film" were resurrected as "Two Hours to Curtain" in *Guilty Pleasures* (1974) and reprinted in *The Teachings of Don B.* (1992), and still others were incorporated into *The Dead Father* (1975). Roughly half of the story has never appeared except in its original form.

Perpetua
First published in *The New Yorker*, June 12, 1971. Reprinted in *Sadness*.

Edward and Pia
First appeared in *The New Yorker*, September 25, 1965. Reprinted in *Unspeakable Practices, Unnatural Acts* (1968).

Notes

The Piano Player
First appeared in *The New Yorker*, August 31, 1963. Reprinted in *Come Back, Dr. Caligari* (1964).

Henrietta and Alexandra
First appeared as "Alexandria and Henrietta" in *New American Review* 12 (1971). Reprinted with significant changes and its new title in *Overnight to Many Distant Cities* (1983).

Presents
First published in *Penthouse*, December 1977. It was subsequently published in 1980 in a limited edition of 376 copies by Pressworks, and included Barthelme's own collages. Sections of "Presents" subsequently appeared as an interchapter in *Overnight to Many Distant Cities*, which itself was reprinted as "A woman seated on a plain wooden chair . . ." in *The Teachings of Don B.* Readers of *Not-Knowing* will recognize that most of one of the later paragraphs was reprinted in that collection as "Bliss . . .". "Presents" in its entirety is previously uncollected.

Among the Beanwoods
This story is previously unpublished, and was probably written sometime in the early 1970s. There are two typescript versions of the story, one titled "Among the Beanwoods," and the other, "The Beanwoods." The version published here is slightly longer and appears to be the later of the two.

You Are as Brave as Vincent Van Gogh
First appeared in *The New Yorker*, March 18, 1974. Reprinted in *Amateurs* (1976).

The Agreement
First published in *The New Yorker*, October 14, 1974. Reprinted in *Amateurs*.

Basil From Her Garden
The story appeared in *The New Yorker*, October 21, 1985. It includes some material later incorporated into *Paradise*, which was published late in 1986. Previously uncollected.

Notes

Paradise Before the Egg
The story was published in *Esquire* in August 1986, and was adapted from Barthelme's novel *Paradise*, then completed and published about a month later. The story is uncollected in this form.

Three
Published in *Fiction* 1 (1973). Previously uncollected.

Up, Aloft in the Air
First appeared in *Come Back, Dr. Caligari.*

Bone Bubbles
First appeared as "Mouth" in *Paris Review* 48 (1969), then under its current title in *City Life* (1970).

The Big Broadcast of 1938
First appeared in *New World Writing* 20 (1962). Reprinted in *Come Back, Dr. Caligari.*

This Newspaper Here
First published in *The New Yorker*, February 12, 1966. Reprinted in *Unspeakable Practices, Unnatural Acts.*

Tales of the Swedish Army
First published in *Great Days* (1979).

And Then
First appeared in *Harper's*, December 1973. Reprinted in *Amateurs.*

Can We Talk
First appeared in *Art and Literature* 5 (Summer, 1965). Reprinted in *Come Back, Dr. Caligari.*

Hiding Man
First appeared in *First Person* 1 (Spring/Summer, 1961) as "The Hiding Man." Reprinted with its current title in *Come Back, Dr. Caligari.*

The Reference
First appeared in *Playboy*, April 1974. Reprinted in *Amateurs.*

Edwards, Amelia
Published in *The New Yorker*, September 9, 1972. Previously uncollected.

Marie, Marie, Hold On Tight
First appeared in *The New Yorker*, October 12, 1963. Reprinted in *Come Back, Dr. Caligari*.

Pages from the Annual Report
Published under the pseudonym "David Reiner" in The University of Houston *Forum* 3 (March, 1959). It is, arguably, the first of Barthelme's published stories. Previously uncollected.

The Bed
Published in *Viva* 1 (March, 1973). Previously uncollected. A fragment of "The Bed" appears in "The Sea of Hesitation."

The Discovery
First published in *The New Yorker*, August 20, 1971. Reprinted in *Amateurs*.

You Are Cordially Invited
First appeared in *The New Yorker*, July 23, 1973. Previously uncollected.

The Viennese Opera Ball
First appeared in *Contact* 10 (June, 1962). Reprinted in *Come Back, Dr. Caligari*.

Belief
First appeared in the *University of Houston Forum* 13 (Winter, 1976). Reprinted in *Great Days*.

Wrack
First appeared in *The New Yorker*, October 21, 1972. Reprinted in *Overnight to Many Distant Cities* (1983).

The Question Party
First appeared in *Great Days*.

Notes

Manfred (with Karen Shaw)
In February 1976, *The New York Times Magazine* ran the beginning of a yet unnamed story written by Barthelme. Readers were invited, in Barthelme's own words, "to complete it in not more than 750 words . . . as an experiment in literary collaboration." Barthelme hoped that the entries would be "serious, rather than parodies or burlesques." He added, "I have done the easiest part, the beginning; you are asked to provide the terrifying middle and the subtle, incomparably beautiful ending. God be with you." The "terrifying middle" and "incomparably beautiful ending" were provided by Karen Shaw, for which she won $250. Barthelme's beginning encompasses the story's first three paragraphs, Shaw provides the last eight, and the final version was published in *The New York Times Magazine* on April 18, 1976. It is previously uncollected.

A Man
Published in *The New Yorker*, December 30, 1972. Previously uncollected.

Heather
This story is previously unpublished. The date of its writing has been impossible to determine with any precision, though it appears to have been written sometime during the middle to late 1970s.

Pandemonium
"Pandemonium" was among the stories that Barthelme was working on at the time of his death in 1989. It is probably unfinished, and appears here for the first time.

A Picture History of the War
First appeared in *The New Yorker*, June 20, 1964. Reprinted in *Unspeakable Practices, Unnatural Acts*.

The Police Band
First appeared in *The New Yorker*, August 22, 1964. Reprinted in *Unspeakable Practices, Unnatural Acts*.

The Sea of Hesitation
First appeared in *The New Yorker*, November 11, 1972. Reprinted in *Overnight to Many Distant Cities*.

Notes

The Mothball Fleet
First appeared in *The New Yorker*, September 11, 1971. Reprinted in *Overnight to Many Distant Cities*.

Subpoena
First published in *The New Yorker*, May 29, 1971. Reprinted in *Sadness*.

The New Member
First appeared in *The New Yorker*, July 15, 1974. Reprinted in *Amateurs*.

To London and Rome
First appeared in *Genesis West* 2 (Fall, 1963). Reprinted in *Come Back, Dr. Caligari*.

The Apology
First appeared in *The New Yorker*, February 20, 1978. Reprinted in *Great Days*.

Florence Green Is 81
First appeared in *Harper's Bazaar*, April 1963. It was the lead story in *Come Back, Dr. Caligari*.

Tickets
Published in *The New Yorker*, March 6, 1989, his last story for the magazine. Previously uncollected.

About the Author
DONALD BARTHELME published seventeen books, including *City Life,*
one of *Time Magazine*'s Best Books of the Year, and *Sixty Stories,* which
was nominated for the National Book Critics Circle Award, the PEN/
Faulkner Award, and the Los Angeles Times Book Prize. He was a long-
time contributor to *The New Yorker* and a winner of the National Book
Award. He was a founder of the University of Houston Creative Writing
Program where he taught for many years. He died in July 1989.

About the Editor
KIM HERZINGER is a critic and fiction writer (winner of a Pushcart
Prize), and writes on minimalism and other contemporary literary phe-
nomena. He's edited two previous collections of Barthleme's writing,
Not-Knowing: The Essays and Interviews and *The Teachings of Don B.*
He taught at the University of Southern Mississippi and now owns and
operates Left Bank Books, specializing in modern first editions and qual-
ity used books, in New York City.

THE BRIDGE BETRAYED

Comparative Studies in Religion and Society

MARK JUERGENSMEYER, editor

THE BRIDGE BETRAYED

Religion and Genocide in Bosnia

Michael A. Sells

UNIVERSITY OF CALIFORNIA PRESS

Berkeley   Los Angeles   London

96

niversity of California Press
erkeley and Los Angeles, California

niversity of California Press, Ltd.
ondon, England

1996 by
he Regents of the University of California

brary of Congress Cataloging-in-Publication Data

lls, Michael Anthony.
    The bridge betrayed : religion and genocide in Bosnia /
Michael A. Sells.
        p.   cm. — (Comparative studies in religion and
society ; 11)
    Includes bibliographical references (p.   ) and index.
    ISBN 0-520-20690-8 (alk. paper)
    1. Yugoslav War, 1991– —Atrocities.   2. Yugoslav
War, 1991– —Bosnia and Herzegovina.   3. Yugoslav
War, 1991– —Destruction and pillage—Bosnia and
Herzegovina.   4. Muslims—Bosnia and Herzegovina—
History—20th century.   5. Genocide—Bosnia and
Herzegovina—History—20th century.   6. Persecution—
Bosnia and Herzegovina—History—20th century.
7. Bosnia and Herzegovina—History—1992–   I. Title.
II. Series.
    DR1313.7.A85S45   1996
    949.702'4—dc20   96-4854
                                                              CIP

Printed in the United States of America
9 8 7 6 5 4 3 2 1

RECEIVED

DEC   4 1996

Kennedy School Library

*This book is dedicated to the tens of thousands
of Bosnian civilians who are now missing;
and to the effort to find them if they are alive,
to account for their fate if they are not, to
bring to justice those who harmed them; and
to the possibility of a genuine peace.*

*In memory of my mother,
Simona Sally Trbovich
(1926–1961).*

CONTENTS

GUIDE TO PRONUNCIATION

j = English "y"
The names Lejla and Jasmina are pronounced LAY-la and YAS-min-a.

ć = English "ch"
Jović, a last name, is pronounced YO-vich. Some Slavs in the West add an "h" to make the pronunciation clear, while others keep the original spelling.
Mihajlovic (Michaelson) is pronounced Mi-HAY-lo-vich.

č = a slightly different form of English "ch"
The town of Foča is pronounced FO-cha.

š = English "sh"
Pašić and Bašić (common last names derived from the Ottoman honorific title "Pasha") are pronounced PAH-shich and BAH-shich. Mušanović (Moses-son) is pronounced Mu-SHA-no-vich.

ž = French "j" or "z" as in "azure"
The southeast Bosnian town of Žepa is pronounced ZHEH-pa.

k = English "k"

c = English "tz"
Stolac, a town in Herzegovina, is pronounced STO-latz.

Map 1. Yugoslavia, 1945–1991

PREFACE

The story told here is not one I wish to believe or to tell. My mother's family is Serbian American, and I know personally that Serbs have suffered in the Bosnian war—some of my Serb relatives in Bosnia and in Krajina (the Serb-occupied area of Croatia) have been killed, some are missing, and others are living in refugee camps. However, the evidence in Bosnia leads to conclusions that are as unavoidable as they are unpalatable. Genocide has occurred. It has occurred with the acquiescence of Western governments, in violation of the United Nations Charter and the Geneva Convention on Genocide of 1948. It has been motivated and justified in large part by religious nationalism, fueled financially and militarily from Serbia and Croatia, and grounded in religious symbols. And the primary victims have been Bosnian Muslims, selected for destruction because of their religion.

In situations of genocide a disengaged, purely objective stance would be inhuman. Yet precisely to the extent that genocide demands a response, it also demands a continual willingness to examine and reexamine the evidence. For over three years the atrocities were documented by refugee workers, human rights groups, and war crimes investigators (see the Note on Sources). That evidence shows a religious violence far more systematic than the media accounts of the shellings in Sarajevo have suggested.

A particular abuse of history, "Balkanism," has been used to justify the genocide in Bosnia by suggesting that people in the Balkans are fated, by history or genetics, to kill one another. It is true that, like the rest of Europe, Bosnia was caught up in the violence of World War I, World War II, and earlier conflicts. But just as Germans, Dutch, French, and British today live together peacefully, only a few years ago Bosnians had every reason to believe the peace they had enjoyed for fifty years would continue.* That their friends and neighbors would one day seek to destroy them, that their family members would be sent to concentration camps, that their cultural heritage would be methodically burned and dynamited—such possibilities seemed remote to most of the people of Bosnia-Herzegovina.

A resurgence in religious violence has caught the post–cold war world off guard. From the subways of Tokyo to the ruins of a mosque in India, from the World Trade Center and the federal building in Oklahoma City to a Jerusalem rally for the Israeli prime minister, religious militants have transgressed the boundaries of civil society in pursuit of their aims. Bosnians have faced the most brutal religious violence unleashed in the aftermath of the cold war, but the forces that assaulted Bosnia are not due to "age-old antagonisms" peculiar to Balkan peoples, as the cliché would have it. They are forces with us all.

The story told here has clear historical parallels with earlier periods of European history. At the heart of the religious nationalism used to motivate and justify the assault on Bosnia, and

---

*Bosnians are defined in this book as all residents of the internationally recognized sovereign nation of Bosnia-Herzegovina, regardless of their religious affiliation, who consider themselves Bosnian, that is, who remain loyal to a Bosnian state built on the principles of civic society and religious pluralism.

on Bosnian Muslims in particular, is the same myth of the Christ killer that was exploited in the past to instigate attacks on Jews. How Muslims, a people whose religion began six centuries after Jesus, could have been singled out for genocide as Christ killers and race traitors is a tale this book seeks to tell.

The ancient bridge at Mostar, destroyed by Croat religious nationalists on November 9, 1993, has come to symbolize the multireligious character of Bosnia. But it symbolizes something larger as well: the ability of a culturally pluralistic society to flourish for almost five centuries, despite the very real tensions among the different religious groups. For those who choose a pluralistic society where different religions coexist—whether in Banja Luka, London, or Los Angeles—the struggle to rebuild that bridge is not something occurring over there and far away, but something frighteningly close to home.

I wish to thank Mark Auslander, Amila Buturovic, Carin Companick, Deborah Cooper, Vanja and Mirza Filipović, Bridget Gillich, Laurie Kain Hart, Nader Hashemi, Richard Hecht, Mark Juergensmeyer, Walter Lee, Kathleen MacDougall, Janet Marcus, Aida Premilovac, Emran Qureshi, András Riedlmayer, Ellen Schattsneider, and the Haverford College community for support in writing this book, and the Greek Studies Yearbook for permission to reprint the lithograph of Adam Stefanović's *The Feast of the Prince*. Special thanks to Douglas Abrams Arava, Reed Malcolm, and Marilyn Schwartz of the University of California Press for their encouragement, judgment, and care during the preparation of this book.

CHAPTER ONE

FIRE IN THE PAGES

RAIN OF ASH

"It was the most apocalyptic thing I'd ever seen," said Aida Mušanović, an artist from Sarajevo, describing the burning of the
National Library in Sarajevo.[1] For days, a thick black cloud of ash
hung over the city and residents would find pieces of charred paper or ashes of burned books and manuscripts in their hair and
on their clothes.

On August 25, 1992, the Serb army began shelling the National Library of Bosnia-Herzegovina in Sarajevo from positions
on the mountainside directly in front of it. In the next few days,
in the largest book-burning in modern human history, over a million books, more than a hundred thousand manuscripts and rare
books, and centuries of historical records of Bosnia-Herzegovina
went up in flames. Volunteers formed a human chain to rescue
what they could. One of them, a graduate student at the University of Sarajevo, never made it home.

What was in the pages of those manuscripts and rare books, survivors of centuries of peace and war, that the Serb army was determined to destroy? What was there in those burning pages that many Sarajevans—Croats, Serbs, Muslims, and Jews—were willing to risk their lives to save?

The destruction of the National Library was one component of a systematic campaign of cultural eradication. Three months earlier, on May 17, 1992, the Serb army had targeted the Oriental Institute in Sarajevo, which housed the largest collection of Islamic and Jewish manuscripts in southeast Europe. More than five thousand manuscripts in Hebrew, Persian, Arabic, Turkish, and Adžamijski (Slavic in Arabic script) were incinerated.

The Serb army then turned its fire on the National Museum, hitting it repeatedly and destroying much of its contents. One special item was saved: an ancient Jewish prayer book used for celebration of the *seder* or Passover feast. The *Sarajevo Haggadah*, with its exquisite Hebrew calligraphy and colored illustration, had been created in fourteenth-century Spain. Jewish refugees from the Inquisition in Spain had brought it to Bosnia. During World War II the *Sarajevo Haggadah* had been preserved by a Muslim curator who hid it from Nazi soldiers. In 1992, it was saved at great personal risk by a team of Bosnian museum workers that included a Muslim, an Orthodox Serb, and a Catholic. The *Haggadah* has thus survived three historic persecutions: the expulsion of the Jews from Spain in 1492, the Holocaust, and what has been called "ethnic cleansing" in Bosnia.[2]

The shelling of these cultural institutions was purposeful. They were chosen for destruction and shelled in a precise manner. Areas around them were left untouched. During one particular shelling of the National Museum, the Serb gunners missed and struck the Holiday Inn directly in front of it. Kate Adie, a BBC reporter, interviewed the Serb officer afterward. When she asked him why he had been shelling the Holiday Inn, the major hotel for journalists in Sarajevo, the officer apologized, explaining that he had been aiming at the museum and had struck the Holiday Inn by mistake.[3]

Since April 1992 the Serb army has targeted for destruction the major libraries, manuscript collections, museums, and other cultural institutions in Sarajevo, Mostar, and other besieged cities. What the Serb artillery missed, the Croat nationalist militia known as the "Croatian Defense Council" (HVO) took care of.

Where the Serb and Croat armies have been able to get closer than shelling range, the destruction has been even greater. The Croatian Defense Council dynamited mosques and Orthodox churches throughout the regions controlled by the Croat military. Serb militias have dynamited all the mosques (over six hundred) in areas they have occupied, some of them masterworks of European architecture such as the sixteenth-century Ferhadija Mosque in Banja Luka and the Colored Mosque in Foča built in 1551. Between them, the Croat and Serb nationalists have destroyed an estimated fourteen hundred mosques. In many cases the mosques have been ploughed over and turned into parking lots or parks; every evidence of their existence has been effaced. Graveyards, birth records, work records, and other traces of the Bosnian Muslim people have been eradicated.[4]

Western political leaders have spoken of "ancient animosities," portraying Bosnians as a group of Balkan tribal killers who have hated one another for centuries and who are incapable of living in peace. In the fires of the National Library, the irony of that portrayal becomes apparent. What the Serb and Croat armies were destroying, there and elsewhere, was the graphic and palpable evidence of over five hundred years of interreligious life in Bosnia. Despite the wars and strife of the past, religious monuments and houses of worship in Mostar and Sarajevo had been built next to one another and shared the same skyline. It is this architectural, literary, and human evidence—the monuments, the books, and the people who treasured them—of a flourishing multiconfessional culture that ethnoreligious militants have sought to efface.[5]

The northeast Bosnian town of Zvornik was known for its heritage of Bosnian Muslim poets, saints, rebels, and mystics. From April through July of 1992 the Serb military killed or expelled the entire Muslim population. After all the mosques in the primarily Muslim town were dynamited and ploughed over, the new Serb nationalist mayor declared: "There never were any mosques in Zvornik." Destroyed with those mosques was the evidence not only of the Muslim heritage of Zvornik but also of five hundred years of shared living between Christians and Muslims. History could now be rewritten according to the desires of those who wished to claim that this land was always and purely Christian Serb. In May 1993 to celebrate Zvornik's new status as 100 percent "pure" and cleansed of all Muslims, the mayor dedicated a new church, renamed a local, formerly Muslim village "Saint Stephen," and kissed a crucifix.[6]

Aida Mušanović, the artist who described the burning of the National Library, had visited the hospital in Sarajevo and seen the carnage brought by the war. Yet the burning of the library struck her with a special horror. In the fire of the National Library, she realized that what she was experiencing was not only war but also something else. The centuries of culture that fell back in ash onto the besieged city revealed a secret. The gunners on the hills above Sarajevo did not seek to defeat an enemy army; at that time, there was no organized, opposing army. They sought to take territory, but not only territory. They sought political concessions, but also something more. Their goal was the eradication of a people and all evidence of that people's culture and existence.

WHO ARE BOSNIANS?

In 1945, communist guerrilla fighter Josip Broz Tito, better known as Marshal Tito, reestablished the Yugoslav federation, which had existed from 1918 to 1941 and then had been dismembered by Nazi Germany. The constituent nations of the reconstituted Yugoslavian republic were Macedonia, Serbia, Montenegro, Bosnia-Herzegovina, Croatia, and Slovenia (see Map 1).

The word "Yugoslavia" means "land of the South (Yugo) Slavs." The central part of Yugoslavia was populated by three major groups (Serbs, Slavic Muslims, and Croats), all of whom spoke the same South Slavic language, until recently called Serbo-Croatian. The vast majority of Croats were Roman Catholic and lived in Croatia, Bosnia-Herzegovina, and some parts of Serbia. The vast majority of Serbs were Orthodox Christians and lived in Serbia, Montenegro, Macedonia, and parts of Croatia and Bosnia known as the Krajina. The Slavic Muslims were concentrated in Bosnia-Herzegovina, the adjacent areas in Serbia and Montenegro, and in Macedonia. Croatians used a Latin-based script, while Serbs preferred a Cyrillic script (based on Greek characters), but despite dialectical differences, Serbs,

Croats, and Bosnian Muslims spoke the same language. Many Serbs and Croats were devoted to the ideal of a multireligious and multiethnic Yugoslavia. Religious nationalists, however, desired religiously homogeneous national states, a greater Catholic Croatia and a greater Orthodox Christian Serbia. Slovenes and Macedonians spoke South Slavic languages distinct from but belonging to the same language family as Serbo-Croatian. The non-Slavic Albanians were primarily Muslim and resided in Macedonia and a region in Serbia known as Kosovo, adjacent to the independent nation of Albania. A large Hungarian population lived in another province of Serbia, Vojvodina.

Like the rest of Europe, Yugoslavia had been torn apart in World War II. Slovenia had been made part of the Greater German Reich. Croatia and Bosnia-Herzegovina had been incorporated into a puppet state of Nazi Germany. Italy had occupied parts of the coastline. Germany had occupied and ruled Serbia through a collaborationist Serbian regime. The "independent" Croatian state, aligned with Nazi Germany, was controlled by a fascist militia known as the Ustashe, dedicated to an independent "Greater Croatia." In 1941 the Ustashe began a campaign to "cleanse" Croatia of Serbs either by forcing them to convert to Roman Catholicism or by killing and expelling them. Various groups of Serb fighters organized themselves as a nationalist guerrilla force, called the "Chetniks," loyal to the Serb royal dynasty. Some Chetniks espoused the idea of a "Greater Serbia" and carried out atrocities against non-Serbs. Tito's army of Partisans, on the other hand, was made up of people from all the major Yugoslav religious and ethnic groups and fought for a unified Yugoslavia under communist rule. At the end of the war, the Partisans carried out mass executions against both their Ustashe and Chetnik enemies.

After the war Tito set out to reestablish Yugoslavia and to balance the various nationalities. "Brotherhood and Unity" was the slogan meant to replace calls for independent and greater Croatia and Serbia. By the 1970s Tito had positioned Yugoslavia as a communist state independent of the Kremlin and a leader of the nonaligned movement—finding a strategic niche between Soviet and Western spheres. Yugoslavia was relatively robust economically. The hatreds and tragedies of World War II began to fade, particularly in the new generations, and intermarriage increased. The 1984 Winter Olympic Games brought thousands of visitors to Sarajevo; many came away enchanted by the culture they found.

After Tito's death in 1980, Yugoslavia was ruled by a rotating presidency; each term would be filled by a representative of a different Yugoslav republic. In the late 1980s Serbs became involved in a bitter struggle with Albanians in the region of Kosovo. As Serb nationalists demanded a Greater Serbia in ways that would never have been tolerated under Tito, the other republics, especially Slovenia and Croatia, became fearful. By 1987 a Serbian communist party official, Slobodan Milošević, used the Serb nationalism to dominate Yugoslavia. The Slovenes and Croats declared independence from Yugoslavia in 1991 and Yugoslavia disintegrated.[7]

The Yugoslav army invaded Slovenia but retreated; there were few Serbs in Slovenia and Serbia had no territorial ambitions in it. Croatia was different. The new Croatian president, Franjo Tudjman, countered Milošević's aggressive Serb nationalism with an aggressive Croat nationalism. Tudjman refused to acknowledge the full extent of Ustashe persecution of Serbs during World War II. While moderate Croats and Serbs tried to prevent war, the nationalists associated with Tudjman and Milošević stoked it. The result was a brutal conflict between the Yugoslav army with its allied Serb militias on one side and the new Croat army on the other.

The people of Bosnia, especially the Muslims, were caught in the middle. Croat and Serb nationalism is based upon an identification of nationhood with a particular branch of the Christian religion. In such religious nationalism, a Muslim is treated as a second-class citizen at best. The majority of Bosnian Muslims and many of the other Bosnians—Serb, Croat, Jew, Gypsy, and others—rejected the identification of religion and nationhood. These people considered themselves Bosnian. A Bosnian is any resident of Bosnia-Herzegovina who seeks a nation based not on exclusive religious affiliation but on constitutional rule and respect for differing religions.

If Bosnians refused to fight in the Yugoslav army against Croatia, they were labeled as traitors by Serb militants. If they fought in the Serb-dominated Yugoslav army, they were considered enemies by Croat nationalists. The president of Bosnia-Herzegovina, Alija Izetbegović, had seen this trap and had opposed the independence of Croatia until these explosive issues could be resolved.[8] When war in neighboring Croatia broke out, the Bosnian government was faced with a further trap. If it tried to procure arms, the Yugoslav army and the Serb nationalist militias would interpret the effort as aggression and would attack. If Bosnia refrained from arming itself, Croat nationalists would set up their own militias in Bosnia and any attack by the Serb army would be justified by blaming the Bosnians for not being better prepared. The final trap was the issue of independence. If Bosnia remained in Yugoslavia, Serb nationalists could persecute non-Serbs in Bosnia and say to the world that the persecution was an "internal affair." If Bosnia declared independence, it would face assault by the heavily armed Yugoslav army and the Serb militias.[9] In a chilling speech before the Bosnian Assembly, a Serb religious nationalist by the name of Radovan Karadžić pointed out the vulnerability of the Muslim population and what lay in store for them if they opposed him: "Do not think that you will not lead Bosnia-Herzegovina into hell, and do not think that you will not perhaps make the Muslim people disappear, because Muslims cannot defend themselves if there is war."[10]

On April 6–7, 1992, after Bosnians had voted for independence in a referendum, the European Community and the United States recognized Bosnia-Herzegovina as a sovereign state. Meanwhile, Bosnian Serb nationalists had declared their own independent "Republika Srpska" (Serbian Republic) and set up their headquarters in the town of Pale, not far from Sarajevo, with Karadžić as their president and backed by Serbia. The Yugoslav army and the Serb militias invaded the new nation from all sides: from the Serb-controlled areas of Croatia known as Krajina, from Serbia, and from Montenegro. Units of the Yugoslav army stationed in Bosnia had ringed the hills around Sarajevo with massive artillery, ostensibly as a "training exercise." And local Bosnian Serb extremists had been armed in advance by agents of Serbian militias and the Yugoslav army. By the fall of 1992, the Serb military had occupied 70 percent of Bosnia-Herzegovina, after rolling over towns and villages that were lacking in basic defense capability. Bosnians had expected an attack by the Serb military; what occurred after Serb nationalists gained military control over most of the country was not expected, however, and to many, inconceivable.

WHAT CANNOT BE SAID

The careful use of the term "genocide" represents a fragile yet critical strand in the fabric of internationally shared and legally recognized values. Genocide is a term that can be manipulated and misused. It is also a name for something that seems to elude naming. It is embodied in the Geneva Convention of 1948 outlawing genocide. That convention also requires signatories not only to prevent genocide when it occurs but to punish it, a provision that can provide a disincentive to speak out and name genocide when it does occur.

The problem of language is illustrated by the case of the invisible mass killings. On October 18, 1995, a front-page headline in the *New York Times* indicated that there had been new "mass killings" of civilians in the Banja Luka region of northern Bosnia. The story described the last phase of the four-year "cleansing" of Banja Luka, during which some 500,000 non-Serbs were killed or expelled. The final phase involved the last 20,000 non-Serbs, mostly Bosnian Muslims. They had survived over three years of atrocities and use as slave laborers by Serb nationalists.

As the Bosnian and Croat armies closed in to within a few miles of the Banja Luka area, the final killings were launched. In late October 1995, women and children were brutally expelled. Serb militias selected out men and boys (twelve years and older) and led them away. Refugee workers on the scene warned of a mass killing similar to that carried out earlier by Serb army forces at the UN "safe area" of Srebrenica.

Despite its placement on the front page of a leading American newspaper, the story did not register. In the aftermath of the NATO air strikes of September 1995, which broke the siege of Sarajevo, a statement by NATO that mass atrocities were a cause for resumption of air strikes would have been enough to forestall any killings and probably secure release of the captives. No such statement was given.[11] The last surviving non-Serb population of the Banja Luka region was being taken away, before the eyes of the world, yet unnoticed. For three years the phrases "civil war," "age-old antagonisms," "blame on all sides," and a coded set of stereotypes about Muslims had helped make the killing of Bosnian Muslims appear natural and helped naturalize the refusal to stop it.

What has been called "ethnic cleansing" is not only invisible but also unspeakable. To describe it is to be forced to use a language from which any compassionate human being recoils. Herein lies the irony: the more obscene the crime, the less visible it is. The human capacity for acknowledging religiously based evil is particularly tenuous. The crime is committed by those who appeal to religiously sanctioned absolutes to justify their behavior. Then it is condoned by those who base their response, in part, on religious stereotypes.

For a moment what was being committed in Bosnia became visible. On August 6, 1992, the camps of Omarska and Trnopolje, near Banja Luka, appeared on television screens around the world. We saw those skeletal figures, eyes riveted to the ground, too terrorized to lift their gaze. We knew what had happened there. And when the television crew persisted in demanding access to the camp and the manager of the camp patiently insisted that it was not a camp, but a center, we knew of what kind of realm Omarska was the center. Subsequent reports indicated that those who perished at Omarska would have been saved if the United Nations and the NATO nations, which had had information on the camps for months, had revealed them. We knew what the repression of the reports entailed.[12]

That moment of visibility at Omarska was made possible, in part, by recent meditations on the Holocaust, the extermination of six million Jews by Nazis and their collaborators in World War II. It was not in a house of worship, then, that the truth was most effectively spoken. It was during the dedication to the Holocaust Museum on April 22, 1993, that Holocaust survivor Elie Wiesel could turn to President Clinton and demand that the killing be stopped. What was happening in Bosnia was not the Holocaust or Shoah. Yet much of the response to the atrocities exemplified by Omarska has appealed to categories of value shaped in response to that event, which entered its final phase fifty years earlier. To be faithful both to those who perished in the Holocaust and to those who perished in Bosnia, however, we need to deepen our understanding of all acts of genocide. Then the phrase "Never again" might be retrieved as meaningful.

THE EUPHEMISM

What do we call Omarska and the network of other such places throughout Serb army–occupied (and, for a time, Croat army–occupied) Bosnia-Herzegovina? The evidence gathered by human rights reports and war crimes investigators shows that most of those taken to Omarska were not expected to emerge alive.

Detention was not the object of such places.[13] The existence of Omarska came to light as a result of a series of articles for *New York Newsday* written by the reporter Roy Gutman. It was both the use of the term "death camp" and the content of the articles that finally forced Bosnian Serb leaders to allow a television crew into Omarska, but not until after they had spent time cleaning up and disposing of the most mutilated prisoners.[14]

Unlike Auschwitz, Treblinka, Sobibor, Chelmo, or Belzen, Omarska had no gas chambers and lacked the mechanized mass-killing and disposal methods associated with Nazi death camps. The killings at Omarska were personalized, entailing prolonged beating and torture, frequently by former associates of the victim. How can we grasp the meaning of Omarska and the realm of which it is the center?

The word "ethnic" in "ethnic cleansing" is a euphemism. Bosnian Serbs, Croats, and Muslims all speak the same language, despite the fact that for political reasons they each call it now by a different name.[15] They all trace their descent to tribes that migrated to the area around the sixth century and were Slavic in language and culture by the time they settled in the area.[16] Those who have been singled out for persecution have fallen on the wrong side of a dividing line based solely on religious identity.

As in most wars, innocent civilians from all sides have suffered in the war, the quest for territory, and population expulsions. But Bosnian Muslims—and those who would share a body-politic with them—have been the victims of a consistently more brutal and more methodical violence. Even in the context of the conflict between Croatian and Serb nationalists, who engage in expulsions and atrocities against each other's population as a continuation of the conflict of World War II, the Muslim population has been separated out and treated (by both Croat and Serb nationalists) with particular cruelty. Most victims were Bosnian Muslim noncombatants in areas taken by Serb and Croat militias without significant combat.[17]

In such cases, Muslim religious identity was determined by strictly extrinsic criteria. A Bosnian Muslim in a Serb or Croat camp was there not because of any particular act, expression, or thought. Some in the targeted population defined themselves as Muslims according to the Islamic testimony of belief in one deity and in Muhammad as the messenger of the one deity. Some were observant, for example, keeping the required fast during the Islamic holy month of Ramadan or the prohibition against pork and alcohol. Some were unobservant. Many Bosnian Muslims were atheists. Many were observant of some of the Islamic practices such as the Ramadan fast but considered themselves religious skeptics and their observances cultural. Some supported the political leaders of the Bosnian government; some did not. Some were indifferent to politics.[18]

In the 1971 census a new national category of "Muslims" in Bosnia was recognized by the Yugoslav government. This nationality label led to numerous contradictions within Yugoslavia: an Albanian Muslim was not considered to be a "Muslim" in the Yugoslav census of nationalities, but many Bosnians of Muslim background who considered themselves atheists or skeptics declared themselves "Muslim" in the census to avoid the categories of "Serb" and "Croat," both of which had religious implications. For those who wanted a Bosnian nationality to be affirmed, alongside those of Croat, Slovene, Macedonian, Serbian, and Albanian, this classification of "Muslim" was problematic; it finally gave Bosnian Muslims a political voice alongside Catholics and Orthodox Serbs, but it did so at the cost of further reinforcing the identity between religion and nationality.[19]

In the world of Omarska, if an inhabitant of Bosnia had a name identifiable as Muslim or parents with names identifiable as Muslim, that was considered guilt enough, whatever the beliefs or practices of that individual and whether or not that person was categorized as "Muslim" in the nationalities census. Those organizing the persecution, on the other hand, identified themselves and their cause through explicit religious symbols. The symbols appeared in the three-fingered hand gestures representing the Christian trinity, in the images of sacred figures of Serbian religious mythology on their uniform insignia, in the songs they memorized and forced their victims to sing, on the priest's ring they kissed before and after their acts of persecution, and in the formal religious ceremonies that marked the purification of a town of its Muslim population. The term "ethnic" in the expression "ethnic cleansing," then, is a euphemism for "religious." It entails a purely extrinsic yet deadly definition of the victim in terms of religious identity; the intrinsic aspect— in the form of religious mythology—becomes the motivation and justification for atrocities on the part of the perpetrator.

THE REALM OF OMARSKA

Vladimir Srebrov was one of the founders, along with Radovan Karadžić, of the Serbian Democratic Party (SDS) in Bosnia. In early 1992 Srebrov became aware of a plan within the Yugoslav army, supported by his colleagues in the party, to destroy the Muslim population of Bosnia as part of a partition of the country between Serbia and Croatia. When he attempted to leave Sarajevo to plead with Serb nationalists to abandon the planned killings, he was arrested by Serb militiamen, placed in the Kula prison, and tortured.[20] Srebrov is one of many Serbs who have refused the nationalist program of the Serb governments. He is also one of a number of Serbs who have risked their lives and the lives of their families to protect non-Serbs, to denounce the "ethnic cleansing," and to call for a civil society that is not confined to one particular religious group.

Osman and Sabiha Botonjić were a middle-class Muslim couple in the town of Sanski Most, not far from Banja Luka. In the spring of 1992 the Serb army had occupied their town with little military resistance. Osman was met at work by a former colleague and told to come to the police station for a few questions. He was first held in a small cell jammed with prisoners, without food or water. Beatings were continual. After several days the prisoners were taken out and thrown onto a truck to be driven to a concentration camp at Manjača. Of the sixty-five prisoners in the truck, forty-seven survived the journey. Others, weakened by beatings, died of suffocation, thirst, trauma, or blood loss. Osman was held at Manjača, where prisoners slept on bare ground coated with sheep dung washed in by each new rain. Osman said that many survivors of Manjača had lost feeling in parts of their body because of prolonged exposure to the cold. A special room in Manjača was used for torture.

For most of this period, Sabiha and her daughters had no idea where Osman was and whether or not he was alive. As the terror increased, Sabiha was more and more reluctant to leave the house. Yet she had to go out to find food for her children. Sabiha was further burdened with the knowledge of what happened to Muslim girls if they were picked up by Serb militias. Muslims were required to display identification marks: white armbands or white marks on their homes. When standing in line for food, Muslims were required to give up their place to Serbs. Sabiha spent one whole morning in line as one after another of her Serb neighbors took places in front of her, until all the stocks were gone.

In 1993 Osman, Sabiha, and their daughters started a new life in the United States as refugees. In the fall of 1995 they heard that the last surviving Muslims in Sanski Most had been expelled or killed just before the town was retaken in the final Bosnian army offensive. The Botonjić family's experience illustrates what has been endured by a great many Bosnian Muslims except that they were fortunate enough to have survived intact as a family.[21]

What happened to Vladimir Srebrov and the Botonjić family exemplifies twin policies of religious-based violence in Bosnia-Herzegovina: elimination of all dissent within a particular religious group and destruction of the people outside of it. While the media focused global attention upon the shelling of Sarajevo, major events were occurring in the countryside, away from television cameras. Evidence and testimonies collected by the UN Special Rapporteur for Human Rights in the Former Yugoslavia, the UN Commission of Experts on War Crimes in the Former Yugoslavia, human rights groups such as Helsinki Watch, Doctors without Borders, and Amnesty International, and the International Criminal Tribunal on War Crimes in the Former Yugoslavia indicate systematic, widespread, and methodical persecution beyond anything the popular media has shown.[22]

These sources report that in each area occupied by the Serb army, killing camps and killing centers were established

Map 2.   Genocide in Bosnia-Herzegovina, 1992–1995

and individual massacres were carried out.[23] The term "killing camps" indicates those camps (such as Omarska, Brčko-Luka, Sušica, and the industrial site of the Keraterm company in Prijedor) where the primary object of detention was killing. Many of the prisoners appear to have been beaten to death over a period of hours or days. The killing went on daily and nightly. The term "killing camp" is meant to avoid false identification with the death camps of the Holocaust, while at the same time avoiding falsifications and euphemisms such as "detention camp." Manjača (the camp in which Osman was held), Trnopolje, Batković, and other smaller areas were concentration camps; killings and torture were common, but the majority of detainees did survive.[24]

"Killing centers" were places where the victims were brought for immediate or nearly immediate execution. Thus the famous Drina River bridge in the eastern Bosnian town of Višegrad was used for nightly executions and "sport atrocities" against Bosnian Muslims by Serb militiamen; the victims would be tortured and then thrown off the bridge and shot as they fell down into the Drina River.[25] Similar centers were found in Zvornik, Foča, and most other centers of Bosnian Muslim population occupied by the Serb army.[26]

Massacres, one-time acts of mass killing at discreet locales, occurred in every area occupied by the Serb army. There were various basic forms of massacre: those that took place as Serb militias entered a village or town; those that took place against unarmed civilians behind Serb lines during the time an area was already occupied and fully under the control of Serb forces; those committed against Bosnian villagers in deportation transit; and those committed against Bosnian prisoners of war. Even when

captives thought they were being released, they were often disabused of their hope. In the Vlašić mountain massacre, busloads
of Bosnians who had been released from the Trnopolje camp
were stopped by Serb soldiers and killed.[27]

In late 1992, after the Serb army had consolidated the 70 percent of Bosnian territory it controlled, the mass killings changed
into steady, individualized killings and rapes. In the fall of 1994,
the International Committee of the Red Cross (ICRC) made an
extraordinary appeal to world leaders to stop the atrocities. The
appeal was ignored.[28]

When a town fell to the Serb army, the first inhabitants to be
targeted were intellectual and cultural leaders: religious authorities, teachers, lawyers, doctors, business people, artists, poets,
and musicians. The object of such "elite-cide" was to destroy
the cultural memory of the Bosnian Muslims and Bosnians who
would live with them. Gradually, acts of cruelty and massacre
took on an interior momentum and logic of their own. In many
cases, the Serb population was alerted to leave a village before
the killing began.

Because the Serb governments have refused UN war crimes
investigators access to alleged killing sites and have tampered
with mass graves, it is impossible to calculate the number of
dead. Whatever the final number, given the small size and
population of Bosnia (only four million total population), the
primitive methods used for the killings, and the interference by
reporters and refugee workers, the killing was methodical, systematic, and of a tragic enormity.

In 1993, when Croat religious nationalists saw that Serb army
aggression and atrocities were not being punished but were be-

ing rewarded by international peace negotiators with territorial concessions, they began their own persecution of Bosnian Muslims, modeled on the actions of the Serb militias.

GYNOCIDE

The following testimony was offered by a survivor of the Sušica camp in eastern Bosnia, whose commandant, Dragan Nikolić, has been charged by the International Criminal Tribunal with crimes against humanity. The witness was testifying about several young women who had been "selected" from other refugees: "They started selecting young women. The first was only 14, the second could have been 16 or 17. . . . I knew them all, they were from Vlasenica. . . . Then they started yelling: 'We want the Muslims to see what our seed is.' The women were never seen again. . . . We know that Dragan Nikolić knows about it very well. That's what he did. . . . He told us himself: 'I'm the commander of the camp. I'm your God and you have no other God but me.'"[29]

In one sense, the rapes in Bosnia are a manifestation of the toleration for and condoning of rape throughout history. Rape is also a feature of warfare, and some have argued that it is a rationale for war—that a purpose of war is the free rein it gives to rape.[30] But the use of rape against Muslim women in Bosnia has been overwhelming even by the bleak standards of war. In one town, Foča, a rape center was set up in the former Partizan Sports Hall in May 1992. Muslim girls and women were held there, underwent continual rape and other physical violence, and also were sent out to apartments where they were held for several days and then returned to the Partizan Hall.[31] The organized rape of Muslim women took place throughout the portions of Bosnia occupied by the Serb military, as well as in areas controlled by Croat nationalist forces.[32] Militiamen boasted about their gang rapes of Muslim women.[33] Human rights reports also show rapes of Christian women, but to a lesser extent and apparently without organization and planning.

The organized rape of Bosnian women was gynocidal—a deliberate attack on women as childbearers. In this connection, Serb and Croat nationalists were aware of two facts. The first fact was that the birthrate for Muslims in Yugoslavia was higher than that of Christians, and in some rural places, such as Kosovo province, this birthrate differential was dramatic. Birthrate became so heated an issue that Serb nationalists charged Muslims with a premeditated plot to use their higher birthrates to overwhelm and ultimately destroy the Christian Serbs.[34]

The second fact was that in traditional, Mediterranean societies women who have been raped are often unable to find a husband and have a family. Patriarchal traditions of shame and honor make it difficult—and in some cases, impossible—for women who have been raped to be accepted as wives and mothers. The organized rapes were meant to destroy the potential of the women as mothers. The statements attributed to many rapists—that the victim would bear "Serb seed"—are the flip side of this ideology: forced impregnation of Serb nationhood, a bizarre mixture of religion and biology that can only be understood against the underlying religious mythology.

The rapes were a form of desecration, closely related to the desecration of the sacred spaces symbolized by mosques. The term for sacred space in Islam is *ḥaram*, originally an Arabic term that Serb nationalists associate with one small aspect of Islamic sacred spaces, the women's quarters. Fantasies of "the harem" were commonplace among Serb nationalist clergy, academics, and soldiers. The commander of the Manjača camp, for example, justified the attack on Muslims on the grounds that the Bosnian Muslims had a plan to seize Serb women and put them in harems.[35] Serb religious nationalists used radio broadcasts to spread the charge that Bosnian Muslims were plotting to put Serb women in harems. Many Bosnian Serbs believed, or claimed to believe, these charges despite their being wildly, even ludicrously, inconsistent with the marriage practices of their Bosnian Muslim neighbors.[36] The harem fantasy involves a particularly cruel version of the use of women's bodies as a battlefield. The phrase allegedly used by Dragan Nikolić, "I am your God and you have no other God but me," appears to be a play upon the Islamic declaration of faith, "There is no god but God."[37]

A final dispossession awaited Bosnian Muslim women. Buses of refugees expelled from Serb army territory were stopped by militias and army units. From these refugees, who had already lost their communities, homes, and household possessions, everything else of possible value was now taken, from hard currency to jewelry of little value and sometimes even shoes. Stolen wedding rings—of little monetary value in relation to the enormous booty taken by the militias—represented the last symbol of group identity as well as a symbol of a future procreative possibility. The symbolism of a procreative future seems to be behind the curious obsession of some Serb religious nationalists with stealing wedding rings from Muslim women and giving them to their own girlfriends.[38]

GENOCIDE

The term "genocide" was coined by the jurist Rafael Lemkin as part of an effort to learn from the experience of the Holocaust and to develop an international legal consensus about certain kinds of systematic atrocities.[39] In 1948 the term was formally adopted in the Geneva conventions, and the act of genocide was prohibited. All contracting parties, which included the NATO nations, agreed that "it is a crime under international law which they undertake to prevent and to punish." Genocide was specifically defined as acts committed to "destroy, in whole or in part, a national, ethnic, racial or religious group, as such." Such acts include killing, torture, and efforts to prevent the procreation and regeneration of the targeted people.

Lemkin emphasizes that the term does not necessarily mean the immediate destruction of an entire nation. Rather, it entails "a coordinated plan of different actions aiming at the destruction of essential foundations of the life of national groups." Among the targets for destruction in such a plan, Lemkin lists institutions of culture, language, and national feelings, and the security of property, liberty, health, dignity, and human life. The key criterion for genocide, according to Lemkin, is that it be "directed against the national group as an entity"; violence against individuals is directed against them "not in their individual capacity, but as members of the national group."[40]

The organized persecution in Bosnia from 1992 to 1995 was

an effort to destroy both Bosnian Muslim culture and Bosnian multireligious culture and to destroy the Bosnian Muslims as a people. The campaign was made up of interlocking elements: cultural annihilation, mass killings, organized rape, and a code of euphemisms. Although Bosnian Muslims may have survived as individuals within refugee camps, they would be destroyed as a people and culture, and Bosnia could be partitioned between the religiously purified Christian states of Serbia and Croatia.

For the NATO powers to acknowledge genocide in Bosnia would have been to acknowledge that not only were they breaking the Geneva Genocide Convention by refusing to prevent and punish genocide, but also that they were rewarding genocide by ceding territory to forces that carried it out. The UN-imposed arms embargo had locked into place the vast Serb-army advantage in heavy weapons, violating Article 51 of the UN Charter, which guarantees every recognized nation the right to defend itself; the embargo reinforced the power imbalance that allowed genocide to be carried out with impunity.

Many have denied, without reference to the history and definition of the term, that genocide has occurred in Bosnia.[41] These denials have done harm. No one wants to believe that a people are being exterminated because of race, religion, or ethnic identity and that governments who have the power to stop it refuse to do so. If an entire people are being killed, then on some level we may wish to believe, as we are constantly being told about Bosnia, that "there are no innocents in this war," that the people suffering deserve what they get. To acknowledge even the possibility of genocide, the mass killing of people simply because of who they are, calls into question fundamental beliefs about the possibility of a just foundation to our existence. Denial, however thinly argued, can be effective in lessening public appetite for the difficult process of enforcing the Geneva Genocide Convention.

At the time of this writing, eight major nationalist Serb and Croat military and civil leaders and numerous lower-level soldiers and civilians have been indicted by the International Criminal Tribunal on multiple charges of crimes against humanity. Five have been indicted on the charge of genocide by the tribunal, made up of distinguished jurists from around the world. In all the indictments for genocide, the vast majority of victims were Muslims. The indictments are based upon meticulous investigations. Much of the vast collections of evidence and testimony have been available to the public since the summer of 1992.[42] In this sense, the genocide was committed in full view of the world.

Srebrenica has become the symbol of the failure to enforce the Geneva Convention on Genocide. Srebrenica, a Muslim-majority town on the Drina River, was an ancient center of civilization in Bosnia. In 1992, as the Serb army burned its way through eastern Bosnia, thousands of refugees fled to the Srebrenica area. On April 16, 1993, as the Serb army entered the Srebrenica enclave, the United Nations declared Srebrenica a "safe area" and empowered the United Nations Protection Force in Bosnia (UNPROFOR) to supply humanitarian aid and to use the power of NATO to protect it. Less than a month later, five other besieged cities were declared safe areas.[43]

For more than a year, the Muslims in Srebrenica lived in hunger and fear as the Serb army blocked most UN convoys into the besieged enclave, and the UN commanders refused to use their authorized "necessary means" to break the blockade. A UN report suggesting the enclaves should be abandoned—despite the solemn UN resolutions—served as a green light to Serb army commanders. In the summer of 1995, the Serb army entered Srebrenica and another safe area, Žepa, as UN officials turned down requests for NATO air support. After the safe areas were overrun, Serb general Ratko Mladić drank a toast with the Dutch commander of the Srebrenica UN contingent, at the same time that Mladić's men were selecting out thousands of boys as young as twelve years of age, men, and some young women for torture, rape, and mass killings. Mass graves have been identified, but Serb nationalist authorities have refused war crimes investigators access to the graves. An estimated 8,000 people are missing, but after serious grave tampering, it is impossible to determine how many were killed.[44]

RELIGION AND THE IDEOLOGY OF GENOCIDE

Many deny a religious motive in the assault on Bosnia and upon Bosnian Muslims in particular and in the three-year refusal by the major powers of the Christian world (Britain, France, the U.S., Canada, Germany, and Russia) to authorize NATO power to stop it or allow Bosnians to defend themselves. This book explores religious dimensions of the genocide. The focal point is a national mythology that portrays Slavic Muslims as Christ killers and race traitors. When that national mythology was appropriated by political leaders, backed with massive military power, and protected by NATO nations, it became an ideology of genocide.

"Ideology of genocide" means a set of symbols, rituals, stereotypes, and partially concealed assumptions that dehumanize a people as a whole, justify the use of military power to destroy them, and are in turn reinforced by the economic, political, and military beneficiaries of that destruction. It is the development and function of this ideology of genocide that the succeeding chapters will explore.

CHAPTER TWO

CHRIST KILLERS

THE CHRIST-PRINCE LAZAR

The Good Friday story of the crucifixion of Jesus has been a central, enduring, and powerful symbol within Christianity. The story of the sufferings and death of Jesus Christ, the divine Son in the belief of many Christians, is ritually performed and re-enacted in masses and services, in sermons, in literature, and particularly during the Good Friday commemorations in Easter week in the practice of meditating on the Stations of the Cross and in solemn Good Friday mass. In the Middle Ages, the story was formally performed, with actors on a stage, in passion plays.

The word "passion" refers to what a person suffers or undergoes, what happens to a person. Yet the word also has a much more active meaning, referring to the most powerful drives and emotions, the passions of life. In the performance of the passion play, the sufferings of Jesus Christ, the Son of God, become universal. As the Son of God carries the cross, he carries the sins and sorrows of the entire cosmos. At the moment of his death, those who participate in the passion play die with him and are reborn three days later with his resurrection.

As the innocent victim is sacrificed, there is a moment of intense catharsis. All the fears, sorrows, and sins of the audience are evoked, called out, and purged. This is one of the most emotive moments in human experience. In performance of the Passion, time is collapsed; the event long ago and far away is made present and immediate. The boundary between audience and actors is also effaced. Those who act the evil characters in passion plays know that a quick exit from the stage may be necessary to prevent a pummeling at the hands of an audience for whom temporal boundaries and differences between event and representation have broken down. The power evoked in the passion play can be and has been used for both good and evil.

In the Good Friday mass, in the sermons that relate the Good Friday story from the Christian gospels, and in the narratives of the medieval passion plays, Jews play a central role in the death of Jesus. For those who wish to harness the emotion of the Passion for their own purposes, the charge that the Jews were the killers of Christ, the killers of the Son of God, has been easy to fabricate and manipulate. Words from the New Testament account of the condemnation of Jesus, such as "Let his blood be on us, and on our children" (Mt. 27:26) could be taken out of context and applied to all Jews, with devastating implications. From the time of the first Crusade in 1096, the charge that Jews were Christ killers was used to foment attacks on Jewish communities, attacks that frequently reached genocidal proportions. As formal Good Friday celebrations of the passion play developed in Europe, attacks on Jews became a standard feature of

Easter week, and up until World War II, Jews in Europe would stay inside during Easter week to avoid being attacked.[1] In the Nazi-organized destruction of Jewish communities, the Christ-killer charge was also evoked; it was particularly effective in inflaming European churches and individual Christians to collaborate with the persecutions.

At the heart of the agitation by Serb radicals against the Muslims of Yugoslavia there has been a mythology which presents Slavic Muslims as Christ killers. How could members of a religion which began six centuries after the death of Jesus be responsible for his death?

The answer lies in the central event of Serb national mythology, the martyrdom of Prince Lazar. In 1389, the forces of the Ottoman Turkish Sultan Murat clashed at Kosovo with the Serb army led by Prince Lazar. Both Lazar and Murat were killed. In the view of Serb tradition, the death of Lazar marked the end of Serb independence and the beginning of five centuries of rule by the Ottoman Empire.[2]

During the nineteenth century, Serbian nationalist writers transformed Lazar into an explicit Christ figure, surrounded by a group of disciples, partaking of a Last Supper, and betrayed by a Judas. Lazar's death represents the death of the Serb nation, which will not be resurrected until Lazar is raised from the dead and the descendants of Lazar's killers are purged from the Serbian people. In this story, the Ottoman Turks play the role of the Christ killers. Vuk Branković, the Serb who betrays the battle plans to the Ottoman army, becomes the Christ killer within. In the nationalist myth, Vuk Branković represents the Slavs who converted to Islam under the Ottomans and any Serb who would live with them or tolerate them.[3]

BOSNIA IN MYTH AND HISTORY

The ancestors of the South Slavs arrived in the Balkans in the sixth and seventh centuries.[4] By the ninth century, the South Slavs were converting in large numbers to Christianity. Credit for the conversion is given to two Christian saints, Methodius and Cyril. The Bible was translated into a liturgical South Slavic language (Church Slavonic). Followers of Cyril are credited with the invention of the Cyrillic script, based upon Greek characters, used in Serbia and Russia today.

The South Slavs were divided by the split or Great Schism in Christianity between the Catholic Church of the West, which recognized the authority of the Pope in Rome and used Latin, and the Orthodox Churches of the East, which refused the priority of the Bishop of Rome and used Greek or other languages in religious texts and practices. The South Slavs inhabiting the northern areas, the Slovenes and Croats, became Catholic and those in the southern and eastern areas, the Serbs, became Orthodox. In 1159 a Serbian dynasty was founded. In 1346, under the Emperor Stefan Dušan, a Serbian Orthodox Church Patriarchate was established, with its seat in the Kosovo region of present-day Serbia. Serbia's rise as a powerful state is expressed in the art and architecture of its many monasteries.

Adjacent to the Serbian kingdom was Bosnia. The early period of Bosnian history is an enigma. What remains as witness to this period are *stećaks*, large funerary monuments decorated with enigmatic, sculpted symbols. Bosnia grew powerful as a crossroads for trade between the flourishing city-state Ragusa (present-day Dubrovnik) and Constantinople, the capital of the eastern Roman Empire and the Orthodox Christian world. Bos-

nia also had mineral wealth in gold and silver. The city of Srebrenica (the name comes from the South Slavic word for silver)
was particularly famous for its mines. The Bosnian state reached
a high point under the rule of King Tvrtko (crowned in 1377),
who ruled at the same time as Prince Lazar of Serbia and who
sent troops to fight at Lazar's side at the battle of Kosovo in June
of 1389.

In medieval Bosnia there were three churches: the Catholic
Church, the Orthodox Church, and a third Christian Church,
called the Bosnian Church, which was independent from both the
Catholic and the Orthodox worlds. The Bosnian Church was accused of heresy and associated by its enemies with heretics from
Bulgaria called Bogomils. Bogomils were accused of being Mani-
chean dualists, that is, believing in two equal principles of good
and evil and rejecting the world as being of the evil principle.

The Catholic rulers of Hungary persuaded the papacy to sanction attacks on Bosnia in order to extirpate the heresy. The papacy also authorized the Franciscan order of friars to establish
monasteries in Bosnia and bring the adherents of the Bosnian
Church back to Catholicism. The Orthodox Church was also involved in persecuting adherents to the Bosnian Church.

The world of the South Slavs was soon to be transformed by
a new force. Ever since the tenth and eleventh centuries, Turkic
tribes from Central Asia had been gaining power in the Islamic
Middle East. By the fourteenth century, one of those Turkic
tribes, the Ottomans, gained ascendancy in Anatolia and began
constructing a major world empire. After the battle of Kosovo,
the Ottomans pursued their advance and in the year 1453 they
captured Constantinople, the capital of the eastern Roman Empire and Orthodox Church. By 1483 they had captured Bosnia.

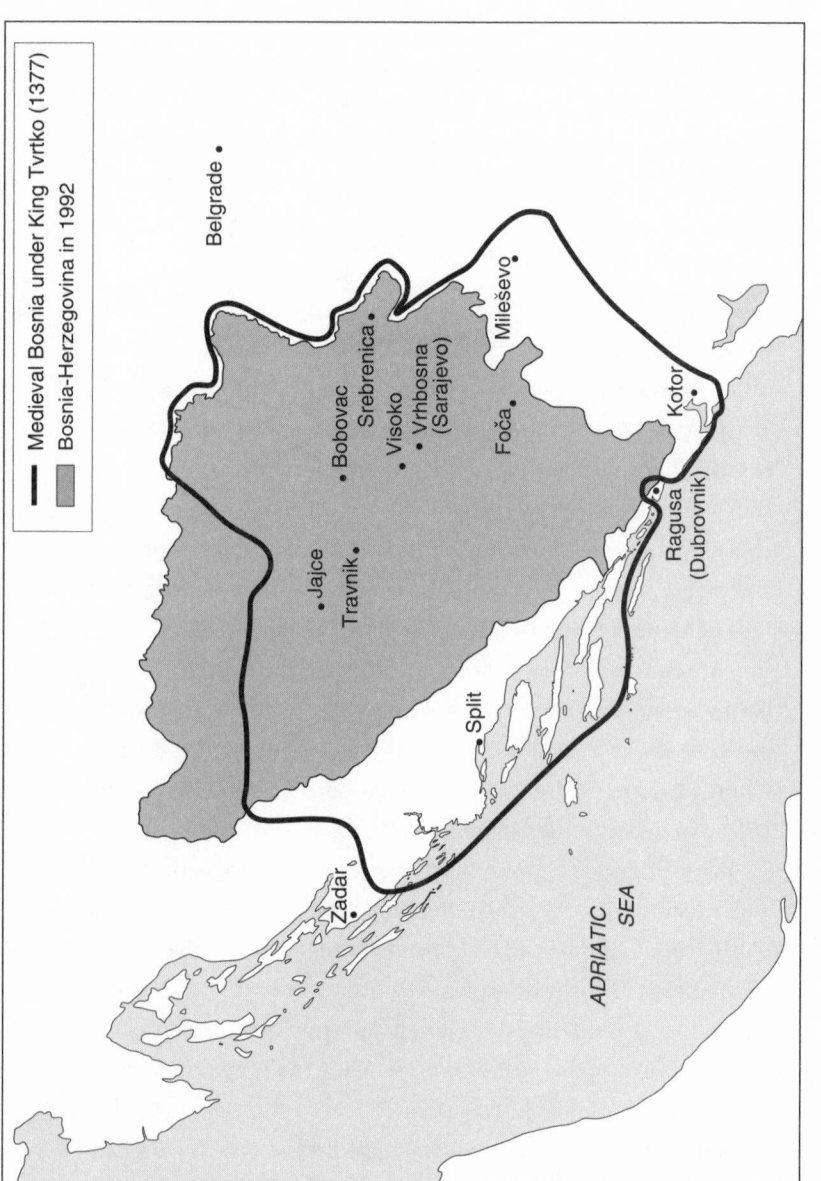

Map 3. Medieval and Modern Bosnia

In the reign of Sultan Suleiman the Magnificent (1520–1566), they were at the gates of Vienna. The Ottomans transformed small villages into the new Ottoman-style cities of Sarajevo, Mostar, and Travnik. Roads, bridges, marketplaces, and inns were constructed throughout the region. As Bosnia grew and prospered, Bosnians converted to Islam in a higher proportion than Serbs or other South Slavic groups.

The conversion of such a large number of Bosnians to Islam has been a major issue in Croatian and Serbian national mythologies. For Croat and Serb nationalists, only the weak and the cowardly converted to Islam; conversions to Islam must have been the product of force or opportunism. Such a mythology is just as distorted as its implied counterpart mythology, that the Slavs who converted to Christianity in the ninth century did so without any economic or political pressures or enticements. Conversion is a complex process, involving intricate interconnections (and sometimes contradictions) between individuals and wider forces in society. Most Bosnians believe that the largest number of converts to Islam were from the Bosnian Church, who were persecuted as Christians and whose beliefs were supposedly more compatible with those of Islam. Historians have challenged this theory, however, showing that there is no evidence that the Bosnian Church in fact was Bogomil and that the patterns of conversion were far more complex than the supposed mass conversion of Bosnian Bogomils to Islam.

Also exposed as historically untenable are the national myths that ethnic groups are or ever were stable entities that remain fixed down through the centuries, or that the Orthodox Serbs, Catholic Croats, and Muslims of Bosnia today are direct descendants through stable ethnoreligious communities of ancient Orthodox, Catholic, and Muslim ancestors. The various loyalties in Bosnia were complex and shifting, and conversions followed many patterns. Orthodox Christians converted to Catholicism, Catholics converted to Orthodox Christianity, Orthodox Christians and Catholics converted to Islam. Some Muslims converted to different forms of Christianity.

The final mythic figure of Croatian and Serbian religious nationalism is the evil Ottoman. No occupied nation thinks kindly of its colonizer and the Ottomans were no doubt capable of cruelty and oppression. Yet the stories of Ottoman depravity at the heart of nationalist mythology cannot match the evidence. If, as Croatian and Serbian religious leaders and academics claim, the Ottomans were constantly massacring Christians, how is it that such large groups of Catholics and Orthodox Christians not only survived, but in some cases grew and flourished under Ottoman rule? If, as today's national myths would maintain, the Ottomans spent five hundred years busily eradicating all traces of Christianity, how is it that such a magnificent ancient heritage of Catholic and Orthodox Christianity—manuscripts, art, and architecture—survived Ottoman rule so well? If Islam is an inherently persecuting religion based on forced conversion, how is it that the Catholic and Orthodox populations not only maintained themselves for five centuries under Ottoman rule, but grew?

In the nineteenth century, the three myths—conversion to Islam based only upon cowardice and greed, stable ethnoreligious groups down through the centuries, and complete depravity of Ottoman rule—became the foundation for a new religious ideology, Christoslavism, the belief that Slavs are Christian by nature and that any conversion from Christianity is a betrayal of the Slavic race.

THE CURSE OF KOSOVO

Western policy makers maintain that the conflict in the Balkans is "age old." Yet contiguous ethnic and religious groups throughout the world have old antagonisms. Armed conflict between Serbs and Croats is confined largely to this century. The conflict between Serbs and Slavic Muslims dates back to the Ottoman conquest of the Balkans in the fourteenth and fifteenth centuries. However, the development of the Kosovo story in which Slavic Muslims and Serbs are ancient and fated enemies is more recent; it was constructed by nationalist Serbs in the nineteenth century and projected back to the battle of Kosovo in 1389, and then back further, even to the very creation of the universe. It is this rather recent national mythology which was revived in the late 1980s in Yugoslavia.

Until the nineteenth century, the battle of Kosovo was not the central theme of Serbian epic. Rather than Prince Lazar, the main Serbian epic hero was Marko Kraljević, a Serb vassal of the Ottomans. Because he fought both for and against his masters in Istanbul, Prince Marko has served as a figure of mediation between the Serbian Orthodox and Ottoman worlds. In the epic literature, Marko stands in contrast to the polarizing figures identified with the battle of Kosovo as it was configured by nineteenth-century Serbian nationalists.

The reconstruction of Serbian mythology took place during the Serb revolt against Ottoman occupation and under the influence of the German romantic nationalism of Johann Gottfried Herder. The key figure in the Serb romantic literary movement was Vuk Karadžić (1787–1864), viewed by many Serbs as the founder of modern Serbian literary consciousness. Karadžić set out to produce a Serb collection of folk literature that would rival collections such as Herder's *Stimmen der Völker* (*Folk Voices*).[5] He collected popular songs and epics and published them in a four-volume set that became, for Serb nationalists, the canonical source and voice of the "national spirit."[6] Karadžić succeeded in forming a linguistic canon based upon certain dialects, which he deemed linguistically and ethnically pure of foreign contamination. In his view, all speakers of the South Slavic dialects, whether Catholic, Muslim, or Orthodox, were considered Serbs; Serb nationality was a function of the language. For Vuk Karadžić and many of his admirers down to the present day, Serbia exists wherever the Serbian language (what was later called Serbo-Croatian) is spoken.[7]

As Vuk Karadžić carried out the canonization of the folk epic, selecting those poems that were to be identified with the Serb nation as a whole, Serb revolutionaries were moving Serbia toward political independence. The revolt of Karadjordje against the Ottomans began in 1804, and in 1806 Karadjordje took Belgrade. In 1829, Serbia was granted autonomy from Ottoman rule in the Treaty of Adrianople and in 1830 Miloš Obrenović founded the first modern Serb dynasty. The Kosovo legends became part of the Serbian revolutionary movement and those parts of the tradition especially meaningful for such a movement were preserved and emphasized.

As early as 1814, Vuk Karadžić had begun to emphasize the importance of the story of Lazar and Kosovo when he published a first version of the famous curse of Kosovo: "Whoever will not fight at Kosovo / may nothing grow that his hand sows, / neither the white wheat in the field / nor the vine of grapes on his mountains."[8] In 1845, Vuk Karadžić published another version of the curse:

> Whoever is a Serb of Serbian blood
> Whoever shares with me this heritage,
> And he comes not to fight at Kosovo,
> May he never have the progeny
> His heart desires, neither son nor daughter;
> Beneath his hand let nothing decent grow
> Neither purple grapes nor wholesome wheat;
> Let him rust away like dripping iron
> Until his name be extinguished.[9]

Karadžić also emphasized the importance of Miloš Obilić, the assassin of Murat, comparing him to Achilles.[10]

Despite Karadžić's public pronouncements on its importance, Kosovo plays a relatively minor role in the poems he collected. The portrayal of Lazar as a Christ figure, Kosovo as a Serb Golgotha, and Muslims as the evil brood of "cursed Hagar" was to be found in sermons and chronicles.[11] However, the Kosovo legend, as a story that would fix Slavic Muslims as Christ killers and race traitors, was still not fully realized.

The Christological imagery solidified after the middle of the nineteenth century. In the art and literature of late nineteenth-century Serb romanticism, Lazar is depicted at a Last Supper, surrounded by knight disciples, one of whom (Vuk Branković) will betray the Christ-Prince. Lazar mistakenly accuses another disciple, Miloš Obilić, of being the traitor. During the ensuing battle, Miloš avenges Lazar by assassinating the Sultan, only to be cut to pieces in turn by the Sultan's guard.[12] Miloš Obilić, who killed the Sultan to avenge Lazar, became the role model for all Serbs.

EXTERMINATION OF THE TURKIFIERS

Montenegro is the small mountainous nation adjacent to Serbia, with a coastline on the Adriatic Sea. While the area of present-day Serbia was occupied by the Ottomans until the revolutions of the nineteenth century, Serbs in the area of Montenegro were able to use the rugged terrain to carve out more independence from the Ottoman Empire. The leader of the Montenegrin Serbs

Fig. 1. Prince Lazar as Christ at the Last Supper: *The Feast of the Prince* by Adam Stefanović, lithograph, 1870s. From Wayne S. Vucinich and Thomas A. Emmert, *Kosovo: Legacy of a Medieval Battle* (Minneapolis: University of Minnesota Press, 1991).

had the title of *vladika*, which indicated a combination of the roles of prince and bishop.

The key figure in the reconstruction of the Lazar story was *vladika* Petar II Petrović (1813–1851), better known through his pen name of Njegoš. Njegoš's key work is *The Mountain Wreath* (*Gorski vijenac*), published in 1847 and considered by many Serb nationalists to be the central work of all Serbian literature.[13] The work, a historical drama in verse, portrays and glorifies the Christmas Eve extermination of Slavic Muslims at the hands of Serb warriors. It is based upon the legend of a campaign said to have been carried out against Slavic Muslims in early eighteenth-century Montenegro.

Njegoš's drama opens with Bishop Danilo, the play's protagonist, brooding on the evil of Islam, the tragedy of Kosovo, and the treason of Vuk Branković. Danilo's warriors suggest celebrating the holy day (Pentecost) by "cleansing" (*čistiti*) the land of non-Christians. The chorus chants: "The high mountains reek with the stench of non-Christians." One of Danilo's men proclaims that struggle will not end until "we or the Turks [Slavic Muslims] are exterminated."[14] The references to the Slavic Muslims as "Turkifiers" (*Poturice*) or as "Turks" crystallizes the view that by converting to Islam from Christianity, the Muslims had changed their racial identity and joined the race of Turks who killed the Christ-Prince Lazar. Throughout the Bosnian genocide of 1992–1995, the Serb nationalists and Serb clerics referred to Bosnian Slavic Muslims as Turks, even though all political ties with Turkey ended with the demise of the Ottoman Empire after World War I.

Western military and political leaders often maintain that the killing in Bosnia is a continuation of an ancient blood feud.[15] In *The Mountain Wreath*, however, the "extermination of the Turki-fied" is placed explicitly *outside* the category of the blood feud. In tribal societies of Montenegro and Serbia, a blood feud, however ruthless and fatal, could end in reconciliation. The godfather (*kum*) ceremony was the vehicle through which clans who had fallen into blood feud could reconcile with one another.[16] In *The Mountain Wreath*, when the Muslims suggest a *kum* ceremony, Danilo's men object that the ceremony requires baptism. The Muslims offer an ecumenical alternative, suggesting that the Muslim hair-cutting ceremony is a parallel to the tradition of baptism. Danilo's men respond with scatological insults against Islam, its prophet, and Muslims. With each set of insults, the chorus chants "*Tako, već nikako*" ("This way; there is no other") to indicate the act that must be done. The Muslims have two choices: be baptized in water or in blood.

Njegoš's story moves the conflict from the realm of blood feud into a cosmic duality of good and evil; Slavic Muslims be-come the "other." The sympathetic qualities of the Muslims are Danilo's last temptation. However sympathetic in person, Mus-lims are Christ killers, "blasphemers," "spitters on the cross." In quieter scenes, *The Mountain Wreath* offers a brooding lyricism in which a cosmic duality of good (Serb) versus evil (Muslim) is reinforced through metaphor, historical analogy, and explicit as-sertion. The antagonism in this representation is not just "old"; it is eternal.

The necessity to purify the Serb nation of the pollution of non-Christians is stated in powerful terms by the anonymous chorus that accompanies the dance (*kolo*), a choir portrayed as the voice of the people. The last hesitation of Bishop Danilo has been overcome by Abbot Stefan, who urges Miloš Obilić as a model and who rejoices openly in killing. *The Mountain Wreath* ends with the Christmas Eve extermination of the Slavic Muslims—men, women, and children. On return from the slaughter, Serb warriors take communion, without going to confession, which was mandatory after acts of blood vengeance.

Acts of blood vengeance were believed to cause religious defilement that rendered the actor ineligible to receive the Eucharist. By offering the Serb warriors communion without requiring their confession, the Serb Orthodox clergy take the "extermination of the Turkifiers" out of the category of blood vengeance. Instead, they present it as an act sacred in itself, with the implication of baptism by blood. Here, however, there is a twist. In the Christian doctrine of baptism by blood, it is the martyr whose sins are washed away by the baptism. In the extermination of the Turkifiers the killers who are baptizing the Turkifiers in blood are rendered worthy of communion and receive a full forgiveness for all their sins. Killing Turks or Turkified ones becomes not only worthy, but sacred, raised to the same level of sacrality as baptism or confession.

As *The Mountain Wreath* and the national mythology it expressed became more popular, Slavic Muslims were placed in a particularly impossible situation. By the linguistic standards of Vuk Karadžić, since the Slavic Muslims spoke South Slavic dialects Vuk Karadžić labeled Serb, they were considered Serbs. But by the standards of *The Mountain Wreath*, all Serbs had to be Christian, and any conversion to Islam was a betrayal of Serb blood and entailed a transformation from Slavic to Turkish blood. Slavic Muslims could not escape being considered Serb because of the Vuk Karadžić linguistic criteria, but as Serbs they had to be considered traitors according to the Njegoš mythology. They were delegitimized as a group and dehumanized as individuals. Finally, in the words of an influential Orthodox bishop, Njegoš portrays Miloš Obilić, the symbol of revenge, as "some kind of divinity; this is why we speak of Obilić's altar."[17]

Shortly after the appearance of Njegoš's *Mountain Wreath*, the feast day of St. Lazar, which had never before been recognized in Church calendars as a holy day, began to take on increased importance. In the 1860s the feast day of Prince Lazar was combined with the feast day of Vid (or Vitus), a pre-Christian Slavic god. In 1889, the 500th anniversary of Kosovo increased the interest in Vid's Day (*Vidovdan*). In 1892 Vid's Day appeared for the first time as an official holiday in the Church calendar as "Prophet Amos and Prince Lazar (Vid's Day)."[18]

The political and religious significance of the day increased in the twentieth century. It was on Vid's Day in 1914 that Gavrilo Princip, who had memorized Njegoš's *Mountain Wreath*, assassinated Archduke Ferdinand and set off World War I.[19] The 1921 constitution of Yugoslavia was called the Vidovdan constitution because it was proclaimed on June 28, Vid's Day. Vid's Day also became the day on which the school year ended throughout Yugoslavia, marking the death of Lazar in a conspicuous manner for all people in Yugoslavia, not just for Serbs. The more militant aspects of the Lazar story continued to grow in importance.

Although the day is Vid's Day, it is the death of the Christ-Prince Lazar that is at the center of the observance.[20] On the occasion of the 600th anniversary of Lazar's martyrdom, the resurgent Serb nationalists began to harness the excitement in order to heighten the symbolism of the event. At the same time there was a revival of interest in Njegoš. Pictures of Njegoš and posters with his verses were in wide circulation. A Serb writer exclaimed in 1989, "Is there anything more beautiful, more sincere and more profound than those pictures and verses [of Njegoš] written out from memory, not dictated by learned people or copied out of collected words. . . . Njegoš was resurrected in the memory of the people."[21] Njegoš, the poet of the death and resurrection of the Serb nation, was himself resurrected.

CHRISTOSLAVISM

"Race betrayal" is a key theme of *The Mountain Wreath* and the strand of Serbian literature it represents. By converting to Islam, Njegoš had insisted, Slavic Muslims "turkified." To "turkify" was not simply to adopt the religion and mores of a Turk, but to transform oneself into a Turk. To convert to a religion other than Christianity was simultaneously to convert from the Slav race to an alien race.

This ideology, originally set forth in the nineteenth century, found a new and powerful form in the work of Ivo Andrić (1892–1975), Yugoslavia's Nobel laureate in literature. Even more explicitly than Njegoš, Andrić presents religious conversion to Islam as conversion to the Turkic race. In his doctoral dissertation of 1924, Andrić makes the following statement about Njegoš and "the people": "Njegoš, who can always be counted on for the truest expression of the people's mode of thinking and apprehending . . . [described] the process of conversion thus: 'The lions [those who remained Christians] turned into tillers of the soil, the cowardly and covetous turned into Turks (*isturčiti*).'"[22] Andrić ascribes to "the people" Njegoš's judgment that Slavic Muslims who converted to Islam were the "cowardly and covetous" who "turned into Turks." Bosnian Slavic Muslims are thus doubly excluded from "the people": first, they became an alien race by converting to Islam; and second, it is the judgment of "the people"—not of one nationalist writer—that they have changed race along with religion.

The verse quoted by Andric´ ("the cowardly and covetous turned into Turks") is followed immediately in Njegoš's *Mountain Wreath* by the curse: "May their Serb milk be tainted with the plague." Few Serb readers of Andrić would be unfamiliar with the famous line about "Serb milk." Njegoš had applied the curse of Kosovo, leveled against those who refused to fight at the battle of Kosovo in 1389, to all Slavic Muslims. Andrić revived this curse and reinstated Njegoš's chorus as the "voice of the people." This voice of the people excludes all Slavic Muslims from the people, and curses them to disappear through a lack of progeneration.

Andrić finds a historical rationale for such exclusion in the belief that the Slavs who converted to Islam were primarily Bogomil heretics from the Bosnian Church. For Andrić, the ancient Bosnian Church showed a "young Slavic race" still torn between "heathen concepts with dualistic coloring and unclear Christian dogmas."[23] Andrić portrays the Bosnian Slavs who converted to Islam not only as cowardly and covetous and the "heathen element of a young race," but finally as the corrupted "Orient" that cut off the Slavic race from the "civilizing currents" of the West.[24]

The notion that the Bosnian Slavs who embraced Islam in the fifteenth and sixteenth centuries did so out of cowardly and covetous reasons is based upon a particular ideology of conversion held by Christian nationalists in the Balkans. As explained earlier, a Slav who converted from Christianity to Islam must have done so out of greed or cowardice. Yet such terms are never applied to the conversion of the Slavs to Christianity, believed to have occurred around the eighth century. It is a premise so basic that its authors do not even bother to argue that conversion to Christianity is based upon genuine religious sentiments.[25] Slavs are racially Christian. The conflation of Slavic race and Christian religion is illustrated in Andrić's popular historical novels.

Andrić's most famous novel centers on the bridge constructed over the Drina River at the eastern Bosnian town of Višegrad.[26] The bridge was commissioned by Mehmed Pasha Sokolović, the Bosnian who had become a vizier or minister to the Ottoman Sultan in Istanbul. According to popular legend, as related by the narrator of the novel, the fairies (*vile*) thwart the bridge's construction, causing all kinds of disasters and accidents. It is learned that for reasons unexplained the fairies will only be mollified if two Christian babies are walled up inside the bridge. Later generations of folk interpret the two holes in the bridge as the place where the infants' mothers would suckle their infants. The essentially Christian race of Slavs is trapped within the monumental structures of an alien religion.[27]

For Andrić, the evil is represented by the practice known as *devşirme*. In this practice, the Ottomans would select young boys from all over the empire to be taken to Istanbul, brought up in the court, and serve as soldiers, bureaucrats, and sometimes high officials. Although in Bosnia both Muslims and Christians were taken, and although the reaction of the boy's family could range from horror at the loss of a son to joy at the possibility of future high position, the Serbian nationalists portrayed the system as a "child tribute" or "blood tribute" by which the Ottomans

6th–7th centuries	Ancestors of South Slavs enter the Balkans
869	Death of St. Cyril, symbol of the Christianizing of the South Slavs
1159	Stefan Nemanja founds the Serbian dynasty
1219	St. Sava becomes the first Archbishop of the Serbian Orthodox Church
1346	Founding of the Patriarchate of Serbian Orthodoxy
1377	Tvrtko is crowned King of Bosnia
1389	Death of Lazar at the battle of Kosovo
1453	Ottomans take Constantinople and change its name to Istanbul
1459	Last Serb stronghold at Smederevo falls to the Ottomans
1483	Ottomans take control of all of Bosnia and Herzegovina
1531	Gazi Husrev Beg Mosque constructed in Sarajevo, the major mosque in Bosnia
1551	Colored Mosque of Foča is constructed
1556	Construction of the great Mostar bridge
1557	Construction of the Drina River bridge at Višegrad
1804	Karadjordje's revolt against Ottoman rule
1818	Assassination of Karadjordje by rival Miloš Obrenović, founder of the first modern Serbian dynasty
1829	Treaty of Adrianople: Serbia gains autonomy under Miloš Obrenović
1847	Njegoš publishes *The Mountain Wreath*
1864	Death of Vuk Karadžić, collector of Serb poetry and lore
1878	Treaty of San Stefano: Ottomans cede Bosnia to Austro-Hungarian control
1903	Descendants of Karadjordje establish a new dynasty in Serbia
1917	Union of South Slavs is declared
1918	Kingdom of Serbs, Croats, and Slovenes (later to be called Yugoslavia) is established under the authority of King Peter I of Serbia

would sap the blood of Christians by stealing their children. The novel's hero represents this image of blood tribute. In history, Sokolović led a fabled life. From the humble town of Višegrad, he rose to become the grand vizier (prime minister) to the greatest empire of the time and married Sultan Suleiman's granddaughter, Princess Esmahan. He endowed his town with great monuments, such as the bridge. According to some accounts, he placed a relative, Makarije, in the position of patriarch of the Serb Church, and thus his family remained thoroughly interreligious. In the novel, however, Mehmed Pasha, despite personal and family success, can never escape the sadness inside; the Christian boy is entombed within the Islamicized man.

The key event in *The Bridge on the Drina* is the impaling of a Serb rebel who tried to destroy the bridge by the Turks and their helpers, Bosnian Muslims and Gypsies. The scene contains a long, anatomically detailed account of the death of the heroic Serb, with explicit evocations of the crucifixion. The scene fits into that genre of Christian literature that details the sufferings and torments of Jesus. It is a scene that is constantly evoked by readers of Andrić as one of the most memorable, if not the most memorable, passage in all of Andrić's writings.[28]

Serb and Croat nationalists have turned the practice of impalement to punish those who defied their authority into a symbol of Turkish and Muslim depravity, despite the fact that the punishment of impalement was also practiced in Christian Austria and elsewhere in Europe at that time. Followers of Serb nationalist leaders in Bosnia have evoked the Ottoman use of impalement in justifying the attacks on Bosnian Muslims who are alleged to be Turks because of the conversion of their ancestors to Islam. Ironically, the most famous impaler of all time was the fifteenth-century Prince Vlad of Moldavia (transformed by later legend into Count Dracula), whose victims were dissidents and Turks.[29]

Andrić's works are characterized by a command of local setting, a sense of the power of myth and folklore, and skill in historical fictive narration.[30] Indeed, it is their literary quality that has given Andrić's views on race betrayal such a key place within the Serb nationalist tradition.[31] The one Ottoman monument that remains intact in areas occupied by Serb nationalists today is the sixteenth-century Višegrad bridge on the Drina that Andrić made famous. Serb nationalists chose that same bridge as a killing center for Muslims in the spring of 1992.

TIME AND THE PASSION PLAY

Radovan Karadžić, President of the Republika Srpska, likes to appear in public with a *gusle*, the stick-fiddle used by bards to recite epic poetry. He makes a point of visiting the countryside frequently, where, he believes, the true Serb folk spirit can be found, unpolluted by the ethnic and religious mixing of the cities. His soldiers are accompanied by *gusle* players. As the *gusle* player sings, the Serb soldiers pass around an alcoholic drink and make the sign of the cross before drinking. They sing: "Serb brothers, wherever you are, with the help of Almighty God / For the sake of the Cross and the Christian Faith and our imperial fatherland / I call you to join the battle of Kosovo."

Karadžić explains that his favorite epic is "The Last Supper": "It has something to do with Jesus Christ, symbolizing Serbian faith after that last supper—so we lost our empire." Radovan Karadžić speaks with pride of his ancestor, the linguist and collector of folk epic, Vuk Karadžić. Vuk, he says, "reawakened the spirit of the Serbian culture that had been buried in the memory of the Serb people during long centuries of Turkish occupation." He speaks of the *gusle* epics as being songs of "our people" (that is, Serbs as opposed to Bosnian Muslims) thus using them to divide Serb from Slavic Muslim. Such a definition of "our people" ignores the fact that the *gusle* epics were a major aspect of folk culture for both Muslim Slavs and Orthodox Serbs, who shared the same epic traditions, conventions, and sensibility.[32]

Christoslavism—the premise that Slavs are by essence Christian and that conversion to another religion is a betrayal of the people or race—was critical to the genocidal ideology being developed in 1989. Christoslavism places Slavic Muslims and any Christian who would tolerate them in the position of the Judas figure of Kosovo, Vuk Branković. It sets the Slavic Muslims outside the boundaries of nation, race, and people. As portrayed in *The Mountain Wreath*, it demonstrates what can be done to those defined as nonpeople and what is, under certain circumstances, a religious duty and a sacred, cleansing act. It transfers the generalized curse of Kosovo onto Slavic Muslims in particular, a curse against the natal milk that will allow them to progenerate. In their acts of genocide from 1992 through 1995, Radovan Karadžić and his followers integrated the Kosovo tradition, as it was handed down through Vuk Karadžić and transformed by Njegoš and Andrić, into the daily rituals of ethnoreligious purification.

Milovan Djilas, Tito's colleague in the Partisans, a chronicler of the events of World War II in Yugoslavia, and a famous critic of the later Tito regime, was an admirer of *The Mountain Wreath*. In his book on Njegoš, he argued that the historical extermination of Montenegrin Muslims, the *istraga Poturica*, was a "process" rather than a single "event" and that Njegoš had shaped it into a single act for literary and ideological purposes.[33] We can only speculate what Njegoš himself would have thought had such an event occurred during his own life. The mounting evidence from human rights reports and war crimes testimony suggests powerfully that it did occur from 1992 to 1995.

To understand the full violence of the Christoslavic ideology unleashed by Serb nationalists at Kosovo in 1989, it is necessary to show how the contemporary conflict with Albanians in Kosovo and the atrocities committed by the Croat fascist state in World War II were incorporated into the Kosovo pageant.

CHAPTER THREE

PERFORMING THE PASSION

SERB JERUSALEM

In 1989, the "Kosovo question" did not refer directly to the ancient battle of 1389 or to the feast day of Lazar and Vid. It referred to a political crisis in the Serbian province of Kosovo, a crisis that enraged Serb nationalists and tore apart the Yugoslav federation. Kosovo is more than the site of the archetypal founding event in Serb romantic mythology. It is also the center of many of Serbia's greatest works of religious art and architecture and the ancient seat of the Serb Orthodox leadership. Some call it the "Serb Jerusalem."[1]

The Serb Patriarchate (the institutional heart of Serb Orthodox Christianity) was established at Peć in the Kosovo region in 1346. It was abolished after the Ottoman conquests in the fifteenth century. The Patriarchate was reestablished in 1557 by Mehmed Pasha Sokolović, the famous Bosnian who became the grand vizier at the court of the Ottoman Sultan Suleiman the

Magnificent. The first occupant of the newly reestablished position of Patriarch is believed to have been a relative of Mehmed Pasha. The restored Patriarchate lasted until 1765 when Ottoman authorities abolished it on the grounds that it offered support to anti-Ottoman revolutionary activity.

During most of the past three hundred years, the province of Kosovo has been inhabited primarily by Albanians. Albanians are not a Slavic people; they speak a completely different language from the other inhabitants of Yugoslavia. Most Albanians traditionally profess Islam, but during the cold war Albania was ruled by an antireligious Stalinist regime; Albanians in Kosovo were less brutally but still effectively secularized under Tito's moderate communism.[2]

After the Balkan wars at the beginning of the twentieth century, Kosovo was recaptured by Serbian patriots and made part of the modern Serb state. During the period between the two world wars, Serbia colonized Kosovo, pushing Albanians out and bringing in Serb settlers. When Tito reestablished Yugoslavia, he was concerned to avoid ethnic and religious conflict and so abandoned the Serb colonization of Kosovo. Serb nationalists complained that Serb settlers who had fled Kosovo during World War II were not allowed to return. In 1974 Tito promulgated a constitution that offered Kosovo and Vojvodina the status of autonomous provinces within Serbia. These two provinces were administratively still part of Serbia, but they were given a vote in the Yugoslav presidency equal to the constituent nations of Yugoslavia (Slovenia, Serbia, Bosnia-Herzegovina, Croatia, Macedonia, and Montenegro). The logic behind this arrangement was that both provinces had large populations of non-Serbs and deserved a measure of autonomy.

The new constitution enraged Serb nationalists. After World War II, the Albanian population in Kosovo had increased in proportion to the Serbian population. Kosovo was the poorest region of Yugoslavia; some Serbs migrated to better employment and living opportunities available for them elsewhere, while Albanians tended to remain in an area where their language was spoken. Impoverished Kosovo Albanians also had one of the highest birthrates in Europe, and the Serbs, already a minority in Kosovo, began to look at the large Albanian families with demographic fear.

In 1981 Albanian students demonstrated over conditions at the University of Priština, the major university in Kosovo province. Serbs in Albania complained of harassment by young Albanian men and of pressure to leave the province. After Serb nationalists revoked Kosovo's autonomy in 1987, Albanians in Kosovo protested the harsh rule of the Serb-dominated Yugoslav police. Albanian protestors began to demand the status of a republic for Kosovo within the Yugoslav federation. A republic had the constitutional right to secede, and Albanians were an increasing majority in the province; for many Serbs a Kosovo republic was just a step toward independence, a merger with the neighboring nation of Albania, and the formation of a "Greater Albania."

In 1986 Serb clerics and nationalists orchestrated the charge that Albanians were engaged in genocide against Serbs. Serb nationalists alleged that the high Albanian birthrate was part of the genocide, a *"dirty demographic war for an ethnically pure Kosovo* [italics in original]."[3] Serb women and girls, Serb nationalists contended, were targeted for rape as part of the genocidal Albanian policy. Continuous references to the birthrate differences between Albanians and Serbs contributed to a gynecological hatred against Albanians within portions of the Serb population. Serb nationalists alleged that Albanian women were "breeding machines" that would destroy Serbs, while Serb women were supposedly exposed to an ethnically based genocidal assault. Albanians were accused of a plot to eradicate Serb cultural heritage in Kosovo by destroying monasteries. The Muslim identity of most Albanians led Serb nationalists to conflate anti-Albanian and anti-Muslim stereotypes.

As the conflict intensified, Serbian intellectuals and clergy claimed an Albanian plot to "ethnically cleanse" Kosovo, unite it with Albania proper, and create a "Greater Albania" and an "ethnically pure Kosovo."[4] In January 1986, two hundred Belgrade intellectuals signed a petition to the Yugoslav and Serbian national assemblies known as the "Serbian Memorandum."[5] The guiding force behind this movement was the novelist Dobrica Ćosić, a former communist who had become an ethnoreligious zealot. The Memorandum demanded a restructuring of the relationship of the autonomous province of Kosovo to Serbia. It condemned the autonomy and majority rule in Kosovo, established in the constitution of 1974, as national treason. It argued that the treason was part of an anti-Serb plot to keep Serbs disunited and separate.[6] It made reference—as if to a known fact that needed no elaboration—to the "genocide" in Kosovo. On a like note, a Serb intellectual complained of an atrocities rate in Kosovo "unprecedented in the twentieth century."[7]

What was the truth of the charges that galvanized Serbian nationalism within Yugoslavia and led to movements of secession in Slovenia and Croatia? According to police records, the incidence of rape in the Albanian region of Kosovo was at a rate *be-*

low that of Serbia proper. According to the same records, there was only one recorded instance of the rape of a Serb by an Albanian.[8] When proponents of the genocide charge in Kosovo were confronted with these facts, they had no answer. Instead they claimed, without evidence, a plot by the Albanian leadership to create an "ethnically clean" Kosovo.[9] Serb nationalists also charged, without evidence, that not only did Albanians side with Italy and Germany during World War II, but that a pro-Nazi organization, the Balli Kombetër, was still playing a key role in Albanian politics. The allegation contained two elements central to the ideology of genocide. First, Serb nationalists attached generic blame to entire peoples (Albanians, Croats, Slavic Muslims) for the acts of some during World War II. Second, Serb nationalists charged, without evidence, that pro-Nazi organizations were still operating within generically defined ethnic groups.

The gap between actual incidents of vandalism and the language used to depict them is vividly illustrated in one essay, in which the undemonstrated tales of ethnically based rape and genocide are placed next to a year-by-year ledger from 1969 to 1982 of the supposed systematic effort by Albanians to annihilate Serb cultural heritage. The list shows several incidents of vandalism per year: cutting of trees on monastery property, writing of graffiti, breaking of windows—hardly the kind of systematic cultural annihilation that was to occur in Bosnia in 1992.[10] As for charges that Albanians were being given lenient treatment, Amnesty International reported that Albanians, 8 percent of the population of Yugoslavia, accounted for 75 percent of prisoners of conscience.[11]

The escalation of charges to false accusations of genocide is especially clear in the language of the Christian Orthodox clergy. In 1969, the Holy Council of Serbian Orthodox Bishops wrote to Yugoslav President Tito to express concern about the neglect of Serb religious property by the state, the vandalism of Serb property by Albanians, and intimidation of Serbs in Kosovo. The language was specific and the concerns were grounded in factual incidents that were described without ethnic or religious vilification or generic blame against all Albanians.[12] By 1982, in a Good Friday appeal by Serb priests and monks, the language had changed. With repeated allusions to the "crucifixion" of the Serb nation, the battle of 1389, a centuries-long plot by Albanians to exterminate Serb culture, and the depravity of the Ottoman Turks, the appeal culminated in the charge of genocide: "It is no exaggeration to say that planned GENOCIDE [emphasis in original] is being perpetrated against the Serbian people in Kosovo! What otherwise would be the meaning of 'ethnically pure Kosovo' which is being relentlessly put into effect through ceaseless and never-ending migrations?"[13] In 1987, 60,000 Serbs signed a petition protesting the "fascist genocide" in Kosovo.[14] In 1988, Serb Orthodox bishops in New Zealand, Europe, and the Americas published a petition entitled "Declaration of the Bishops of the Serbian Orthodox Church Against the Genocide Inflicted by the Albanians on the Indigenous Serbian Population, Together with the Sacrilege of their Cultural Monuments in their Own Country."[15] None of these appeals offered any evidence for the charges that there was an Albanian plot to create an "ethnically pure" state in Kosovo, or that 250,000 Albanians had migrated to Kosovo from Albania.

The charges became more and more extreme. One writer asserted that 300,000 Albanians in Kosovo are refugees from Albania proper and should be forcibly returned. His call for ethnic expulsion was grounded in a quote from Njegoš: "We [Serb and Slavic Muslims] must fight until one of us is exterminated."[16] He went on to ridicule "brotherhood and unity," an ideal that had helped keep the fragile Yugoslav federation together since the end of World War II: "Do not pretend that you [Albanians] love us, because we do not love you. We have long ago eaten up the moldy pretzel of internationalism that falsely joins us in brotherhood and falsely unites us." The writer concludes with an open-ended threat: "We are neither brothers nor are we united, but let us examine how we shall . . . [ellipsis part of original]."[17] Such language was dominating the most prestigious publications of Serbian writers and intellectuals. By 1989, references to the crucifixion of Serbia mixed with threats of revenge. Those who engineered the "Serbian Golgotha," the writer warned, forget that executioners can become victims.[18]

Although the hate was directed at Albanians in Kosovo, the literature and archetypes made Slavic Muslims (rather than specifically Albanian Muslims) particularly vulnerable. It was Slavic Muslims who were associated by Njegoš with the treason of Vuk Branković, an association renewed in the novels of Ivo Andrić. It was the Slavic Muslims who were portrayed as Turkifiers and still called Turks in a national mythology that saw the Turks as the killers of the Christ-Prince. The Serb nation was again being crucified; the archetype of national myth was tied into the actual situation in Kosovo province. The relics of Lazar were paraded around the province of Kosovo as a reminder of the killing of the Christ-Prince and as a territorial claim.

From within such a perspective, there is no safety. Even the peaceful smile is the smile of the traitor. One poem, based upon the art within the Peć monasteries, meditates on the figure of Christ while "In the neighboring nave / Judas threatens him with a knife / the eye's calm smile." The poem appeared in a volume of hate literature published in 1989 by the Serbian writers union as part of the celebration of the 600th anniversary of Kosovo.[19] When through historical circumstance such rage was diverted from the Albanians in Kosovo to Slavic Muslims in Bosnia, there was nothing the Bosnian Muslims could possibly do to convince their attackers of their peaceful intent; even their peaceful smile could be read as the smile of a Judas.

RETURN OF THE USTASHE

The village of Jasenovac stands near the border between Bosnia and Croatia in an area known as Western Slavonia. From 1991 to 1995 this area was held by Serb rebels and formed part of the self-declared "Serbian Republic of Krajina."

During World War II, Jasenovac was the site of the largest death camp in Yugoslavia for Serbs as well as Jews, Gypsies, dissident Croats, and others deemed undesirable by the Croat nationalist forces known as the Ustashe. The Ustashe regime lasted from 1941 to 1944 and was kept in power through its patron, Nazi Germany. The brutality of the Ustashe was such that even some Nazis complained about it.

The role of the Catholic Church in the atrocities of the Ustashe state has been a source of deep bitterness to Serbs. The highest-ranking Catholic at the time, Bishop Stepinac, was a Croat nationalist who celebrated the coming to power of an independent government. When the depravity of the Pavelić regime began to show itself, Stepinac was slow to condemn it and slow to condemn the role of many Catholic priests in instigating the killings and, in numerous cases, actually supervising or carrying them out. After the war, a Croat monastery in the Vatican became the center for the smuggling of Ustashe war criminals to safety. Stepinac (who had been elevated to cardinal) never really came to grips with the open participation of many Croat priests in the religious-based genocide or with his own weak response to the atrocities of the Pavelić regime. Even after the war, he failed to show empathy with the hundreds of thousands of Serbs killed, referring to the killings as "errors." In the early 1980s, Serb Orthodox clergy asked the Catholic clergy of Croatia for dialogue on this issue. The Croatian bishops refused. The Catholic Church generally has refused to fully acknowledge the Ustashe genocide.[20]

Parallel to their construction of an alleged genocide in Kosovo, Serb nationalists began alleging the imminent repetition of the Ustashe genocide of World War II, which was all too real and all too recent. The atrocities of World War II were relived continually in the Belgrade media along with the standard use of generic blame familiar from Kosovo. Just as Kosovo Albanians were, as a group, held responsible for German collaborators in World War II, all Croats came under suspicion for Ustashe activities in World War II. Both sides manipulated numbers. Serb nationalists claimed that anywhere from 700,000 to more than a million Serbs were killed at Jasenovac. Croat nationalist and historian Franjo Tudjman started low (60,000) and kept revising downward. In such an environment, every sign becomes a symbol, every symbol becomes charged. Thus, a provocative ruling by the newly independent Croatian state limiting the official use of the Cyrillic alphabet, used by Serbs in certain areas, inflamed

Serb fears and angers. The adoption by the Croat state of a flag based upon the checkerboard pattern was, for Croat nationalists, an assertion of an ancient Croatian symbol dating back into the medieval times; for many Serbs, the checkerboard was the prime symbol of their Ustashe persecutors of World War II.

Serb clergy and Serb nationalists began to disinter the remains of Serb victims of the Ustashe in World War II. Ignoring the fact that thousands of Croats fought against the Ustashe and Nazis in World War II, Serb nationalists used this grim exercise to reiterate their charge of generic Croat responsibility for collaboration with the Nazi regime. The Croatian people were genocidal by nature, the Serb nationalists maintained, and would carry out their genocide again; indeed, they were already planning a repeat of Jasenovac. As late as 1995, Bosnian Serb President Radovan Karadžić contended that in 1992 Croatians were prepared to repeat the World War II genocide against the Serbs.[21]

The Bosnian Muslims were also targeted with the generic blame of Serb nationalism. During World War II, Bosnian Muslims were caught on all sides of the battle lines; some fought with the Ustashe, many with the Partisans, and many others were massacred by both Ustashe and Chetniks. Indeed, the proportion of Bosnian Muslims killed in World War II rivaled that of the Bosnian Serbs. The Nazis recruited Bosnian Muslims into two divisions of the SS. Those two divisions have been used as an emblem to identify Bosnian Muslims with Nazi atrocities of World War II, ignoring the major role played by other Bosnian Muslims in the Partisan resistance and in saving the lives of Jewish and Serb neighbors.[22] The writings of politician Vuk Drašković were especially important in stirring up hatred against all Croats and Muslims. Drašković portrayed Muslims as Serbs who betrayed their race by converting to Islam and, within the context of World War II, as sadistic monsters.[23]

Lazar's bones were paraded around Bosnia, tying the bones of the victims of the Ustashe to the bones of the Christ-Prince. The pain and anger of living memory (most Serbs had family members who perished in World War II) combined with the pain and anger of mythic time; Jasenovac and 1389 were brought into a single moment in the present. Accompanying the procession of Lazar's relics in Bosnia was a proclamation about enemies of "long-suffering Serbs": "We will do our utmost to crush their race and descendants so completely that history will not even remember them."[24]

APPROPRIATING THE PASSION

The genocide charges against Kosovo Albanians, the alleged Ustashe nature of all Croats, and the alleged race betrayal of Slavic Muslims formed a lethal brew.[25]

The work of political cartoonist Milenko Mihajlović offers a taste of this brew. In May 1989, at the height of the Kosovo dispute and Serb anger over the Albanian birthrate, Mihajlović published a cartoon showing throngs of Albanian babies with demented, leering grins swarming out from behind Marshal Tito, who is depicted as a queen bee. In September of the same year, Mihajlović depicted Ustashe members fishing for Serb babies with barbed fishing line. As the Serb media stepped up its accusations that all Croats were genocidal, Mihajlović published a cartoon in January 1990 showing a Roman Catholic prelate with a rosary made out of the eyeballs of Serb children; the Serb infants with their eye sockets empty surround the priest. The deadly

Fig. 2. Religious nationalist cartoon by Milenko Mihajlović: a Catholic cleric and a Muslim cleric fight over a Serbian baby; the Muslim wields a circumcision knife. From *The New Combat*, September 1990.

position of Bosnian Muslims appeared in a Mihajlović cartoon of September 1990. In the cartoon, a Roman Catholic prelate and a fez-topped Muslim leader argue over a Serb baby. The prelate wants to baptize the baby, the Muslim to circumcise him. The second frame shows the prelate gouging out the baby's eyes, while the Muslim stretches out the foreskin under a large knife. It is a measure of the degree to which nationalism had degraded Serb culture and civic values that the cartoons of Mihajlović were published not in some obscure journal but in the *Literary Gazette (Književne novine)* of Belgrade, the official arm of the Association of Serbian Writers.[26]

By 1992, the charges against Albanians, Croats, and Slavic Muslims had been woven together into a claim of both actual and imminent genocide against Serbs by a worldwide Islamic conspiracy aided by Germany and the Vatican. The charges were repeated by Serb Church leaders such as Metropolitan Amfilohije Radović in cosmic terms reminiscent of Njegoš: orthodoxy in the Balkans was "the last island of holiness, of untroubled and unpolluted truth," against which "all the demonic forces are directed."[27] Fears of a demographic plot by Muslims were exploited to spur a higher Serb birthrate. Serb Orthodox Bishop Vasilije, of the Zvornik–Tuzla area in northeast Bosnia, warned of catastrophe from the low Serb birthrate. The Serb Orthodox Church offered medals to Serb mothers for bearing many children. A Serb artist demanded that Serb women give birth every nine months. If a woman refused, "We will hand her over to the *Mujahidin* (Islamic fighters) from the [United Arab Emirates]. Let her have them inseminate her."[28]

By the time the Bosnian conflict began, the national mythology, hatred, and unfounded charges of actual genocide in Kosovo and imminent genocide in Bosnia had been shaped into a code: the charge of genocide became a signal to begin genocide. In 1992, witnesses began to notice a pattern in the atrocities by Serb forces in Bosnia. A massacre would take place in a village immediately after the local news announced that the Croats and Muslims were about to exterminate Serbs.

José Maria Mendiluce, an official of the UN High Commission for Refugees, was witness to the organized killing of un-armed Muslims in the town of Zvornik. He observed that they fit a pattern of atrocities carried out by the militia of Serb religious nationalist Vojislav Šešelj: "For days, the Belgrade media had been writing about how there was a plot to kill all Serbs in Zvornik. The authorities in Zvornik realized that the point in question was a typical maneuver by Šešelj's Radical Volunteers. This maneuver always precedes the killing of Muslims, as had already happened in Bijeljina and many places along the left bank of the Drina River."[29] An overlapping and robust ideology had taken shape. To refute any part or even most of the Serb radical position would only lead to new charges and channel the rage in new directions. In justifying the atrocities in Bosnia, Serb nationalists would point to atrocities by Croatian army forces in World War II or in the 1991 Serb-Croat war. When it was pointed out that the largely Muslim population selected for extermination had nothing to do with the Croat army and indeed had been attacked by the Croat army in 1993, Serb nationalists would shift to blaming all Muslims for the acts of those who fought with the Ustashe in World War II. When it was pointed out that many of the families who suffered worst in the Serb army onslaught in Bosnia were families of World War II Partisans who fought against the Ustashe, Serb nationalists would shift to claims of Ottoman depravity and treat the Muslims as Turks. When it was pointed out that the Slavic Muslims were just as indigenous to the region as Orthodox Christians or Catholics, the discussion would then shift to allegations that the Bosnian Muslims were fundamentalists and that Serbia was defending the West against the fundamentalist threat of radical Islam. When it was pointed out that most Bosnian Muslims were antifundamentalist by tradition and character, the Serb nationalist would move to the final fallback position: that this was a civil war in which all sides were guilty, there were no angels, and the world should allow the people involved to solve their own problems.[30] Hatred of Albanians, hatred of Croats, hatred of Muslims (both Albanian and Bosnian) were combined and reinforced through endless loops of victimization not accountable to evidence or reason. Then the language of eternal victimization was flipped into a code in which charges of genocide against Serbs became a signal to begin genocidal operations against Bosnian Muslims.

In 1987, a Serbian communist party official by the name of Slobodan Milošević was upbraided by Serb nationalists in Kosovo for not attending to Serb concerns in the province. Milošević returned to a tense meeting with Kosovo Serbs. A large Serbian crowd surrounded the building in which the meeting was held. When Milošević emerged, a vulnerable-looking elderly Serb ran up and shouted that the Albanian-dominated Kosovo police were beating people in the crowd.

"These people will not beat you again!" The response by Milošević was shown throughout Serbia on all the major television networks. What the viewers were not shown was how the incident was staged. Serb nationalists, with Milošević's approval, had supplied the crowd with truckloads of heavy stones. At a given moment the crowd threw the stones directly into the face of police who had been standing by. The violence was instigated through crowd manipulation and exploited through media manipulation, tactics Milošević would refine during his rise to absolute power.[31]

On June 28, 1989, the Serb Orthodox Patriarch led a procession of three hundred Serb priests in scarlet robes at the Gračanica monastery in Kosovo. They were marking the 600th anniversary of the death of Lazar at the battle of Kosovo. The Patriarch lit two ten-foot candles in honor of the martyrs of the battle of Kosovo and then stored the candles away until they could be lit in another century on the 700th anniversary. For a week, Serb pilgrims had gathered at the monastery to pray before the relics of Lazar.[32]

Nearby, on the plain of Gazimestan where the battle had taken place, a vast crowd of pilgrims estimated at between one million and two million gathered for the commemoration of the battle of Kosovo.[33] On this occasion, June 28, 1989, Serb President Slobodan Milošević consolidated three years of effort to instigate and appropriate radical nationalist sentiment.

Serbia was accustomed both to a cult of mythic personality (Miloš Obilić, Lazar) and the cult of personality under Tito, whose image adorned homes and businesses throughout Yugoslavia. As he stood on the podium before the massive throng at Kosovo on June 28, 1989, Milošević could see the evidence that he had become the bridge between the Titoist Great Leader and the Serb nationalist icon; in the crowd, next to pictures of Lazar, were pictures of Slobodan Milošević. Before the vast and euphoric throng, Milošević spoke of ancient battles to defend Europe and warned of battles to come.

Three vectors of mythic power came together in the 1989 passion play performance. The fourteenth-century ancestors of Slavic Muslims were characterized as Christ killers and then, through temporal collapse effected by the performance, identified with present-day Slavic Muslims in Bosnia. The hatred of Albanians in Kosovo province in 1989 was fused with the hatred of Slavic Muslims. And the atrocities of World War II were resurrected and attributed to Croats and Muslims as entire peoples.

Three streams of rage—disinterment of remains of Serb victims of genocide in World War II, procession of Lazar's relics through Bosnia and around Kosovo, and pilgrimage of Serbs to visit the relics in Kosovo—were channeled into a single raging torrent. Within three years, those who directed the festivities in 1989 were organizing the unspeakable depravities against Bosnian civilians.[34]

IN THE CROSSHAIRS OF THE SNIPER

In December 1993, a resident of Sarajevo walked out of his home. He was the father of the graduate student who had been killed trying to save books during the burning of the National Library in August 1992. He had fought against the Nazis in World War II as part of the Partisan resistance, alongside Croats, Serbs, Slovenians, and others. After the war, he had been imprisoned by Tito's secret police. In his fedora, he was a handsome man with kind eyes and a thin, hawkish nose.

Some said that of all the tragedies he lived through, the killing of his daughter on the way back from the library was the first thing to shake him. Some thought he was tired of the constant humiliation faced by Sarajevans, having to crawl along walls to avoid the constant sniper fire. As he opened his door that day in December and walked out without taking cover, someone had him in the crosshairs of his rifle.

Those crosshairs were a nexus of myth and symbol: the Christ killer myth constructed in the nineteenth century and brought back into the present through the 600th anniversary of Lazar's death, a fabricated genocide against Serbs in Kosovo, and manipulation of Serb suffering in World War II to indict all Croats and Muslims and instill fear that another genocide was imminent. Yet the rifle sights were not enough to cause the shot. Someone had to load and distribute the guns and give the order to fire.

CHAPTER FOUR

MASKS OF OTHERNESS

By 1992, a series of ominous developments had occurred: a language of extremist paranoia had emerged; allegations were made that an ethnoreligious group was plotting and carrying out genocide; militias were arming to battle the federal government, which was allegedly supporting the genocidal plot; a battle was looming to save Christian values and identity; a violent text—read and memorized by militia members—recounted the plot against Christians, the battle to save Christendom, and the punishment in store for race traitors; bombings, shootings, and other terrorist acts carried out by such militias were on the increase . . .

Such was the background to the bombing of the Federal Building in Oklahoma City, on April 19, 1995, carried out by men associated with the militias of the Christian Identity movement. The prime suspect in the bombing, Timothy McVeigh, had studied the "bible" of the Christian Identity movement, William Pierce's *The Turner Diaries*, which contains a fanciful account of an ethnoreligious plot against Aryan Christians, the war by militias to save their Christian identity, the bombing of federal buildings, and the hanging of women who violate the purity of their race by marrying Jews or blacks.[1]

Imagine that such extremists had control over major U.S. media, which for three years broadcast alleged atrocities of non-Christians and non-Aryans against the Aryan Christians. Imagine that such extremists had a high-level supporter in the U.S. military who supplied them not only with assault rifles but with tanks and heavy artillery. Many Americans dismiss the threat of such groups and the possibility of such an ethnoreligious war. In the former Yugoslavia, the extremists were dismissed in the same way. Few imagined that in just a few years neighbors and friends would be shelling them with mortars or tormenting them in killing camps.

CREATING THE PERPETRATOR

Explosive as they were, the symbolic forces marshaled at the Kosovo celebrations of 1989 were not capable alone of producing genocide. The fuse needed to be lit. Serb nationalist forces, protected by Serb President Slobodan Milošević, worked carefully to light it. Milošević and Serbian nationalists had used mob intimidation and media exploitation to overthrow Serbian President Ivan Stambolić and purge the communist party and governments in Serbia's autonomous regions of Vojvodina and Kosovo and in Montenegro. In 1990 Milošević began using purges to transform the Yugoslav Army into a Serb-nationalist controlled implement of the struggle for a "Greater Serbia."[2] In 1991, he used attacks in Belgrade on demonstrators for freedom of the press and the war in Croatia to harden the soldiers. In May

1992, Milošević pretended to withdraw the Yugoslav army from Bosnia but in fact simply transferred all the Bosnian Serb soldiers in the federal army and vast amounts of weapons to the Bosnian Serb army, whose expenses Milošević subsidized from the Yugoslav federal budget.[3] Milošević gave militia leaders such as Vojislav Šešelj and Arkan access to the media, secret police, military command, and arms depots.[4] These men built private militias and collaborated closely with regular Serb forces to spread terror throughout eastern and northern Bosnia.[5]

Serbs who refused to participate in the persecution of Muslims were killed. In a Serb-army occupied area of Sarajevo, Serb militants killed a Serb officer who objected to atrocities against civilians; they left his body on the street for over a week as an object lesson. During one of the "selections" carried out by Serb militants in Sarajevo, an old Serb named Ljubo objected to being separated out from his Muslim friends and neighbors; they beat him to death on the spot.[6] In Zvornik, Serb militiamen slit the throat of a seventeen-year-old Serb girl who protested the shooting of Muslim civilians. In the Prijedor region, Serb militants put Serbs accused of helping non-Serb neighbors into the camps with those they tried to help. Similar incidents occurred throughout areas controlled by the Bosnian Serb military.[7]

Serb militants tried to provoke revenge attacks by Muslims against Serbs still living in Bosnian-controlled territory. The theory was that such attacks would drive the remaining Serb population out of Bosnian government areas, thus creating two ethnoreligiously pure entities, one Serb, one Muslim. The claim of extreme religious nationalists that Serbs could never live safely with Muslims would be validated.[8] During the "cleansings" of the Bijeljina area in 1994, Muslim survivors of the operation were driven toward the Bosnian-controlled city of Tuzla, which has a large Serb population. Young men were taken to slave labor camps. Their families were told that if they wanted to see those taken to the camps alive again, they should take the houses of Serbs in Tuzla, expel the Serbs into territory held by the Serb army, and then the other captives would be released.[9] Although one attack in Tuzla against Serbs did occur when the first wave of traumatized refugees from the overrun enclave of Srebrenica came into the city in 1993, the Tuzla authorities, against all odds, have maintained a multireligious city.

Serb army officers used alcohol to break down the normal inhibitions of the young men in their commands. Serb soldiers were kept drunk night after night, weeks at a time; military convoys were accompanied by truckloads of plum brandy (*šljivovica*). In Sarajevo, there was an evening *šljivovica* hour during which Serb soldiers would get drunk and broadcast over loudspeakers, in grisly detail, what they were going to do to the Bosnian civilians when they got hold of them. Survivors of mass killings reported that once soldiers began drinking, the atrocities followed.

Commanders of the killing camps made a practice of opening them to local Serb radicals, gangsters, and grudge-holders, who would come each night to beat, torture, and kill the detainees.[10] This practice had the effect of spreading complicity throughout the neighboring area. Distribution of stolen and abandoned goods also spread complicity. Every town "cleansed" meant the availability of automobiles, appliances, stereo and television equipment.[11] Once a family had in their home something that had belonged to a neighbor, they were less likely to object to the "ethnic cleansing."

Militia leaders worked to instill an ethos of brutality. Arkan, the leader of the Tiger militia, used his headquarters in the city of Erdut as a training ground. Serb recruits were taught that in fighting the enemy, they had no right to spare children, women, or the aged.[12] Serb military commanders showed reporters and their own troops how to slit a throat by having pigs killed as demonstrations.

The final dehumanization of the perpetrator occurred in rit-ualized fashion, when young soldiers were forced to watch tor-ture, gang rape, and killings and forced to participate. To refuse was to risk death. To participate was to learn to believe that the victims were not truly human anyway.

Dehumanization of the victims was achieved through a vari-ety of methods. Captives would be held for months in extremely cramped quarters without toilets or sanitary facilities. Women spoke of the shame of being forced to wear clothes stained with menstrual blood. Weeks of a starvation diet, lack of water, and lack of hygiene would turn captives into filthy, emaciated shad-ows of the persons they had once been. Cities the Serb army did not capture were blockaded. Few convoys were allowed in, and some safe areas, such as Srebrenica, Žepa, and Bihać, became abodes of misery, what one refugee worker called UN concen-tration camps.[13]

Dehumanizing labels were also important in motivating geno-cide. In Serb-occupied areas, Bosnian Croats were invariably called Ustashe, in reference to the fascist units of World War II. Muslims were called Turks (a term of alienation and abuse when used by Serb and Croat militants), Ustashe, and "balije." The origin of the term "balija" (plural "balije") is obscure. Some

Fig. 3.   Masks and religious terror: Arkan's Tiger Militia. Ron Haviv, SABA Press Photos, 1990.

believe it is related to the South Slavic term for spit or mucus (*bala*); others suggest different etymologies. Bosnian Muslim survivors of the "ethnic cleansing" reported that nationalist Serbs would "spit" the term out at them.[14] A popular song in Belgrade was based on the rhyme "Alija" (the first name of Bosnian President Alija Izetbegović) and "balija."

In both the Republika Srpska and Serbia proper, militia leaders became patrons in their community through their control over the real estate and moveable properties of the killed or expelled non-Serbs. As the Serb economy faltered under the strain of war expenditures, corruption, and economic sanctions, the person who could get what was needed—extra food, medicine, gasoline, or a new stereo—was the militia leader. No need to ask where the goods came from.

The use of masks symbolized the methods used by the organizers of the genocide. When the fighting broke out in Croatia in 1991, Serb irregular militiamen wore ski-masks or face paint. Survivors of atrocities reported trying to discern the accent of their masked torturers to determine where they came from. Sometimes a victim would recognize the voice of a neighbor.[15] In many cases the man behind the mask was content to allow his identity to be known through his voice, and in some cases even taunted his victim with the fact that they knew one another.

The mask transformed identities. Before he put it on, the militiaman was part of a multireligious community in which Catholic Croats, Orthodox Serbs, Slavic Muslims, Jews, Gypsies, and others had lived together. These were his friends, his work colleagues, his neighbors, his lovers, his spouse's family. Once he put on the mask, he was a Serb hero; those he was abusing were *balije* or Turks, race traitors and killers of the Christ-Prince Lazar.

THE FORGOTTEN SERBS

Despite the effort of Serb religious nationalists to dehumanize both their own population and their target population, many Serbs have resisted and kept their humanity. Serbs in Serbia evaded military service in large numbers. Bosnian Muslim survivors commonly reported that a Serb or (in the case of Croat extremist violence) a Croat helped them escape. A soldier or border guard may have turned a blind eye as a Bosnian slipped away from an atrocity or fled to safe territory. A family might shelter a fugitive in their home, at great risk. A Muslim survivor of the killing camp at Sušica mentioned that a Serb priest tried to help him.[16] Bogdan Bogdanović, the Serb former mayor of Belgrade, has spoken out courageously against the systematic annihilation of mosques and other cultural monuments. Many of the stories of resistance and courage cannot be told at this time, because the resisters or their families are still vulnerable to reprisals.[17]

In 1995, the majority of Bosnian Serbs did not live in Serb-army occupied Bosnia but had fled, many of them to Serbia proper. In 1994, President Milošević allowed agents of Radovan Karadžić and militia leaders like Arkan to sweep through Serbia, rounding up thousands of Serbs from refugee camps, abusing them for refusing to fight, and punishing them by sending them to the front lines with little training.

In Bosnian government areas, the Serb Civic Council was formed to work for a multireligious society and to articulate the concerns of those Serbs loyal to a multireligious Bosnia-Herzegovina. The Civic Council pointed out that the total number of Bosnian Serbs living under the control of the Republika

Srpska was less than 50 percent; over 150,000 lived in Bosnian government–controlled areas and some 500,000 had fled abroad. The council criticized the international community for treating the religious nationalist faction as the sole representative of the Serbian people.[18]

THE SERB CHURCH AND THE STEPINAC SYNDROME

In Bosnia, the Serb Orthodox Church made the same mistake the Catholic Church made in Croatia during World War II; it became a servant of religious nationalist militancy. In many instances, Christian Serb clergy have supported the extremists who carried out the genocide in Bosnia and have given ritual and symbolic support to the programs of ethnic expulsion and destruction of mosques.

In the late 1980s, the Serb Orthodox Church collaborated with academics and literati to highlight the motif of Muslims as Christ killers and race traitors. It was a motif that came to dominate the commemoration of the 600th anniversary of the Kosovo battle. Supporters of the Republika Srpska memorized and quoted Njegoš's *Mountain Wreath* and even more violent religious epics as they planned and carried out their genocide. Verses from these epics glorifying the extermination of Muslim civilians were being posted on the Internet even as various villages and cities in Bosnia-Herzegovina were being "cleansed" of Muslims and all evidence of Muslim civilization was eradicated.[19] Militiamen involved in the atrocities wore patches depicting the battle of Kosovo and received medals with the name of Miloš Obilić, the assassin of Sultan Murat.[20] In an Orthodox monastery near Sarajevo, a Serb priest blessed the followers of the ethno-fascist warlord Vojislav Šešelj, after the names of the towns associated with the worst atrocities against Muslims were read aloud in triumph.[21] The chief of police of Banja Luka—the site of massive atrocities against Muslims carried out with the complicity of the Banja Luka police—received a delegation of Greek Church leaders in honor of Saint Michael the Archangel, the "Patron Saint of the Republika Srpska Ministry of Internal Affairs."[22]

When the city of Foča was purged of its Muslim population and all traces of their existence had been dynamited and bull-dozed, the name of the city was changed to Srbinje (Serb Place). More generally, the term *Srbinje* has been shouted at Muslims during killings and expulsions throughout Bosnia ("Serb Place!" "Serb Place!"). The renamed Foča was celebrated with visits by high Church officials. A university professor from Sarajevo, Vojislav Maksimović, explained that "the [Serb] fighters from Foča and the region were worthy defenders of Serbianness and of Orthodoxy."[23] In Trebinje, an Orthodox priest led the way in expelling a Muslim family and seizing their home. Trebinje's 500-year-old mosque and elegant Turkish-style buildings were burned and its Muslim population killed and expelled immediately following celebrations of the feast day of St. Sava, the founder of the Serbian Church. Mirko Jović, leader of the White Eagles terror squad, called for a "Christian, Orthodox Serbia with no Muslims and no unbelievers."[24]

While still an abbot, Serbian Orthodox Bishop Atanasije of Herzegovina characterized the Islamic architectural style of homes with interior courtyards enclosed by walls as a sign of Islamic "primitivism" from "Bihać to Baghdad to Belgrade."[25] The official Serbian Orthodox Church journal promoted the

writings and the cult of personality of militia leader Vuk Drašković, a major instigator of anti-Muslim atrocities; another Serb
Church publication condemned those who would not join the
armed struggle against the "evil forces that are opposed to God
(and by the same token to humanity)."[26] The sustained attacks
on Muslims by Serb Orthodox clergy were based on global stereotypes of Muslims as a people; the complex and variegated nature of Bosnian Islam was ignored. Metropolitan Christopher, a
Serb Church leader in the United States, gave a list of stereotypes about Muslims, implying they were all like the radical followers of Iran's Ayatollah Khomeini. When someone asked him
whether Muslims in Bosnia were Sunnites or Shiites, he said:
"I don't know very much about Muslims in Bosnia, but they
are Muslims."[27] Vasilije, Bishop of the Zvornik–Tuzla area, offered up the bizarre notion that for Muslims in Bosnia, the
more unbelievers they kill, the closer they get to heaven.[28] Religious stereotypes met psychological stereotypes; Jovan Rašković,
a mentor to Radovan Karadžić, claimed that Muslim ablutions
before prayer showed the "anal-analytic" nature of Muslims as a
people.[29]

A worldwide Serb Orthodox campaign was mounted to fi-
nance a massive new cathedral in Belgrade. Serb Orthodox
Church officials promoted the project with constant references
to the fact that this church was to be constructed on the very
spot on which Ottoman Turks had burned the bones of St. Sava,
the founder of the Serbian Church.[30] Serbian religious leaders
lauded those Serbian officials responsible for designing and im-
plementing the policy of "ethnic cleansing." On Orthodox Easter
1993, Metropolitan Nikolaj, the highest-ranking Serb Orthodox
Church official in Bosnia, stood between Radovan Karadžić and

General Ratko Mladić and spoke of the Bosnian Serbs under their leadership as "following the hard road of Christ." Karadžić suggested the problem in Bosnia could be solved if Muslims would just convert to Serb Orthodoxy.[31]

What Serb dissidents have called the clericalist faction of Serb militants is clearly dramatized in the figure of Arkan, who is both a friend and ally of Karadžić and a protégé of Serb President Slobodan Milošević. After the Russian neo-Nazi Vladimir Zhirinovsky had embraced the highest-ranking living Nazi SS officer in Austria, he was given an adoring welcome in Arkan's stronghold of Bijeljina in eastern Bosnia. Arkan led Zhirinovsky on a tour, showing him the parking lot where a mosque once stood.[32]

Serb priests waved incense and offered blessings over a boxing match at a casino owned by Arkan. Serb clergy presided over Arkan's 1995 marriage, staged in public with great fanfare, to a Serb popular music star by the name of Ceca. For the ceremony, attended by Christian Orthodox bishops from Serb-controlled Bosnia and Croatia, Arkan wore an old Montenegrin warrior costume festooned with a huge cross, as his supporters waved paper flags with an Orthodox cross and nationalist slogans. Ceca was dressed as "The Maid of Kosovo" (*Kosovka djevojka*), the Mary Magdalene figure who nurses the Kosovo martyrs as they lie dying on the battlefield. Of the atrocities in Bosnia, Arkan said: "We are fighting for our faith, the Serbian Orthodox Church."[33]

Orthodox Christian clergy sit as elected members of the parliament of the Republika Srpska. When General Ratko Mladić, indicted by the International Criminal Tribunal on multiple counts of genocide, came under criticism, the Serb clergy rallied to his defense. Yet the Orthodox Church has been slow to minister to the Serbs in Bosnian government areas, where churches are intact but priests are lacking. A Serb priest teaches that Croats and Muslims have a genocide plan against Serbs and that "one who forgives is worse than one who did the bad deed in the first place."[34] Orthodox Bishop Atanasije attacked those who criticized expulsions of Muslim civilians and the burning of mosques in the Herzegovinan town of Trebinje.[35]

In 1994, negotiators for the "Contact Group" (Britain, France, the U.S., Russia, and Germany) suggested a peace plan that would give to the 32 percent of Bosnians who were Serb 49 percent of the land, including the areas on which they had carried out the most systematic "ethnic cleansing"; the Serbian Orthodox Church attacked the peace plan as unfair, to Serbs.[36] Both Metropolitan Nikolaj and Radovan Karadžić demanded that Sarajevo be the capital of the Republika Srpska. Karadžić stated that Sarajevo had "always" been a Serb city; since Slavic Muslims were originally Serbs who had converted to Islam, Serbs were "there" first and Slavic Muslims had no rights to Sarajevo. Nikolaj advanced the same specious argument.[37]

Patriarch Pavle, the leader of the worldwide Serbian Orthodox Church, had a different view. Pavle claimed that Serbs were native to Bosnia-Herzegovina, whereas the Muslims had arrived with the Ottoman invasion. Pavle's confusion of religion and ethnic identity was outdone only by the racial theory of Serb religious nationalist Dragoš Kalajić. Kalajić claimed that Slavic Muslims did not belong to Europe, that their culture was an unconscious expression of "semi-Arabic subculture," and that the Slavic Muslims of Bosnia inherited an inferior "special gene" passed on by the Ottomans from North African Arabs.[38]

In fact, the ancestors of both the Bosnian Serbs and the Bosnian Muslims had lived in the area long before the Ottoman conquest. Sarajevo was established by the Ottomans as a major economic, cultural, and political center. But the mythologized history and racial logic of Karadžić and Nikolaj, and their alternate version promulgated by Patriarch Pavle, are based on claims that Slavic Muslims had no right to land in Bosnia because they lacked ethnoreligious priority. People whose ancestors arrived with the ancestors of their Serb neighbors were relegated to a permanent alienness and denied any claim to existence in the region.

After the revelations of the killing camps, organized rape, and systematic destruction of mosques, the Serbian Orthodox Church led the way in denial. The church's government body, the Holy Episcopal Synod, stated: "In the name of God's truth and on the testimony from our brother bishops from Bosnia-Herzegovina and from other trustworthy witnesses, we declare, taking full moral responsibility, that such camps neither have existed nor exist in the Serbian Republic of Bosnia-Herzegovina." The Synod also wrote a protest against the European indifference to genocide in Bosnia—the alleged genocide against Serbs. The document was composed in May 1992 while the Serb armies were rampaging triumphantly through Bosnia and hundreds of thousands of non-Serbs were being killed and driven from their homes, before the eyes of local Serbian Orthodox priests and bishops.[39]

Some have defended the Serb Church leadership by pointing to its criticism of Serb President Slobodan Milošević. Serb Church criticism of Milošević only began, however, when he retreated from the extreme nationalist position he held up until 1994. Bishop Atanasije of Herzegovina urged Serbs not to "capitulate to the world as Milošević has. The vultures from the West will not get our signature [on the peace plan]."[40] While some Orthodox Christian leaders have offered a general condemnation of nationalism as a "sign of apostasy,"[41] they have refused to condemn specific crimes committed in the name of Serb Orthodoxy; others have supported Serb extremists. As the International Criminal Tribunal conducted an investigation that would lead to the indictment of Radovan Karadžić on multiple counts of genocide, the Greek Orthodox Church appointed Karadžić to the 900-year-old "Knights' Order of the First Rank of Saint Dionysius of Xanthe," declaring him "one of the most prominent sons of our Lord Jesus Christ working for peace."[42]

Some Orthodox Christians have appealed to the Serbian Orthodox Church to take a strong stand against the violence in Bosnia.[43] Yet, one of the authors of that appeal defended Patriarch Pavle from his harsher critics by pointing to a letter Pavle wrote condemning the killings of non-Serbs and burning of Catholic churches in Banja Luka.[44] In it Pavle laid the responsibility for the Banja Luka atrocities on refugees from western Slavonia who had fled the Croat army offensive in the spring of 1995. These acts were unjustifiable, he argued, but understandable as acts of refugees in a state of "vengeful despondency." In fact, the killings and destruction of mosques and churches in Banja Luka were organized by Serb civil and military groups at the very start of the occupation of Banja Luka in April 1992. By the time Pavle expressed his condemnation, all the mosques in the Banja Luka region had been dynamited (a fact he did not mention), and the religious terror had been denounced by international refugee workers for years. The destruction of Catholic churches and the attacks on some Croats may have been carried out in part by Serbian refugees, but they were carried out as part of a consistent policy of religiously based persecution. To hold refugees from western Slavonia responsible is to refuse to confront the authorities of Banja Luka with the truth about their three-year role in organizing religious persecution.

The editor of the religious journal *Orthodoxy* (*Pravoslavlje*) proclaimed that "The patriarch [Pavle] is right. . . . It's still too early to tell who's done what to whom. In this war, everyone is guilty."[45] That everyone is guilty in the "war" has been the consistent stance of Slobodan Milošević. The "everyone is guilty" position is a moral obfuscation. If it is based on a reading of the Christian doctrine of original sin, the question must be raised as to whether such a reading is not to be approached with caution; if everyone is guilty, is anyone really guilty of anything specific? If everyone is guilty, is anything done to any person that is undeserved? Generalized guilt allows a convenient avoidance of the stubborn fact that in genocide, innocents suffer and their suffering is inflicted upon them deliberately.

ONLY UNITY SAVES THE SERB

On June 28, 1989, a vast crowd began to assemble on the plain of Gazimestan, the plain at Kosovo at which Lazar was slain. Slobodan Milošević mounted the stage. On the enormous backdrop behind him were depictions of peonies, the flower that symbolized the blood of Lazar. Above the peonies was a Serb nationalist emblem: an Orthodox cross with a Cyrillic C (equivalent to Latin S) at each of the four corners of the cross. The CCCC symbol stands for the slogan "Only Unity Saves the Serb" (*Samo sloga Srbina spašava*). The meaning of *sloga* (unity, harmony) was key to interpreting the slogan. As Milošević began to speak of the necessity for battles—"not armed battles yet, though it may come to that"—the unity was being defined as the unity of Serb against Albanian, and by extension, against all others.[46] It was natural for a former communist official, raised in the personality cult surrounding Marshal Tito, to move easily into another kind of personality cult. As the communist party crumbled, Milošević had adroitly transformed himself into an ethnoreligious nationalist. At the 600th anniversary of Lazar's death the crowd chanted "Kosovo is Serb." Other rallies included slogans such as: "We love you, Slobodan, because you hate the Muslims."[47] During the same period that Milošević stood at Kosovo in front of the CCCC symbol, that same symbol and other symbols of Serbian religious nationalism such as the Kosovo maiden and the double-headed eagle were reappearing in Serbian communities around the world.[48]

Milošević's abandonment of the goal of Greater Serbia in the negotiations leading up to the Dayton accords of 1995 as well as the attacks of his wife (Mirjana Marković) upon the clericalist movement within Serb nationalism suggest that Milošević has no deep ethnoreligious convictions. Yet, to say that Milošević's aggression was not motivated by personal religious concerns is not to say that the forces he unleashed were not deeply, even fanatically, religious. Many Serb and Croat religious nationalists are not religious in the sense of observing regular religious practice.

It is important to distinguish between an observant religious behavior and what is popularly called fundamentalism. The term

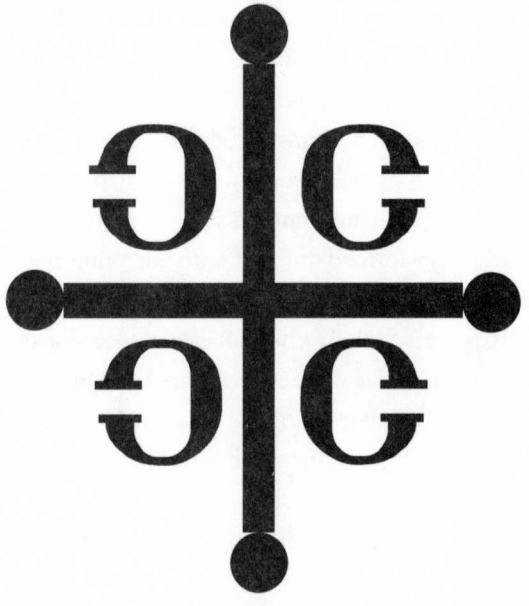

Fig. 4. Symbol of Serbian religious nationalism: The CCCC cross.

"fundamentalism" has been criticized as a cross-cultural category on the grounds that it is rooted in a particular religiosity that has little to do with many of the movements in the world today given that name.[49] Popular usage frequently creates new meanings, and in replying to accusations that Bosnian Muslims were a fundamentalist threat, it is necessary to define the popular meaning. In popular usage, fundamentalism indicates a person's absolute conviction that he knows the truth or at least the way to the truth, an inability to engage in self-criticism, a violent intolerance of those who disagree, and a zeal to use the full power of the state to enforce beliefs and practices deemed proper. In some cases religious fundamentalism is at odds with nationalism and attempts to abolish national states. In other cases, as with Serb and Croat Christoslavism, the fundamentalism and nationalism reinforce one another and merge. In this popular sense, the clericalist wings of both Croat and Serb nationalism are fundamentalist, while personalities like Milošević merely exploit fundamentalism for their own political gain.

Scholars are now studying fundamentalism or religious nationalism as a cross-cultural phenomenon, its distinctive features, and its relationship to modernity and traditionalism.[50] Christoslavic religious nationalism will certainly need to be examined for its similarity and difference from the other contemporary manifestations of religious militancy throughout the world. The goal here is simply to demonstrate what has so repeatedly been denied concerning the genocide in Bosnia: that it was religiously motivated and religiously justified.[51] Religious symbols, mythologies, myths of origin (pure Serb race), symbols of passion (Lazar's death), and eschatological longings (the resurrection of Lazar) were used by religious nationalists to create a reduplicating Miloš Obilić, avenging himself on the Christ killer, the raće traitor, the alien, and, ironically, the falsely accused "fundamentalist" next door. The ideology operated not only in speeches and manifestos, but in specific rituals of atrocity. Survivors of concentration camps report that during torture sessions or when they begged for water, they were made to sing Serbian religious nationalist songs, reworded to reflect the contemporary conflict. One of the songs concerned Bosnian President Alija Izetbegović:

> Oh Alija, oh Alija
> If we go to battle
> It's you I'll kill,
> You I'll slaughter,
> Just like Miloš once
> Got rid of Murat. . . .
>
> See the Turk at her Mosque bowing,
> Her love to Serbs only swearing.[52]

The religious ideology of the violence was complex. It was at once part of a modern surge in religious militancy after the cold war, a reappearance of a Serbian nineteenth-century ideology that constructs an "age-old antagonism" between Muslim and Christian in which the Muslim is a race traitor, and a new manifestation in a history of assaults on non-Christian populations in Europe grounded in manipulation of the Christ-killer charge.[53]

Whether such an ideology reflects the Serb Orthodox faith or is instead a perversion of it, is a question that Serb tradition will answer. Serb religion, history, literature, art, and culture have been used to justify a crime the true proportions of which the world has yet to grasp. In a retrieved Serbian Orthodox tradition, the real traitor of Kosovo would not be the non-Christian next door but rather those who used Kosovo and all of Serbian heritage to incite crimes against humanity. In such a retrieval, Serbia might revalidate the more humane aspects of the Lazar tradition, those that present the sorrow of Kosovo not as the property of Serb militancy but as Serbia's distinctive contribution to a shared human understanding.[54]

Christian scholars have been addressing the problem of the Christ-killer theme in the New Testament in light of the Holocaust and its implications for Christian anti-Semitism. The use of a Christ-killer motif in the Bosnian context poses a theological challenge not only to the Serb Orthodox tradition. The silence of self-identified Christian leaders in many parts of the world in the face of the Bosnian genocide makes it clear that the issue demands attention by the wider Christian community as well. If many Serbs have either supported or remained silent in the face of religiously motivated genocide, the same can be said for most nations.

Certainly no one writing from the United States, founded on territory "cleansed" (with religious sanction) of its native inhabitants and built with the labor of another people seized as slaves from their ancestral homeland, could possibly claim a shred of moral superiority. Nor could anyone watching the Christian Identity movement's instigation of racial and religious warfare find any cause for comfort.

To acknowledge the responsibility for genocide within our own traditions is not to abandon the right and the duty to resist new forms of genocide. Indeed, that resistance can be authentic only to the extent that it is rooted in the willingness to confront our own demons. Such resistance is doubly imperative because of the complicity of Western and Christian powers, through the UN Security Council and NATO, in the destruction of Bosnia, a complicity that will be examined in the final chapters of this book.

No account of the fate of Bosnia can be complete without an examination of the role of Croatian Christoslavism in supporting the destruction of the Bosnian people. While the religious element in Croatian nationalism has been more subtle than Serbian religious nationalism, it has been no less effective. It is symbolized in the 1993 destruction of the Old Bridge at Mostar.

CHAPTER FIVE

THE VIRGIN AND THE JEWEL OF HERZEGOVINA

BRIDGE KEEPER

"It is not enough to cleanse Mostar of the Muslims," said a Croat militiaman as his unit worked to destroy the bridge; "the relics must also be destroyed."[1] On November 9, 1993, in a final barrage, the sixteenth-century bridge, which had withstood months of shelling, collapsed into the Neretva River.

Mostar takes its name from its magnificent old bridge. Under Ottoman patronage, Mostar became a major cultural and economic center in the sixteenth century. The Ottomans built bridges, inns, marketplaces, and mosques. By 1987 the old city had been reconstructed and Mostar was an important tourist site. The city was filled with architectural masterworks like the sixteenth-century Karadjoz Beg Mosque.[2] Its skyline was dominated by an Orthodox church, a Catholic bell tower, and a Muslim minaret, testimony to centuries of living among three religious groups.[3]

At the center of Mostar was the "old bridge" (*stari most*), its high-arched, dizzying vault gracefully linking the two sides of the city. The bridge, which dated from 1561, had been designed by Hajruddin, a pupil of the great Ottoman architect Sinan. The construction project was multireligious with engineers and artisans from around the region. The bridge had survived four centuries and thirty earthquakes.

Mostar is the capital of Herzegovina, a term that means "dukedom." Herzegovina occupies the southwest section of Bosnia-Herzegovina, and for some periods in medieval times it had a separate administrative identity from Bosnia proper. The geography, dialect, customs, and cultural personality of the area are distinctive. Particularly striking are the white-bouldered mountains, craggy gorges, pre-Ottoman tombs, and Ottoman fortresses. Other towns in Herzegovina include Stolac and Trebinje (the once-classic city plundered and burned by Serb nationalists in 1992). Of special interest is Počitelj, with its centuries-old mosques, minarets, and Ottoman-style homes perched along a steep hillside like a Herzegovinian Positano or Amalfi.

EUROPEANIZING THE BOSNIANS

Croatian President Franjo Tudjman had fought in World War II with Tito's Partisans. By the time of Croatia's independence in 1991, he had changed from a communist into a religious nationalist. In his 1990 book *Wastelands of Historical Reality*, Tudjman revealed an anti-Semitic tendency. He suggested that Jews are genocidal by nature and that Jews were the major executioners in the Ustashe death camp of Jasenovac where an estimated

300,000 Serbs, Jews, and Gypsies were killed.[4] Earlier Tudjman had claimed that as few as 60,000 people died in all the camps in Croatia during World War II, a number far below the estimates by serious scholars of the Holocaust.[5] The problems of the Jews are of their own making, Tudjman implies; Jews could have avoided them had they heeded what he calls, vaguely, "the traffic signs."

A clue to what Tudjman means by "traffic signs" can be found in his views on Muslims. In 1991, Tudjman stunned U.S. Ambassador to Yugoslavia Warren Zimmerman with his ignorance of and contempt for Bosnian Muslims and with his plan to carve up Bosnia between a "Greater Croatia" and a "Greater Serbia."[6] Tudjman wanted Croatia to be considered part of Europe. He wanted to eradicate what he sees as contamination by the "Orient" (Turkish and Islamic cultures). In September 1995, after his forces had destroyed much of the interreligious culture of Bosnia-Herzegovina, Tudjman asserted that "Croatia accepts the task of Europeanization of Bosnian Muslims." The task, Tudjman claimed, was undertaken at the behest of the Western European powers.[7]

It is now well documented that at a meeting with Serbian President Slobodan Milošević in the town of Karadjordjevo, Tudjman and Milošević decided on a plan to partition Bosnia between Croatia and Serbia and to neutralize any political or social aspirations of Bosnia's Muslim community.[8] Tudjman began his "Europeanization" with the establishment of the Croatian Defense Council (Hrvatsko Vijeće Obrane, or HVO), as the military arm in Bosnia for his political party, the Croatian Democratic Union (Hrvatska Demokratska Zajednica, or HDZ).

The HVO was formed outside of the Bosnian army, on the pretext that it would fight to repel aggression by the Serb army. The underarmed Bosnians had no choice but to accept the arrangement.

The alliance between the HVO and the Bosnian government succeeded in the spring of 1992 in repelling the Serb army's assault on the city of Mostar. In July 1992, however, Croat nationalists declared their own "Union of Herceg-Bosna," a Croat state in Bosnia based upon the same ideals of ethnoreligious purity espoused by the Republika Srpska, only in the name of Catholicism rather than Serb Orthodoxy. Tudjman helped overthrow the moderate Bosnian Croat leader, Stjepan Kljuić, who had been elected Bosnian representative of the HDZ. Kljuić was replaced with nationalist warlord Mate Boban.

In May 1992, Boban had met with Radovan Karadžić in Graz, Austria, to draw up plans for dividing Bosnia between Croat and Serb nationalists. By October 1992, Boban had given up all pretense of alliance with the Bosnian government and ceased all hostilities with the Serb radicals of Radovan Karadžić. In late October 1992, Croat religious nationalists took over much of the town of Novi Travnik. They attacked the town of Prozor, engaging in killing, raping, destroying mosques, and burning Muslim property, in imitation of Serb nationalist actions in eastern Bosnia. Spokesmen for Boban's government of Herceg-Bosna and for Tudjman's government in Croatia claimed that Muslims had attacked Croats and that some Muslim property had been damaged in the fighting. What reporters saw in Prozor contradicted this story: burned-out Muslim homes and businesses sat ruined next to intact Croat structures. When asked why only the

Muslim properties were damaged, a Croat militiaman grinned and said: "The Muslims burned their own homes down with candles."⁹ Before Serb nationalist attacks on Muslim populations, Serb inhabitants were told to evacuate; similarly, Croats in Prozor were ordered to leave before the killing began.

For the next eighteen months, Croat and Serb religious nationalists collaborated in "Europeanizing" Bosnia. As the HVO attacked from the west, the Serb army moved in on the last remaining Muslim enclaves in eastern Bosnia: Goražde, Žepa, Cerska, and Srebrenica. Since spring 1992, these towns had held out against the Serb army and had taken in tens of thousands of refugees driven from the surrounding areas. Day by day, mosques were dynamited by the advancing Croat and Serb militias. Tudjman's "Europeanization" was a euphemism, like "ethnic cleansing," for the annihilation of Slavic Muslim people and culture and the creation of pure Christian states on the rubble of the once multireligious Bosnia.

It is too late for the Muslims of Stolac to "heed the traffic signs." Stolac was a magnificent small town, built along a rushing river beneath rugged hills with ancient Ottoman fortifications and ancient pre-Ottoman Bosnian tombstones known as *stećaks*. It was also known for its exquisite, small-scale, seventeenth-century mosques. Stolac was occupied in 1992 by the Serb army; when Serb forces were driven out, they began shelling the town from nearby mountains. Then the HVO, wearing the masks favored by Serb militias during such operations, turned on the people it had helped save from the Serb army only months before. Here is an account from the UN High Commission for Refugees: "On 23 August 1993, four mosques in Stolac were blown up. That night, witnesses said, military trucks carrying [Croatian] soldiers firing their weapons in the air went through the town terrorizing and rounding up all Muslim women, children, and elderly. The cries and screams of women and children could be heard throughout the town as the soldiers looted and destroyed Muslim homes. The soldiers, who wore handkerchiefs, stockings or paint to hide their faces, took the civilians to Blagaj, an area of heavy fighting northwest of Stolac."[10]

THE MADONNA

The Madonna was said to have appeared to six Catholic children, four girls and two boys, at the small village of Medjugorje in Herzegovina on June 24–25, 1981. This village subsequently became one of the world's more popular pilgrimage sites. Millions have made their way to Medjugorje, which means "between the hills." Pilgrims would see the shimmering light, the strange phenomenon around the sun, an intense feeling of both attraction and fear of looking, but only a select group of young visionaries were able to hear the Virgin Mary speak and transmit her message to the rest of the world. Most of the messages were general messages on the need for world peace.

At the time the Virgin was appearing in Medjugorje, the Bishop of Mostar, Monsignor Pavao Žanić, had been attempting to wrest control of some parishes from some local friars of the Franciscan order. Among the first champions of the authenticity of the Virgin's appearances were local Franciscans. When the Virgin was asked by one of her interlocutors about the case of two Franciscans who had been punished by the bishop, she replied that the bishop had made a mistake. The bishop worked tirelessly to have the visions condemned as a fraud.[11]

Various interpretations have been given for the visions, which were declared to be authentic by influential Catholics, including the theologian Hans von Balthasar. Those who interpret the visions psychologically suggest that the vision of the Madonna calling for peace is a return of repressed memories. Herzegovina was the scene of some of the worst atrocities of World War II, with gruesome killings by Catholic Ustashe of Serbs in the very locale of Medjugorje itself. During World War II, the Bishop of Mostar wrote to Archbishop Stepinac of Zagreb, the highest ranking cleric of the Catholic Church in Croatia, describing the slaughter of Serb men, women, and children by the Ustashe, who threw hundreds of women and children over a cliff to their deaths.[12] After the war, Serbs and Croats went back to living side by side; discussion of the atrocities of World War II was forbidden in the Tito era.

Herzegovina is dominated by Croat religious nationalists, who are divided into two political factions. The HVO worked to partition Bosnia with Serbia, destroy Bosnian Muslims, and integrate most of the Croats of Bosnia into a larger Croatian nation. The other faction, the HOS (Croatian Armed Forces), worked to drive Serbs out of Bosnia-Herzegovina and integrate Bosnia into a "Greater Croatia" modeled on the World War II fascist state. Its motto was the Ustashe slogan "ready for the homeland" (*Za dom, spremni*). With the backing of Tudjman's government and the regular Croatian army, the HVO took over Herzegovina and absorbed the HOS.[13] It was out of these elements that Croatian President Franjo Tudjman forged the knife he was to plunge into the back of Croats, Muslims, and Serbs who desired a multireligious Bosnia.

THE CONVOY OF JOY

At the London Conference of 1992, the Western powers condemned ethnoreligious terror, pledged to support Bosnia's territorial integrity, and rejected the use of force to change boundaries. The conference appointed two negotiators to work for peace in Bosnia: Cyrus Vance was to represent the United Nations and David Lord Owen the European Community. The Vance-Owen plan divided Bosnia-Herzegovina into ten cantons with a dominant ethnic group in nine of the cantons. The area designated for Croat control was very generous. The Herceg-Bosna regime used the Vance-Owen map to justify an attack on Muslim communities; where the map said "Croat control," they seized control by disarming Bosnian Muslims and destroying their communities.[14]

While Croats and Bosnians had agreed to the Vance-Owen plan, the Republika Srpska leaders stalled as their army seized more territory. Then in May 1993, they rejected the plan. Owen and Thorwald Stoltenberg, Vance's successor as UN negotiator, then came up with a map that in Owen's phrase, recognized "reality on the ground" and was based on a map drawn by Croatian President Tudjman and Serbian President Milošević. The plan gave Serb nationalists control of almost all the territories they occupied, including the former Muslim-majority cultural centers.[15] The proposed territorial division based upon reality on the ground became a signal that ethnoreligious expulsions would be rewarded by the international peace negotiators. When the

HVO saw that the Serb army would be rewarded for its atrocities, it began copying them, turning its original aggression at places like Prozor into a systematic campaign modeled on the Republika Srpska aggression against the Bosnian Muslims.[16] Bosnia was under enormous pressure to capitulate and accept a plan that would put Bosnian Muslims into religious ghettoes. The pressure was increased when a Muslim businessman, Fikret Abdić, supported by both Croatian and Serbian nationalists, declared his own statelet in the Bihać area, fragmenting further what was left of Bosnia.

By the summer of 1993, Bosnia was on the edge of annihilation. After the HVO attacked Muslims in the ancient Muslim-majority city of Travnik, the underarmed Bosnian army fought back; as the HVO retreated, many Croats fled Travnik to HVO-controlled territory. In many cases it was the HVO that forced Croats to leave areas controlled by the Bosnian army, although there were also cases in which Muslim militias forced Croats to leave.[17] The Bosnians were opposed to religious expulsions as a matter of policy; indeed, Bosnia was constitutionally defined as a multireligious nation. Yet the Owen-Stoltenberg rules of reality on the ground rewarded religious expulsions with territorial concessions and, in effect, punished any party that refused to engage in them.

As Bosnians struggled to survive, the only ones to come to their defense were a few contingents of *Mujahidin*, veterans of conflicts in Afghanistan and elsewhere in the Middle East. The volunteers came both to help save a Muslim population from extermination and to lead them back to what they believed was a more proper version of Islam. Even though most Bosnians resisted such missionary work, the militant and intolerant behavior of the *Mujahidin* became a propaganda bonanza for Serb and Croat nationalists and their European and North American supporters who had claimed that Bosnian Muslims were fundamentalists. By contrast, the many Greek and Russian volunteers fighting for the Republika Srpska aroused little attention in the West.[18]

In April 1993, in the Lašva Valley of Bosnia, the HVO launched a wave of terror. Entire families were burned alive in their homes. In the southern Herzegovinian town of Čapljina, Muslim civilians were raped and confined in concentration camps. The HVO openly collaborated with the Serb army in an assault on the town of Žepče.[19]

The "Convoy of Joy" has become the abiding symbol for the betrayal of Bosnia. In June 1993, the HVO and the Croatian army authorized a humanitarian convoy to pass through Croat military lines to relieve the city of Tuzla, in Bosnian government territory. Once the convoy had passed into HVO-controlled territory, the HVO attacked it. HVO militiamen shot the Muslim drivers or pulled them out of the trucks and slit their throats. The HVO invited local villagers to loot the trucks. For several days the convoy was attacked and pillaged as British UN peacekeepers, who were on the spot, observed but refused to intervene. Only when the peacekeepers themselves were attacked did they fire on the HVO.

Bosnian Muslims were caught in the middle of a family quarrel between Croat and Serb Christian nationalists. However violent that quarrel was between the two parts of the family, the violence was greater when displaced upon those considered to be alien. It is always dangerous for a third party to come near to an intrafamily dispute. The violence can easily be turned toward the alien; once the alien is dispensed with, the family can resume its dispute. The Serb-Croat dispute was bitter. Even so, for some Croats the Serbs were still fellow Christians, while Muslims are all Turks.

In 1993, Christoslavic hatred of Muslims was being stoked by Croatian President Franjo Tudjman and his anti-Muslim Minister of Defense Gojko Šušak. As the government-dominated news media in Croatia hammered home stereotypes about Muslims, some parts of Croatian society turned hostile. One Croatian writer recalled a cold reaction by friends in Zagreb when she declined to wear the jewelry crosses that had come into fashion; she was accused of subversive attitudes.[20] Many Muslim refugees were told they were no longer allowed to study or work in Croatia. In some cases, Muslims who did not eat pork or drink alcohol were called Turks and disowned by their own Catholic relatives.[21] Tudjman himself reviled Bosnian President Alija Izetbegović for not drinking alcohol. A 1992 article in the popular Catholic magazine *Veritas* rejoiced that the cross of Christ stood next to the Croatian flag, a Croatian bishop next to the Croatian minister of state, and "guardsmen wore rosaries around their necks."[22]

After finishing with Stolac in August 1993, the HVO turned to Počitelj. In September, Počitelj's sixteenth-century masterworks of Islamic art and architecture were dynamited and its Muslim population driven off to detention camps.[23] To mark the expulsion of the Muslims and destruction of the Islamic monuments, a huge cross was erected on the roadside next to the town.[24] Just as Serb religious nationalists first expelled the Muslims from Foča and Zvornik, then dynamited all the mosques, and then declared there never had been any mosques in the

Fig. 5. Počitelj old town: Islamic monuments constructed in 1563 and destroyed by Croatian religious nationalists in 1993. From Husref Redžić, *Studije o Islamskoj arhitektonskoj baštini* (Sarajevo: Veselin Masleša, 1983).

towns, so the Herceg-Bosna authorities are now attempting to rewrite the history of Počitelj. In spring 1996, a conference was organized in nearby Čapljina on the "Historical Development of Croat Počitelj." There are reports that a Catholic church will be built on the ruins of the destroyed mosque.[25]

In the same month, images of skeletal prisoners at the HVO

concentration camp at Dretelj reminded the world of earlier images from the Serb nationalist camp of Omarska. The prisoners at Dretelj had been starved, forced to drink their own urine, and tortured sexually. As at Omarska, local criminals were invited in to kill Muslim captives.[26]

After watching the HVO and Croatian army attack Bosnian Muslims for more than a year and a half, the Western powers tired of the spectacle. Western diplomats threatened Croatia with a withdrawal of support and on March 18, 1994, the Clinton administration brokered an agreement between Bosnia and Croatia. The Croatian government ceased hostilities and agreed to a federation between Bosnian Croats and the Bosnian government, and a confederation between Croatia proper and the new federation of Bosnia-Herzegovina.[27]

THE MADONNA AND THE
CONCENTRATION CAMPS

In Croatia and central Bosnia, Catholic church leaders, particularly Cardinal Kuharić of Zagreb, Archbishop Puljić of Sarajevo, and Father Petar Andjelković OFM, the superior of the Franciscan Province of Bosnia, have specifically and courageously condemned the crimes of Croat religious nationalists. In Herzegovina, however, the Catholic clergy played a different, more troubling role.

The view of Slavic Muslims put forth by some Herzegovinian clergy differs little from nationalist Serb views. A local Herzegovinian priest offers a pilgrim to Medjugorje a portrait of Herzegovina under the Ottomans that differs little from the history of Ottoman occupation given by the Serb clergy: lurid tales of torture without acknowledgment of the long history and complexity of the relationship between the Franciscans and the Ottomans.[28] When European mediators attempted to reconcile the Catholic and Muslim population of Mostar, they were opposed by elements within the local Catholic clergy such as Tomislav Pervan, the provincial superior of 250 Franciscan friars in the Mostar region, who repeated the Tudjman propaganda that the Bosnian Muslims wanted an Islamic state. Friar Pervan went on to say that "Islamic states don't have free speech, democracy, or freedom of religion," ignoring the irony of such a statement made in the wake of the brutal persecution of Bosnian Muslims by Serb and Croat religious nationalists, in the name of Christian states.[29] In the Herzegovinian town of Bobani, a Franciscan priest, the Rev. Vinko Mikolić, compared the Bosnian government to the "Turkish occupiers." In the same town, the Catholic church features a large mural behind the altar showing the suffering of the Croat people, with portraits of a World War II Ustashe militiaman, Ranko Boban, hanging nearby. Portraits of the leader of Ustashe Croatia, Ante Pavelić, one of the most ruthless war criminals of the Nazi empire, are displayed in the homes of local Catholic priests.[30]

Not only Serb religious nationalists but Croat nationalists as well subscribed to the view of novelist Ivo Andrić that only weak and cowardly Slavs converted to Islam. Andrić drew on both the nineteenth-century Christoslavism of Serbian Orthodox Bishop Petar II (Njegoš), as well as an older tradition of Croat Christoslavism. In his dissertation, immediately after citing—as "the people's" judgment—Njegoš's caricature of Slavic Muslims as greedy and cowardly, Andrić cited Franciscan Friar Franjo Jukić as an exponent of the "spirit" of popular Christian perception:

"They [Bosnian Muslims] sprang from bad Christians who turned Muslim because only thus could they protect their land."[31]

As the visions at Medjugorje gained wider recognition, they were "nationalized" by Croat politicians. For example, the independence of Croatia was announced on June 25, 1991—the tenth anniversary of the apparitions. The Franciscans at Medjugorje favored an association between the Virgin and the independent Croat state and were proud of it.[32] Franciscans are especially prominent in Grude, the city in which the Christoslavic state of Herceg-Bosna was proclaimed. In 1993, as the HVO was turning Herzegovina into flames, a journalist reported that: "In the souvenir shops [of Medjugorje], statuettes of the Madonna were on sale with swastikas, Maltese Crosses and other Nazi regalia." The city had also become a major center for the warlords and gangsters known as the Herzegovinian mafia, who terrorized Muslims, Serbs, and any Croat who stood in their way. When the visions of the Virgin first occurred at Medjugorje, local Muslims (who also revere the mother of Jesus) came to visit the site. The religious nationalization of Medjugorje was complete when the HVO proclaimed that "anyone found sheltering Muslims in the Holy City would have their homes blown up."[33]

The continuing atrocities by the HVO were opposed by Cardinal Kuharić of Zagreb, who appealed to the Herceg-Bosna warlord Mate Boban to seek peaceful coexistence with the Muslims and warned (accurately) that those responsible for the violence could be charged in the future with war crimes. Boban responded to the cardinal's letter: "This is not a time of coexistence [with Muslims]. It is time for something else."[34] Despite his own earlier Croat nationalist statements dismissing the Ustashe atrocities of World War II and glorifying Croatia's thirteen-hundred-year Catholic history, by the summer of 1993 Kuharić was resisting the militant religious nationalism of Boban and his hard-line Franciscan backers in Herzegovina, as well as the nationalist circle around Tudjman and Šušak.[35] On September 13, 1993, Kuharić appointed a new bishop of Neum (the only Bosnian town on the Adriatic sea) to whose installation ceremony Muslim clerics were invited and which they attended.[36]

The papal response is difficult to evaluate. Pope John Paul II called a conference at Assisi in January 1993 dedicated to seeking peace in the former Yugoslavia. In contrast to the statements of the Serb Orthodox leaders, the Assisi conference participants did not single out for attention members of their own flock (in this case Catholics), but spoke with equal fervor of the suffering of all peoples in the region.[37] Even so, the Pope never publicly denounced the role of Herzegovinian clergy in supporting the violent religious nationalism of the Herceg-Bosna militias. Nor did the Pope, who has been forceful in his visits to Latin America in reshaping the hierarchy according to his own views, exert an effective force on the Mostar clergy or visit Mostar, a few minutes' flight from Rome, to demand an end to the persecutions.[38] Whether or not they could have been better supported by the Roman Catholic hierarchy, the moderate elements of the Bosnian Croat church and society had been marginalized by the late summer of 1993 and could only try to ameliorate, not stop, the ongoing persecutions.

Meanwhile, the struggle between the Bishop of Mostar and the Herzegovinian Franciscans was intensifying. The religious nationalists supported the Herzegovinian Franciscans and threatened to blow up the Mostar Cathedral. In November 1995, the

Map 4. Herzegovina

CROAT NATIONALIST OFFENSIVE, *1991–1993*

1991

| June 25 | Independence of Croatia declared on tenth anniversary of Medjugorje visions |

1992

April	Bosnia-Herzegovina is recognized by the EC and the U.S. Croatian nationalists form the Croatian Defense Council (HVO)
May	Graz partition plan between Mate Boban and Radovan Karadžić
July	Mate Boban declares the Union of Herceg-Bosna
	Stjepan Kljuić ousted from elected post in the Croatian Democratic Union (HDZ)
October	Radovan Karadžić and HVO cease all hostilities
	Croat nationalist assault on Prozor
	Croat-Muslim fighting in Novi Travnik

1993

January	Vance-Owen plan is announced
April	HVO massacres at Ahmići and across the Lašva Valley
	Franjo Tudjman tours Herceg-Bosna to support the HVO campaign
June	Convoy of Joy
	HVO force near Travnik is rescued by the Serb army
	HVO and Serb army cooperate in besieging the Bosnian town of Maglaj
	HVO reign of terror against Muslims in Čapljina
August	Muslims driven from Stolac
	European mediators pressure Bosnians to accept the Owen-Stoltenberg plan
September	HVO concentration camp at Dretelj
	Bosnian army revenge atrocity at Uzdol

	HVO destroys the old town of Počitelj and expels its Muslims
October	Fikret Abdić declares an "Independent Republic" in the Bihać region
November	HVO destroys the Mostar bridge on 55th anniversary of Kristalnacht

Pope sent a special delegate, a papal nuncio, to urge the Franciscans of Čapljina to cede their parish to the bishop's control. Anti-Muslim extremist Gojko Šušak, the Croatian Defense Minister, visited the meeting in an apparent show of support for the Franciscans.[39]

On November 13, 1995, two high Croat officials in Herzegovina were indicted by the International Criminal Tribunal for organizing the slaughter of Muslims in fourteen Muslim villages in the Lašva Valley. After the indictments, Croatian President Tudjman announced that rather than arresting indicted war-criminal General Tihomir Blaškić, he was promoting him. Tudjman made the announcement in Dayton, Ohio, where he had promised to cooperate with the International Criminal Tribunal and to detain suspects for trial. The other suspect, Dario Kordić, had been placed by Tudjman at the head of the HDZ in Herzegovina over more moderate candidates; after the Lašva Valley atrocities, he was decorated for increasing Croatia's "position and prestige."[40]

By November 1993, after eighteen months of shelling, first by the Serb army and then by the HVO, the multireligious heritage of Mostar was reduced to rubble. As a final gesture, Christoslavic forces supported by Franjo Tudjman destroyed the Old

Fig. 6. The Old Bridge (*Stari most*) in Mostar: symbol of a multireligious heritage, constructed in 1561 and destroyed by Croatian
religious nationalists in 1993. From Husref Redžić, *Studije o Islamskoj
arhitektonskoj baštini* (Sarajevo: Veselin Masleša, 1983).

Bridge of Mostar, which had stood since 1561 as a symbol of Bosnia's role in bridging cultures. The destruction fit Tudjman's desire to be accepted by Europe and to cut his Catholic Croat nation off from any association with the "Orient" of Serbs, Muslims, and Jews. Tudjman depends upon the major Western European powers for economic, political, and cultural support. After "Europeanizing" Bosnia, he awaits his reward.

Herzegovinian Catholics call the Madonna of Medjugorje *Gospa* (Lady). Catholic theologians maintain that a true vision will lead to changed and morally responsible behavior on the part of those who experience it.[41] If the Madonna of Medjugorje did insist on peace one wonders why those who heard her message gave such little thought to the Muslims confined to concentration camps at Gabela, Čapljina, Dretelj, Ljubuški, and Rodoč, all within a few miles of Medjugorje. Did those busloads of pilgrims, filled with inner light and joy, hear the screams from the other side of the Medjugorje hills?

DIVING FROM THE BRIDGE

Amir Pašić is a native of Herzegovina. An architect and city planner, he won an international award in 1987 for his work in reconstructing the old city of Mostar. The historic core of the city, which had been in decline, was reconstructed with sensitivity to both historical detail and social viability. Residents of the old city were not priced out of their property. They were encouraged to open businesses and museums that would serve the tourists expected to come to a revived Mostar. The plan worked, and before the war broke out in neighboring Croatia in 1991, Mostar had a strong tourist economy and a vital old town.

When Mostar came under attack, Pašić escaped to Istanbul with detailed plans of the city. He now directs an institute with graduate students from around the world dedicated to rebuilding Mostar yet again, with attention to both historical detail and social vitality. When people start talking about religious and political exclusivity, he just changes the subject back to rebuilding this great city. He has given out invitations printed up for the reopening of the reconstructed city in the year 2004.

One Mostar tradition is the annual bridge dive. Daring young men and women would dive off the high-arched old Ottoman bridge, far down into the Neretva River. In the summer of 1994, in the wake of the siege, when east Mostar had been pummeled into ruin and its inhabitants starved, shelled, and confined to cellars for months, the people came out for the annual event. The spectators got out their swimsuits and sat along the banks of the river. An improvised, temporary bridge was placed over the blasted-out central section of the great bridge, and the divers dove.

CHAPTER SIX

MASKS OF COMPLICITY

ARMING THE AGGRESSOR

For almost two years, since the summer of 1992, the continuing atrocities in Bosnia had been denounced by officials with the UN High Commission for Refugees. Louis Gentile, the UNHCR head of operations in Banja Luka, was prompted to make the following statement: "It should be known, and recorded for all time, that the so-called leaders of the Western world have known for the past year and a half what is happening here. They receive play-by-play reports. They talk of prosecuting war criminals but do nothing to stop the continuing war crimes. May God forgive them, may God forgive us all." [1]

For months Gentile had been reporting on systematic atrocities against non-Serb civilians in Banja Luka. For months his appeals to stop the killings had been ignored by Western leaders. It is common to ask whether the West, the United Nations, or the Christian world failed in Bosnia, or worse, whether the Christian West was complicit in the evil that occurred there. Terms like "the West," however, are abstractions. The work of the UNHCR workers like Louis Gentile, Western news reporters, UN war crimes investigators, and some Western public officials may have prevented genocide from attaining even greater proportions. Despite these efforts, the conditions reported by Gentile were not only allowed to occur but were made possible by particular Western policy makers. Just as the ethnoreligious militants donned masks and face-paint to allow themselves to transform their former colleagues into disposable aliens and themselves into epic champions of their race and religion, so have many in the Western Alliance created their own masks to justify a policy that has allowed what Gentile called "beyond evil" to flourish. At the heart of the complicity was a policy that denied the Bosnians the right to defend themselves, while at the same time refusing to enforce UN resolutions authorizing NATO power to protect them.

A weapon is not a particular tool or device, but a disparity between one tool and another. Against a Goliath with a club, a slingshot is a weapon. Next to a tank, a slingshot is a toy. In 1991, the NATO nations armed the Serb militants, not with arms sales as in the Iran-Iraq war or the Rwanda genocide, but with a UN declaration.

During the cold war, the Yugoslav army, supported and financed by the Western powers, had stockpiled immense stores of weapons in hardened bunkers and had constructed weapons factories throughout Yugoslavia, especially in Bosnia-Herzegovina, in anticipation of a Soviet invasion that never came. In 1991, Serb nationalists seized control of most of those weapons. The advantage of the Serb army in heavy weapons over the Bosnians was estimated at anywhere from 20–1 to 100–1. When the Serb army attacked Sarajevo in the spring of 1992, the Bosnian government was so poorly armed that it was gangs of criminals and black marketeers—the only groups with the weapons and organization needed to set up barricades and capture Serb armaments—that saved parts of the city from the genocidal assault.[2]

On September 25, 1991, British Foreign Minister Douglas Hurd orchestrated passage of UN Security Council Resolution 713, an arms embargo on the former Yugoslavia by the UN Security Council, a resolution that the Milošević regime was seeking. The five permanent members of the Security Council—U.S., Britain, France, Russia, and China—all voted for the resolution. The embargo locked into place a radical arms disparity between the Serb army and Bosnian army; in effect, it armed the Serb militants.[3]

What occurred from April through October of 1992 has been labeled a war and even a civil war. A war, however, is a conflict between armed adversaries. The Serb army took towns and villages that lacked significant military defenses. Where there was any Bosnian defense at all, Serb militants used heavy artillery to shell the defenders into submission. Once the town or village was taken, the killings of civilians would begin.

This was not war but organized destruction of a largely unarmed population. With weapons and weapons factories under their control and with the arms embargo in place and stubbornly maintained for years, Serb militants were able to carry out their program with impunity.

ORIENTALISM

In 1970, Yugoslavia was experiencing a form of *glasnost;* writers took up previously taboo subjects such as religion. A Sarajevo lawyer named Alija Izetbegović published a document entitled "The Islamic Declaration." The document, an anticommunist assertion of religious rights, spelled out the conditions for a just Islamic society and contained several provocative statements concerning the incompatibility of Islam with other systems. The principles of an Islamic state were discussed in an abstract manner, without specifying any particular nation. A few years later, Izetbegović wrote a more extensive work, *Islam between East and West,* which suggested two models—Islam and European liberal democracy—as antidotes to the problems besetting Europe at the time.[4]

When Izetbegović became president of Bosnia in 1989, most Bosnians had never read his Islamic Declaration. But Serb militants not only read it, they published a Belgrade edition of it and used it to claim that Bosnian Muslims were radical fundamentalists or "Islamists," that is, Muslims who desired a state based on Islamic religious law (*sharia*).

The charge that Bosnians were Islamists was combined with the charge that they were plotting to re-create the Ottoman rule over Bosnia. Serb radicals claimed that Bosnians wished for a state based on the leadership of religious scholars and a new Ottoman sultanate based upon imperial rule. Bosnian Muslims were accused of plotting to steal Serb women for their harems (Bosnian Muslims do not take more than one wife) and of drawing up lists of viziers (ministers in the Ottoman Sultanate) to rule the country.[5] Croatian Defense Minister Gojko Šušak claimed that 110,000 Bosnians were in Egypt studying to become fundamentalists.[6]

The representation of the Muslim as an alien "other" has been called Orientalism. During the Christian Middle Ages, Muslims were viewed as perverted heretics and frequently associated with Jews and persecuted with them. During the period of European colonialism, Western scholars, artists, and other intellectuals reflected the ideology of the age: the need for Western colonial rule to "civilize" barbaric Oriental lands. Orientalism abounds in contradictions. Muslims were portrayed as mysterious, sensuous, and sexually obsessed (the harem fantasy in Western writing). At the same time they were portrayed as sexually repressed, authoritarian, rote-learners, and lacking in all creativity and imagination.[7]

Religious nationalists in Croatia and Serbia used such Orientalist stereotypes both for home consumption and for the audience in the wider Christian world. Those who spread hate are seldom concerned about logical consistency, and stereotypes are not fashioned to appeal to reason but rather to semirepressed fears and hatreds. The contradictions of Orientalism appeared in a vicious and dehumanizing new form. Now Serb Orientalists had come up with the Islamist vizier, without the slightest embarrassment over the fact that modern Islamist ideologues believe in a state run by religious scholars and despise as corrupt and anti-Islamic the former imperial Ottoman structure with its sultans and viziers which collapsed in World War I. Similarly, the language of hate lacks even a basic concern with plausibility. Thus Šušak claimed that 110,000 Bosnian Muslims were studying fundamentalism in Egypt—a number that would represent 5 percent of the *entire* Bosnian Muslim population.

Religious nationalists in Serbia then charged a plot between Libya and Bosnian Muslims. During the 1970s Yugoslavia and Libya had been partners in the nonaligned block of nations that refused allegiance to either the Western Alliance or the Soviet Bloc. Through cultural, educational, and economic interchanges, many Yugoslavs of all ethnic and religious backgrounds worked or studied in Libya, including Bosnians such as Haris Silajdžić, who went on to become Prime Minister of Bosnia.

According to the religious nationalists, Silajdžić and other Bosnians who had visited Libya were trying to set up a fundamentalist *Jamhariyya* ("People's State," a word used by Libya's Qaddafi to describe his regime) without noting the difference between Qaddafi's Arab nationalism (based on the socialist ideas of Jamal Abdul Nasser of Egypt) and modern Islamist militants (who oppose Qaddafi and whom Qaddafi suppresses).

According to Tanjug, the news service controlled by Slobodan Milošević, one of the most enthusiastic supporters of Milošević's Yugoslavia has been none other than Muammar Qaddafi, President of Libya. By December 3, 1994, Tanjug was reporting on the visits to Libya of high-level Serbian officials. Praise for close cooperation between the two states, both of them outcasts from the international community, resounded through Tanjug reports.[8] The same Serb nationalists who attacked Bosnian Muslims for alleged involvement with Libyans were posting Tanjug's effusive reports on Serbo-Libyan cooperation.[9]

In 1994, Bosnian Minister of Culture Enes Karić defended a Muslim cleric who had discouraged mixed marriages and criticized the playing of enemy (i.e., Serb) music. His provocative statements were denounced by a wide range of government and extragovernment leaders, including Haris Silajdžić, the Prime

Minister. Yet Karić's statements were enough to set off announcements by Western observers that multireligious Bosnia was now dead and that Bosnia should therefore be partitioned along ethnoreligious lines.[10]

Particularly galling to many Bosnians is the phrase, popular among diplomats and newscasters, "Muslim-dominated government of Bosnia-Herzegovina." The Bosnian executive branch of government is made up of two Catholic Christians, two Serb Orthodox Christians, and three Muslims; the Bosnian parliament and diplomatic corps contain Muslims, Jews, Serbs, Croats, and atheists. It is true that Muslims are in the majority in Bosnia and that, as large numbers of Croats and Serbs choose or are compelled by their own nationalist leaders to live under all-Croat and all-Serb governments in Herceg-Bosna and the Republika Srpska, the percentage of Muslims has increased. Yet Bosnians ask why there are not references to the "Protestant-dominated government of the United States" or the "Anglican-dominated government of Britain."

Behind much of the official, governmental propaganda were academics. University of Belgrade Professor Miroljub Jevtić, for example, wrote of the imminent threat to Europe posed by Muslims and also wrote of Balkan Muslims as having the blood of the martyrs of Kosovo on their hands—an almost direct copy of the blood-libel, that European Jews had the blood of Christ on their hands, used to persecute Jews from the time of the First Crusade in 1096.[11] Dr. Aleksandar Popović wrote of Islam as a "totalitarian" religion because it embraces all aspects of life.[12] His use of the term "totalitarian" evokes Stalinist and Nazi totalitarianism, mentions of which are still painful in the former Yugoslavia. Belgrade academician Darko Tanasković described Bosnia as the scene of a struggle between fundamentalist Muslims on the one hand and Serbs dedicated to keeping Church and State separate on the other. He thereby reversed the reality in which a clericalist Republika Srpska had eradicated every trace of peoples and cultures outside of Serbian Orthodox Christianity, while the Bosnian government struggled to maintain a multireligious culture.[13]

The refusal of European governments to either defend Bosnians against genocide or allow them to obtain arms to defend themselves has been based in part on stereotypes about Islam. The attitudes of policy makers in Europe and North America are also influenced by a nativist backlash against immigrant communities, especially non-Christian immigrant communities, and an environment of increasing global tensions between some Muslim governments and the West.[14] As Croatian President Franjo Tudjman noted, he had taken his mission to Europeanize Bosnian Muslims from the expressed desires of Western European leaders. Serb President Slobodan Milošević was equally desperate to play up to European leaders and be accepted by them. In his 1989 Kosovo speech Milošević stated that Prince Lazar's battle six hundred years before had been a battle to defend Europe from Islam, that Serbia was the bastion of European culture and religion, and that Serbia's future actions would demonstrate that now as in the past, Serbia was always a part of Europe. Tudjman and Milošević felt a duty as Europeans to destroy the Bosnian Muslims and felt that doing so would facilitate their acceptance by Europe.[15]

Central to the Orientalist stereotype is a confusion in the presentation of Islam between religious observance and religious militancy. While few would argue that the militant wing of the

Irish Republican Army represents all observant Catholics, the association of observant Muslims with religious militancy is widespread. Some defenders of Bosnia have fallen into this trap, arguing that Bosnian Muslims are not "real Muslims" since many of them eat pork or drink alcohol and dress in Western fashion. The implicit logic seems to be that if Muslims in Europe eat pork, they deserve to exist. Desperate to counter false charges that they were fundamentalists, there were Bosnian Muslims who used the same logic, arguing that some of them also ate pork and drank alcohol, or were religious skeptics. Ironically, while European powers out of prejudice against Muslims and fears of fundamentalism tried to prevent Bosnia from attaining arms to defend itself, support in the Islamic world was slow in coming, partly because some Muslim leaders viewed Bosnians as not rigorous enough practitioners of Islam. A particularly sad absurdity awaited many Bosnian refugees in Western nations. Having been driven out of home and country for being Muslim, the refugees sometimes find themselves castigated for not observing what certain Muslims in the West deem proper Islamic observance, dress, or behavior.[16]

The stereotypes of Orientalism did not have to be subtle to be effective. However crude the presentation of Islam, however filled with interior contradictions, they provided a justification for many among Christian Croat and Serb populations for what was done to their Muslim neighbors, and they worked outside the region to militate against any effective, coordinated action by Western powers to stop the aggression.

As evidenced by those commentators who immediately assumed that the terrorist behind the Oklahoma City bombing was a Muslim, when it turned out the suspect was a follower of the

Christian Identity movement, a militant anti-Islamic prejudice has now pervaded much of Western society, subduing any popular sentiment for protecting "them," the religiously "other" in Bosnia.[17] Tragically, the betrayal by Western powers of Bosnian Muslims into the hands of genocide will only strengthen the argument of Islamic militants that the West is by nature inimical to Islam, thus further polarizing elements of Muslim and Christian populations.[18]

BALKANISM

Bosnian Muslims are also objects of a dehumanizing discourse about Balkan peoples which portrays Bosnians as Balkan tribal haters outside the realm of reason and civilization.

"They have been killing each other with a certain amount of glee in that part of the world for some time now," asserted former U.S. Secretary of State Lawrence Eagleburger in July 1995 just after the betrayal of Srebrenica.[19] The phrase "in that part of the world" provides to the domestic audience an immediate, nongeographical excuse to feel alienation: these people are not our concern because they are "other," "foreign," "different." In view of the domestic audience's deep-seated (though not always admitted) prejudices against non-Christians in general and Muslims specifically, vague references to "that part of the world" tap into both anti-Balkan and anti-Islamic sentiments.

"Ancient Balkan hatreds" has become a standard cliché in debate on Bosnia. The Balkans are historically and geographically too close to the Orient (read Islam) to be a true part of Europe, we are told. The 1992 book by Robert Kaplan, *Balkan Ghosts*, referred to the border with Turkey as Europe's "rear door."[20] The book popularized the caricature of Balkan peoples as locked in unending hate and revenge.

Balkanism is the distorted depiction of the people of southeastern Europe as barbaric with the implication that violence, even genocide, is inevitable there and part of the local culture. Balkanist comments were pervasive after the revelations of the horrors of Omarska in August 1992. Western officials had been holding back news of such camps.[21] The press revelations caught the major players off guard. Western leaders came under pressure by the press and public to liberate the killing camps. During this period, all the major figures of the foreign-policy team of U.S. President George Bush repeated Balkanist stereotypes.[22]

One stereotype was the superhuman Serb warrior. In World War II Serbs had tied down many Nazi divisions, we were told by Pentagon planners and by experts at military think tanks. No effort was made to distinguish between the anti-Nazi fighters of World War II, who were a multiethnic and multireligious group, and the Serb militias of fifty years later. Ignored also was the decidedly unheroic behavior of the Serb military in 1992: attacks with massive heavy weaponry against lightly defended villages and retreats when faced with serious military confrontation.

Public comments from the U.S. Defense Department also violated a key military principle: Never tell an aggressor what you may and may not do. Even if you are not going to act, never let an aggressor know what to expect. The comments from the Pentagon on the uselessness of air power to deter genocide and on the impossibility of stopping it with anything less than massive casualties were a signal that the U.S. and the NATO powers would not respond, no matter how heinous the assault—a "green light" for further genocide.[23]

In September 1995, the NATO powers tried air strikes. After three weeks of very selective bombing, the siege of Sarajevo was broken and NATO became concerned that further strikes would utterly destroy the Serb army in Bosnia. For three years, experts had declared the Serb army to be invincible and impervious to air power. After three weeks of air strikes, NATO feared that the same Serb army would collapse, causing a "destabilizing" shift in the balance of power.[24]

BALKANISM AS A MASK

How Balkanism functions as a code for political decisions can be seen in the statements of U.S. President Bill Clinton. As candidate for president in 1992, Bill Clinton proposed the use of NATO air power to save Bosnians from "deliberate and systematic extermination based on their ethnic origin."[25]

On February 10, 1993, President Clinton still acknowledged massive human rights violations but spoke of "containing" the conflict. Containment had been the policy of the Bush, Mitterrand, and Major administrations. The policy served, in effect, to turn Bosnia over piece by piece to Serb and Croat army conquest. On April 25, 1993, Clinton proclaimed that "Hitler sent tens of thousands of soldiers to that area and was never successful in subduing it." He was ignoring the fact that the Bosnians had never asked for Western ground troops, only for a lifting of the arms embargo and for air support.[26] On May 7, 1993, U.S. Secretary of State Warren Christopher returned from Europe with a Balkanist stereotype to explain the refusal by the NATO powers to stop the killings. In testimony before the U.S. Congress, he referred to "ancient antagonisms" and spoke of the Bosnian catastrophe as a "problem from hell."[27]

Another Balkanist claim, advanced by Serb President Slobodan Milošević, Bosnian Serb President Radovan Karadžić, and the British government, was that the violence was a "civil war," an "interior affair," or an "ethnic war." Among the most zealous Balkanists were the Serb nationalists, who asserted that the Bosnian conflict was part of an age-old pattern of ethnic war, that outsiders could not understand it and should leave the people of Bosnia to solve it for themselves (while keeping in place the arms embargo).[28] By May 1993, Clinton was calling the conflict a civil war, even though Croat and Serb forces had crossed the borders into Bosnia and were fueling the violence. Clinton next spoke of a "conflict" in Bosnia that is "ultimately a matter for the parties to resolve." On February 10, 1994, Balkanism reached its conclusion: "Until these folks get tired of killing each other," Clinton said, "bad things will continue to happen."[29] The stage was set for Srebrenica.

After Srebrenica, the U.S. Senate passed by an overwhelming margin the bipartisan Dole-Lieberman bill requiring the United States unilaterally to lift the arms embargo against the Bosnians. Both the vote and the speeches that accompanied it were a historic bipartisan repudiation of the foreign policy of an American president still in office.[30] The Europeans had threatened to withdraw their peacekeepers from Bosnia if the arms embargo were violated. Clinton had promised to send U.S. troops to aid in any evacuation of peacekeepers. A withdrawal would have led to a crisis in Bosnia before the 1996 presidential elections.

The Clinton administration was finally moved to act. Backed

by NATO air strikes on Serb army munitions dumps and communication facilities in Bosnia, Assistant Secretary of State Richard Holbrooke led negotiations that resulted in the Dayton peace agreement of November 22, 1995. Soon after, Deputy Secretary of State Strobe Talbot denounced the idea that the Bosnia tragedy was the inevitable result of "ancient hatreds"—the Balkanist stereotype that had been propounded by the same administration for two years.[31]

The Balkanist mask, donned and removed by the Clinton administration, was put back to work by the isolationist wing of the Republican party. All of Bosnia (and its four million human lives) was not worth one American soldier, exclaimed one candidate for the Republican presidential nomination.[32] One congressman proclaimed that "they have been fighting" in the Balkans for fifteen hundred years, oblivious to the fact that none of the major religious and ethnic groups in Bosnia had yet settled in the Balkans by that time. The culmination of the Balkanism frenzy was reached by Congressman William Goodling of Pennsylvania, who announced it "all began in the fourth-century split of the Roman Empire."[33] These congressmen had now embraced the mythology propounded by British policy makers and pundits such as Sir Crispin Tickell, who claimed that the hatreds among Yugoslav peoples extended back "thousands of years."[34]

PASSIVE VIOLENCE AND
FALSE HUMANITARIANISM

Western policy makers also manipulated the language of pacifism to justify maintaining an arms embargo against the Bosnians while refusing to use force to help them. The same leaders have authorized arms sales throughout the world. British Foreign Secretary Douglas Hurd stated that to lift the arms embargo would be to create a "level killing field."[35] When the existence of the concentration camp at Omarska was revealed in August 1992, President Bush, proud author of Operation Desert Storm against Iraq, consistently refused to advocate lifting the arms embargo on the grounds that more arms in the area would increase the violence.

NATO policy makers had a moral and legal duty to uphold Article 51 of the UN Charter guaranteeing the right of a nation to defend itself, as well as the 1948 Geneva Convention requiring all signatory nations not only to prevent genocide but to punish it. By refusing either to allow the Bosnians to defend themselves or to use NATO power to defend them, these leaders engaged in a form of passive violence, setting the parameters within which the killing could be and was carried out with impunity.[36]

Despite the extraordinary efforts of many individuals and small congregations, influential Christian church leaders and organizations also opposed both lifting the embargo and the use of NATO force to save the Bosnians and have offered little in the way of an alternative.[37] The position of many church groups that the best way to stop the violence was by "tightening" the arms embargo neglected the fact that the Serb army had enough weapons and weapons factories to last years. One of the few influential Christian leaders to speak out against the acquiescence of major church leaders and organizations in the assault on Bosnia has been Adrian Hastings, emeritus professor of theology at Leeds University. Hastings remarks that "If those in need are mostly Muslims who have lived peaceably for generations with their Christian neighbors but are now being destroyed by nominal Christians, that is all the more reason for Christians to come to the rescue." He remarks on the silence of the archbishops of Canterbury, York, and Westminster and the British Council of Churches in view of the greatest moral outrage in Europe since World War II. He then draws a historical parallel: "Bishop George Bell of Chichester was a lonely voice 50 years ago when he spoke up for the Jews. Where is a Bishop of Chichester today?"[38] Sarajevo Archbishop Vinko Puljić, who has so courageously struggled for a multireligious Bosnia, approaches the topic with devastating understatement: "I think we had expected much more energetic voices against injustice from Western churches."[39] While it is true that differing churches have widely different views on the issue of just war and justified use of force, what was indisputable was the reluctance of major Christian church leaders to call the crimes in Bosnia what they were, genocide, and to demand a stop to them. To the extent that church statements showed only a generalized concern over suffering in Bosnia without an urgent demand to stop genocide, they can be justly accused of refusing to speak truth to power, or in Hastings's term, of speaking platitudes.

To the passive violence of the Western policy makers was added a false humanitarianism. By focusing the UN mission on the supply of humanitarian aid while refusing to stop the campaign of genocide, the UN Security Council created a system that put UN peacekeepers as suppliers of humanitarian aid to Bosnia—as hostages. Whether or not they were actually detained by radical Serb militias was not important. They could be detained at will and thus served as hostages whether or not they were confined. The Serb army was able to violate with impunity dozens of UN resolutions demanding free flow of humanitarian aid, liberation of concentration camps, access to camps by war crimes investigators, and protection of civilians.[40] By requiring a dual key for any action by NATO (approval by both the UN military and civilian commanders and the NATO commander), the Security Council prevented any effective deterrence to hostage-taking. Some people were fed who would otherwise have starved but, as Bosnians commented, they were being fed for the slaughter.

For three years the UN struggled to get a basic minimum of food to the enclaves of Srebrenica and Žepa. After some peacekeepers were taken hostage and others threatened with being taken hostage, the people in the safe areas who had been forbidden adequate weapons to defend themselves and had been kept alive by UN humanitarianism were turned over to the Serb army for mass killings.[41] In September 1995, when NATO did use air strikes to break the siege of Sarajevo, total casualties to NATO forces were two French pilots missing. Had those strikes, or a credible threat of strikes, been used to prohibit any genocidal act by any party in 1992, not only would untold numbers of Bosnians (of all religions) have been saved, but the lives of more than two hundred UN peacekeepers as well.

It is impossible to know the personal motivations of those who for three years manipulated a language of pseudopacifism and false humanitarianism to justify a policy that rewarded aggression and punished its victims; who recognized Bosnia's sovereignty and pledged to defend it, then broke their own pledges; who declared a "no-fly zone" in October 1992, refused to authorize any enforcement for months, then refused to enforce it anyway; who declared six cities safe areas but refused to protect them; and who authorized "all necessary means" to get humani-

Fig. 7. British UN General Michael Rose (*right*) shares a laugh with Serbian General Ratko Mladić (*left*) as Mladić's forces close in on UN designated safe areas. Reuters/Stjepanovic, 1995.

tarian convoys through to starving civilians but refused to use the means available.[42]

For some, the degradation of the notion of peacekeeping is encapsulated in a particular incident. In the summer of 1992, UN peacekeepers under the command of Canadian General Lewis MacKenzie frequented the rape camp known as Sonja's Kon-Tiki, in the town of Vogošća near Sarajevo. Even after they learned that the women at the Kon-Tiki were Muslim captives held against their will, abused, and sometimes killed, UN peacekeepers continued to take advantage of the women there and to fraternize with their Serb nationalist captors. Only 150 yards away from Sonja's, scores of Muslim men were being held in inhuman conditions, but the peacekeepers took no notice.[43]

For others, the degradation of the peacekeeping role culminated on January 8, 1993. A French contingent of UN peacekeepers was escorting the Bosnian Deputy Prime Minister Dr. Hakija Turajlić into Sarajevo. They were stopped at a Serb army checkpoint. When the Serb soldiers asked the French peacekeepers to open up the armored car—against their orders and with the certain knowledge of what would follow—they complied, then stood aside and watched as a Serb soldier shot the unarmed Dr. Turajlić dead. When the same French peacekeepers came home to France, they were decorated for heroism.[44]

A Serbian religious nationalist put into one formula the manipulations of the language of nonviolence and humanitarianism that have been so often used by Western policy makers in regard to Bosnia and by doing so demonstrated the moral equalizing to which such language leads. The nationalist claimed that Christianity was superior to Islam because Christianity forbids all violence, even in self-protection. When asked why he justified as self-defense the violence of Serb nationalists, he responded: "We are all sinners."[45]

MORAL EQUALIZING

"There are no angels in this conflict" has been a slogan used for the refusal to stop the killing—as if angels, rather than human beings, deserve our empathy and support. In July 1992, British Foreign Secretary Douglas Hurd patronized victims along with perpetrators: "Where there is no will for peace we cannot supply it."[46] The Balkanist stereotype was continually used to imply that all sides were equally guilty.

No party in any war has ever been free of blame. But the blame-on-all-sides position falsified important differences between the methodical genocide carried out by Serb nationalists, the predatory aggression of Croat nationalists, and individual crimes committed by Bosnian soldiers, crimes that were not related to any overall criminal policy and that have been punished.[47]

Moral equalizing led to political equalizing. After the London Conference of 1992 affirmed the territorial integrity and legitimacy of Bosnia, NATO powers shifted to a competing language in which the Bosnian government was one of three "warring factions."[48] When Bosnian leaders held out against aspects of peace plans that rewarded the atrocities of Serb and Croat nationalists with territorial concessions and left Bosnia open to future destruction, Western diplomats leaked statements to the effect that the Bosnians were "sore losers" and would not accept the fact that they had "lost"—as if genocide were some kind of football game.

In 1993, David Owen stated that Serbs had controlled 60 percent of pre-war Bosnia, a claim used by Serb militants to justify their claim that most of Bosnia should be given to the 31 percent of the country that was Serb.[49] The last land registers before the war, however, showed 50 percent of Bosnia was public land and that Serb landowners controlled 23 percent. In April 1995, Thorwald Stoltenberg made the astonishing announcement that Bosnian Muslims were actually Serbs; it was a Serb extremist dream-come-true. If Bosnian Muslims were Serbs, then they had no reason to reject Serb military occupation and since (according to the extremists) Serbs were either Orthodox Christian or traitors, there was no reason Bosnian Muslims shouldn't be treated as traitors.[50] The two men entrusted by the Western powers to protect the sovereignty of Bosnia were adopting the most spurious and fatal claims of the radical religious nationalists among the Serbs.

Moral equalizing could be achieved by portraying all sides as inhuman savages; it could also be achieved by ignoring atrocities. According to a senior fellow at the Brookings Institution and a senior advisor to Yasushi Akashi, the chief of the UN operation in Bosnia, the problems in Bosnia were not the result of age-old tribal hatreds but rather the effects of organizational breakdown—within both international and Yugoslav institutions—following the cold war. There was no crime and, it was implied, no one really was responsible.[51]

A final way of avoiding moral distinctions was to demonize an entire people. Phrases such as "Serb aggression" and "Serb atrocities" ignore any Serb opposition to genocide. The group demonization is based upon a view of the Serb people as a homogenous mass—a view shared by Serb militants. For Republika Srpska President Radovan Karadžić, for example, any Serb who does not support the attack on Bosnia is not a true Serb and any criticism of Karadžić's policies is a criticism of "Serbs" in general.

Peter Brock published a piece in the journal *Foreign Policy* asserting that the Western media had exaggerated the atrocities committed by Serbs while refusing to report atrocities against Serbs.[52] The article ignored the massive evidence in the human rights reports and war crimes investigations of organized genocide by the Serb militants. Multiple flaws in the Brock article were soon demonstrated. Even so, it was a propaganda bonanza for Serb religious nationalists.[53] For many Serbs and others who wish to believe that the genocide was a fabrication of Western media, the Brock article was a citation from an establishment journal. At the base of the Brock article was the notion that criticism of the leadership of the Republika Srpska was a slur against *all* Serbs; Radovan Karadžić couldn't have said it better.

NATIONAL INTERESTS

Western officials such as U.S. Secretaries of State Lawrence Eagleburger and Warren Christopher had trouble seeing a vital interest in acting to prevent genocide in Bosnia, beyond "containment" of the violence within the boundaries of Bosnia. At this time, it is still unclear whether the Dayton accords will be enforced or whether the NATO operation to support them will be degraded in the manner of the UN mission from 1992 to 1995. The outcome will affect the security of peoples and nations outside of Bosnia in profound ways.

In 1948, the first Arab-Israeli war left 750,000 Palestinian refugees. The "Palestinian problem" led to three more major Middle East wars, the destruction of Lebanon, East-West geopolitical conflict, proliferation of nuclear weapons by Israel and its enemies, and billions of dollars in U.S. foreign aid to the Middle East. In July 1995 there were more than twice as many Bosnian refugees as there were Palestinian refugees in 1948, and they have suffered atrocities beyond description. The consequences of allowing Bosnia to be destroyed will begin to appear in the second and third generations of children born in refugee camps, and they will be incalculable.

GENOCIDE IN BOSNIA, *1992-1995*

1989

June 28	Milošević speaks at the 600th anniversary Kosovo celebration

1991

September 25	UN Security Council Resolution 713: Arms embargo on all parties in the former Yugoslavia

1992

March 27	Republika Srpska declared
April 6–7	Bosnia-Herzegovina is recognized by the EC and U.S.
April 3–17	Serb military begins genocide in Zvornik, Višegrad, Foča, and Bijeljina areas
April 21	Siege of Sarajevo begins
May	Bosnian government pleads in vain for military help or a lifting of the arms embargo
May 17	Serb army destroys Oriental Institute in Sarajevo
May 19	Yugoslav Army claims it is "withdrawing" from Bosnia, transferring soldiers and weapons to the control of the Bosnian Serb army
May 27	Bread-line shelling in Sarajevo
May 30	UN Security Council Resolution 725: Sanctions against Yugoslavia (Serbia and Montenegro)
June 19	Union of Herceg-Bosna declared
August 3	Bosnian President Izetbegović appeals in vain for an end to the arms embargo
August 4–6	Televised pictures of Omarska and Trnopolje concentration camps
August 25–28	London Conference: NATO nations affirm Bosnia's territorial integrity
	Serb army burns the National Library in Sarajevo

1993

January 2	Unveiling of the Vance-Owen plan
January 8	UN gives over the Bosnian Deputy Prime Minister to Serb soldiers, who kill him on the spot
January 15	Water-line shelling in Sarajevo
March–April	Serb army takes Cerska and threatens Goražde, Srebrenica, and Žepa
April 16	UN Security Council Resolution 819: Declares Srebrenica a safe area
May 5	The Republika Srpska rejects the Vance-Owen plan
May 22	Bihać, Tuzla, Žepa, Goražde, and Sarajevo declared safe areas along with Srebrenica
June–September	Owen-Stoltenberg partition of Bosnia, based on a map drawn by Tudjman and Milošević
June 30	UN Security Council rejects a proposal to lift the arms embargo
July	Joint Croat-Serb nationalist attacks on Bosnian Muslims
September	HVO forces destroy Počitelj's Old Town and expel its Muslims
September 6	Izetbegović pleads for the UN Security Council to lift arms embargo
September 27	Fikret Abdić declares an autonomous state in the Bihać pocket
November 9	HVO destroys the Mostar Old Bridge
November 17	UN War Crimes Tribunal authorized

1994

February 5	Marketplace shelling in Sarajevo; NATO pressure leads to temporary relief from shelling
April 4–15	Serb army shells Goražde, enters the safe area, and burns Muslim homes. British UN General Michael Rose refuses to protect the safe area

May	Contact Group plan to partition Bosnia with 49 percent of the territory to go to the Republika Srpska
August– September	Vojkan Djurković phase of expulsions and religious terror in Banja Luka and Bijeljina
September– November	Yugoslavia claims it has closed its border with Bosnia
November	Bihać attacked by Serb forces from Bosnia and Croatia, and by Abdić rebels. British UN General Michael Rose renounces further NATO air strikes to protect Bihać

1995	
July 11–21	UN hands over safe areas of Srebrenica and Žepa to Serb army; mass killings ensue
July 26	U.S. Senate passes Dole-Lieberman bill to lift arms embargo against Bosnia
July–August	Croatian regular army crushes the Serb Krajina Republic in "Operation Storm"
August 28	Second Sarajevo marketplace shelling leads to NATO bombing
November 22	Peace agreement initialed in Dayton, Ohio

At the end of the cold war, NATO changed its mission from defense against the Soviet Union to protecting the peace and security of Europe. Failure to fulfill that mission in Bosnia will weaken and may destroy an alliance that has been critical to stability in Europe and to which all the NATO nations have contributed enormous resources.

Sarajevo is at the center of ethnic and religious fault lines that stretch around the world: the Slavic and Orthodox Christian world extends to the east and northeast; the Muslim and Turkic worlds extend to the east and southeast across central Asia and to the west along North Africa; the Catholic world extends to the west and northwest from Austria to Latin America; the Protestant world begins its arc not far north of Sarajevo. Rewarding genocide in Bosnia will send a message to the many potential antagonists: strike first and strike ruthlessly and you will get what you want.

In 1993, the extremist Hutu leadership of Rwanda was plotting genocide. They had every reason to expect that if genocide could be carried out with impunity in Europe, right in front of NATO, it could be carried out in Central Africa, far from any force like NATO. A final failure in Bosnia will send an ominous message to any other group in the world (and there will be many) who might contemplate genocide.

A geopolitical cold war between Islam and the West would be more intractable and more dangerous, perhaps, than the cold war between the West and the Soviet Bloc. Muslims around the world were stunned by Western acquiescence in the genocide, and by the passivity of pro-Western Islamic governments. A final failure in Bosnia will only strengthen the claim of Islamic militants who argue that the West wishes to destroy Islam. It will weaken the position of Muslims who seek peaceful relations with the Western world.

Religious violence has broken out globally: a Buddhist group's poison gas attack against Tokyo; the April 1995 Oklahoma City bombing by followers of the Christian Identity movement; the attack on Muslim holy sites by Hindu militants; the attack on the World Trade Center in New York City by Islamic radicals; the celebration by Jewish militants of the mass murder of Muslim Arabs in Hebron and the killing of Prime Minister Yitzhak Rabin in Israel. Rewarding genocide in Bosnia will make such violence a model for success.[54]

For some, it may well be in the national economic interest for a major arms producer like the United States to allow or even foster such strife and conflict. It assures markets for a major export item, keeps a military industrial complex in a state of readiness, and keeps a large army as a safety valve in a time of increasing unemployment; a conflict with the Islamic world would create a new global enemy; outside enemies help interior cohesion. The practitioners of *realpolitik* do not make these arguments so baldly, but they intimate them. Ultimately, whether preventing genocide is in our national interest depends on our definition of "interest"; that definition depends in turn upon what kind of nation and what kind of world we wish to inhabit.[55]

NOT TWO CENTS

"I don't give two cents about Bosnia. Not two cents. The people there have brought on their own troubles." This statement by *New York Times* columnist Thomas Friedman was made on June 7, 1995. It marks the logical end of moral equalizing, the equating of the victim and the perpetrator and the devaluing of both.[56]

In theological terms, the moral and political equalizing was embodied in the statement by the Serb Church spokesman that "everyone in this war is guilty."[57] The ramifications of such a statement go beyond theological doctrines of original sin. The notion that everyone is guilty in the Bosnian conflict is a generalized statement that leads downslope to the conclusion that

Bosnian people are in some sense getting what they deserve. Indeed, the view that the victims of genocide deserve what they get is more often a subtext of the language of moral and political equalizing; only rarely does an influential columnist such as Thomas Friedman articulate the message directly. In the less restrained world of Internet newsgroups, posters often state a version of the slogan, "Let them keep on killing one another and the problem will solve itself," a statement that is a more honest version of the phrase popular among political commentators: "Contain the problem to Bosnia and let it burn itself out."

Albert Speer, the architect of much of Nazi Germany's industrial machine, spent twenty years in prison. In his memoirs, he stated that he never accepted responsibility for the evil he had caused despite the vast number of victims. Then he saw a photo of a family being taken to a death camp. With that glimpse of suffering on an individual scale, he began to understand the evil of which he had been part.[58]

In Bosnia, witnesses to the violence have focused on individual cases in order to touch somehow a world that seemed not to wish to care. A reporter noted that after the second Sarajevo market massacre on August 28, 1995, a Bosnian child turned to her mother saying "Mommy, I've lost my hand," as her mother, herself grievously wounded, moaned "Where is my husband, I've lost my husband." After the Serb army shelling of a Sarajevo suburb in 1992, a reporter wrote of a young boy found next to his dead mother, repeating, "Do you love me, Mommy?" After the Srebrenica shelling massacre of 1993, in which the Serb army opened fire on a group of Muslim civilians waiting to be evacuated by the United Nations, an official with the UN High Commission for Refugees told of a young girl who had half her face

Fig. 8.   Who was she? Refugee from Srebrenica after the safe haven
was turned over to the Serb army in July 1995. AP/Wide World
Photos.

blown away. He said that her suffering was so intense, he could do nothing but pray that she would die soon, which she did.[59]

In some cases, images that intimate rather than demonstrate have allowed people to see beyond the masks to what is at stake in Bosnia. A young woman from Srebrenica hanged herself after the enclave was turned over to the Serb army; a picture of her allowed U.S. Senator Dianne Feinstein, who had been using the language of Balkanist "ancient animosities" mythology to excuse the violence, to understand the human element of the genocide. Feinstein asked a series of questions about the young woman: What was her name, where was she from, what humiliations and depravations did she suffer, had she been raped, did she witness loved ones being killed? It was what the picture left unsaid that allowed the senator to look beyond the linguistic masks of "warring factions" and "guilt on all sides" to the reality that this young woman was most likely not warring, not guilty, not an ancient antagonist or hater, and that her act was "not the act of someone who had the ability to fight in self-defense."[60]

The violence in Bosnia was a religious genocide in several senses: the people destroyed were chosen on the basis of their religious identity; those carrying out the killings acted with the blessing and support of Christian church leaders; the violence was grounded in a religious mythology that characterized the targeted people as race traitors and the extermination of them as a sacred act; and the perpetrators of the violence were protected by a policy designed by the policy makers of a Western world that is culturally dominated by Christianity.

In the case of religious genocide, moral distinctions are particularly difficult to maintain; the basis of much moral thinking is to be found within religions, but in religiously motivated violence, religions are being manipulated to motivate and justify the evil. One response is to reform religions from within, in dialogue with other religions. Religious leaders of each tradition need to better understand and more clearly explain the full humanity of those who embrace other religions and the variety and richness within other traditions. Another response is to begin with a basic premise—that needless, willfully inflicted human suffering cannot and should not be explained away. The two responses may complement one another.

A counterreading to the manipulation of the Good Friday story by religious nationalists might be found in the refusal of "doubting Thomas" to accept the risen Jesus until he had put his hands into the wounds. There are those who will refuse to accept the suffering of their fellow human beings even if they were to put their hands into the wounds; in the case of Bosnia the doubters might include Western political leaders and a segment of the public.

The story of Thomas may be a story about how difficult it is to recognize the wounds of another and how such recognition is necessary in order to see the resurrected Jesus. The Bosnian Muslim has been the "other" for much of the Christian world. The genocide in Bosnia was grounded in a particular version of the Good Friday story; it remains to be seen whether other readings of that story will contribute to a decision to stop the genocide, and whether that decision will occur before it is too late.

CHAPTER SEVEN

THE BRIDGE

THE WOUNDING SKY

Before Aida Mušanović spoke of the cloud of ashes that hung over Sarajevo for three days after the Serb army burned the National Library, she told another story. She had gone to the Oriental Institute, one of the central resources for the history and development of Bosnian culture. It was the day after the institute had been completely destroyed by Serb army gunners. She stood on the ground floor of what used to be a six-floor building and looked up at the open sky.

Bosnian culture has always resisted being reduced to a single religion or ethnicity. In pre-Ottoman times, Bosnia was the home of three churches: Orthodox, Catholic, and the independent Bosnian Church. Since Ottoman times, Islam, Orthodoxy, and Catholicism have made up the large pattern of Bosnian cultural heritage. After the expulsion of the Jews from Spain in 1492, many Sephardic Jews who had been offered refuge in the Ottoman Empire came to Bosnia; Ashkenazi Jews from northern and eastern Europe also settled in Bosnia. The Roma (Gypsy) population of Bosnia-Herzegovina is divided between adherents of Islam and Christianity.

The specific character of Bosnia's heritage is reflected in its tradition of love lyric, among the world's most sophisticated. The native love song is the *sevdalinka*, which can be composed in Croatian, Bosnian, and Serbian and written in either the Latin alphabet, Cyrillic alphabet, or as Adžamijski (Slavic in the Arabic alphabet).[1] The *sevdalinka* involves the timeless lyrics of unrequited love. It is called "the woman's song" because by convention it is sung by a woman to her male beloved. The woman poses as a male lover in the song, singing to his female beloved. This complex gender interplay is further enhanced when male singers sing the woman's song. There is one account of six Muslim *ulema* or religious scholars on their way to the pilgrimage in Mecca, singing *sevdalinkas*.

The love lyric is about love, but it is also about loss and exile. During the shelling of Sarajevo, one of the most popular lyrics, based on an ancient *sevdalinka*, concerned Mt. Trebević, the mountain above Sarajevo from which Serb army gunners were shelling the city. In the old *sevdalinka*, Mt. Trebević was the mountain of the love fairy. The love song took on new meaning during the siege of 1992–1995, when Sarajevans listened to a *sevdalinka*-based popular song lamenting the unrequited love of the maiden of Sarajevo: "A fair lady's crying from Mount Trebević where it used to be."[2]

In addition to composing *sevdalinkas* in South Slavic, Bosnian poets composed them in the languages of the Ottoman empire: Ottoman Turkish, Persian, or Arabic. They also combined the native *sevdalinka* themes with themes from the Ottoman Islamic world and from the Petrarchan sonnet. Many poets composed in all the languages of the region. Some of the more popular poems, composed in Persian or Ottoman Turkish (or in interlocking verses of Persian and Ottoman Turkish), were translated into South Slavic, and in some cases the South Slavic versions are now better known than the Persian and Ottoman Turkish originals. The manuscripts containing this intricate multilingual tradition of Bosnian love lyric were one part of the cultural treasure that went up in flames on May 17, 1992.

Bosnia has a culture rich in transitions and translations. Those looking for the essence of culture and language in ethnic, racial, or religious purity will find Bosnia incomprehensible. On the other hand, those who see culture as a creative process that by its very nature involves intermingling and creative tension among different elements will treasure Bosnia-Herzegovina.

Sarajevo was at the center of such a pluralistic culture. Its mosques, synagogues, Catholic and Orthodox churches stand side by side. Its people are skilled at languages and navigating the concourses of differing traditions—as many discovered when they visited the city for the Winter Olympics in 1984. Bosnia-Herzegovina could be a bridge between the increasingly polarized spheres of East and West and could play an important role in preventing a war between the majority Christian world and the majority Islamic world, a reversion to the Crusades. It is the polarized world of the Crusades that religious nationalists presuppose and desire and that the complex culture of Bosnia-Herzegovina contradicts.

The sounds of that polarized world are clear in the lyric sung by Radovan Karadžić's soldiers, accompanied by the *gusle*—the stick fiddle used with classical South Slav epics—as they trained their guns down from the mountains above Sarajevo:

Oh, beautiful Turkish daughter
Our monks will soon be baptizing you,
Sarajevo, in the valley,
The Serbs have you encircled.[3]

THE EXECUTION OF CULTURE

In the fall of 1995, former U.S. Secretary of State Henry Kissinger proclaimed that "there is no Bosnian culture." The context for Kissinger's claim was his proposal that Bosnia should be partitioned between Serbia and Croatia and that the Muslims (and presumably anyone else who did not want to be part of ethnically pure Greater Croatia and Greater Serbia) should be placed in a "Muslim state." Partitioning Bosnia and putting the Muslims in a religious ghetto was the original goal of the Serb and Croat nationalists.[4]

Those who have done the most to disprove Kissinger's claim that there is no Bosnian culture are Ratko Mladić and Mate Boban, the Serb and Croat nationalists who devoted such extraordinary energy to destroying the vast testimony to Bosnian culture: the National Library, the Oriental Institute, and the National Museum, all in Sarajevo; the archives of Herzegovina; music schools; local museums; graveyards; ancient bridges and clocktowers; entire historic districts; covered marketplaces; and of course thousands of churches, synagogues, and mosques, from masterworks of South Slavic architecture to the humble, local houses of worship.

One incident, recounted by the Bosnian writer Ivan Lovrenović, captures the frenzy of this campaign of cultural annihilation. A Serb army officer had entered the home of a Sarajevan artist, who happened to be Serb. Among the works of art, he saw a piece that depicted a page from the Qur'an. Infuriated, he had all the artwork taken out into the street, lined up, and shot to pieces with automatic weapons fire.[5]

What is behind such a seemingly lunatic obsession with destroying culture? Why would Croat and Serb nationalists spend almost four years destroying a culture that did not exist in the first place? The four years of destruction were an attempt to eliminate something that does exist and continues to exist. Testimony to that existence is to be found in the people and cultural world that has survived, and in the empty spaces throughout Bosnia-Herzegovina where so many human lives and cultural monuments used to be.

The armies of the Serb and Croat religious nationalists targeted Bosnian culture, monuments, cultural leaders, teachers, and students, so that someday advocates of religious apartheid in Bosnia could declare: "There is no Bosnian culture." People looking at the parking lots where mosques and churches and art museums and music schools and libraries and manuscript collections once stood would say: "I guess Kissinger was right." The argument then becomes plausible. As the mayor of the newly "cleansed" and 100 percent pure Serb Orthodox city of Zvornik said, after all of the city's mosques had been dynamited, "There never were any mosques in Zvornik." If there is no Bosnian culture, why not divide Bosnia between Croatia and Serbia, and herd the Muslims into a central ghetto?

The same reasoning was used by advocates of apartheid in South Africa. There was no African culture, they said, so why not put Africans on reservations called homelands and institute an apartheid state? The same approach was used during the extermination of the American Indian nations. There was no Native American culture, so why not "cleanse" the American Indians and put the survivors on reservations?

Since the First Crusade in 1096, non-Christian communities in Europe have been subject to annihilation. Throughout the Crusades, Jewish communities were attacked and burned, visited with the kind of atrocities that have occurred in Bosnia-Herzegovina. In 1492, exactly five hundred years before the beginning of the attack on Bosnia, Queen Isabella of Spain ordered her kingdom "cleansed" of its Jewish population. In 1609, those to be "cleansed" were the Moriscos, all those who kept the customs of the Muslims of Spain, whether or not they were practicing Muslims. A new word, "pogrom," came into our vocabulary to explain the fate of Jewish communities in eastern Europe for several centuries. Then there was the Holocaust. To advocate the driving of Bosnian Muslims into a Muslim state surrounded by two heavily armed nationalist armies that have tasted blood is to advocate, if a ruthlessly consistent European history tells us anything, the probable destruction of that people. Those who advocate a ghetto for Bosnian Muslims may suggest that the UN and NATO would give the ghetto security guarantees—like those given to the "safe area" of Srebrenica.

Like culture in the United States, Bosnian culture cannot be defined by the linguistic and religious criteria of nineteenth-century nationalism. Just as Americans share a language with the British and Australians, so Bosnians share a language with Serbs and Croats. Just as the United States has no single, official church, so Bosnia is made up of people of different religious confessions, and within those confessions, vastly different perspectives. If Bosnia has no culture, then the United States has no culture. If Bosnia should be partitioned into religiously pure apartheid states, then the same logic leads to the idea, proposed by the Christian Identity movement, that the United States should be divided into apartheid states of different races and religions.

CREATION IN THE FIRE

After recounting her experiences of the destruction of culture in Sarajevo, Aida Mušanović explained the exhibit she was organizing, entitled Expo/Sarajevo 92. It consists of eighteen engravings made by distinguished Sarajevan artists during the worst of the shelling of Sarajevo. The names of the artists (Serb, Croat, and Muslim) and the styles of their art reflect the mosaic of cultures, religions, and influences that comprises Sarajevo. Radoslav Tadić's work, "Echo 92," shows the silhouette of a building in which Catholic, Serbian Orthodox, and Muslim architectural and sacred figures blend into, grow out of, and complement one another. Mustafa Skopljak's "The Cry" offers piercing emotion transmuted through semi-anthropomorphic shapes reminiscent of those of Joan Miró. Sead Čizmić's "Sarajevo Sera" depicts a calm evening with a Mediterranean atmosphere, with a darkness on the horizon. Zoran Bogdanović's "Homage to Alija Kućukalić" is calm solemnity, a grief too deep for words or movement. Nusret Pašić's "Witnesses to Existence" depicts human figures in elongated shapes partially reminiscent of German expressionism.[6]

The artists decided to use engraving not only because prints are replaceable and thus not vulnerable to total destruction but also because of the social aspect of engraving. Because of the shelling, the artists were often forced to stay overnight or for several nights at a time in their studio (an old evangelical church). In their catalogue comments the artists trace the line of teachers and traditions that religious nationalists wished to destroy.

Why would people risk their lives to produce a work of art? Why did that doctoral candidate at the University of Sarajevo give her young life to try to carry some small part of the cultural heritage of Bosnia out of the flames of the National Library?[7] Several months after the death of her father at the hands of a sniper, the student's sister in Canada received in the mail some letters from the dead father; because of the siege of Sarajevo they had been delayed en route. At the time of their delivery, she said, she had not been able to open them. I do not know what the letters might have said, whether they discussed the death of his daughter. From the testimony of hundreds of Bosnians, I imagine one theme would be this: It is not tolerable to live as a captive, to sneak along alleys and walls to receive a UN food handout. To live is to create. To create or protect culture is an act of living.

One participant in the discussion of Expo/Sarajevo 92 suggested that the engravings do not represent a cultural reality that could exist independently and prior to them.[8] Rather, it may be that through such art a culture like that of Bosnia—a culture not defined by notions of ethnic and religious purity—can exist. In the act of creating culture, the overlapping boundaries and claims of different languages, religions, and traditions can find a space in which otherwise competing worlds are on common ground.

When Slobodan Milošević stood at the Kosovo field in 1989, he told the crowd that Serbia "was a fortress defending European culture and religion." The Serbian Orthodox Church leaders and academics in Belgrade speak of a defending wall against the Asiatic aliens. Croat religious nationalists destroyed the Mostar bridge as they "Europeanized" Bosnian Muslims. After the Dayton treaty proposed a unified Sarajevo, Radovan Karadžić demanded a walled Sarajevo patterned on the Berlin of the cold war.

Those who want a wall between Europe and an allegedly alien and inferior "Orient," a wall between Christian and Islamic worlds, face one problem: the stubborn propensity of Bosnians to think in terms of bridges instead of walls and their courageous effort to save or rebuild their bridges. Cultures are hard to kill. Fire meant to destroy them may steel them instead.

A DANCE

In a city in North America, a family of exiles from Sarajevo had invited a group of friends to a dinner party before they moved to another city. The family, of mixed religious background—primarily Serbian Orthodox, with relatives in the Muslim and Croat Catholic communities—had struggled to survive for three years of separation and persecution. Guests included Serbs, Croats, and Muslims from Bosnia as well as Americans of many religions and ethnic backgrounds.

At such events there is a moment when the evening comes together in a special way. That moment occurred as someone put popular music from Sarajevo on the cassette player. The song was an old *sevdalinka* in popular music form. Jasminka, who had spent three years in exile struggling to reunite her family, stood up and began to dance. Soon her daughter joined her. At such times, as separation is mourned and reunion celebrated, joy and sorrow have a way of blending into one.

NOTE ON SOURCES

The charge of genocide almost always generates disputes over data and numbers killed and charges that the other side engaged in equal atrocities. False charges of genocide can be used to foster and motivate actual genocide, as Chapter 3 demonstrates.

Even the most clearly established cases of genocide, such as the Holocaust or the genocide perpetrated by the Khmer Rouge in Cambodia, have frequently been denied. Given the human tendency to deny, evade, excuse, or ignore something as profoundly evil as genocide, a few denials in the right place at the right time can effectively disrupt efforts to halt genocide in progress.

The claims in this book are based on the following types of sources: (1) human rights reports by organizations that are not attached to any government, that have reported on human rights practices of any and all governments, and whose credibility has been established by vindication of their reporting over long periods of time; (2) evidence collected by the International Criminal Tribunal in The Hague (authorized by the United Nations on November 17, 1993) and indictments issued by the tribunal; (3) eyewitness accounts by refugee workers in Bosnia, who have no political interest in either maximizing or minimizing the abuses they witnessed; (4) interviews by this author with Bosnian refugees and survivors; (5) reports in the press insofar as they are corroborated by evidence from one or more of the first four categories; and (6) negative evidence, revealed in glaring contradictions within the denials of atrocities by those alleged to have committed them or in the refusal by those accused to allow access to independent investigators or to cooperate with the International Criminal Tribunal.

Of special importance is the corroboration of evidence from more than one source and more than one kind of source. It is possible even for trained human rights investigators to make a mistake in a particular case. Cross-corroborated evidence and evidence gathered not from a single incident but from a pattern are more reliable. An example of how cross-corroboration works can be found in the case of the Čelopek Cultural Center killings near Zvornik. Survivors from Zvornik testified that Serb militiamen detained, raped, tortured, and killed Muslim civilians at the Čelopek Cultural Center outside town. This evidence was later corroborated by a trial in Yugoslavia, reported by the dissident Serb journalists of *Vreme News Digest*, in which an alleged perpetrator admitted the crimes but excused them on the grounds that he was drunk. Later, when the issue of possible involvement by the Yugoslav secret police was raised, the Yugoslav government shut down the trial. Serb nationalist authorities in Zvornik have refused to cooperate with or grant access to International Criminal Tribunal investigators and human rights groups. It is often difficult to prove rape and torture to those who discount the testimonies of survivors, but the physical testimony of dynamited mosques is hard to dispute. The accounts of genocide in Zvornik, as elsewhere, weave accounts of attacks on persons with descriptions of the systematic destruction of mosques. When it turns out that every mosque in Zvornik and every mosque in the Republika Srpska has been destroyed, the evidence of systematic, organized genocide is reinforced.

Negative evidence is important in view of demands that the point of view of the other side be respected and heard and that coverage should be "balanced." The point of view of Serb and Croat religious nationalists has indeed been taken into account very carefully; it has impeached itself in the following ways: (1) through internal contradiction based on obvious stereotypes and ignorance, as in the accusations by Serb religious nationalists that Bosnians are Muslim fundamentalists who aim to establish an Islamic state ruled by religious scholars, on the one hand, and are plotting to reestablish the viziers and other accouterments of imperial Ottoman rule, on the other; (2) through contradictory responses to the same accusation, as when Serb authorities defended shelling refugees in Srebrenica in 1993 by saying they were shooting at a Bosnian tank and accidentally hit the refugees, while at the same time maintaining that there was no shelling at all but that the incident was staged by Bosnian and UN officials using the bodies of Serbs who had been tortured to death; (3) through a pattern of repeated falsehoods, as with the three-year history of denial by Republika Srpska officials that ethno-religious expulsions were taking place or that refugee convoys were being blocked in the face of massive eyewitness testimony to the contrary; (4) through glaring falsehood in individual instances, such as the claim by Yugoslav diplomat Vladislav Jo-vanović in his December 1995 letter to the UN Security Council that the thousands of Bosnian Muslims missing from the safe areas of Žepa and Srebrenica were killed by their own soldiers, despite overwhelming evidence to the contrary; or the Croatian government's claim that the property of Muslims in Prozor was damaged during a fire fight, when photos and eyewitness accounts showed burned-out Muslim businesses and residences scattered throughout town next to undamaged businesses and residences of Catholic Croats; and (5) through refusal to allow claims to be verified, as has been the case throughout the Republika Srpska: Serb nationalists claimed that prisoners were treated according to the Geneva conventions but refused access to the International Red Cross, war crimes investigators, and other human rights monitoring organizations.

Religious nationalists in the former Yugoslavia have specialized in the control of the media. Atrocities by their own forces are never mentioned; alleged atrocities by their enemies are repeated continually. Are there people of good will in these territories who truly believe the views presented to them with such an air of authority? Is it possible for them not to have noticed the interior contradictions in such propaganda or how the boasting of local militia leaders in their own town or village contradicts it? In writing a book like this one, I take it as a moral challenge to be open to the possibility that I have been deceived and to reexamine continually the account I give. To those who maintain total skepticism, however—and with it, reject any moral responsibility to stop the genocide if it is occurring—I would say this. The possibility of deception can never be ruled out completely, but the willingness to accept an unpleasant, even devastating truth, when we are faced with it, is necessary if we are to become truly human.

SOME BASIC SOURCES

Publications by Governments and International Organizations

Amnesty International: *Bosnia-Herzegovina: Gross Abuses of Basic Human Rights* (New York: 1992); *Bosnia-Herzegovina: Rana u duši—A Wound to the Soul* (New York, 1993).

Helsinki Watch: *War Crimes in Bosnia-Hercegovina* (New York: Human Rights Watch, 1992); *Letter to President of Serbia and JNA Chief of Staff* (New York, 1992); *War Crimes in Bosnia-Hercegovina*, Vol. 1 (New York, 1992); *War Crimes in Bosnia-Hercegovina*, Vol. 2 (New York, 1993); *Abuses Continue in the Former Yugoslavia: Serbia, Montenegro and Bosnia-Hercegovina* (New York, 1993); *Prosecute Now!: Helsinki Watch Releases Eight Cases for War Crimes Tribunal on Former Yugoslavia* (New York, 1993); *Procedural and Evidentiary Issues for the Yugoslav War Crimes Tribunal: Resource Allocation, Evidentiary*

Questions and Protection of Witnesses (New York, 1993); *Abuses by Bosnian Croat and Muslim Forces in Central and Southwestern Bosnia-Hercegovina* (New York, 1993); *The War Crimes Tribunal: One Year Later* (New York, 1994); *War Crimes in Bosnia-Hercegovina: Bosanski Šamac* (New York, 1994); *War Crimes in Bosnia-Hercegovina: U.N. Cease-Fire Won't Help Banja Luka* (New York, 1994); *Sarajevo* (New York, 1994); *"Ethnic Cleansing" Continues in Northern Bosnia* (New York, 1994); *War Crimes Trials in Former Yugoslavia* (New York, 1995).

UN Security Council: *Annex I: European Community Investigative Mission into the Treatment of Muslim Women in the Former Yugoslavia, Report to the European Community Foreign Ministers*, Vol. S/25240, February 3, 1993 (New York: United Nations, 1993).

U.S. Congress: *Genocide in Bosnia-Herzegovina: Hearing Before the Commission on Security and Cooperation in Europe, One Hundred Fourth Congress*, Vol. CSCE 104-1-4 (Washington, D.C.: U.S. Government Printing Office, 1995).

U.S. Department of State: "War Crimes in the Former Yugoslavia": This consists of eight U.S. State Department War Crimes Commission Reports found in *U.S. Department of State Dispatch*, 3.39, 3.44, 3.46, 3.52 (1992); 4.6, 4.15, 4.16, 4.30 (1993). This author has edited the reports into a form more easy to cite, by numbering each entry. The edited versions are available on the World Wide Web:

URL:http://www.haverford.edu/relg/sells/reports.htm/

Electronic Bulletin Boards

Tribunal Watch World Wide Web Site on Major War Criminals/Suspects: Information and documents are from Helsinki Human Rights Watch, International Criminal Tribunal in The Hague, UN Special Committees for War Crimes in the former Yugoslavia, and other international organizations and sources including referenced articles from newspapers:

http://www.cco.caltech.edu/~bosnia/criminal/criminals.html

United Nations International Criminal Tribunal for the Former Yugoslavia:

http://www.igc.apc.org/tribunal/

Court TV: War Crimes Tribunal Page (especially useful for description of the tribunal jurists and personnel):

http://www.courttv.com/casefiles/serb/docs/

Human Rights Watch/Helsinki Watch:

gopher://gopher.igc.apc.org:5000/11/int/hrw/helsinki/bosnia

Commission of Experts on the Former Yugoslavia Established Pursuant to Security Council Resolution 780 (1992):

http://www.cij.org/cij/commission.html

War Crimes Investigators' Open Source, Factual and Legal Resources:

http://www.his.com:80/~cij/investigations.html

Reports of Thaddeus Mazowiecki, Special Rapporteur on Human Rights to the United Nations:

http://www.emse.fr/~maillot/HTML/PERSO/E/YUGO/ MAZOWIECKI

gopher://gopher.igc.apc.org:5000/11/int/hrw/helsinki/bosnia

Physicians for Human Rights:

gopher://gopher.igc.apc.org:5000/11/int/phr

ICRC Operations in Western and Central Europe and the Balkans (with details on the Manjača and Mostar-area camps):

http://www.icrc.ch/icrcnews/opeuroc.htm

Efforts to Resist Cultural Genocide and Destruction of Manuscripts:

http://www.acs.supernet.net/manu/ingather.htm

AN EXAMPLE OF SOURCE CROSS-CORROBORATION: OMARSKA

The Omarska camp offers one example of how the various sources can be used in cross-corroboration. Following are the sources used by this author in depicting the camp at Omarska. Similar cross-corroborated evidence was used in discussion of the other camps and killing sites.

U.S. Department of State: "War Crimes in the Former Yugoslavia: Submission of Information to the United States Security Council in Accordance with Paragraph 5 of Resolution 771 (1992)." The original publications of these reports are difficult to cite, since they are scattered over eight issues of a publication. The citation below is based upon an index prepared by Aida Premilovac and Michael Sells and posted, with the full text, on the World Wide Web site listed above: 1:20, 2:13, 2:15, 2:16, 2:17, 2:24, 3:4, 3:7, 3:8, 3:9, 3:11, 3:12, 3:17, 3:18, 3:21, 3:24, 3:36, 4:3, 4:9, 5:15, 6:1, 6:2, 6:6, 6:7, 7:7, 7:14, 7:16, 8:6, 8:10, 8:13, 8:14.

Helsinki Watch: *War Crimes in Bosnia-Hercegovina* vol. 1 (New York, 1993), 87; vol. 2 (1994), 163.

Indictments: (1) The International Criminal Tribunal for the Former Yugoslavia, The Prosecutor of the Tribunal

[Richard Goldstone], Against Dušan Tadić, a.k.a. "Dule" Goran Borovnica, *Indictment*. Includes eight sets of charges, each set detailing up to fifty-four specific incidents. Tadić was a local official allegedly invited into the Omarska camp on a regular basis to commit atrocities. (2) The International Criminal Tribunal for the Former Yugoslavia, The Prosecutor of the Tribunal [Richard Goldstone], Against Željko Meakić [Commander of Omarska] and eighteen other named Omarska personnel. Includes thirteen sets of charges.

Books, Reports, Diaries, and Interviews: Roy Gutman, *Witness to Genocide* (New York: Macmillan, 1993); Rezak Hukanović, "Eyewitness to Hell: A Survivor's Diary of the Serb Concentration Camp at Omarska," *The New Republic*, 12 February 1996, 24–29; Ed Vulliamy, *Seasons in Hell* (New York: St. Martin's Press, 1994); Radovan Karadžić's public statements on Omarska; Televised reports (ITN) of visits to Omarska and Trnopolje; Reports by the UN High Commission for Refugees for the Banja Luka region (site of Omarska); Published interviews with Omarska survivors and survivors of nearby camps where some Omarska prisoners were transferred; Personal interviews with refugees whose family members were last seen being taken to Omarska.

NOTES

CHAPTER ONE

1. Aida Mušanović, "Bosnian Culture under Siege: Artistic Responses" (paper presented at the 1995 Annual Gest Symposium on the Cross-Cultural Study of Religions, "Art, Religion, and Cultural Survival," Haverford College, October 29, 1995).

2. On Passover, April 15, 1995, the *Haggadah* was ceremonially opened for the third time since it entered the National Museum's collection a hundred years ago, during an interreligious service at which Jews, Croats, Serbs, Muslims, and other Bosnians reaffirmed their commitment to a multireligious society. See Roger Cohen, "Bosnia's Jews Glimpse Book and Hope," *New York Times*, 16 April 1995. For the *Haggadah*, see Mirza Filipović, ed., *The Sarajevo Haggadah* (Sarajevo: Svjetlost, 1988).

3. András Riedlmayer, *Killing Memory: Bosnia's Cultural Heritage and Its Destruction*, Haverford: Community of Bosnia Foundation, 1994, videocassette.

4. Riedlmayer, *Killing Memory;* and *idem*, "The War on People and the War on Culture," *New Combat* (Autumn 1994): 16–19; B. Bollag, "Rebuilding Bosnia's Library," *Chronicle of Higher Education* (13 January 1995): A35–37; *Warchitecture* (Sarajevo: OKO, 1994); Karen Detling, "Eternal Silence: The Destruction of Cultural Property in Yugoslavia," *Maryland Journal of International Law and Trade* 17 (Spring 1993): 41–74. See also the essay by the Serbian architect who served as mayor of Belgrade from 1982 to 1986 and who has been kept under house arrest for his opposition to radical Serb nationalism: Bogdan Bogdanović, "Murder of the City," *New York Review of Books* 51 (27 May 1993): 20.

For a scholarly exposition of the "Colored Mosque of Foča," dynamited and turned into a parking lot in 1992, see Andrej Andrejević, *Aladža džamija u Foči* (Belgrade: Institute for the History of Art, 1972).

5. For Bosnia's religiously pluralistic art and architecture, see Mirza Filipović, ed., *The Art in Bosnia-Herzegovina (The Art Treasures of Bosnia and Herzegovina)* (Sarajevo: Svjetlost, 1987); and idem, *Yugoslavia* (Sarajevo: Svjetlost, 1990).

6. Carol Williams, *New York Times*, 28 March 1993; and Roger Cohen, *New York Times*, 7 March 1994, "In a town 'cleansed' of Muslims, Serb Church Will Crown the Deed." For an account based upon the eyewitness testimony of José Maria Mendiluce, an official of the UN High Commission for Refugees in Zvornik, see the video series *Yugoslavia: Death of a Nation* (BBC/Discovery, 1995) and the accompanying book, Laura Silber and Allan Little, eds., *Yugoslavia: Death of a Nation* (New York: TV Books, 1995): 222–25. See also the eight *U.S. State Department Reports on War Crimes in the Former Yugoslavia Submitted to the United Nations Security Council in Accordance with Paragraph 5 of Resolution 771 (1992)*, which have been published under the title "War Crimes in the Former Yugoslavia" in the *U.S. Department of State Dispatch* 3.39 (28 September 1992): (first report) 732–35; 3.44 (1992): 802–6 (second report); 3.46 (16 November 1992): 825–32 (third report); 3.52 (28 December 1992): 917–22 (fourth report); 4.6 (8 February 1993): 75–79 (fifth report); 4.15 (12 April 1993): 243–52 (sixth report); 4.16 (19 April 1993): 257–69 (seventh report); 4.30 (26 July 1993): 537–48 (eighth report). The incidents in these eight reports are not numbered, but listed by dates, which makes them difficult to reference. I have edited them, adding incident numbers, and indexed them by number, for clear citation. See the World Wide Web at URL: http://www.haverford.edu/relg/sells/reports.htm/.

These reports are village by village reports of crimes against humanity researched and written in response to UN Resolution 771 demanding access for international organizations to detention camps in the former Yugoslavia and authorizing the collection of information on human rights violations (see n. 22 below). They are not to be confused with the annual State Department reports on human rights in countries around the world, which are far less detailed. In all subsequent references to the eight reports I will simply refer to the eight U.S. State Department Reports on War Crimes in the Former Yugoslavia, and give the number of the report and the incident number. In the three years since these reports have been compiled, the validity of the testimony has been verified continually by independent investigations. For Zvornik then, the testimonies are found in the following reports and incidents: 1:19, 3:13, 4:11, 5:11, 6:15, 6:45, 7:16, 8:16, 8:22, 8:28, 8:63. See also Helsinki Watch, *War Crimes in Bosnia-Hercegovina* (New York: Human Rights Watch, 1994), vol. 2, 220 ff, "Forced Displacement."

7. For one of the clearer accounts of these events, see *Yugoslavia: Death of a Nation;* this video series and accompanying book are based upon interviews with the principals in the drama, including Serb and Croat nationalists who are proud of their role in destroying Yugoslavia and quite explicit about the various stages in their program.

8. David Owen, *Balkan Odyssey* (New York: Harcourt Brace Jovanovich, 1995), 10, 40.

9. For the details in the events of 1991 and early 1992, see Paul Shoup, "The Bosnian Crisis in 1992," in Sabrina Petra Ramet and Ljubisa S. Adamovich, eds., *Beyond Yugoslavia: Politics, Economics, and Culture in a Shattered Community* (Boulder: Westview Press, 1995), 155–88.

10. Izetbegović replied to the Assembly that Karadžić's words "illustrate why others refuse to stay in this Yugoslavia." The exchange took place on October 14, 1991. See Silber and Little, *Yugoslavia: Death of a Nation,* 215.

11. President Milošević of Serbia had made it clear he was willing to go to great lengths to secure a peace and to remove sanctions on Serbia and Montenegro that had been imposed by the United Nations. The protégé of Serb President Slobodan Milošević, the militia leader Arkan, was implicated in the expulsions and brutalities. Yet Milošević was issued a visa to the United States not conditioned upon the release of this last remnant of Bosnian non-Serbs in the Banja Luka region.

12. See Richard Rubenstein, "Silent Partners in Ethnic Cleansing:

The UN, The EC, and NATO," *In Depth: A Journal for Value* 3.2 (1994), 51 ff. Even after the camps were revealed in news reports, Western nations refused to act promptly to save lives. The Serb authorities offered to release the prisoners if Western nations would take them as refugees. For several critical days, many Western nations delayed. As a result of the delay, many prisoners are thought to have perished.

13. See the eight U.S. State Department Reports on War Crimes in the Former Yugoslavia 1:20, 2:13, 2:15, 2:16, 2:17, 2:24, 3:4, 3:7, 3:8, 3:9, 3:11, 3:12, 3:17, 3:18, 3:21, 3:24, 3:36, 4:3, 4:9, 5:15, 6:1, 6:2, 6:6, 6:7, 7:7, 7:14, 7:16, 8:6, 8:10, 8:13, 8:14. Other, corroborating testimonies on Omarska are so extensive that, rather than listing them in this note, I have offered a separate discussion of them above in the Note on Sources. For an extended account by one survivor, see Rezak Hukanović, "Eyewitness to Hell: A Survivor's Diary of the Serb Concentration Camp at Omarska," *The New Republic*, 12 February 1996, 24–29.

14. Roy Gutman, *Witness to Genocide* (New York: Macmillan, 1993), author's note. Cf. Edward Vulliamy, *Seasons in Hell* (New York: St. Martin's Press, 1993), 97–111, 320–41.

15. Thus, Serb nationalists call the language spoken in Bosnia "Serbian" and consider Bosnian Muslims and to some extent even Bosnian Croats to be Serbs who have fallen away from their true identity. Similarly, Croat nationalists speak of the language as "Croatian." Caught in between the two nationalist terminologies, which are based on visions of an identity among religion, language, and nation, Muslims in Bosnia and those Croats and Serbs who do not identify with Croat and Serb visions of a Greater Croatia and a Greater Serbia now speak of the Bosnian language. As the conflict continues, the artificial differences in the languages are reinforced by a politically correct vocabulary for each grouping. Certain key words can determine whether one is speaking Serbian, Croatian, or Bosnian—even though, from the standpoint of linguistic comprehension, all three are the same language.

16. Some scholars believe the tribes that later became the Croats

and Serbs migrated originally from Central Asia and gradually became absorbed by the Slavic cultural and linguistic worlds.

17. Areas of mass killings carried out against Muslim civilians include Sanski Most, Ključ, Banja Luka, Prijedor, Kotor Varoš, Bosanski Šamac, Zvornik, Vlasenica, Zaklopača, Rogatica, Višegrad, Gacko, and Trebinje (by Serb nationalists); and Stolac, Čapljina, Počitelj, Ahmići, Stupni Do, Prozor, and Vitez (by Croat nationalists).

18. There were also major differences between Muslims in villages and those in the cities. For a glimpse into one Muslim community in Bosnia, see Tone Bringa, *Being Muslim the Bosnian Way: Identity and Community in a Central Bosnian Village* (Princeton: Princeton University Press, 1995).

19. For the background and implications of the designation of the "Muslim" national category in Bosnia, see Noel Malcolm, *Bosnia: A Short History* (New York: New York University Press, 1994), 119 ff.

20. See the interview in *Vreme News Digest* 213 (30 October 1995).

21. This summary is based upon personal interviews with Osman and Sabiha and upon Osman's article, written under the pen name Orhan Bosnević, "The Road to Manjača," in Rabia Ali and Lawrence Lifschultz, eds., *Why Bosnia? Writings on the Bosnian War* (Stony Creek, Conn.: The Pamphleteer's Press, 1993), 103–13.

22. In August 1992, in response to the media revelations about the concentration camps, the UN Security Council enacted Resolution 771 authorizing the collection and collation of human rights data, under which the U.S. State Department authored and submitted its eight reports. In September 1992, the United Nations Human Rights Commission appointed Polish Prime Minister Tadeusz Mazowiecki as Special Rapporteur for Human Rights in the Former Yugoslavia. The United Nations Commission of Experts was established at the request of the UN Security Council on 6 October 1992, Security Council Resolution 780. The Commission of Experts was empowered to gather evidence but not to prosecute. In a separate resolution on 25 May 1993 (Resolution 827) the Security Council authorized the establishment of an In-

ternational Criminal Tribunal on War Crimes with prosecutorial powers. The U.S. State Department human rights investigation group, the Rapporteur, the Commission of Experts, and the International Criminal Tribunal are, therefore, separate entities. The U.S. State Department, the Rapporteur, and the Commission of Experts have turned over to the tribunal their information, and some of that information is available to the public (see n. 6 above and Note on Sources above). The International Criminal Tribunal, based in The Hague, has made its own information available in two forms: in public indictments and in Rule 61 hearings that expose further evidence against indicted criminals who have not yet been taken into custody.

23. The following depiction is based on the sources listed in the previous note, detailed articles on war crimes in the journal *Vreme News Digest*, written by Serb human rights activists, and other sources listed below under each aspect of the "ethnic cleansing" program.

24. The first week of August saw mass killings at Manjača, but at other periods the killings were less frequent and methodical than at camps such as Omarska. See the eight U.S. State Department Reports on War Crimes in the Former Yugoslavia: 1:1, 1:25, 1:42, 2:26, 3:24, 6:1, 6:6, 6:11, 7:14, 7:16, 8:6, 8:14, 8:17, 8:23, 8:24, 8:51; Helsinki Watch, *War Crimes in Bosnia-Hercegovina* (New York: Human Rights Watch, 1994), vol. 2, 133 ff.

25. For the persecution of Muslims in Višegrad, see Peter Maass, *Love Thy Neighbor: A Story of War* (New York: Knopf, 1996), 8–15; Chris Hedges, "From One Serbian Militia Chief, A Trail of Plunder and Slaughter," *New York Times*, dateline Višegrad, 21 March 1996, A1, A8.

26. Such centers included the Drina River bridge at Višegrad, the Drina bridge at Foča, the stadium at Bratunac, and schools, mosques, stadiums, and roadsides throughout Serb-army occupied Bosnia-Herzegovina. For the killings and other abuses at Foča, see the eight U.S. State Department Reports on War Crimes in the Former Yugoslavia: 2:28, 4:8, 5:18, 6:14, 7:4, 7:5, 7:17, 7:19, 7:20, 7:21; Helsinki Watch, *War Crimes in Bosnia-Hercegovina*, vol. 2: 237, 257. Particularly

well documented are the killings that took place at the Čelopek cultural center near Zvornik. See the exposé in *The Weekend Australian,* 2–3 March 1996. One of the many Serbian militia taking part in the Zvornik killings was a group called the Yellow Wasps. Dušan Vuković, a member of the Yellow Wasps, was arrested and tried in Serbia for crimes in Zvornik, in an attempt by the Milošević government to show that it was capable of prosecuting Serbs for crimes in Bosnia. The trial was delayed, however, when questions about the relationship of Vuković and the Yellow Wasps to the Serbian secret police began to emerge. Vuković has acknowledged rape and multiple killings and even his defenders admit that he may have been involved in the killing of over one hundred civilians. See *Vreme News Digest* 156 (19 September 1994); 157 (26 September 1994); 164 (14 November 1994); 166 (28 November 1994); 178 (27 February 1995); 200 (31 July 1995).

27. An example of the first type occurred on May 16, 1992, in the village of Zaklopača in eastern Bosnia, where up to a hundred Muslims were killed as the Serb militias entered the town, which had previously disarmed itself under the orders of local Serb nationalist officials. See Helsinki Watch, *War Crimes in Bosnia-Hercegovina,* vol. 1: 50–53; Malcolm, *Bosnia: A Short History,* 245. An example of the second type was the days-long spree of rape, torture, and murder in the village of Liskovac. See Sally Jacobs, "Terrified, trapped in Bosnia: After a murderous attack, Liskovac Muslims want to leave," *Boston Globe,* 8 August 1993.

28. The ICRC appeal was made during the ethnic terror associated with Vojkan Djurković, an associate of the Serb militia leader Arkan. The appeal was made by International Red Cross president Cornelio Sommaruga. UN human rights rapporteur Tadeusz Mazowiecki also demanded a stop to the persecutions. The UN chief of civil affairs in Bosnia, Sergio de Mello, said Republika Sprska leader Karadžić had given him guarantees that the evictions would halt, but the expulsions and atrocities continued. See the Associated Press report of 9 September 1994 and *New York Times,* 18 October 1994. Many of those evicted were sent to the Lopare slave labor camp near Brčko.

29. From the testimony at the International Criminal Tribunal in The Hague, Netherlands.

30. Susan Brownmiller, *Against Our Will: Men, Women, and Rape* (New York: Simon and Schuster, 1975).

31. See the Pulitzer Prize winning reports of Roy Gutman, which appeared originally in *New York Newsday* and have been included in Gutman, *Witness to Genocide*, 157–63.

32. Other major sites of organized rape include the camps at Trnopolje and Manjača, various locales in Višegrad, Rogatica, Vogošća, Grbavica (a district in Serb army–occupied Sarajevo), Zvornik, Vlasenica, and the nearby camp at Sušica. The most notorious area of organized rape by Croatian religious nationalists was the Čapljina region of Herzegovina. See the eight U.S. State Department reports, the reports of Helsinki Watch, and the other sources listed above in the Note on Sources.

33. See Paul Mojzes, *Yugoslavian Inferno* (New York: Continuum, 1994), 231: *"Muslimanka sva u krvi, Srbin joj je bio prvi"* ("The Muslim woman is all bloody; a Serb was the first to spoil her"). The Serbian Guard militia boasted of gang-raping a 13-year-old Muslim girl in the Bosnian town of Gacko, attaching her to a tank, and riding around until there was nothing left of her but the skeleton. The boast was made public by Danica Drašković, wife of Vuk Drašković, who founded the Serbian Guard. See Norman Cigar, *Genocide in Bosnia: The Policy of "Ethnic Cleansing" in Eastern Europe* (College Station: Texas A & M University Press, 1995), 104–5.

34. See the discussion of Kosovo in Chapter 3 for detailed examples.

35. Božidar Popović, commander of the concentration camp at Manjača, in comments to Richard Cohen, *Philadelphia Inquirer*, 19 December 1992.

36. See the illuminating conversation of Peter Maass with a Bosnian Serb woman who maintains the absolute truth of the allegation about the harem plot that was broadcast on the radio. Maass, *Love Thy Neighbor*, 112–14.

37. The Qur'anic phrase chanted five times a day from the mosque

is: *la ilaha ill Allah.* The word "Allah" is a personal name believed to be derived from a combination of *al* (the) and *ilah* (god). Thus the testimony means: no "ilah" but "allah," or no god but God.

38. For just one example, see the U.S. State Department Report on War Crimes in the Former Yugoslavia 7:19, recounted by a woman who survived the atrocities at Foča.

39. "The Convention on the Prevention and Punishment of the Crime of Genocide," 78 U.N.T.S. 277, adopted by Resolution 260 (III) A of the General Assembly of the United Nations on December 9, 1948.

40. Rafael Lemkin, *Axis Rule in Occupied Europe: Laws of Occupation, Analysis of Government, Proposals for Redress* (New York: Howard Fertig, 1973), 79. See also L. L. Bruun, "Beyond the 1948 Convention: Emerging Principles of Genocide in Customary International Law," *Maryland Journal of International Law and Trade,* 17.2 (Fall 1993): 196–98.

41. The denials are usually based on the assumption that anything less than Auschwitz is not genocide. The 1948 Geneva Convention banning genocide was an effort, however, to avoid the conflation of all organized destruction of people with the Holocaust, while still learning from it. See for example Charles Krauthammer, "Drawing the Line at Genocide," *Washington Post,* 11 December 1992. Krauthammer denies that violence in Bosnia was genocidal but never mentions the criteria for genocide set in the Geneva Convention or in the definition by Lemkin. See also George Kenney's denial as cited in Owen, *Balkan Odyssey,* 80.

42. See n. 22 above for a list of the major sources of information. Charged with genocide for activities in Bosnia-Herzegovina are Republika Srpska President Radovan Karadžić, Serb army General Ratko Mladić, Bosnian Serb Security Chief Mićo Stanišić, Dušan Sikirica, commander of the Keraterm killing camp in Prijedor, Goran Jelišić, commander of the Brčko-Luka killing camp, and Željko Meakić (a.k.a. Mejahić), commander of the Omarska killing camp near Prijedor. A Rule 61 hearing has been held on the case of Dragan Nikolić, com-

mander of the Sušica camp, who has been indicted on multiple counts of crimes against humanity.

The term "genocide" was invented as a response to the Holocaust and has been inscribed within the articles of international law. During the cold war period, the genocides that existed (in Guatemala and Uganda, for example) were partially protected by a cold war rivalry that prevented coordinated international efforts to enforce the Geneva Convention. With the end of the cold war, the genocides in Bosnia and Rwanda have led to the creation of an International Criminal Tribunal in The Hague and have become the focal point for the effort to reestablish the Geneva Convention criminalizing genocide and to provide judicial, diplomatic, and economic disincentives to those who would practice it.

43. UN Security Council Resolution 819. On May 6, 1993, the Security Council passed Resolution 824, declaring Bihać, Sarajevo, Žepa, Goražde, and Tuzla as safe areas along with Srebrenica.

44. In addition to the International Criminal Tribunal indictments, and evidence presented to the UN Security Council (including satellite and spy plane photos of Muslim prisoners held in stadiums and of mass graves), there have been investigative reports in the press. See the reports of David Rhode of the *Christian Science Monitor*, who was captured by the Serb military as he investigated a mass grave (16, 17, 20, and 21 November, 1995); the *Monitor*'s reports on Srebrenica are available on the World Wide Web at http://www.cs monitor.com/bosnia/winning.html. See also the special report, "Srebrenica: The Days of Slaughter," *New York Times*, 29 October 1995.

CHAPTER TWO

1. For the development of the notion of "the Jews as Christ killer" see Cecil Roth, "The Mediaeval Conception of the Jew," in *Essays and Studies in Memory of Linda R. Miller*, ed. Israel Davidson (New York: Jewish Theological Seminary of America, 1938), 171–90; Jeremy Cohen, *The Friars and the Jews: The Evolution of Medieval Anti-Judaism* (Ithaca:

Cornell University Press, 1992); and *idem*, "The Jews as Killers of Christ in the Latin Tradition, from Augustine to the Friars," *Traditio* 29 (1983): 1–28. For the wider ideological and institutional forms of persecution, see R. I. Moore, *The Formation of a Persecuting Society* (New York: B. Blackwell, 1987).

2. For the legacy of Kosovo in the Serb tradition, see Thomas A. Emmert, *Serbian Golgotha: Kosovo, 1389* (New York: East European Monographs, 1990) and Wayne S. Vucinich and Thomas A. Emmert, eds., *Kosovo: Legacy of a Medieval Battle* (Minneapolis: University of Minnesota Press, 1991).

3. The power of passion commemoration, for good or evil, is not limited to Christianity, of course. In the passion of Shiite Islam, Husayn, the grandson of the Prophet Muhammad, is being opposed in his rightful role as leader and guide (Imam) of the Islamic community by the wicked Caliph Yazid. Yazid's army surrounded Husayn and his family and followers at the battle of Karbala in 680. Husayn and most of his family were killed in cruel fashion by the Caliph's soldiers. Each year the martyrdom of Husayn is reenacted during the commemorations known as the *ta'ziyya*. Some Islamic radicals used the *ta'ziyya* performances in Iran to demonize Americans, Jews, Bahais, and others as the killers of Husayn in a manner similar to the way Serb radicals used the Kosovo passion play to demonize Slavic Muslims. For example, see Ruhollah Khomeini, *Imam Khomeini's Last Will and Testament* (Washington, D.C.: Embassy of the Democratic and Popular Republic of Algeria, Interests Section of the Islamic Republic of Iran, 1989).

4. Some believe that the migrating South Slavic tribes that settled in Bosnia were originally Iranian tribes from the Inner Asian steppes, but little is known about this period.

5. See Alexander K. A. Greenawalt, "The Nationalization of Memory: Identity and Ideology in Nineteenth Century Serbia" (bachelor's thesis, Princeton University, 1994), 34–63. For Karadžić's interest in Herder, see ibid., 45.

6. Vuk Stefanović Karadžić, *Srpske narodne pesme* (Belgrade: Prosveta, 1985).

7. Greenawalt, "The Nationalization of Memory," 54.

8. Anne Elizabeth Pennington and Peter Levi, *Marko the Prince: Serbo-Croat Heroic Songs* (London: Duckworth, 1984), 15.

9. Milorad Ekmečić, "The Emergence of St. Vitus Day," in Vucinich and Emmert, *Kosovo: Legacy of a Medieval Battle*, 355. Cf. Greenawalt, "The Nationalization of Memory," 54.

10. Greenawalt, "The Nationalization of Memory," 53.

11. For the development of the Kosovo legend in the literature of chronicles and sermons, from the fifteenth to the nineteenth centuries, see Emmert, Serbian Golgotha, 61–142.

12. From the point of view of the Lazar legend, the religious element in nineteenth-century Serbian nationalism is far more important than works like Benedict Anderson's *Imagined Communities* might lead us to expect. While linguistic purification was crucial to the nineteenth-century construction of the Serb nation, the religious element was also crucial. See Greenawalt's "The Nationalization of Memory," 20–33, for an explicit critique of *Imagined Communities* on this point. The difference between historical event and the literary construction of "age-old antagonism" can be seen in the contrast between Vuk Branković and Marko Kraljević. Marko was a Serb vassal of the Ottomans and yet he is celebrated within the tradition of Serb heroic poetry. Vuk Branković (who many historians believe did not betray Lazar at Kosovo) has been identified with the Judas figure and used as a coded symbol since the nineteenth century to stigmatize Slavic Muslims.

13. Bishop Petar II Petrović (Njegoš), *The Mountain Wreath (Gorski vijenac)*, trans. and ed. Vasa D. Mihailovich (Irvine, Calif.: Charles Schlacks, Jr., 1986). The explicitly Christological patterning of Njegoš's portrayal of the Kosovo myth was echoed in other art and literature produced or collected during the late nineteenth-century Romantic period. A description of a particular fragment of poetry, known (among other epithets) as the "Last Supper," depicts Lazar's banquet on the eve of the battle. Lazar's Last Supper is represented in Adam Stefanović's lithograph "The Feast of the Prince [Lazar]" with Lazar in the center of the banquet table surrounded by figures posed as Christ's dis-

ciples, with light suffusing the prince, and the traitor Vuk brooding in the background (see Fig. 1) (Ljubica Popovich in Vucinich and Emmert, *Kosovo: Legacy of a Medieval Battle*, fig. 21, p. 287).

14. Njegoš, *Mountain Wreath*, verses 95, 284.

15. See George Bush, "Remarks and an Exchange with Reports on Departure from Colorado Springs," 6 August 1992. *Public Papers of the Presidents of the United States. George Bush, 1992–93, Book II: August 7, 1992, to January 20, 1993* (Washington, D.C.: Office of the Federal Register, National Archives and Records Administration, 1993), 1393.

16. Christopher Boehm, *Blood Revenge: The Enactment and Management of Conflict in Montenegro and Other Tribal Societies* (Philadelphia: University of Pennsylvania Press, 1984).

17. Bishop Nikolaj Velimirović, *Religija Njegoševa* (Belgrade: Izdanje S.B. Cvijanovica, 1921), 166.

18. Branimir Anzulović, *The Triumph of the War God: Violence in Serbian Life and Culture* (unpublished manuscript, 1995), chap. 17.

19. Emmert, Serbian Golgotha, 134.

20. The Reverend Dr. Krstivoj Kotur writes of the Kosovo story as a Good Friday story, "with suffering, death, resurrection, and ascension, which experiences accrue to the poet from the ancient cosmic-ontological spiritual motivation." Kotur cites with approval the characterization of the Kosovo legend as "a nationalized Christ-epic: sacrifice, physical death, a defeat now in exchange for a future ascension to Heaven; Lazarus perishes, the heroes with him; even the traitor is there, and the premonition of treachery is at hand, as well, during the Last Supper." Kotur writes of Christian belief as a battle, of the day before St. Vitus's day—the eve of Vidovdan—as the Last Supper, of Vuk Branković as Judas, of Lazar as Christ, of Miloš as St. Peter, of Kosovo as an analogy of Golgotha, the mount on which Jesus was crucified.

See Rev. Dr. Krstivoj Kotur, *The Serbian Folk Epic: Its Theology and Anthropology* (New York: Philosophical Library, 1977) and Vladimir Dvorniković, *Karakterologija Jugoslavena* (Characteristics of the Yugoslavs) (Belgrade, 1930), 969.

21. Pavle Zorić in Alek Vukadinovic, ed., *Kosovo 1389–1989: Special*

Edition of the Serbian Literary Quarterly on the Occasion of 600 Years since the Battle of Kosovo (Belgrade: Serbian Literary Quarterly, 1989), 79.

22. Ivo Andrić, *The Development of Spiritual Life in Bosnia under the Influence of Turkish Rule* (Durham: Duke University Press, 1990), 20. Andrić's dissertation was composed in German and presented to the dean of the faculty of philosophy at the Karl-Franz University in Graz, Austria on May 14, 1924, under the title *Die Entwicklung des geistigen Lebens in Bosnien unter der Einwirkung der türkischen Herrschaft.*

23. Ibid., 12.

24. Ibid., 16 ff. For careful revision of the Bogomil thesis see John Fine, *The Bosnian Church: A New Interpretation* (Boulder: East European Quarterly, 1975; distributed by Columbia University Press).

25. John Fine dismantles national mythologies that portray Slavic Muslims, Croats, and Serbs as unchanging entities. See John Fine, "The Medieval and Ottoman Roots of Modern Bosnian Society," in M. Pinson, ed., *The Muslims of Bosnia-Herzegovina: Their Historic Development from the Middle Ages to the Dissolution of Yugoslavia* (Cambridge: Harvard University Press, 1993), 1–21. Both Fine and Noel Malcolm, *Bosnia: A Short History* (New York: New York University Press, 1994) show that the Orthodox Christians in Bosnia only in the postmedieval period came to identify themselves explicitly as Serbs.

26. Ivo Andrić, *The Bridge on the Drina*, trans. Lovett F. Edwards (New York: Macmillan, 1959; Chicago: University of Chicago Press, 1977). *Na Drini ćuprija* was originally written in 1942.

27. Ibid., 35–37.

28. Ibid., 37–52. See the comments by John Matthias, "Introduction," in *The Battle of Kosovo*, trans. John Matthias and Vladeta Vuckovic (Athens, Ohio: Swallow Press/Ohio University Press, 1987, 15–16). Matthias chooses the Andrić impalement scene as the single image "most resonant of the suffering by the Christian Slavic population during the long night of Turkish rule in the Balkans." One American reader told this author that by the time she finished the impalement scene of *The Bridge on the Drina*, she was trembling all over; the horror of the scene never left her.

29. Prince Vlad was a Vlach, an ethnic group closely intertwined with Serbs and allied with Serbs through the shared Orthodox Christian faith. Prince Vlad is a hero to some supporters of the Republika Srpska.

30. They are also characterized by monodimensional characters. Muslim Slavs fall into one of a series of types: the evil Turk, the good Turk (dull, uncreative, but not cruel), and the janissary (brilliant, gifted, with the sadness of the loss of Christian essence always in his soul). These types are portrayed through the voice of an omniscient narrator who presents their thoughts through a stereotyped notion of Islam. Also in *The Bridge on the Drina* (written in 1942 while Gypsies were being exterminated in Europe), Gypsies are portrayed generically as vile.

31. In addition to a revival in the cult of Njegoš, the late 1980s experienced a revival of interest in Andrić from both Serb and Croat nationalists. For the revival and nationalistic politicization of the works of Andrić and Njegoš, see Sabrina Petra Ramet, *Balkan Babel: Politics, Culture, and Religion in Yugoslavia* (Boulder and Oxford: Westview Press, 1992), 28–29 and Misha Glenny, *The Fall of Yugoslavia* (London: Penguin, 1992), 22. This brief reading of Njegoš and Andrić cannot do justice to the range of their work. It is meant to demonstrate that religion is a key element in the tragedy and to identify how that element is used.

32. For the *gusle* verses and the statement of Karadžić, see the film *Serbian Epics*, produced and directed by Paul Paulikawski (BBC, 1992).

33. Milovan Djilas, *Njegoš: Poet, Prince, Bishop* (New York: Harcourt Brace Jovanovich, 1966), 310–96.

CHAPTER THREE

1. For the Serbian art and monuments of Kosovo, see the sumptuously illustrated collection of essays, *Kosovo*, comp. William Dorich, ed. Basil W. R. Jenkins and Anita Dorich (Alhambra, Calif.: Kosovo Charity Fund, 1992).

2. The Islamic tradition of Albania differs from that of the Slavic Muslims of Bosnia. The differences between Albanian Muslims and Bosnian Muslims would not be recognized within the stereotypes of

religious nationalists. For a scholarly discussion of Albanian Islam, see Frances Trix, *Spiritual Discourse: Learning with an Islamic Master* (Philadelphia: University of Pennsylvania Press, 1993).

3. Marko Mladenović, "Counter-Revolution in Kosovo, Demographic Policy and Family Planning," in Alek Vukadinović, ed. *Kosovo 1389–1989: Special Edition of the Serbian Literary Quarterly on the Occasion of 600 Years since the Battle of Kosovo* (Belgrade: Serbian Literary Quarterly, 1989), 141–50, cf. Milan Komnenić, "The Kosovo Cataclysm," in Vukadinović, *Kosovo 1389–1989*, 67–80. For the pervasiveness of this claim among Serb nationalists, see Robert Duff, "The Resurrection of Lazar," *The Spectator*, 8 July 1989.

4. Branko Kostić, "The Yugoslav Programme on Kosovo," in Gordana Filipović, *Kosovo: Past and Present* (Belgrade: Review of International Affairs, 1989), 309.

5. "Memorandum on the Position of Serbia in Yugoslavia" (Belgrade, 1986). The document was authored by members of the Serbian Academy of Sciences and Arts, but the names were not made public, and the Memorandum was never officially published but leaked to the nationalists in the media.

6. For the problems of the 1974 constitution analyzed from a scholarly perspective, see Vojin Dimitrijević, "The 1974 Constitution and Constitutional Process as a Factor in the Collapse of Yugoslavia," in *Yugoslavia: The Former and the Future*, ed. Payam Khavan and Robert Howse (Washington: The Brookings Institute, and Geneva: The United Nationalist Research Institute for Social Development, 1995), 45–74.

7. Milan Komnenić in Vukadinović, *Kosovo 1389–1989*, 69. The denunciation of Albanians is from a speech given by Milan Komnenić at the meeting "Serbians and Albanians in Yugoslavia Today," April 26, 1988. It was incorporated into a memorial volume on the 600th anniversary of the battle of Kosovo, as a special issue of the *Serbian Literary Quarterly*.

8. See Branka Magaš, *The Destruction of Yugoslavia: Tracking the Break-up 1980–92* (London: Verso, 1993), 49–73.

9. Mihajlo Marković, then a professor at the University of Pennsylvania and a founder of the philosophical journal *Praxis*, was exposed by Michele Lee with his allegations unproved. See Magaš, *The Destruction of Yugoslavia*, 57–58; and *Vreme News Digest* 208 (25 September 1995).

10. A. Dragnich and S. Todorovich, *The Saga of Kosovo: Focus on Serbian-Albanian Relations* (Boulder: East European Monographs, 1984), 170–72.

11. Amnesty International, *Yugoslavia: Ethnic Albanians—Victims of Torture and Ill-Treatment by Police* (New York, 1992). Cf. Helsinki Watch reports on Kosovo for the years 1986, 1989, and 1990. In addition to lacking any evidence, the genocide charges were filled with interior contradictions. Serb nationalists insisted that Albanians were never prosecuted in Kosovo for individual crimes against Serbs, yet in one complaint a Serbian nun denounced the sentences leveled against a group of teenagers convicted of setting a fire; the sentences ranged from five years to twelve years (Rada Saratlić in Vukadinović, *Kosovo 1389–1989*, 151–61). In an article entitled "Violated Culture" (Petar Šarić in Vukadinović, *Kosovo 1389–1989*, 159–61), a Serb nationalist claimed that the lack of road signs to monasteries implied an ominous intent on the part of the Albanian populace and that the lack of signs in the Cyrillic alphabet was a manifestation of "cultural violation." The writer recalled that a traveler in Serbia proper had expressed surprise "that no road sign or name of the city, dwellings or a river was in Cyrillic writing." He concluded, "It is not hard to imagine what the situation in Priština, Djakovica, Prizren, Uroševac [towns in Kosovo] is. . . ." After implying that the lack of Cyrillic signs in Kosovo is an aspect of the Albanian policy to "violate" Serb culture, the Serb nationalist states (as if it bolstered his own case) that a traveler could find no Cyrillic signs in Serbia proper, dominated and controlled by Serbs.

12. Holy Council of Bishops, 1969, in G. Filipović, *Kosovo: Past and Present*, 354–55.

13. Appeal by the Clergy in G. Filipović, *Kosovo: Past and Present*, 355–60.

14. Ibid., 360–63.

15. *Srbobran*, 2 November 1988.

16. Njegoš, *Mountain Wreath*, verses 131–32.

17. Komnenić in Vukadinović, *Kosovo 1389–1989*, 70.

18. Ibid., 71. A participant in the events has offered the following synopsis of the manipulation of Kosovo genocide claims (Azem Vllasi in *Vreme News Digest* 208 (25 September 1995). The author asked police for crime figures and found that the lowest number of cases in Yugoslavia was in Kosovo and Montenegro. There were five interethnic murders in all of Kosovo during the period from 1981 to 1987, two in which Albanians murdered Serbs and three in which Serbs murdered Albanians. Cf. Mark Thompson, *A Paper House: The Ending of Yugoslavia* (New York: Pantheon, 1992): 129–30. In reference to calls for the expulsion from Kosovo of 360,000 alleged Albanian immigrants, the police files showed a total of 813 Albanian immigrants in Serbia.

The manipulation of the term "genocide" during the Kosovo dispute came full circle in 1995. After NATO air strikes were called against Serb army anti-aircraft positions and munitions dumps, Serb Orthodox clergy and activists railed against this alleged genocide of the Serbian people. See *Srbobran*, September–October 1995.

19. Adam Puslojić, "On the Way," in Vukadinović, *Kosovo 1389–1989*, 114.

20. Stepinac was tried after the war for complicity in the crimes of the Ustashe regime, but his conviction was marred by Tito's attempt to pressure Stepinac into forming a Catholic Church in Croatia more independent of the Vatican. See Richard West, *Tito and the Rise and Fall of Yugoslavia* (New York: Carroll and Graf, 1995), 212–361. The most famous clerics involved in World War II atrocities were Catholic Archbishop of Sarajevo Ivan Šarić, an anti-Semite and admirer of Ustashe chief Ante Pavelić, and Franciscan Friar Filipović-Majstorović, known as "Brother Devil," a killer in the Jasenovac camp. For the role of Catholic leaders in the protection of Ustashe criminals after the war, see M. Aarons, M. and J. Loftus, *Unholy Trinity: The Vatican, the Nazis, and*

Soviet Intelligence (New York: St. Martin's Press, 1991). For the Croatian bishops' refusal (with the significant exception of Bishop Pihler) to address the Ustashe genocide, see Paul Mojzes, *Yugoslavian Inferno* (New York: Continuum, 1994), 129–35 and Gerald Schenk, *God with Us: The Role of Religion in Conflicts in the Former Yugoslavia* (Uppsala: Life and Peace Institute, 1993).

21. Interview, *Sixty Minutes*, 17 June 1995.

22. Milovan Djilas, *Wartime* (New York: Harcourt Brace Jovanovich, 1977), 139. For Tito's recollection of his shock at the massacre of Foča Muslims, see V. Dedijer, *Novi prilozi za biografiju Josipa Broza Tita*, 1 (Zagreb: Mladost, 1980), 557; trans. Paul Garde, *Vie et mort de la Yougoslavie* (Paris: Fayard, 1992), 81.

23. Vuk Drašković, *Nož* (Knife) (Belgrade: Zapis, 1982). One Serb commented that on reading Drašković he would become enraged and go out immediately to attack Croats and Muslims; see Norman Cigar, *Genocide in Bosnia: The Policy of 'Ethnic Cleansing' in Eastern Europe* (College Station: Texas A & M University Press, 1995), 25.

24. Muharem Durić and Mirko Carić, *"Kako srpski nacionalisti odmažu srpskom narodu i šta prati mošti kneza Lazara"* (How Serbian Nationalists Are Hindering the Serbian People and What Accompanies the Relics of Prince Lazar), *Politika*, 17 September 1988, 7. Cited and translated in Cigar, *Genocide in Bosnia*, 35. Cf. Milan Milošević and Dragoslav Grujié in *Vreme News Digest* 145 (4 July 1994): "At about the same time the Serbian Orthodox Church carried the relics of Grand Duke Lazar (the leader of the Kosovo battle) around the Serb lands, and religious services were held over the remains of the victims of genocide of a half a century ago that were retrieved from mass graves for that purpose."

25. V. Gagnon, "Roots of the Yugoslav Conflict," *International Organizations and Ethnic Conflict*, ed. M. J. and S. T. Esman (Ithaca: Cornell University Press, 1995), 180–97, especially 191–92.

26. Ivo Banac, "Serbia's Deadly Fears," *New Combat* 3 (Autumn 1994): 36–43.

27. Cigar, *Genocide in Bosnia*, 78.

28. For these instances and others, ibid., 80.

29. Cited in *Vreme News Digest* 170 (26 December 1994). At this stage, the Serb militias allowed camera crews to videotape their work. For the video footage, commentary by Mendiluce, and Šešelj's discussion of his and Serb President Slobodan Milošević's roles in what he calls the "separations" at Zvornik, see *Yugoslavia: Death of a Nation* (BBC production aired 26–30 December 1995 on "Discovery Journal"), part 3.

30. These last two positions are also part of an international discourse of complicity discussed in Chapter 6.

31. See *Yugoslavia: Death of a Nation*, part 3, for an interview with Miroslav Šolević, the Serb nationalist who helped stage the incident and is proud of his achievement. Cf. Laura Silber and Allan Little, *Yugoslavia: Death of a Nation* (New York: TV Books, 1995), 37–38. See also Beverly Allen, *Rape Warfare: The Hidden Genocide in Bosnia-Herzegovina and Croatia* (Minneapolis: University of Minnesota Press, 1996).

32. These events received little journalistic notice at the time. Among the available descriptions, see Barney Petrovic, "Serbia Recalls an Epic Defeat," *Guardian*, 29 June 1989, 9; Robert Duff, "The Resurrection of Prince Lazar, *Spectator*, 8 July 1989, 9–11.

33. Noel Malcolm, *Bosnia: A Short History* (New York: New York University Press, 1994), 213 ff and *Vreme News Digest* 145 (4 July 1994).

34. Misha Glenny, *The Fall of Yugoslavia* (London: Penguin, 1992), 39.

CHAPTER FOUR

1. See Klanwatch, *Intelligence Report*, 79 (August 1995) and 80 (October 1995) and "Neo-Nazi Novel a Blueprint for Hate," in the Southern Poverty Law Center, *SPLC Report*, 25.3 (September 1995), for detailed information on William Pierce's *The Turner Diaries* and its role in the Christian Identity and militia movements. For branches of self-

styled Christian militancy, see Ronald Holmes and Stephen Holmes, *Murder in America* (Thousand Oaks: Sage Publications, 1994), 55–70. McVeigh tried to call Pierce just before the destruction of the Oklahoma City Federal Building.

2. V. Gagnon, "Roots of the Yugoslav Conflict," *International Organizations and Ethnic Conflict*, ed. M. J. and S. T. Esman (Ithaca: Cornell University Press, 1995), 180–97, especially 195–96.

3. The role of Milošević in the destruction of Yugoslavia and in the violence in Bosnia was discussed in a book by a former political ally of his, Borisav Jović, *The Last Days of the Socialist Federation of the Republic of Yugoslavia.* See Jane Perlez, "Serb Chief Painted as Warmonger by Ex-Aide," *New York Times*, 16 December 1995.

4. These groups are mentioned in Misha Glenny, *The Fall of Yugoslavia* (London: Penguin, 1992), but to understand their close cooperation with the Yugoslav army and security forces, one needs to consult *Vreme News Digest* (1993–1995, *passim*) and see the comments of the militia leaders themselves in Laura Silber and Allan Little, eds. *Yugoslavia: Death of a Nation* (New York: TV Books, 1995), 222–50. An example of the cooperation between the regular army and the irregular genocide squads occurred after the Yugoslav army took the city of Vukovar in 1991. Colonel Veselin Šljivančanin was filmed refusing the International Red Cross access to over 200 prisoners that had been taken from the hospital at Vukovar. Also on camera are Chetnik irregulars, with beards, backpacks, and rifles. According to one of the few survivors, the prisoners were handed over by the Yugoslav army to the irregulars for torture and execution. A mass grave has been found at the nearby village of Ovčara. Šljivančanin has been indicted by the International Criminal Tribunal.

5. Jezdimir Vasiljević is considered to be one of Arkan's financial backers. After his bank collapsed, he fled with the savings of thousands of innocent Serb civilians (*Vreme News Digest*, 1993–1994, *passim*).

6. U.S. Department of State Report on War Crimes in the Former Yugoslavia 4:12.

7. For other examples, see Norman Cigar, *Genocide in Bosnia: The Policy of "Ethnic Cleansing" in Eastern Europe* (College Station: Texas A & M University Press, 1995) 84.

8. See the comments by Radovan Karadžić, who considers all Serbs living in Bosnian government areas to be "ethnic hostages" (David Binder, "Bosnian Serb Leader Says His People Fight Out of Fear and in Self-Defense," *New York Times*, 5 March 1993). The Croat population in eastern Bosnia was small, so that Serb extremists were mainly preoccupied with what they called the "separation" of Muslims from Serbs.

9. Ljuljeta Goranci, "1,300 Weeping Muslims Forced from Homes in Serb-Held Bosnia," Associated Press, *Philadelphia Inquirer*, 19 September 1994. In the article, Vasvija Mulasalihović, 39, is quoted as saying that the leader of the expulsions, Vojkan Djurković, told her and other women whose sons, brothers, and husbands were being taken away that they should to go to Tuzla (in Bosnian-government controlled territory) and attain the expulsion of 150 Serb families. Upon doing that, they would get their loved ones back.

10. The practice was later adopted by Croat commanders of camps for Muslims. See Chapter 6, below.

11. For a chronicle of the economics of looting in Serbia and in the Republika Srpska, see *Vreme News Digest* 104 (20 September 1993); 108 (18 October 1993); 147 (18 July 1994); and 156 (19 September 1994).

12. Cigar, *Genocide in Bosnia*, 65.

13. The effect of such dehumanization was clear at Srebrenica, where before the Dutch UN battalion handed over the town to the Serb army, a Dutch soldier expressed contempt for Muslims because they were "smelly." It evidently did not occur to him that people living in concentration-camp conditions are not able, as part of a deliberate policy, to practice normal hygiene.

14. In interviews with the author, Haverford College, 1993.

15. When Sanski Most was retaken by the Bosnian army in the fall of 1995, a mask was found that had been used during killing sprees carried out against Muslim civilians.

16. Dragan Nikolić, Rule 61 Hearing, International Criminal Tri-

bunal, The Hague, 10 October 1995. The *müfti* (Muslim religious leader) of Banja Luka has survived the persecution there and acknowledged those courageous Serbs who sheltered or rescued their Muslim and Croat neighbors.

17. Serbian-Americans have tended either to remain silent or to support the religious nationalists. For a denunciation of the Serbian-American refusal to recognize and condemn the slaughter organized by Serb religious nationalists in Bosnia, see George Mitrovich, "Serbian-Americans should Condemn Nazi-style Savagery," *Philadelphia Inquirer*, 2 September 1993.

18. Dr. Mirko Pejanović, President of the Serb Civic Council of Bosnia and a member of the collective seven-member presidency of the Republic of Bosnia-Herzegovina, in an interview in Washington by Umberto Pascali of *Executive Intelligence Review*, 19 September 1995.

19. On the newsgroup soc.culture.bosna-herzgvna from 1993 to 1995.

20. See Serbian Republic News Agency (SRNA) report of 20 November 1995 for Karadžić's presentation of Obilić decorations in Bijeljina and 3 December 1995 for the Obilić awards in the district of Nevesinje.

21. Paul Holmes, Reuters, 15 May 1993, "Serbian Extremists Gather in Bosnia to Honour Fighters": "In Knezina, a mountain village 60 km (40 miles) east of Sarajevo, Šešelj invested 18 Chetnik fighters with the old Serbian title of 'military duke' (*vojvoda*) at a candlelit ceremony in the small stone monastery of the Sacred Lady. . . . The battlegrounds reeled off in the citation included towns shattered by Serb artillery and purged of non-Serbs in almost two years of war—Brčko, Srebrenica, Foča and Višegrad in Bosnia. . . . They kissed a silver crucifix and a copy of the bible before they were blessed by Father Voja, a Serbian Orthodox priest."

22. SRNA, dateline Banja Luka, 20 November 1995.

23. Vojislav Maksimović, "Podseća na robovanje" (It is Remindful of Slavery), *Evropske Novosti*, 27 January 1994, 18, cited and translated by Cigar, *Genocide in Bosnia*, 61. For the role of Maksimović at Foča, see

Gutman, *Witness to Genocide*, 157–63. Cf. BBC broadcast, 7 January 1994, from the Belgrade Newspaper *Borba* (5 January 1994), "Foča Becomes Srbinje"; BBC, 3 October 1994, "Serbian Orthodox Patriarch Meets Karadžić on Tour of Bosnian Serb Republic," based upon the Yugoslav Telegraph Service news agency, Belgrade, 30 September 1994; Inter Press Service, 13 January 1995. For the term "Srbinje" used during expulsions, see the *Cleveland Plain Dealer*, 2 April 1995.

24. Duško Doder, Special to the *Boston Globe*, "On Serb Holy Day, Hellfire for Foes," 10 February 1993. For the Mirko Jović remark, see Cigar, *Genocide in Bosnia*, 35. Many examples could be given. Thus, after the slaughter of Muslims from the safe area of Srebrenica, a Serb priest disagreed with local Serbs who condemned the killings, stating that he would gladly kill a "Turk." *New York Times*, 29 October 1995.

25. For Bishop Atanasije's remark, see Cigar, *Genocide in Bosnia*, 30. The remark is part of an interview published in Rajka Radivojić, "Zavodjenja za Golešplaninu" (Leading Astray to Mount Goleš), *Intervju*, 9 December 1988, 27).

26. In *Glas Crkve*, cited by Cigar, *Genocide in Bosnia*, 31–32.

27. Metropolitan Christopher, *The Historical Background of the Contemporary Situation of the Orthodox Church in Yugoslavia* (Belleville, Mich.: Firebird Video, 1992), videocassette.

28. Interview in *Evropske Novosti*, 4 March 1993, 10, cited in Cigar, *Genocide in Bosnia*, 66. Zvornik was the first Muslim-majority city in Bosnia to become 100 percent "cleansed" of Muslims and to have a new church commissioned in memory of this accomplishment.

29. Christopher Bennett, *Yugoslavia's Bloody Collapse: Causes, Course and Consequences* (New York: New York University Press, 1995), 126–29.

30. *Los Angeles Times*, 12 August 1995.

31. Cited in Cigar, *Genocide in Bosnia*, 59.

32. The SS officer was Edwin Neuwirth, who treated Zhirinovsky to two days at his retreat in the Austrian Alps; see Craig Whitney, "Russian Rightist Angers Germans," *New York Times*, 24 December 1992. For Zhirinovsky in Bijeljina, see *Washington Post*, "Bosnian Serbs Hail Russian Nationalist," 1 February 1994, A16.

33. See the three articles in *Vreme News Digest* 178 (27 February 1995): Alexander Cirić, "Turbo Land: Machine Gun Wedding (with Singing)"; Dejan Anastasijević, "Željko Ražnjatović Arkan: The Groom," and idem, "Ceca Veličković: The Bride." See also Roger Cohen, "Serbia Dazzles Itself: Terror Suspect Weds Singer," *New York Times*, 20 February 1995; and John Kifner, "An Outlaw in the Balkans Is Basking in the Spotlight," *New York Times*, 23 November 1993.

34. Rev. Djordje Ilić cited in B. Demick, "Bosnian Serbs Nurture Anger: A Town United in Acrimony," *Philadelphia Inquirer*, 26 September 1995, A1, A9. Demick goes on to show how Father Ilić's teachings affect a young Serb man, Drago Konstantinović. Konstantinović grew up with Muslims and Croats as friends and dated a Muslim girl named Amela. He is shown kissing Father Ilić's ring and states to the journalist that if he saw his former Muslim and Croat friends now, he would kill them.

35. See Milan Milošević, "Conflict within the Serbian Church: Pavle versus Atanasije," *Vreme News Digest* 221 (25 December 1995). The politicians who had protested atrocities against Muslims in Trebinje and Gacko were none other than Dobrica Ćosić and Vuk Drašković, whose virulent anti-Muslim writings had created the climate for the atrocities; but Ćosić and Drašković at least were able to reject the worst extremes committed by their militias and followers, while Bishop Atanasije's support of extreme religious nationalism has never wavered.

36. BBC Monitoring Summary of World Broadcasts, 7 July 1994, "Yugoslavia: Serb Bishops Appeal for Rejection of Contact Group's Maps" (Tanjug news agency, Belgrade, 5 July 1994). In urging rejection of the peace plan, the synod stated that it was speaking not just as a political party, but as "Christ's church of this God-loving people at a time of serious temptations for our history and the history of humankind"— to the people it has guided upon "Christ's Via Dolorosa for centuries."

37. Radovan Karadžić interview, on Paul Paulikawski, *Serbian Epics* (BBC, 1984). For Nikolaj's argument, advanced in his condemnation of the Dayton accords, see *SRNA Bulletin*, 26 November 1995. In fact, the first Orthodox church in Sarajevo was built in the 1530s at the order of

the Ottoman governor, almost a century after the Turkish conquest of the region.

38. Kalajić is a mentor for the White Eagles militia (*Beli orlovi*), associated with some of the most inhuman atrocities in Bosnia; it is commanded by a historian on Kosovo, Dragoslav Bokan, and Mirko Jović, the chairman of the Serbian Popular Renewal Party. See Dragoš Kalajić, "Kvazi Arapi protiv Evropljana" (Semi-Arabs versus Europeans), *Duga*, 13–19 September 1987, 14–15, translated and cited by Cigar, *Genocide in Bosnia*, 26. For the genetically caused flaws supposedly resulting from this "special gene" of Ottoman soldiery, see Cigar, *Genocide in Bosnia*, 26–27. In a September 1995 issue of *Duga*, Kalajić also celebrates Serb army destruction of Bosnian cities, claiming that since Homer, true Europeans have hated cities.

39. See "The Extraordinary Session of the Holy Episcopal Synod of the Serbian Orthodox Church in Response to the False Accusations against the Serbian People in Bosnia-Herzegovina," *Pravoslavni misionar*, June 1992, 250–51, cited by Cigar, *Genocide in Bosnia*, 89; and Memorandum of the Holy Episcopal Synod's session of May 14–20, 1992, *Pravoslavlje*, 1 June 1992, 2, in Cigar, *Genocide in Bosnia*, 78.

40. *Los Angeles Times*, 12 August 1995, reporting on a statement made in a recent issue of the weekly *Pogledi*.

41. See the statement from the Syndesmos Conference on Nationalism and Culture held in St. Petersburg in July 1994, quoted in *In Communion: Journal of the Orthodox Peace Fellowship of the Protection of the Mother of God*, 1995, 6.

42. Edward Sorel, "Religion in the News," *The Nation*, 11 October 1993, 380. See also Martin Peretz, "Cape Cod Diarist: Symbolic Politics," *The Nation*, 5 September 1994, 50. Peretz compares Karadžić's honor to Pope John Paul II's awarding of the Knight of the Ordine Piano for "outstanding service to Church and society" to Kurt Waldheim, the former Nazi officer in Yugoslavia who lied about his Nazi connections and later was elected president of Austria. (Waldheim was awarded the Order of King Zvonimir by Ustashe leader Ante Pavelić for

his work with Nazi Group E, which supervised massacres in the Kozara region of Bosnia). See also Marlise Simons, "At a Crossroads, Rifts Pull at Orthodox Churches," *New York Times*, 5 November 1995.

43. For a summary of this appeal, see *Syndesmos, The World Fellowship of Orthodox Youth*, Orthodox Press Service 70 (31 August 1995). Among the signatories were Bishop Kallistos Ware of Diokleia (UK), Professor Olivier Clement (France), Professor Nicholas Lossky (France), and James Forest (USA), Secretary of the Orthodox Peace Fellowship.

44. See James Forest, "We Drink the Same Water and Pray to the Same God, an Orthodox Response to the War in Former Yugoslavia," *In Communion: Journal of the Orthodox Peace Fellowship of the Protection of the Mother of God*, 1995, 1–3. After opposing a succession of peace plans and supporting Karadžić and Mladić, Pavle refused to oppose the Dayton accords. For this he was condemned by other Serb bishops for betraying the Serb cause. Belgrade, December 20, 1995, from a report by Serb independent agency BETA.

45. Živica Tucić quoted in *Los Angeles Times*, 12 August 1995.

46. For Milošević's language of battles to come, see Silber and Little, *Yugoslavia: Death of a Nation*, 72.

47. Cigar, *Genocide in Bosnia*, 33. Other slogans included "I'll be the first, who'll be second, to drink some Turkish [Muslim] blood?" "Europe, remember who we are fighting for," and simply, "We want arms."

48. See the "Serbian Pride" t-shirts advertised in *Srbobran*, 19 April 1989, with designs including the maiden of Kosovo and various versions of the CCCC flag upon a shield on the breast of the double eagle.

49. Mark Juergensmeyer, *The New Cold War* (Berkeley: University of California Press, 1993), 4–5.

50. For a few examples, see Martin Marty and Scott Appleby, eds., *Fundamentalisms Observed* (Chicago: University of Chicago Press, 1991); Bruce Lawrence, *Defenders of God* (New York: Harper and Row, 1989); John Voll, in John Esposito, ed., *Voices of Resurgent Islam* (New York: Oxford University Press, 1984); and Juergensmeyer, *The New Cold War*.

51. The denial of the religious element in the genocide in Bosnia is

pervasive. For just one example, see Susan Woodward, *Balkan Tragedy: Chaos and Dissolution after the Cold War* (Washington, D.C.: The Brookings Institution, 1995), 243: "The victimization of Muslims through ethnic cleansing was also a result of the political contest behind the wars, not ethnic or religious hatreds."

52. Rezak Hukanović, "Eyewitness to Hell: A Survivor's Diary of the Serb Concentration Camp at Omarska," *The New Republic*, 12 February 1996, 29. For accounts of such forced singing at other concentration camps and torture centers, see the eight U.S. State Department Reports on War Crimes in the Former Yugoslavia 2:5, 5:11.

53. An extended investigation of this nexus of issues might begin with Gavin Langmuir's important study, *History, Religion, and Antisemitism* (Berkeley: University of California Press, 1990).

54. In the realm of the visual arts, for example, see Petar Palavicini's relief, "The Mother of the Jugovići" and Ljubinka Jovanović's work of the same title (Ljubica D. Popovich in Wayne S. Vucinich and Thomas A. Emmert, *Kosovo: Legacy of a Medieval Battle* (Minneapolis: University of Minnesota Press, 1991), figs. 34 and 35, pp. 300–301.

CHAPTER FIVE

1. See András Riedlmayer, "Killing Memory: The Targeting of Libraries and Archives in Bosnia-Herzegovina," *MELA Notes: Newsletter of the Middle East Librarians Association* 61 (Fall 1994): 3. See also Riedlmayer, *Killing Memory: Bosnia's Cultural Heritage and Its Destruction* (Haverford: Community of Bosnia Foundation, 1994), videocassette.

2. For the Islamic monuments in Bosnia-Herzegovina and a report on their destruction, see Amir Pašić, *Islamic Architecture in Bosnia and Hercegovina* (Istanbul: Research Centre for Islamic History, Art, and Culture, 1994). Of 29 major Islamic monuments in Mostar, dating from 1552 to 1651, Pašić lists 27 as totally destroyed.

3. See Riedlmayer, *Killing Memory*.

4. Franjo Tudjman, *Bespuća povijesne zbiljnosti* (Wastelands of Historical Reality) (Zagreb, 1990), 318–19.

5. Franjo Tudjman, *Nationalism in Contemporary Europe* (Boulder: East European Monographs, 1981; distributed by Columbia University Press), 162–63, cited by Richard West, *Tito and the Rise and Fall of Yugoslavia* (New York: Carroll and Graf, 1995), 364. Cf. Richard West, "An Apologist for Hitler," *The Guardian*, 21 October 1991, 23.

6. Warren Zimmerman, "The Last Ambassador: A Memoir on the Collapse of Yugoslavia," *Foreign Affairs* 74.2 (Spring 1995). Zimmerman recounts a meeting with Tudjman during which Tudjman "erupted into a diatribe against Izetbegović and the Muslims of Bosnia." Tudjman accused them of being fundamentalists trying to establish a beachhead in Europe and appealed to "civilized nations" to stop them.

7. Interview with *Le Figaro*, 25 September 1995. See also Christopher Hitchens, "Minority Report," *The Nation*, 18 December 1995.

8. See Laura Silber and Allan Little, eds. *Yugoslavia: Death of a Nation* (New York: TV Books, 1995), 131–32.

9. Edward Vulliamy, *Seasons in Hell* (New York: St. Martin's Press, 1994), 221–34; John Burns, "Croats Wield the Guns in 'Cleansed' Bosnian Town," *New York Times*, 30 October 1992.

10. András Riedlmayer, "The War on People and the War on Culture," *New Combat* 3 (Autumn 1994): 23, quoted from a UNHCR report of August 23, 1993.

11. See Mary Craig, *Spark from Heaven: The Mystery of the Madonna of Medjugorje* (Notre Dame: Ave Maria Press, 1988), 67–103; Wayne Weible, *Medjugorje: The Message* (Orleans, Mass.: Paraclete Press, 1989), 274–95; Mar Bax, *Medjugorje: Religion, Politics, and Violence in Rural Bosnia* (Amsterdam: VU Uitgeverij, 1995).

12. The World War II Bishop of Mostar, Dr. Alojzije Mišić, was horrified by the methods used by the Ustashe in carrying out forced conversions. Stepinac's response to the letter was to blame the Serbs for their own persecution. See West, *Tito*, 94–96. Mišić described how mothers, girls, and children under eight were taken from six railway wagons and thrown alive down the cliffs into ravines.

13. Vulliamy, *Seasons in Hell*, 214–24.

14. The relationship between the Vance-Owen map and the HVO

military operations against Bosnian Muslims is clearly illustrated in a booklet drawn up by the followers of Mate Boban in defense of the "cleansing" campaign against Muslims: Croatian Community of Herceg-Bosna, *Ethnic Cleansing of Croats in Bosnia and Herzegovina 1991–1993* (Mostar, August 1993). The booklet uses the Vance-Owen map in claims that Herceg-Bosna is entitled to land inhabited by Muslims and, at the very time of its publication, being purged of Muslims.

15. In his own account, Owen vehemently maintains that the original Vance-Owen plan was subverted by the U.S. State Department. He acknowledges that he and Stoltenberg then tried to persuade the Bosnian Muslims to accept a plan based upon a revised version of the Milošević-Tudjman map, but insists that the plan should not be called the "Owen-Stoltenberg" plan. See David Owen, *Balkan Odyssey* (New York: Harcourt Brace Jovanovich, 1995), 89–225. It may be true, as Owen maintains repeatedly, that the U.S. State Department helped kill the Vance-Owen plan, but Owen refused, continually, to confront the reality that after months of stalling, it was the Bosnian Serb parliament that killed the Vance-Owen plan formally. The Serb government in Pale allowed the Vance-Owen plan to be used as a pretext for avoiding a credible use of force to stop the genocide, and then, when they were finally forced to make a decision, they rejected it, first by refusing to endorse it and then by engineering a referendum of Bosnian Serbs in which the plan was presented as a sell-out and overwhelmingly defeated. Whatever the virtues of the Vance-Owen plan itself, Owen cannot bring himself to confront the reality that the Bosnian Serb side had no incentive to accept a just peace plan as long as it could carry out its aggression with impunity, backed secretly by the regular Serb army and openly by Serb militias, against a Bosnian opponent that was vastly inferior in military strength.

16. In addition to the attack against the Bosnian Muslims at Prozor, the HVO had also engaged in a campaign of cultural destruction and religious expulsion against Orthodox Serbs. An HVO team destroyed the sixteenth-century Orthodox monastery of Žitomislići, south of

Mostar, for example, and blew up the Orthodox Cathedral in Mostar, as well as destroying hundreds of smaller, village Orthodox churches. It should be emphasized immediately that such actions do not mean that all sides are equally to blame: the Bosnian government never engaged in systematic cultural annihilation.

17. HVO soldiers pushed from Travnik and Vareš by the Bosnian army took refuge with the Serb army, indicating their common agenda with the Serb army even as they presented themselves as allies of the Bosnians.

18. In addition to the volunteers from Serbia, Montenegro, Russia, Greece, and other nations with large Orthodox Christian populations, there were Orthodox members of the UN peacekeeping forces who used their position to thwart UN resolutions and aid the Serb militants. In one case, Colonel Viktor Loginov, a Russian officer in UNPROFOR, stated in a December 1992 interview published in the Russian newspaper *Ruski vjesnik* that Russia and Serbia were brothers in a Christian Orthodox war of self-defense against the Vatican and other conspiratorial anti-Orthodox powers. At the same time he was a member of UNPROFOR, Loginov took on a highly paid position with Arkan's Serbian Volunteer Guard and used his position with the UN to smuggle fuel and supplies to Arkan. See Vlastimir Mijovic, "Big Brother is Backing You," in Ben Cohen and George Stamkoski, eds., *With No Peace to Keep: United Nations Peacekeeping and the War in the Former Yugoslavia* (London: Grainpress, 1995), 142–47.

19. See Chuck Sudetic, "Serbs and Croats Mount Joint Attack on Muslim Town," *New York Times*, 28 June 1993, A3. Serb and Croat religious nationalists also cooperated on the siege of nearby Maglaj. Only two years earlier, that Serb army now being aided by the Tudjman-backed HVO had been annihilating the Croatian city of Vukovar.

20. Dubravka Ugrešić, *Have a Nice Day*, trans. Celia Hawkesworth (New York: Viking, 1994), 236–37.

21. From an interview conducted by the author in November 1995 with a Bosnian Muslim refugee. The Bosnian refugee and his family had

come to Croatia to stay with a Croatian relative. When they refused to eat pork, they were called Turks and thrown out onto the street.

22. Josip Beljan, "Priznata vjernost" (Recognition of Faithfulness), *Veritas* 9–10 (September–October 1992): 24–25, translated by Paul Mojzes, *Yugoslavian Inferno* (New York: Continuum, 1994), 130.

23. See Pašić, *Islamic Architecture in Bosnia and Hercegovina*, 218, who lists the following works of major importance annihilated by late summer 1993: Šišman Ibrahim Paša Mosque, Šišman Ibrahim Paša Medresa (school complex), Šišman Ibrahim Paša Han (market complex), Šišman Ibrahim Paša Hamam (Turkish-bath complex), and the Gavran-Kapetanović House.

24. Eyewitness report by correspondent Francois Raitberger, "NATO Lifeline to Bosnia Revives Croatia Port," Reuters, 9 February 1996.

25. For reports on the conference at Čapljina, see BBC Summary of World Broadcasts, 14 February 1996, reporting on a broadcast from Radio-TV Mostar, 13 February 1996. For the report on plans to build a Catholic church on the ruins of the mosque, see Reuters, 17 March 1996; and BBC Summary of World Broadcasts, 6 March 1996, citing a report in the Sarajevo newspaper *Večernje novine* of 5 March 1996. There is no independent confirmation of these reports, but the Herceg-Bosna authorities have not denied them. There is also a report that the Herceg-Bosna authorities wish to change the name of Počitelj to Komušin, again following the example of Serb nationalists who changed the name of Foča to Srbinje. See TWRA press agency, dateline Mostar, 14 February 1996.

26. See Vulliamy, *Seasons in Hell*, 320–41. Vulliamy was among the first press witnesses to Omarska and the Herzegovinian Croat camps.

27. See Owen, *Balkan Odyssey*, 268.

28. Weibel, *Medjugorje*, 105–6. The priest's views are enthusiastically reinforced by the narrator and author, Wayne Weibel.

29. "Croats Accused of Terrorism," *Toronto Globe & Mail*, 5 February 1996, A1, A7.

30. See Mike O'Connor, "Bosnian Croats Resist Peace Accord," *New York Times*, 13 February 1996.

31. Ivo Andrić, *The Development of the Spiritual Life in Bosnia under the Influence of Turkish Rule* (Durham: Duke University Press, 1990), 16.

32. West, *Tito*, 383.

33. Vulliamy, *Seasons in Hell*, 260; Bax, *Medjugorje*, 78.

34. OMRI (Open Media Research Institute) Daily Report, 28 May 1993.

35. For Kuharić's religious nationalism in 1991 and his claim that "only a handful of Serbs" were killed in the Ustashe state during World War II, see West, *Tito*, 372 and the London daily *The Times*, 25 August 1991. For the Boban-Šušak controversy, see OMRI Daily Report, 8 June 1993, 14 June 1993, 28 July 1993, 27 August 1993. While some view Kuharić as genuinely concerned with peaceful coexistence, others have suggested that the Croatian Catholic hierarchy was upset with Boban for losing territory in his attacks on Muslims and for trading other traditionally Catholic territory to Serb nationalists. For a discussion of the various readings of the Boban-Kuharić dispute, see Gojko Berić, "Catholic Church: Setbacks in Bosnia Fuel Boban-Church Conflict," *Balkan War Report* 21 (August/September 1993): 15.

36. OMRI Daily Report, 17 September 1993.

37. See The Catholic Church, *Assisi 1993: Giovanni Paolo II per la pace in Bosnia ed Erzegovina* (Citta del Vaticano: Libreria Editrice Vaticana, 1993). Earlier Vatican documents did focus on the death and destruction suffered by Catholic Croats, especially in Dubrovnik, while still wishing peace for all parties. See *La Crisi Jugoslava: Posizione e azione della Santa Sede* (1991–1992) (Citta del Vaticano: Libreria Editrice Vaticana, 1992).

38. Pope John Paul II visited the Sudan in February of 1993 and protested vigorously the persecution of Christians by the military regime. Alan Cowell, "Pope, in the Sudan, Assails Religious Persecution," *New York Times*, 10 February 1993.

39. Šušak is alleged to have ordered the assassination of moderate

Croat police officials in an effort to provoke war with Serbia in 1991 and to have instigated HVO attacks on Muslims in 1993. For Šušak's role in 1991, see *Yugoslavia: Death of a Nation* (BBC, 1995), part III and Silber and Little, eds., *Yugoslavia: Death of a Nation* 140–46. For Šušak's ties to the Herzegovinian Franciscans, see the account by Gordan Nuhanović, *Globus* 259 (24 November 1995). The Nuhanović article discusses three days of negotiations between Herzegovinian Franciscans and Mostar's bishop. It states that the meeting was called by the Pope and convened by the papal nuncio for Bosnia-Herzegovina, Francesco Monteresi, and that it included a verbal threat, a first in the 700-year-old history of Franciscans in Herzegovina, to shut down the Franciscan order in the province.

While a meeting of Franciscans was in process to discuss the problem, Gojko Šušak (a frequent and welcome guest at Mostar's monasteries) and the director of Croatian Intelligence Service (HIS) Dr. Miroslav Tudjman rang the bell. They had arrived from a celebration of four years of Herceg-Bosna at Grude, founding site of Herceg-Bosna. Originally from the Medjugorje area (before he emigrated to Canada to make his fortune), Šušak is considered an important man around town.

40. OMRI Daily Digest, No. 223, Part II, 15 November 1995, "Croatian President Promotes Indicted War Criminal." See the article by Dubravko Grakalić and Davor Ivanković in *Globus* (258) 17 November 1995, which lists the awards given to Dario Kordić on the day of statehood as the Order of Prince Branimir with Neckband, for "particular merits in advancing the international position and prestige of the Republic of Croatia and its relations with other countries"; the Order of Nikola Šubić Zrinski "for a heroic deed in the war"; and the Order of Petar Zrinski and Fraj Krsto Frankopan with Silver Braid, "for contribution to the maintenance and development of the Croatian state-forming idea, the establishment and betterment of the sovereign state of Croatia." In December 1995, Croat authorities further violated the Dayton accords by releasing Ivica Rajić. Rajić was indicted by the International Criminal Tribunal for crimes against humanity, including

the mutilation and burning-alive of Muslim children at the village of Stupni Do.

41. The relationship of the truth of a vision to its moral efficacy in the lives of those who experience it is also argued by William James, *Varieties of Religious Experience* (New York: Longmans, Green, 1902).

CHAPTER SIX

1. Louis Gentile, *Toronto Globe & Mail*, 13 January 1994. A similar comment by Gentile was quoted by Anthony Lewis, *New York Times*, 25 January 1994: "The leaders of the Western world have received a play-by-play report of what is going on here. It is unforgivable that it has been allowed to go on month after month." See also *New York Times*, 15 February 1994, opinion page. Other UNHCR officials who have been denouncing the systematic atrocities have been Kris Janowski, Larry Hollingsworth, and José Maria Mendiluce.

2. The three most famous gangsters went by the nicknames of Caco, Čelo, and Juka. When the Caco and Čelo gangs began abusing residents of Sarajevo, they were arrested by Bosnian police on October 24, 1993. Čelo (Colonel Ramiz Delalić) and his gang were arrested, but Caco (Colonel Mušan Topalović) was killed during the violence surrounding his arrest.

3. See Mark Almond, *Europe's Backyard War: The War in the Balkans* (London: Mandarin, 1994), 243; Winston Nagan, "Bosnia: A Question of Genocide," talk given 12 September 1994 in Gainesville, Fla.; Carol Hodge, "Hurd Mentality: Britain's Foreign Secretary Bows out in Shame," *The New Republic*, 7 August 1995, 18. Croatia was less affected by the embargo because it could purchase arms on the black market in Eastern Europe. The embargo thus only really harmed the Bosnians; any attempt to send arms to Bosnia would have to run a double gauntlet of Croatian blackmail and "surcharges" and the NATO arms blockade. The most obvious donor of weapons for Bosnia would have been the NATO powers themselves; the arms embargo allowed

them to refuse to arm Bosnians with the excuse that it would be illegal to supply them.

4. "The Islamic Declaration" was not published in the original Serbo-Croatian until 1990: *Islamska deklaracija* (Sarajevo, 1990). An English version appears in the *South Slav Journal*. For the later, more modulated position, see Alija Izetbegović, *Islam between East and West* (Indianapolis: American Trust Publications, 1984). Again, the Serbo-Croatian version appeared after the English version: *Islam izmedju Istoka i Zapada* (Sarajevo, 1988).

5. Amila Buturovic discusses the link between the curse of Kosovo (in which anyone who did not fight at Kosovo would be bereft of children) and the gynocidal assault against Slavic Muslims who were, precisely, viewed by Serb nationalists as Kosovo traitors. Amila Buturovic, "Nationalism and Rape: Gendering 'Ethnic Cleansing' in Bosnia-Herzegovina," paper presented at the conference "The Crisis in Bosnia," 7 November 1995, Keene State College, Keene, N.H.

6. Interview by Batsheva Tsur in the *Jerusalem Post*, 13 November 1992, cited by Cigar, *Genocide in Bosnia*, 124.

7. For the link between anti-Muslim and anti-Jewish prejudice, see Allan Cutler and H. Cutler, *The Jew as an Ally of the Muslim* (South Bend: Notre Dame University Press, 1986). This use of the term "Orientalism" was popularized by the influential book of Edward Said, *Orientalism* (New York: Pantheon Books, 1978). For a specific example of the history of Orientalist scholarship, see Michael Sells, "The Qasida and the West: Self-Reflective Stereotype and Critical Encounter," *Al-ʿArabiyya*, 20 (1987): 307–57.

8. Since May 1992, Yugoslavia has been made up of the two Serb-majority republics of Serbia and Montenegro and has been dominated by Serbian President Slobodan Milošević. In the 25 July 1994 Tanjug news agency release, dateline Tripoli, Yugoslav President Zoran Lilić was reported to have arrived in Tripoli for a friendly visit where he was received "with honors customarily reserved for outstanding officials from friendly countries." Colonel Qaddafi made an unscheduled visit to

the Yugoslavian president, a visit that was considered by the reporter to be a special compliment. See also the Tanjug reports for July 24–27, September 18, and December 5, 1994.

9. Similarly, when the NATO nations refused to lift the arms embargo on Bosnia, the Bosnians accepted military aid from nations such as Iran and the Sudan that were willing to break the embargo. Serb nationalists and Western politicians pointed to such desperate moves as evidence of the militant fundamentalism of the Bosnian Muslims. Yet when Iran was caught breaking the economic embargo against Serbia (with an effort to smuggle a massive oil-drilling complex directly to the Milošević regime), the Serb nationalists in Belgrade escaped being labeled militant Islamic fundamentalists. See Ray Bonner, "U.S. Scrambles to Keep Oil Rigs from Reaching Serbia," *New York Times*, 7 April 1995.

10. See Tanjug reports from the first week of October 1994 for synopses of such articles from the French weekly *L'Evenement de Jeudi*, the Paris daily *Le Figaro*, and the Paris daily *Liberation*, from which the Belgrade daily *Politika* carried an anti-Muslim article as a feature. The point here is not that the Bosnian government or Bosnian Muslim religious leaders should not be criticized, but that the criticism should be kept in perspective. There are some who wish to introduce Islamic symbols into Bosnian public life, but then Christian symbols, slogans, and pledges pervade the public rituals, currency, and public monuments of European and North American nations.

Given the enormity of the assault on Bosnia, the Bosnian people have shown restraint by refraining from retaliation or generic condemnation of all Serbs or all Christians. In World War II, the U.S. government put Japanese-Americans in detainment camps without any due cause and without Japan having occupied any U.S. soil; what might have happened to Japanese-Americans had Japan "ethnically cleansed" 70 percent of the United States? The Bosnian government never considered putting all Serbs in their territory into detention camps.

11. See the translations in H. T. Norris, *Islam in the Balkans* (Co-

lumbia: University of South Carolina Press, 1993), 295–96; and Norman Cigar, *Genocide in Bosnia: The Policy of "Ethnic Cleansing" in Eastern Europe* (College Station: Texas A & M Press, 1995), 29. Cigar provides a series of Jevtić's stereotypes about Muslims.

12. Aleksandar Popović, *Les Musulmans Yougoslaves, 1945–1989: mediateurs et metaphores* (Lausanne: L'Age d'Homme, 1990), 1–10. If the term "totalitarian" is to be applied to Islam because the religion is not restricted to private life, then it also must be applied to Halakhic Judaism, much of Evangelical Christianity, and much of classical Hinduism, Roman Catholicism, Confucianism, and Shintoism.

13. Darko Tanasković, "Religion and Human Rights in the Contemporary Balkans," *The Mediterranean Review*, Winter 1995, 81–96.

14. See Luciano Cheles, Ronnie Ferguson, and Michalina Vaughan, eds., *The Far Right in Western and Eastern Europe* (London: Longman, 1995), chapter 2, "The Dark Side of Nationalism," and chapter 11, "The Extreme Right in France"; and Hans-Georg Betz, *Radical Right-Wing Populism in Western Europe* (New York: St. Martin's Press, 1994), chapter 3, "Immigration and Xenophobia."

15. The speech appears in the Serbian daily *Borba*, 29 June 1989, 1.

16. David Owen recounts of Bosnian President Alija Izetbegović that "there was no outward and visible sign that he was a Muslim. He, his son and his daughter dressed and acted as Europeans"—as if it were surprising that Muslims, who have been inhabiting Europe for twelve centuries, would appear European, or if there were a contradiction between appearing Muslim and appearing European. See David Owen, *Balkan Odyssey* (New York: Harcourt Brace Jovanovich, 1995), 39.

17. For just one example of the construction of Muslims as anti-Western caricatures, see David Pryce-Jones, *The Closed Circle: An Interpretation of the Arabs* (London: Weidenfeld & Nicolson, 1989) and the review of that book by Conor Cruise O'Brien, "Sick Man of the World," in *The Times*, 11 May 1989. O'Brien states: "Muslim threats and incitements following the publication of Salman Rushdie's *The Satanic Verses* have brought home to many people in the West just how inimical to Western values Islamic society actually is." After offering a list of stereo-

types about Muslims, O'Brien states that "It [Muslim society] looks repulsive because it *is* repulsive from the point of view of Western post-Enlightenment values [emphasis O'Brien's]." O'Brien adds: "It remains true that Arab and Muslim society is sick, and has been sick for a long time." After citing a Muslim reformer's statement that the remedy for the ills of Islam is the Qur'an, O'Brien ends: "Unfortunately the sickness gets worse the more the remedy is taken." It would be unimaginable to find such a venomous, purely bigoted portrayal of Christianity, Judaism, or any other major religion in the pages of a leading Western newspaper. It would be naive to think that the attitudes represented by O'Brien did not play a role in the acquiescence by British society and Western society more generally in the assault on Bosnian Muslims.

18. For the anti-Muslim basis of keeping the arms embargo, see Roger Cohen, "West's Fears in Bosnia," *New York Times*, 13 March 1994, and Chris Hedges, "In the Truce Line, a Vast New Divide," *New York Times*, 11 February 1996. Hedges writes: "The possibility that there would be an overtly Islamic state in Europe, allied with Iran, is one of the main reasons the French opposed the establishment of Bosnia in the first place." Willy Claes, NATO Secretary General during much of the Bosnian conflict, wrote of the fundamentalist Islamic threat and of NATO as an alliance committed to "defending the basic principles of civilization that bind North America and Western Europe." See "NATO Chief Warns of Islamic Extremists," *Toronto Globe & Mail*, 3 February 1995. Cf. Edgar O'Ballance, *Civil War in Bosnia 1992–94* (New York: St. Martin's Press, 1995), 79. While policy makers and diplomats do not speak publicly of their motives for allowing the assault on Bosnia to continue with impunity for three and a half years, those not in public office are more open. The Internet discussion groups (soc.culture.bosna-herzgvna, alt.current-events.bosnia, soc.culture.yugoslavia) offer postings angrily questioning why Christians should come to the aid of Muslims. The construction by some Western ideologues of a "green threat" of Islam and the self-fulfilling prophecies of a clash of civilizations, and the mirror construction by some Islamic militants of a Western great Satan—and the way in which the two ex-

treme views reinforce one another—is of course a huge topic. Among the more important recent works is Thierry Hentsch, *Imagining the Middle East* (Black Rose Books, 1992).

19. Televised interview with Charlie Rose, July 13, 1995. For Eagleburger's comment, see Charlie Rose Transcript #1420 (1995 Thirteen/WNET) 5.

20. Robert Kaplan, *Balkan Ghosts* (New York: St. Martin's Press, 1993), 283.

21. See Richard Rubenstein, "Silent Partners in Ethnic Cleansing: The UN, the EC, and NATO," *In Depth: A Journal for Value* 3, no. 2 (1994), 51–52.

22. President Bush, Secretary of State Eagleburger, Secretary of Defense Dick Cheney, National Security Advisor Brent Scowcroft, and Chairman of the Joint Chiefs of Staff General Colin Powell. See President Bush's statement on August 6 after the Omarska revelations: "Now, the war in Bosnia-Herzegovina and Croatia is a complex, convoluted conflict that grows out of age-old animosities." "Remarks and an Exchange with Reporters on Departure from Colorado Springs," August 6, 1992, *Public Papers of the Presidents of the United States. George Bush, 1992–93, Book II: August 7, 1992, to January 20, 1993* (Washington, D.C.: Office of the Federal Register, National Archives and Records Administration, 1993), 1393.

23. See Colin Powell, "Why Generals Get Nervous," *New York Times*, 8 October 1995, opinion page. Powell's statement was published with approval of Secretary of Defense Dick Cheney and the National Security Council, who thus endorsed the signal to the Serb army that the U.S. was not likely to be a threat, no matter what atrocities were committed.

24. For General Powell's own description of his position, see Colin Powell with Joseph Persico, *My American Journey* (New York: Random House, 1995), 291, 558–605. For another claim that NATO air strikes would lead to catastrophe, see Misha Glenny, "Bosnian Quicksand," *New York Times*, 18 February 1994. David Owen, who opposed the use of air power to stop the genocide, is forced to acknowledge that the

three weeks of selective bombing had utterly disoriented the Serb army. See Owen, *Balkan Odyssey*, 336. Owen begins the discussion by saying that Serb General Ratko Mladić "did not fold up with the first wave of NATO bombing as so many commentators had confidently predicted" (as if those arguing for the "lift and strike" option had specified a one-week period). Owen then goes on to admit that after three weeks of the campaign, the communications system of the Serb army was disrupted and the balance of power on the ground shifted in favor of the Bosnian and Croat coalition.

25. Bill Clinton, campaign speech, August 6, 1992, cited by Hanna Rosin in Andrew Sullivan, *Accomplices to Genocide* (Entire August 7, 1995, issue of *The New Republic*) (Washington, D.C.: The New Republic, 1995).

26. President Bill Clinton, cited by Rosin in ibid., 14.

27. As quoted in the Associated Press report by Barry Schweid, *Philadelphia Inquirer*, 19 May 1993, A3. According to the account in Elizabeth Drew, *On the Edge: The Clinton Presidency* (New York: Simon & Schuster, 1994), 157–63, Christopher and his aide Tom Donilon were major figures in persuading Clinton to give up his commitment to the "lift and strike" plan to stop the genocide and to turn to a policy of containment.

28. For the efforts of British Foreign Secretary Douglas Hurd and others in Britain to portray the genocide as a "civil war," see Noel Malcolm, *Bosnia: A Short History* (New York: New York University Press, 1994), 239. Cf. A. M. Rosenthal, "Why Only Bosnia?" *New York Times*, 30 May 1995: "What to do now? . . . Keep American troops out and the [arms] embargo on—against all parties. Tell Bosnians to deal with their own fate, asking for Western diplomatic help if they want it." Rosenthal's solution would likely have led to the rest of Bosnia suffering the fate of Srebrenica.

29. "Our interest is in seeing, in my view at least, that the UN does not foreordain the outcome of a civil war." President Bill Clinton, May 14, 1993, cited by Rosin in Sullivan, *Accomplices to Genocide*, 14. The other Clinton quotes above are taken from the same source. Ser-

bian President Milošević maintained that the Yugoslav army was not involved in Bosnia. By the admission of his assistant, Borisav Jović, the alleged "withdrawal" of the Yugoslav army from Bosnia had been a ruse, a "fast one," and the Serbian government in Belgrade continued to arm, direct, and pay the salaries of Serb soldiers in Bosnia. See *Yugoslavia, Death of a Nation* (BBC, 1995), part III, and Laura Silber and Allan Little, eds., *Yugoslavia: Death of a Nation* (New York: TV Books, 1995), 217–18.

30. For the Senate speeches on S. 21, "The Bosnia and Herzegovina Self-Defense Act of 1995," known as the Dole-Lieberman bill to lift the arms embargo, see the *Congressional Record*, 18–20 July 1995, 10178–10367.

31. Strobe Talbot, "Remarks to the World Affairs Council of Pittsburgh," December 14, 1995. Whether the Clinton administration is committed to enforcing the Dayton accords or merely using them to keep genocide in Bosnia out of the election campaign is a controversial question. The NATO troops are to be withdrawn after the 1996 elections, and there are deep doubts whether or not the Western powers will fulfill their commitment to establish a viable framework for peace during the NATO stay in Bosnia.

32. Senator Phil Gramm in his campaign comments, November 1995.

33. For the notion that "they have been fighting for fifteen hundred years" see Congressman Manzullo of Illinois, address on the House floor, 29 November 1995. For the view that the problem goes back to the fourth-century split in the Roman empire, see Congressman William Goodling, 30 November 1995. Goodling boasted of his background as a history professor while making his speech. For a short piece pointing out the many historical errors in Goodling's speech, see Anthony Bazdarich, "An Open Letter to the Voters of the 19th Congressional District of Pennsylvania," *Zajedničar*, December 20, 1995.

34. See Noel Malcolm, "Impartiality and Ignorance," in Ben Cohen and George Stamkoski, eds., *With No Peace to Keep: United Nations*

Peacekeeping and the War in the Former Yugoslavia (London: Grainpress, 1995), 121.

35. See Carol Hodge, in Sullivan, *Accomplices to Genocide*, 18. For the U.S. arms export industry, see William Hartung, *And Weapons for All: How America's Multibillion Dollar Arms Trade Warps Our Foreign Policy and Subverts Democracy at Home* (New York: Harper Collins, 1995).

36. Bosnian President Izetbegović repeatedly urged Western leaders to either lift the arms embargo or intervene to stop the genocide. In a September 6, 1993 speech to the UN Security Council he pleaded: "Defend us or allow us to defend ourselves. You have no right to deny us both."

37. The Associated Press reported from Geneva on November 24, 1994, that the World Council of Churches, made up of Protestant and Orthodox churches, "demanded renewed enforcement of the U.S. arms embargo to all sides in the conflict."

38. Adrian Hastings, "A Crime that Puts the Church to Shame," *The Guardian*, 3 July 1993.

39. Quoted in the London daily *The Independent*, 17 December 1995.

40. For a list of all the relevant UN Security Council resolutions, see Cohen and Stamkoski, eds., *With No Peace to Keep*, 177–84. For a succinct exposé of the activities of the UN in Bosnia, see David Rieff, "The Institution That Saw No Evil," *New Republic*, 12 February 1996, 19–24.

41. At Srebrenica, British diplomats first watered down the safe area resolution. Next, Yasushi Akashi and other UN officials refused to use all necessary means to get convoys through to the enclave, turning it into an abode of hunger and misery. Then Akashi issued a UN report suggesting that Srebrenica be abandoned—a clear green light to the Serb army. On June 5, 1995, the Serb army violated the safe area and drove two thousand desperate refugees into the center of town, but the UN refused to enforce its mandate to deter attacks. The Dutch officers drank a toast with General Mladić and wrote him a document stating

the civilians had been treated properly, while Mladić had a pig slaughtered before the Dutch commander's eyes as an example of what happened to his "enemies" and as Mladić was having thousands of Srebrenica residents led away for slaughter. The Dutch soldiers retreated in their armored vehicles, running over and killing a number of desperate residents trying to flee the killings. When they returned to the Netherlands, they were decorated for heroism.

42. Of the refusals to protect the UN-declared safe areas, British General Michael Rose's refusal to protect Goražde in April 1994 was among the more ingenious. As the Serb army shelled and killed civilians in the city and burned outlying villages, Rose stated that he had not been authorized to "protect" the safe area, only to "deter" attacks on it. Yet it was Rose who had refused to use a credible threat of NATO air strikes to deter the Serb army from violating the enclave in the first place. See *Yugoslavia: Death of a Nation* (BBC, 1995), part IV.

In November 1993, the Serb armies entered the safe area of Bihać and were on the verge of taking it. Rose and French General Bertrand Lapresle finalized the destruction of any credible NATO deterrence. As the Croatian Serb army violated the no-fly zone and the international border by launching air strikes on Bihać from the Udbina air base in Croatia, Rose and Lapresle authorized an air strike on the Udbina runway—a militarily useless target. The runway was soon repaired, and Lapresle demonstrated to the Serb army just how far he was willing to go to make NATO air power ineffective. It has since been revealed that at the same time, the CIA had intercepted a message from British special forces (SAS) in the area. The SAS were supposed to give NATO coordinates for the air strikes against Serb artillery and anti-aircraft batteries, but they deliberately held back the coordinates or gave false coordinates to thwart the effectiveness of any NATO strikes. See Ed Vulliamy, "How the CIA Intercepted SAS Signals," *The Guardian*, 29 January 1996.

43. See Roy Gutman, "Witnesses Claim UN Forces Visited Serb-Run Brothel," *New York Newsday*, 1 November 1993. Branislav Vlaco, the Bosnian Serb commander of the camp from May to November,

confirmed that UN peacekeepers from various nations frequented Sonja's, but claimed the women there were not captives, but rather "women of low morals." Gutman's account of the captivity of the women at the camp, the gang rapes in which UN personnel took part, and the fraternization of UN personnel with those running the camp are based on the testimony of nine Muslim men from the area who had been held in the bunker and three Muslim women who had been held at Sonja's, two of whom had been raped. The UN ultimately was forced to investigate and a number of UN peacekeepers were disciplined, but the UN refuses to make public its report on the incident. Borisav Herak, a Bosnian Serb militiaman who admitted to raping and killing women at the camp, also charged that General MacKenzie himself visited the camp. Gutman was able to prove this charge wrong; other UN officers may have been mistaken for MacKenzie.

During this same period, General MacKenzie gave numerous interviews in which he patronized the Bosnians and ignored the genocide. After he retired, he was paid $18,000 a day by Serbnet, a lobby for radical Serb nationalists, to propound his views.

44. The incident is described in detail in David Rieff's *Slaughterhouse: Bosnia and the Failure of the West* (New York: Simon & Schuster, 1995), 150–51. Rieff dedicates the book to Dr. Turajlić.

45. soc.culture.bosna-herzgvna, 21 February 1995.

46. *New York Times* (16 July 1992), A8; S. Burg, "The International Community and the Yugoslav Crisis," in *International Organizations and Ethnic Conflict*, ed. Milton Eshman and Shibley Telhami (Ithaca: Cornell University Press, 1995), 254. For the role of Douglas Hurd, see Carol Hodge in Sullivan, *Accomplices to Genocide*, 18–19.

47. The Bosnian army authorized the rebuilding of the Franciscan church in Fojnica damaged by an attack in which two Franciscans were killed. No such gesture has been made by the authorities of the Republika Srpska in connection with any of hundreds of mosques they destroyed.

In addition to the crackdown on the Caco and Čelo gangs (see above, n. 2), the Bosnian government alone of all the parties in the

Bosnian conflict has fully cooperated with the International Criminal Tribunal and other war crimes investigations.

In late March 1996, the International Criminal Tribunal charged three Muslims with war crimes committed against Serbs in 1992 at the Čelebići camp near Konjic: Zejnil Delalić, Hazim Delić, and Esad Landžo. Ironically, according to officials from the tribunal, the indictments were delayed not by the Bosnian government but by the authorities of the Republika Srpska who have refused to allow investigators for the tribunal to interview witnesses in territory controlled by the Serb army. See "In a First, Tribunal Cites Serb Victims," Associated Press, *Philadelphia Inquirer*, 23 March 1996.

Even when moral distinctions were made among different parties, there were suggestions, without evidence, that had Bosnian Muslims been in a position of power, they would have carried out the same atrocities. See Paul Mojzes, "The Reign of 'Ethnos': Who's to Blame in Yugoslavia," *The Christian Century*, 4 November 1992, 996: "If they [Croatians or Muslims] had been more powerful, they would have been the ones carrying out 'ethnic cleansing.'" No evidence is offered that Bosnian Muslims had any notion of committing genocide or ethnic expulsions that would have left them living in a non-Christian ghetto in Europe. The accusation that a victimized people would have been committing the same crime committed against them is a deeply serious accusation; yet this charge against Bosnian Muslims, easily made, has never been demonstrated or even shown to be plausible. The charge was made into a special boldface display quote in the Mojzes article by the editors of *The Christian Century*. Cf. Paul Mojzes, *Yugoslav Inferno* (New York: Continuum, 1994), 171–72. For another unargued claim that the atrocities by Serb nationalists would have been matched by Bosnians had they had the opportunity, see Dimitri K. Simes, "There's No Oil in Bosnia," *New York Times*, 10 March 1993, opinion page.

48. The term "warring factions," which negates the official recognition of Bosnia and equalizes the recognized Bosnian government with ethnoreligious extremist militias, was immediately adopted by the major news media in the U.S., particularly television commentators.

49. Noel Malcolm, "The Whole Lot of Them Are Serbs," *The Spectator* (London), 10 June 1995.

50. Ibid. Malcolm cites the Norwegian historian of the Balkans Professor Monnesland of Oslo University, who characterizes Stoltenberg's ethnoreligious theory as "monstrous" and "absurd." For the claims by Serbian religious nationalists that "In Bosnia the Muslims are really Serbs" and have betrayed their ancestral religion, see Florence Levinsohn, *Belgrade: Among the Serbs* (Chicago: Ivan Dee, 1994), 151, 162; and Branko Grujić, the Serb religious nationalist mayor of Zvornik who celebrated the expulsion and killing of the town's Muslims (see Chapter 1 above) and who stated: "Serbs believe that other Serbs who change their religion are actually worse than Turks," quoted in *Toronto Star*, 28 April 1993.

51. See Susan Woodward, *Balkan Tragedy: Chaos and Dissolution After the Cold War* (Washington, D.C.: The Brookings Institution, 1995), 243. In Woodward's account, the use of passive voice and intransitive verbs strips the discourse of an agent: thus "methods of population transfers varied"; "Muslim elites were murdered or brutally expelled" from some areas, while elsewhere "local rivalries were encouraged to play out."

52. Peter Brock, "Dateline Yugoslavia: The Partisan Press," *Foreign Policy* (Winter 1993–94), 152–72.

53. See Charles Lane, "Brock Crock," *New Republic* 15 September 1994, 19–21. For the use of Brock by Serb church leaders to deny systematic war crimes of the Serb military, see the letter by the Rev. Rade Merich, a Serb Orthodox priest in Ohio and editor of *Path of Orthodoxy*, "Letter to the Editor," 1 December 1994, *Religion in Eastern Europe* 15.3 (June 1995): 41–44.

See also retired General Charles Boyd, "Making Peace with the Guilty: The Truth about Bosnia," *Foreign Affairs* 74.5 (September–October 1994). When criticized by scholars on Bosnia for moral equalizing, Boyd stated (*Foreign Affairs* 74.6, November–December 1994) that he wasn't trying to deny "Serb crimes" and had called them "reprehensible." The term "reprehensible" is hardly adequate; stealing a hubcap is reprehensible—what better example of the extremes to which moral equalizing leads. Boyd also denies the genocide in Bosnia by citing the number killed in Sarajevo, despite the fact that the International Criminal Tribunal indictments for genocide concern crimes committed in northern and eastern Bosnia, as well as in Sarajevo.

54. "We are doing all we can in Bosnia, consistent with our national interests," said Secretary of State Warren Christopher at a news conference July 21, 1994. See Drew, *On the Edge*, 276. Political scientist Michael Mandelbaum suggested that the post-Dayton NATO mission in Bosnia was a form of "social work" rather than protecting the nation's role as a superpower (CNN News, 1 January 1995).

55. The refrain "What about Somalia?" was also used to criticize calls for stopping genocide in Bosnia. The implication was that those who favored stopping genocide in Bosnia were racists who only cared about European victims. Yet some who had used the "what about Somalia" argument against stopping genocide in Bosnia protested the loudest when U.S. troops were sent to Somalia. The intervention saved an estimated 500,000 people from starvation before the operation became politicized and fell apart. In both Somalia and Bosnia, the Western governments were complicit in the original problem, in Bosnia through the arms embargo that in effect armed Serb radicals, in Somalia through massive weapons sales. Activists against the Bosnia genocide were instrumental in getting the genocide in Rwanda added to the agenda of the International Criminal Tribunal and in protecting the tribunal from efforts to sabotage its deliberations and cut off its funding.

56. Thomas L. Friedman, "Allies," *New York Times*, 7 June 1995, opinion page. Friedman goes on: "The Bosnias will come and go, but good friends whom we can count on for solving problems that really do involve our national interest are hard to find." Friedman's comment is especially unintentionally ironic in view of the duplicity of British General Sir Michael Rose and the British SAS in feeding false information to NATO pilots during the Bihać debacle (see above, n. 41).

57. Živica Tucić quoted in *Los Angeles Times*, 12 August 1995, cited above, chapter 4, n. 45. The statement originally appeared in the official

Serb Church journal *Pravoslavlje* and was presented as a paraphrase of the position of Serb Patriarch Pavle, the highest-ranking Serbian Orthodox leader.

58. Albert Speer, *Erinnerungen* (Inside the Third Reich: Memoirs), trans. R. and C. Winston (New York: Macmillan, 1970).

59. For the child whose hand was blown off, see Kurt Schork, Reuters, August 29, 1995. The young boy's words were spoken during the attack on the suburb of Otes, 5 December 1992. The story of the girl of Srebrenica was related by UN relief worker Larry Hollingsworth. See John Burns, *New York Times*, 20 March 1993, A4. A spokesperson for General Mladić claimed that the Serb army had fired in self-defense at a Bosnian tank and hit the refugees by mistake. Belgrade TV has maintained that there was no 1993 Srebrenica massacre of Muslims; the victims were Serbs tortured to death by Bosnian soldiers, dressed up as Muslims and placed around the site of the alleged shelling, a story the refugee workers who witnessed the massacre called preposterous (for the Belgrade TV story, see *New York Times*, 14 April 1993).

60. For Senator Feinstein's remarks, see the *Congressional Record*, 19 July 1995, S 10276–10278.

CHAPTER SEVEN

1. To this tradition was added the influence of both European sonnets and Middle East love poetry. For centuries, Bosnian poets composed in south Slavic as well as in languages of the Ottoman empire. There was a school of Bosnian Persian poetry and a school of Bosnian literary criticism of the international Persian poetic tradition. See Hamid Algar, "Persian Literature in Bosnia-Herzegovina," *Journal of Islamic Studies* 5.2 (1994): 254–67.

2. Amila Buturovic, "Multivocality in the Lyric of Ottoman Bosnia," unpublished paper.

3. Paul Paulikawski, *Serbian Epics* (BBC, 1992), videocassette.

4. Henry Kissinger, Interview with Mortimer Zuckerman, on *The Charlie Rose Show*, September 14, 1995. Among the others who have

proposed forcing Bosnian Muslims into a religiously homogeneous enclave are John J. Mearsheimer, "Shrink Bosnia to Save It," *New York Times,* 31 March 1993; George Kenney, "Bosnia Deadline," *San Diego Union-Tribune,* 20 February 1994; and Ronald Steel, "A Realistic Entity, Greater Sarajevo," *New York Times,* 26 July 1995. Steel, a professor of international relations at the University of Southern California, begins his opinion-page essay with the statement that the turning over of the safe areas of Žepa and Srebrenica to the Serb army—during which thousands of unarmed Bosnians were raped, brutalized, tortured, killed in groups of hundreds, and put into mass graves—"may be a blessing in disguise." None of these proposals acknowledges the history of non-Christian ghettoes within Europe or proposes a viable defense for such a ghetto.

On 12 December 1995, the Croatian daily *Večernji list* ran a piece by commentator Nenad Ivanković on Kissinger's plan in what is believed by some commentators to be a trial balloon, to test a renewed effort at the partition of Bosnia that President Tudjman has always favored.

5. Ivan Lovrenović, "The Hatred of Memory," *New York Times,* 28 May 1994, A15.

6. These brief remarks cannot do justice to the exhibit. They are meant only to illustrate the intersection of artistic creation and a multireligious culture. The other works exhibited are: Josip Alebić, "Aggression"; Seid Hasanefendić, "Destruction"; Dževad Hozo, "12"; Radmila Jovandić, "Les Gens"; Mladen Kolobarić, "Wave of the Devil"; Mirsad Konstantinović, "The Message"; Esad Muftić, "Trace of the Crime"; Aida Mušanović, "Year of All Dangers"; Salim Obralić, "Eclipse of the Spirit"; Mihailo Prica, "Papa, I Don't Want to Be a Refugee"; Petar Waldegg, "Homage to the People of Sarajevo, 1992"; Mehmed Zaimović, "Pain"; and Avdo Žiga, "The Black Sun." See *Expo/Sarajevo 92* (Catalogue for the Exhibit of 2–16 March 1994) (Brussels: Musée Charlier/Charliermuseum, 1994).

7. There are many such stories. Cf. Marian Wenzel, "Obituary: Dr. Riso Sijarić, Director of the Zemaljski Muzej, Sarajevo. Killed in Sarajevo, 10 December, 1993," *Museum Management and Curatorship* 13

(1994): 79–80. For refutations of the notion that Bosnia is artificial as a culture or a nation, see Noel Malcolm, *Bosnia: A Short History* (New York: New York University Press, 1994) and Robert Donia and John Fine, *Bosnia and Herzegovina: A Tradition Betrayed* (New York: Columbia University Press, 1994).

8. Laurie Kain Hart, Response, 1995 Annual Gest Symposium on the Cross-Cultural Study of Religions, "Art, Religion, and Cultural Survival," Haverford College, October 29, 1995.

RECOMMENDED READINGS

The events in Bosnia from 1992 to 1995 have generated a vast literature. The list below is meant to help orient the nonspecialist reader to different aspects of the story. For details on human rights and war crimes sources, see the Note on Sources, above. Sources on specialist issues are listed in the endnotes with full bibliographic information and also can be found in the bibliographies of the works listed below.

For the nonspecialist reader wishing to pursue aspects of the story told here, I would point out the following as particularly useful: Malcolm's *Bosnia: A Short History* for a very readable historical and geographical introduction and a rigorous refutation of standard stereotypes; Gutman's *Witness to Genocide* and Vulliamy's *Seasons in Hell* for works that recorded history in the making and, through the impact of the original articles and stories from which these works were composed, helped change the course of history; Emmert's *Serbian Golgotha* for the Serbian tradition of Kosovo; Filipović's *Art Treasures* and Riedlmayer's *Killing Memory* for the beauty and variety of Bosnia's cultural heritage; Buturovic's articles for Bosnian literature; *Yugoslavia: Death of a Nation* for the intrigue and power plays behind the destruction of Yugoslavia; Ali and Lifschultz's *Why Bosnia?* for selections from Bosnian writers and scholars; Cigar's *Genocide in Bosnia* for the role of Serbian clergy and intellectuals in motivating the violence; Almond's *Europe's Backyard War* and Rubenstein's "Silent Partners" for the complicity of the NATO powers; West's *Tito* for Yugoslavia during and after World War II; Fine's *The Bos-*

nian Church for pre-Ottoman religion in Bosnia and the controversy over the Bogomils; and finally, the journals *Vreme News Digest* and *Balkan War Report* for the most comprehensive ongoing coverage of the events in Bosnia-Herzegovina.

BOOKS, FILMS, ARTICLES, AND SPECIAL ISSUES OF JOURNALS

Ali, Rabia, and Lawrence Lifschulz, eds. *Why Bosnia? Writings on the Bosnian War.* Stony Creek, Conn.: Pamphleteer's Press, 1993.

Allen, Beverly. *Rape Warfare: The Hidden Genocide in Bosnia-Herzegovina and Croatia.* Minneapolis: University of Minnesota Press, 1996.

Almond, Mark. *Europe's Backyard War: The War in the Balkans.* London: Mandarin, 1994.

Andrić, Ivo. *The Bridge on the Drina.* New York: Macmillan, 1959.

———. *The Development of Spiritual Life in Bosnia under the Influence of Turkish Rule.* Trans. Z. Juricic and J. Loud. Durham: Duke University Press, 1990.

Anonymous. "Kosova, the Quiet Siege." *Cultural Survival* 19, no. 2 (1995): 35–42.

Banac, Ivo. *The National Question in Yugoslavia: Origins, History, Politics.* Ithaca, N.Y.: Cornell University Press, 1984.

Bennett, Christopher. *Yugoslavia's Bloody Collapse: Causes, Course and Consequences.* New York: New York University Press, 1995.

Buturovic, Amila. "Producing and Annihilating the Ethnos of Bosnian Islam." *Cultural Survival* 19, no. 2 (1995): 29–33.

———. "National Quest of the Anguish of Salvation: Bosnian Muslim Identity in Meša Selimović's *Dervish and Death.*" *Edebiyat* 7, n. 1 (1996).

———, trans. "Neither a Church Nor a Mosque," by Ćamil Sijarić. *Edebiyat* 7, n. 1 (1996).

Christopher, Metropolitan. "The Historical Background of the Contemporary Situation of the Orthodox Church in Yugoslavia." Belleville, Mich.: Firebird Video, 1992. Videocassette.

Cigar, Norman. *Genocide in Bosnia: The Policy of "Ethnic Cleansing" in Eastern Europe.* College Station: Texas A & M University Press, 1995.

Cohen, Ben, and George Stamkoski, eds. *With No Peace to Keep: United Nations Peacekeeping and the War in the Former Yugoslavia.* London: Grainpress, 1995.

Djilas, Milovan. *Njegoš: Poet, Prince, Bishop.* New York: Harcourt Brace Jovanovich, 1966.

———. *Wartime.* New York: Harcourt Brace Jovanovich, 1977.

Donia, Robert J. *Islam under the Double Eagle: The Muslims of Bosnia and Hercegovina, 1878–1914.* Boulder: East European Quarterly, 1981; distributed by Columbia University Press.

Donia, Robert J., and John Fine, *Bosnia and Hercegovina: A Tradition Betrayed.* New York: Columbia University Press, 1994.

Dorich, William, comp. and Basil W. R. Jenkins and Anita Dorich, eds. *Kosovo.* Alhambra, Calif.: Kosovo Charity Fund, 1992.

Emmert, Thomas A. *Serbian Golgotha: Kosovo, 1389.* New York: East European Monographs, 1990.

Expo/Sarajevo 92. Catalogue for the Exhibit of 2–16 March 1994. Brussels: Museé Charlier/Charliermuseum, 1994.

Filipović, Gordana. *Kosovo: Past and Present.* Belgrade: Review of International Affairs, 1989.

Filipović, Mirza, ed. *The Art in Bosnia-Herzegovina (The Art Treasures of Bosnia and Herzegovina).* Sarajevo: Svjetlost, 1987.

———. *Yugoslavia.* Sarajevo: Svjetlost, 1990.

Fine, John. *The Bosnian Church: A New Interpretation.* Boulder: East European Quarterly, 1975; distributed by Columbia University Press.

Garde, Paul. *Vie et mort de la Yougoslavie.* Paris: Librairie Artheme Fayard, 1992.

Greenawalt, Alexander K. A. "The Nationalization of Memory: Identity and Ideology in Nineteenth Century Serbia" (Bachelor's thesis, Princeton University, 1994).

Gutman, Roy. *Witness to Genocide.* New York: Macmillan, 1993.

Izetbegović, Alija Ali. *Islam Between East and West.* Indianapolis: American Trust Publications, 1984, 1989.

Langmuir, Gavin. *History, Religion, and Antisemitism.* Berkeley: University of California Press, 1990.

Levy, Bernard-Henry, and Gilles Hertzog. "Bosna!" Bosnia-Herzegovina/France: Zeitgeist Films, 1994.

Maass, Peter. *Love Thy Neighbor: A Story of War.* New York: Knopf, 1996.

Magaš, Branka. *The Destruction of Yugoslavia: Tracking the Break-up 1980–92.* London: Verso, 1993.

Malcolm, Noel. *Bosnia: A Short History.* New York: New York University Press, 1994.

Matthias, John, and Vladeta Vuckovic, trans. *The Battle of Kosovo.* Athens, Ohio: Swallow Press, 1987.

Njegoš, Petar II Petrović. *The Mountain Wreath (Gorski vijenac).* Trans. and ed., Vasa D. Mihailovich. Irvine, Calif.: Charles Schlacks, Jr., 1986.

Norris, H. T. *Islam in the Balkans: Religion and Society between Europe and the Arab World.* Columbia: University of South Carolina Press, 1993.

Owen, David. *Balkan Odyssey.* New York: Harcourt Brace Jovanovich, 1995.

Pašić, Amir. *Islamic Architecture in Bosnia and Hercegovina.* Istanbul: Research Centre for Islamic History, Art, and Culture, 1994.

Paulikawski, Paul. *Serbian Epics.* BBC, 1984.

Pinson, Mark, ed. *The Muslims of Bosnia-Herzegovina: Their Historic Development from the Middle Ages to the Dissolution of Yugoslavia.* Cambridge: Harvard University Center for Middle East Studies, 1993.

Ramet, Sabrina Petra. *Balkan Babel: Politics, Culture, and Religion in Yugoslavia.* Boulder and Oxford: Westview Press, 1992.

Riedlmayer, András. *Killing Memory: Bosnia's Cultural Heritage and Its Destruction.* Haverford: Community of Bosnia Foundation, 1994. Videocassette.

Rubenstein, Richard. "Silent Partners in Ethnic Cleansing: The UN, the EC, and NATO." *In Depth: A Journal for Value* 3, no. 2 (1994), 35–57.

Silber, Laura, and Allan Little, eds. *Yugoslavia: Death of a Nation.* New York: TV Books, 1995.

Sullivan, Andrew, ed. *Accomplices to Genocide* (Entire August 7, 1995 issue of *The New Republic*). Washington, D.C.: The New Republic, 1995.

Udovicki, Jasminka, and James Ridgeway. *Yugoslavia's Ethnic Nightmare: The Inside Story of Europe's Unfolding Ordeal.* New York: Lawrence Hill Books, 1995.

Williams, Ian, ed. *The Yugoslav Wars*, special issue of the *The New Combat*, Autumn 1994.

Vucinich, Wayne S., and Thomas A. Emmert, eds. *Kosovo: Legacy of a Medieval Battle.* Minneapolis: University of Minnesota Press, 1991.

Vukadinović, Alek, ed. *Kosovo 1389–1989: Special Edition of the Serbian Literary Quarterly on the Occasion of 600 Years since the Battle of Kosovo.* Belgrade: Serbian Literary Quarterly, 1989.

Vulliamy, Edward. *Seasons in Hell.* New York: St. Martin's Press, 1994.

Warchitecture. Sarajevo: OKO, 1994.

West, Richard. *Tito and the Rise and Fall of Yugoslavia.* New York: Carroll and Graf, 1995.

Yugoslavia: Death of a Nation, four-part video. BBC/Discovery, 1995.

PERIODICALS

American Srbobran. Serbian-American publication, includes issues of *Pravoslavlje (The Path of Orthodoxy)*, an official publication of the Serbian Orthodox Church in the United States.

Balkan War Report: Bulletin of the Institute for War and Peace Reporting.

Vreme News Digest. English language version. Published by Serbian writers committed to a democratic, civil society.

Zajedničar. Official organ of the Croatian Fraternal Union of America.

ELECTRONIC SOURCES

Internet Bulletin Board Newsgroups:

alt.current-events.bosnia

soc.culture.bosna-herzgvna

soc.culture.croatia

soc.culture.yugoslavia

Subscription Newsgroups:

SII (Serbian Information Initiative), Bosnet, Cronet (Subscription information is posted periodically on the Internet newsgroups).

World Wide Web:

See the sites listed in Note on Sources; new sites are being added and are usually announced in the bulletin board newsgroups or the subscription newsgroups.

INDEX

Compositor: G & S Typesetters, Inc.
Text: 10/15 Janson
Display: Hiroshige Sans Black
Printer: Haddon Craftsmen
Binder: Haddon Craftsmen